Collected Stories Of Rhys Davies
Vol. I
Ed. Meic Stephens
Cat : 25825 class ; F

RHYS DAVIES:
COLLECTED STORIES
Volume I

Rhys Davies
Collected Stories

Volume I

compiled and edited by
MEIC STEPHENS

First Impression—1996

ISBN 1 85902 347 9

This volume is published with the support of the Arts Council of Wales.

*Printed in Wales
at Gomer Press, Llandysul, Ceredigion*

Contents

		page
Volume 1		
	Introduction	7
1	Arfon (1931)	17
2	A Woman (1931)	44
From *A Pig in a Poke* (1931):		
3	Revelation	58
4	Death in the Family	67
5	Conflict in Morfa	74
6	Blodwen	81
	from *Love Provoked* (1933):	
7	The Journey	94
8	The Bard	101
From *The Things Men Do* (1936):		
9	The Two Friends	110
10	The Contraption	117
11	Wrath	125
12	Cherry-Blossom on the Rhine	134
13	Glimpses of the Moon	144
14	The Funeral	152
15	Caleb's Ark	158
16	Resurrection	166
17	Half-holiday	172
18	The Farm	178
19	The Skull	193
From *A Finger in Every Pie* (1942):		
20	The Wages of Love	202
21	Abraham's Glory	209
22	Mourning for Ianto	218
23	The Nature of Man	224
24	A Pearl of Great Price	229
25	Nightgown	237
26	Alice's Pint	245
27	The Dark World	248
28	Over at Rainbow Bottom	254
29	The Pits are on the Top	261
30	Weep not, my Wanton	267
31	The Zinnias	273
32	Pleasures of the Table	277
	Editor's Note	287

INTRODUCTION

Rhys Davies was among the most dedicated, prolific, and accomplished of Welsh short-story writers. For more than forty years, with unswerving devotion, he practised the literary form of which he was to become a master, and on which his reputation as a prose-writer now firmly rests. He wrote twenty novels, three novellas, two books about Wales, and an autobiography, but it is for his short-stories—about a hundred in all, published in a dozen main collections—that he is remembered today.

Most of Rhys Davies's stories are set in his native Wales, whether in an unspecified but easily recognizable Rhondda, grimly proletarian, or else in fondly idealized rural parts farther west, and despite the fact that he left home for London as a very young man, it was to those landscapes that he most often returned in his imagination. Some of his later stories have characters and social milieux which are unmistakably English and middle-class, and some are set in France and Germany. Nevertheless, 'There is only one abiding classic,' he once commented, 'Wales'.

On the other hand, his long residence in England, and his refusal to be associated with any literary school or coterie, even to consider himself an 'Anglo-Welsh' writer, was to set him apart from that first generation of Welsh writers in English who came to prominence in the years between the world wars. He was, for a start, unconcerned in his writing with political or social questions, though he claimed to have had a lifelong allegiance to the Labour Party. He may have been fairly typical in his antipathy towards the narrowness of Welsh Nonconformity, and in his ambivalence towards the Welsh language, which he did not speak, but there is something wilfully wholesale about his rejection of so much that belonged to the Wales of his youth. Like Stephen Dedalus, he decided early on to fly by the nets of nationality, language, and religion. His revulsion against what he considered to be 'the tyranny of the chapels' was keenly felt and bordering on the obsessive; only Caradoc Evans was more hostile. One of the characters in his first novel, *The Withered Root* (1927), is made to say, 'You Welsh! A race of mystical poets who have gone awry . . . To me there seems to be a darkness over your land and futility in your struggles to assert your ancient nationality. Your brilliant children leave you because of the hopeless stagnation of your miserable Nonconformist towns; the religion of your chapels is a blight on the flowering souls of your young . . .' On the subject of the language he had this to say: 'To me it is a lovely tongue to be cultivated in the same way as some people cultivate orchids, or keep Persian cats: a hobby yielding much private delight and sometimes a prize at an exhibition.' Not even Caradoc Evans went as far. The price he had to pay for distancing himself by such plain speaking was that readers in Wales never really took him to their hearts: many thought he was out to caricature them for the amusement of an English audience. As a consequence, Rhys Davies's books have for long been out of print and only since his death, in 1978, has he attracted any serious critical attention in the land of his birth.

In England, too, he was always something of an outsider, a role he assiduously cultivated in defiance of all the prevailing fashions and ideologies of the day. His life, which he shared with no other person, was given up entirely to his writing. Except for a stint as a draper's assistant on first arriving in London and a few months of compulsory war-work as a civilian at the Ministry of Information, he lived for many years almost entirely by his pen, his income unsupplemented by any teaching, journalism, or broadcasting, and usually in cheap, rented accommodation. He maintained a rigorous work-schedule—eating, writing and sleeping in one small room—and seldom sought either the company or the opinion of other writers. This professional single-mindedness, which was reinforced by his equanimity, love of solitude, and modest material needs, enabled him to pursue a literary career uninterrupted by any of the emotional or domestic upheavals such as are to be found so often in his stories. The virtues he extolled were those he had learned in his youth—thrift, a horror of debt, and minding one's own business—which he also took, unusually, to be specificaly Welsh characteristics; that is why he disliked the profligate Dylan Thomas. He kept his distance, too, from London Welsh society, though was not averse to meeting other expatriate Welsh writers such as Idris Davies at Griff's Bookshop in Cecil Court. But he preferred the company of London's artistic community, taking delight in some of the more outrageous characters like the boozy Nina Hamnett, 'Queen of Bohemia', and the notorious Count Potocki, pretender to the Polish throne, who paraded through the streets of Soho in a red cloak and with his blond hair falling over his shoulders; in his entry in *Who's Who* Rhys Davies gave his recreation as 'collecting ruined characters', and it seems he had a patient way of dealing with these difficult people. Although sometimes to be seen at the Wheatsheaf, one of Fitzrovia's most famous pubs, he never took to excessive drinking and remained an urbane, mild-mannered, parsimonious man whose only extravagance was sartorial: he had a taste for fine, expensive clothes, almost to the point of dandyism. His sexual orientation was homosexual but he maintained complete discretion, never even writing about it in personal terms. It took the form of

8

platonic friendships with younger men or else was satisfied by fleeting encounters with Guardsmen, usually strangers, about whom he is said to have had an erotic fixation. The enigmatic title of his autobiography, *Print of a Hare's Foot* (1969), is in fact a coded reference to its author's own androgynous nature. The image of the hare, a richly secretive, shape-shifting creature in folklore, was central to both his writing and his life. It also explains to some extent the detached, almost clinical way in which he observed other people and the evasiveness with which he habitually responded to enquiries about himself.

The important facts of Rhys Davies's life are few and plain, but highly relevant to his work because he often drew upon his own experiences in his writing. He was born on the 9th of November 1901 (not in 1903 as he claimed) in Blaenclydach (not Clydach Vale), a side-valley of the Rhondda, in industrial Glamorgan, which rises steeply from the town of Tonypandy. The valley was dominated by the presence of two major collieries—the Cambrian and a drift-mine, known as the Gorki, in Blaenclydach itself, quite close to the house where the author was born; both were the focus of bitter and violent industrial strife. Rees Vivian Davies, as he was christened, was the fourth child of the village grocer and his wife. His father, who voted Liberal, was the son of an illiterate Merthyr collier and his mother an uncertificated schoolteacher from Ynysybwl. On both his father's and his mother's side his people had their remote origins in north-west Carmarthenshire, always for him a lost Arcady, 'everlastingly green and sweet-smelling', despite his tenuous connection with it. The household was strongly matriarchal. Rhys Davies was to create many a female character who was as capable, shrewd, and dignified as his mother, while his men tend to be much weaker creatures, bemused, hapless victims of misfortune. The Davies's small shop, known rather grandly as Royal Stores, was at 6 Clydach Road, Blaenclydach, now a private house distinguished from others in the row only by a commemorative plaque put up by the Rhys Davies Trust in 1995; across the road stands the Central Hotel, which appears in the stories as the Jubilee. One of the Davies sons was killed in the closing weeks of the First World War; they also had three daughters and a younger son, Lewis, who is still alive. Both sides of the family were Welsh-speaking, as were Rhys Davies's parents, but they did not pass the language on to their children, and he grew up with only a few phrases at his command. As a boy he attended services at Gosen Chapel, where Welsh was in regular use, but was soon attracted to the High Anglican rite at nearby St. Thomas's Church. In later life Rhys Davies was to turn against all forms of religious practice and declare himself an atheist. At the age of twelve he became a pupil at Porth County School, which had a reputation as the best school in the Rhondda, but he was not happy there and did not distinguish himself academically. He left two years later, much to the chagrin of his parents for whom education seemed to be the surest way of avoiding the pits, and began helping behind the counter at Royal Stores. His parents' status as shopkeepers set them apart from a community that worked in the coal-industry, to the extent that some of his attitudes in later life were distinctly petit bourgeois, but in the shop's daily routine the boy came into contact with many local people, especially women, for whom he felt a deep affection and whose gossip he relished. One of the recurring references in his prose is to 'the ledger of old accounts' in which his mother kept a record of the villagers' debts and around which more than one drama unfolds. 'I always think of this period as a burial, with myself lying somnolent in a coffin, but visually aware of the life going on around me, and content to wait until the time came for me to rise and be myself,' he told one of his earliest critics. For the next five years, having resisted parental ambition for him to work in a bank, he read avidly, mainly the French and Russian classics, and made his first adolescent attempts at writing poems and stories. A growing awareness of his own sexuality, however, eventually made life in the male-dominated society of the Rhondda unbearable and, daunted by its grime and coarseness, and by what he saw as the narrowness of its chapel-culture, he went to live for a while in Cardiff, where he found work in a corn-merchant's warehouse. He was never to live permanently in the Rhondda again, but its ethos had marked him indelibly and provided him with an inexhaustible source of material for his writing.

Soon afterwards, drawn to London, where he was determined 'to starve and suffer' for his art, he embarked on his literary career. 'I wished for no possessions and, since taking my leap over the mountains, I had learned in my initial year or two how to be alone,' he recalled in his autobiography. One wet Sunday in 1924 he sat down in his dingy lodgings in Manor Park, near Ilford, and wrote three short-stories 'as clear of fat as winter sparrows'. Set in a Welsh mining valley, these 'carnal little stories' owed more to Caradoc Evans than to Maupassant or Chekhov, except that they dealt with a brutish proletariat rather than a venal peasantry. They were first published in a small, left-wing, short-lived, avant-garde magazine, *The New Coterie*, which was distributed by Charles Lahr; a few other stories and novellas appeared in limited private-press editions which have since become collectors' items. Among other contributors to the journal were H. E. Bates, Liam O'Flaherty, and T. F. Powys. It was Lahr, a German-born bibliophile and owner of the Progressive Bookshop at 68 Red Lion Street in Holborn, who introduced Rhys Davies to the literary and artistic world of London. He also served as his amanuensis, typing the manuscript of *The Withered Root*, and publishing his first collection of short-stories, *The Song of Songs*, both of which appeared in 1927. The public response to these books was favourable: they received good reviews and the novel was published in an American edition. The author found himself taken up as an original new talent especially among those who admired the work of D. H. Lawrence, at the time a cult-figure for the young. With an advance on a second novel, Rhys Davies was able to give up the menial jobs on which he had subsisted hitherto and become a full-time writer.

The rest of his life was without great incident. During a visit to the south of France in the winter of 1928 he was invited to spend some time with D. H. Lawrence and his wife Frieda at Bandol, and the two writers, both of whom had grown up in a mining-village and whose mothers had been teachers, took to each other immediately. 'What the Celts have to learn and cherish in themselves,' Lawrence told the impressionable young Welshman, 'is that sense of mysterious magic that is born with them, the sense of mystery, the dark magic that comes with the night . . . That will shove all their chapel Nonconformity out of them.' It was Rhys Davies who smuggled a manuscript copy of Lawrence's *Pansies* into Britain and arranged for it to be published by Charles Lahr. Although his literary output throughout the 'thirties was regular and substantial—he published seven collections of short-stories, six novels (one under the pseudonym Owen Pitman), and three novellas during the decade— financial success eluded him. Unable to settle at any one address, he lived a peripatetic life until he was offered accommodation at the home of Vincent Wells, a wealthy homosexual, in the leafy village of Henley-on-Thames, an arrangement which lasted until 1945, when the house caught fire and many of the writer's papers were destroyed. Whenever his money ran out he would go home to Blaenclydach and immerse himself in his writing, turning out stories and novels with a view to selling them to magazines and publishers in London; there were, of course, no such opportunities in economically depressed Wales. The finest of his stories written at this time appeared in the collection *The Things Men Do* (1936). Much of his energy during the 'thirties, by which time the making of the young writer was virtually complete, went into the writing of a trilogy of novels chronicling life in Blaenclydach from the days of 'sylvan Rhondda', before the discovery of coal, through the years of economic boom and industrial strife—he witnessed the Tonypandy Riots of 1910—down to the onset of economic decline and widespread social deprivation after the General Strike of 1926. The best of these novels is undoubtedly *Jubilee Blues* (1938).

The outbreak of war in 1939 filled Rhys Davies with despondency, and yet the war-years—despite rationing and the blitz—were to be one of his most productive periods. Although paper was in short supply, there was great public demand for reading material, and the short-story flourished in a variety of magazines, which were exempt from rationing. Davies contributed to many of them and, with the publication of *A Finger in Every Pie* (1942), *The Trip to London* (1946), and *Boy with a Trumpet* (1949), his style as a writer of short-stories reached maturity. At about the same time he achieved his only commercial success with a novel, *The Black Venus* (1944), when it was reissued as a paperback; in the same year, however, a stage-musical adapted from his stories, *Jenny Jones*, after a short run in London's West End, turned out to be a flop. For the rest of the 'forties, and particularly after the demise of so many of the magazines where he had found a market for his stories, he concentrated on writing novels. He lived for some years with the Scottish writer Fred Urquhart in a cottage near Tring in the Chilterns, and later with other male friends in Brighton, but by 1955, the year in which his *Collected Stories* appeared, he had returned to London, where he had long felt most at home, and to his old sedentary routine. When I first met him he was living in a studio flat at 15 Russell Court in the heart of Bloomsbury, a small but compact place which he was to occupy for the rest of his life. I found him to be a friendly, courteous but reserved man, and in appearance slim, fine-boned, and with a distinctively Iberian head and complexion. He had been able to afford the flat, I remember him telling me with a wry grin, with the help of money he had inherited from his parents, who had left him a little more than their other four children because he had saved them the expense of higher education. Towards the end of the 'fifties he published a novel, *The Perishable Quality* (1957), and a collection of stories, *The Darling of her Heart* (1958), the last of his books to take the Rhondda and west Wales as their main setting. From now on he would deal with more lurid themes: incest, lesbianism, drug-addiction and murder.

The 'sixties and 'seventies were not productive years for Rhys Davies, but they were not unlucrative. Looking to America for a new market, he had several stories published in such prestigious magazines as *The New Yorker* and *The Saturday Evening Post*, including 'The Chosen One' which won the Edgar Award for Crime Fiction in 1966. Honours came his way, too. In 1968 he was admitted to the Order of the British Empire and, two years later, the Welsh Arts Council made him an award in recognition of his contribution to the literature of Wales. Two more novels appeared—*Nobody Answered the Bell* (1971) and *The Honeysuckle Girl* (1975)—but they were not particularly well received, perhaps because their subject-matter had moved beyond the taste of many of his older readers. Fortunately, he was by now no longer dependent on his books for an income, having been left two more substantial legacies. The first came from half the estate of the writer Anna Kavan, with whom he had shared a curious bond that ended only with her death in 1968. Kavan had been addicted to heroin for more than forty years and had tried several times to commit suicide. Rhys Davies had rescued her after two overdoses and arranged for her to receive medical treatment. The precise nature of the friendship between these two solitaries remains undocumented, since hardly any of their correspondence has survived. Other women had been attracted to Davies and he took pleasure in women's company, but it was perhaps only with the asexual Kavan that he was able to enjoy anything like a close relationship. Yet neither admired the work of the other and Davies turned down a suggestion from Kavan's agent that he should write a biography of her, excusing himself on the grounds that although they had seen a good deal of each other over many years, he did not know enough about her; he nevertheless carried out his duties as her literary heir and executor by editing two posthumous volumes of her work. The second legacy, of sixty thousand pounds, came a few years later from another woman-friend, Louise Taylor, an American who had been the adopted daugher and heiress of Alice B. Toklas, the companion of Gertrude Stein. She and her husband, a painter, had kept a literary and artistic salon in Chelsea, and they had been kind to Rhys Davies. He now found himself with money in the bank for the first time in his life and contemplated a trip to America to see his old friend Philip Burton, the radio producer with whom he had collaborated in the 1950s. But his deteriorating health would not allow it. A lifelong smoker and suffering from severe bronchial attacks, he was diagnosed as having lung-cancer. He died on the 21st of August 1978 at University College Hospital. After a brief secular service at Golders Green Crematorium, his ashes were scattered in the rose garden there in the presence of his brother Lewis and two or three friends, among them Keidrych Rhys.

It was the writer Glyn Jones who was among the first of Rhys Davies's compatriots to recognize his mature talent. In the inaugural issue of Keidrych Rhys's magazine *Wales*, which appeared in the summer of 1937, Glyn Jones reviewed Davies's new novel, *A Time to Laugh*. 'As Welsh writers go,' he commented, 'Rhys Davies is undoubtedly a bigshot, a good bit of a pioneer, one of the first to get the valleys across on the English in the face of indifference, prejudice and a good deal of press-engendered hostility. He has written some of the best short-stories ever published about the valleys; and his virtues, well-known by this time (fancy, salty dialogue, grotesque humour, a robust masculinity of style) are all present in this his latest novel . . . Only philosophy is missing.' He went on to regret the lack of a unifying principle, or tension, which held the characters together in an imaginative world where their co-existence might be more credible. Althought this stricture is much less true of Rhys Davies's short-stories than it is of his novels, it does contain some perceptive criticism of his work as a whole.

Rhys Davies was the first Welsh writer in modern times to live as a full-time writer in London and to exploit his Welsh background fully in his writing. He knew, too, what it was like to feel 'the ancient recoil' of English readers from Welsh life and letters. In an article in *The Literary Digest* published in 1947, one of the rare occasions on which he wrote about his craft, he revealed how conscious he was of the pitfalls lying in wait for the writer who would write about Wales in English. 'There is no decadence in Wales,' he wrote. 'Life there is lived with the bright and hard colouring, and the definite simple principles of conduct, which one sees in a child's picture-book. There are rogues and ogres, true, there is scandalous behaviour. But the Celtic simplicity and wonder lies over all.' Of his fellow-countrymen he added, 'But let a writer go beyond the border and try to shape them into English print and they begin to scowl . . . The life of this fairyland must not be told outside or to foreigners like the English. Alas, that there should be traitors like myself! But I cannot help myself—my passion for Wales, her beauty, her individuality, her quality of perpetual youth . . . must be expressed in the only way I know—words—and as truthfully as I am able.'

One of Rhys Davies's difficulties was that he had few literary models on which to base his treatment of Welsh characters and locations, and that is why so much of his dialogue and some of his plots call to mind the work of Caradoc Evans, the Welsh writer to whom he was psychologically closest. He may not have had the latter's vitriolic turn of phrase but he certainly strove for his economy of style and emulated his attempts at rendering the peculiarities of Welsh speech in English, at least in his early stories. However picturesque or outlandish the effect may have seemed to his first English readers, with its inverted syntax, literally translated idioms, singsong rhythms, and so forth, this local colour can seem dated and tedious now, especially to readers in Wales, but it should not be allowed to spoil our enjoyment of the tale. More seriously, perhaps, is that after long years of residence in England, with only occasional trips back to Wales, by the 'fifties Rhys Davies found that his memories of the Rhondda had begun to fade and date, so that Welsh readers had some difficulty in recognizing the veracity of the people and places he was endeavouring to depict. This sense of not belonging any more is most movingly treated in *The Perishable Quality* (1957), the last of his novels to have a Rhondda setting.

It may be that, in any case, a story's location for Rhys Davies was never as important as characterization and plot, for as a writer he was more interested in the play of human personality than in anything else. Only rarely does he point the moral to his tale and he never condemns his characters, not even the villains among them. He was particularly good at tracing the subtleties of the female psyche and among his most striking portraits are those women in his stories who suffer and triumph in their social and sexual relationships. His own sexual make-up may have been an advantage in this respect. Be that as it may, he is one of the few Welsh writers to have written about industrial South Wales mainly from the point of view of its womenfolk. The plots of his stories often revolve around three sisters, or a young headstrong woman, or a middle-aged spinster, or else a wife fretting against the restrictions of an unhappy marriage, who eventually rise above their circumstances and achieve a kind of liberation. Emma Bovary was ever the heroine whom Rhys Davies most admired. The women in his stories usually achieve their victories by dint of personal revolt against convention, a favourite theme of his, and by embracing the Lawrentian values inherent in a passionate response to life. This leitmotiv is linked in his work to an abhorrence of puritanism and industrialism, and to his belief that one of the specifically Welsh virtues is a joy in the natural world untrammelled by any sense of original sin. 'There is still a primitive shine on Wales,' he wrote in his travelogue *My Wales* (1937). 'One can smell the old world there still, and it is not a dead aroma.' He detected the embodiment of these virtues in the person of his great hero, the eccentric Dr William Price of Llantrisant—quack, druid, Chartist rebel, exponent of free love, nudism and moon-worship, and pioneer of cremation—whom he described as 'the seer who sought to bring back to his people the spirit of an ancient, half-forgotten poetry.' Part of this joy, for Rhys Davies, had its corollary in a fascination with death: there are more fatal accidents, bereavements, widows, murders, corpses, coffins, wreaths, legacies, funerals, cold ham, and mournful hymns in his books than in the work of any other modern Welsh writer. 'Myself, I favour a dark, funereal tale,' he wrote in the preface to his *Collected Stories* (1955), 'but not always.' Fortunately for his readers, his treatment of this theme is not at all morbid; indeed, some of the funniest scenes in his stories—he had a delicious sense of black humour—take place during the rituals of death and burial. At such moments he found his countrymen at their most primeval, their greed and hypocrisy the very stuff of satire. 'Another virtue of the short-story,' he wrote, 'is that it can be allowed to laugh.'

As for his lack of 'philosophy', Rhys Davies defended himself thus in an interview with Denys Val Baker for *John O'London's Weekly* in 1952: 'I become uneasy when a novelist begins to expound, preach or underline, state a case, even briefly, or when he douses his characters with over-personal wealth of vision. This sort of philosophising must be kept, with me, incidental.' He was against the waving of flags in public, of all kinds whatsoever, and never joined any party or group which would have required him to do so. He was, however, prepared to allow a glimpse of his political colours in private: writing to Charles Lahr in 1929, he confided, 'Every night in my devotions I pray for a Labour Government'; and in the magazine *Wales* he once expressed support for the idea of self-government for Wales; but those are his only recorded utterances on the subject. In his stories there is hardly a hint that he had any political opinions and the reader is left to draw whatever inference is preferred. It may be that, like many other satirists, including Caradoc Evans, Rhys Davies was more conservative than his radically-minded contemporaries ever had reason to suspect. His primary aim was objectivity in the delineation of character in which there was no room for anything beyond the strictly individual, and in this he nearly always succeeded. It follows that he set his face against deliberately striving to express a specifically Welsh attitude to life and the world. 'If a writer thinks of his work along these lines,' he replied to a questionnaire from Keidrych Rhys, 'it tends to become too parochial, narrow. But if he is Welsh by birth, upbringing, and selects a Welsh background and characters for his work, an essence of Wales should be in the work, giving it a national slant or flavour.' It is an irony of Rhys Davies's career that in his determination to rebut the charge of parochialism, while at the same time giving so much of his work Welsh settings, he was sometimes considered too English in Wales and too Welsh in metropolitan England.

There is nevetheless a remarkable consistency of quality in Rhys Davies's mature work which puts him in the first rank of twentieth-century short-story writers in English. In his prodigious output he is comparable only with Liam O'Flaherty and A. E. Coppard. Whereas most writers, towards the end of a long writing career, experience a dimunition in their creative powers and tend to lapse into self-parody, often bringing out work that has long been consigned to the drawer, Rhys Davies—with the help of the legacies from Anna Kavan and Louise Taylor—was saved from the necessity of having to publish what he considered third-rate work. He continued writing during the very last years of his life, finishing another novel which was published as *Ram with Red Horns* in 1996. But there were no more short-stories. Nevertheless, he left us enough on which to base our judgement of him as a master of the form. Even in his reliance, in the early work, on melodrama and some pretty unlikely coincidences, he manages to beguile and entertain us. At his best he has an eye for significant detail, an instinct for moments of high drama, an ear for dialogue, and a delight in human nature in all its lovely and unlovely variety, which make his stories compelling reading. In practising the ancient art of the story-teller to such excellent effect Rhys Davies wrote stories that have a timeless and universal quality which will ensure their lasting appeal.

MEIC STEPHENS
Whitchurch, Cardiff   *October1996*

Mr. and Mrs. Edwards did not deserve such a child. There was nothing peculiar about them, they were chapel people and a respected business couple, he selling oil, soap, candles, and oddments from a cart in the streets, and she, a thin, staid woman, making savoury pasties on Tuesdays and Fridays, eight for sixpence and very delicious. So no one could understand why such a funny little boy was born to them.

Odd he was to look at, too. He never grew beyond the stature of a small boy of ten, but his head was ridiculously large, and the expression on his heavy grey face was of such gravity that no one felt at ease in his presence. He would stare at things and people with a prolonged intensity, falling into such depths of brooding meditation, it was not to be wondered at that he had the reputation of being an idiot. They named him Arfon.

His mother and father were convinced he was of idiotic tendencies. Mrs. Edwards never forgave him for appearing in a deformed state. So silly he looked, her only child, with his paltry thin body and massive head, she shut herself away from him in resentment and became angry at the continual ache in her heart when she looked at him. His father roared at him, protruding his thick lips and rolling his violent eyes, beating him for the sulky gravity of his face. Mrs. Edwards blamed her husband for their son's oddness.

'You got funny blood in your family,' she said accusingly; 'blood that's mad and bad. Ha, found out I have that your aunt was put away in an asylum and your grandfather in jail for whatnot. Gipsy blood is in you.'

Mr. Edwards had come to the valley from another part of Wales. She had known nothing of him, but, since he attended chapel regularly, believed him to be a healthy and ordinary man, though she realised afterwards that it was to work up a trade for his new hawking business that he became a faithful member of Soar. She had her own little pasties business before she married him, but her health was not of the best, so when Mr. Edwards paid her a visit, looked over her cottage, and proposed a marriage, she thought it would lead to prosperity. The day after they married, Mr. Edwards took thirty pounds of her money and bought a new horse and cart for his hawking, replacing the old donkey he possessed. He brought her nothing but himself. He bossed her into continuing her pasties business too. Gradually, especially in their mutual disgust over their son, they became of similar temperament, thrifty and mean in the house, regular chapel-goers, and therefore nicely prosperous in their respective business. You took a dish to Mrs. Edwards's kitchen and she filled it with pasties from a big pan.

Arfon always sat in the corner of the fireplace. Sometimes he looked at you with a slow and steady stare. You felt he knew all that there was to know about you. He was like a wise old gnome, sitting on his little stool by the fire. His eyes were sad and beautiful. They were so large and luminous in his heavy-fleshed head. Sometimes his expression was very anxious, as though he badly wanted to please people.

Arfon suffered a great deal. Except for a habit of dreaming visionary dreams and his unusual stature, he was like most other children. Especially when he was born. But as he grew, he found that the world was an ugly place. From the beginning he was aware of contempt and disgust. His mother's resentful rejection of him and his father's bad temper and anger that he would be a burden entered his heart without his being aware what they meant. And the mockery and jeering of the other young people in the place made him quiver with suffering. He had to attend the school on the hillside, and because he hated going among the other children, who poked fun at him mercilessly, he was a fool at the lessons. He would be numb with silent anger and pain. Once, after a particular bout of teasing from the other boys, and fury from the teacher, he had to be sent home with his knicker-bockers dirtied. The boys never forgot that.

He went into himself for sustenance. He dreamed of imaginary worlds where the contacts of people were of a lovelier nature than in this world. He had a talent for drawing, and with a penny box of crayons and a copybook he would be occupied for hours making pictures of his dreams. And as he went further into this imaginary sphere he thought he saw its people all about him. He called them angels. He stood gazing for an hour at an old and sulky plum tree in the garden next door, among whose branches several young angel girls were playing, dressed in frilly puce and golden skirts and bodices of shining silks. They were dainty and elegant in their frolics, leaping with fragile grace from branch to branch. Arfon would have liked to join them. When his mother's harsh voice called him from the garden, the girl angels became startled and whisked themselves with fluttering skirts away through the green leaves.

That was when he was very young. The headmaster of the Council school came to the house and complained to Mr. and Mrs. Edwards that he didn't know what to do with Arfon.

'He is a boy,' said he in his untidy English way, 'that won't make any headway in the world. And he's obstinate as a mule in his dullness. He is unable to do the sums of Standard One even now, and in his geography he is

weaker still. He doesn't seem to belong to this world at all. For why is this?'
The schoolmaster gazed at Mr. and Mrs. Edwards in a sharp and angry way as
though he blamed them or thought them not quite right in the head.

Mr. and Mrs. Edwards were of the simple class that respects schoolmasters
and learning. Mrs. Edwards told him timidly:

'He is fond of his Bible, and a religious boy.'

'You should have him seen to,' declared the schoolmaster with anger. 'Is his
health orl right?'

'A bit of fig syrup I give him often,' said Mrs. Edwards. 'Nothing he needs
otherwise, as far as I can see.'

The schoolmaster became quite furious.

'He didn't ought to be allowed to mix with other boys,' he stormed. 'He's
no good to my school and he won't get anywhere. He ought to be put away
in a reformatory or something. He's not Normal.'

Arfon sat in his corner by the fireplace. His face betrayed no particular
comment on the conversation.

'Something will have to be done about him,' continued the schoolmaster
with aggressive decision. 'He must be medically examined. Institutions there
are for the Not Quite Right. It will do the boy good to go to one. Anyone
can tell only by looking at him what a big dunce he is. He didn't ought to be
in a good, respectable school like mine, really he didn't. Well now, I will speak
to the doctor.'

He was examined by the doctor. Dr. Dan, blowing odours of liquor over
him, made him strip, and handled and did this and that to the boy, afterwards
declaring that, far from seeing anything wrong with Arfon, his body was
perfectly made even though miniature in stature. Mr. and Mrs. Edwards then
begged the chapel minister to interview their son.

Mr. Jeb. Watkin-Watkins, a bad-tempered bachelor of fifty noted for his
fiery sermons, came and sat in the parlour, on the sofa because no chair could
have held him. Snorting and sweating, he fixed his small elephant's eyes on
Arfon and thundered:

'What parts of the Bible can you speak off by heart, boy?'

Arfon at this time was thirteen, and ever since he could read he had been
engrossed in his Bible. He began to recite from the Book, without discrimin-
ation, including a great many verses from the Old Testament. Sometimes Mrs.
Edwards, who sat in the far corner, bowed her head. Arfon went on and on.
The minister's eyes became red, like an infuriated boar's. For some reason or
other he was angry. He thundered:

'A dirty mind you got, boy, loving mischief.' He turned to the mother. 'He
is a cunning lout, and full of mockery. A bad egg you got here.' He shook a

bullying hand at Arfon, as though he would swipe him. The minister's belly bulged out like a hill from the sofa. Arfon scarcely moved his intent stare from it during the whole of the interview.

Mrs. Edwards became very angry, too, in sympathy with the chapel minister. She felt that life had been sore to her.

'Did he ought to be put away?' she asked.

'He is possessed with a devil!' declared the minister. 'Beaten out of him it ought to be. Dangerous he will become. Murder and violent and dirty work he will do unless the fear of God is put in what he is possessed by.' He gathered his massive shanks together and rose, darting vicious glances at the staring Arfon. 'Something must be done about him. He ought to be beaten and put away for a few years.'

He spoke to the police about Arfon and the police spoke to the doctor and the schoolmaster. The schoolmaster for no reason at all complained that the boy 'didn't ought to be about where there were women,' but the doctor had him stripped once more for examination, afterwards insisting again that he was beautifully made if miniature and that the boy was pleasant enough to him. So of course the doctor's word counted and Arfon, feeling ill-used, escaped being put away.

But Mr. Watkin-Watkins, pursuing the matter with the malevolence of the old-fashioned evangelist, declared that the devil possessed in Arfon should be whipped out of him. He coaxed Mr. and Mrs. Edwards to grant him permission to beat the evil thing out, and the parents, frightened of the horrors that, according to the minister, Arfon would commit when he would be a young man, gave way. The minister told them to send the boy down to his house one evening.

Arfon went obediently enough, for at this time he accepted the judgments of the malignant outside world with a frightened silence. Very often his stomach felt sick and his heart as though it were full of evil stuff, but some day, he thought, everything would be clear to him and he would be the master of himself. He hated and was afraid of Mr. Watkin-Watkins, the minister of the chapel, to whom people listened in awe. The sight of the minister was like a bad dream to him. But he was one of the great powers of the world.

So that when Mr. Watkin-Watkins, after lowering the gas-light in his dark, lonely house, went on his knees and invoked God's help in driving out the devil, Arfon waited in an expectant and obedient silence for whatever was to happen. Rising, the minister, who had begun to heave with anger again, told him to take off his clothes. Arfon did so and looked down with meek, silent resignation at his frail little body.

'You lie on that mat,' said the minister sternly. 'And don't you cry out. The hand of God is in this. A sacred task it is and for your benefit. You be grateful now for what I am doing to you. Old as the world is your complaint and as old is this cure for it.'

Arfon waited, lying on his stomach. The minister took a long cane from a cupboard and, muttering imprecations and curses, began to beat Arfon.

'Out, devil, out!' rose Mr. Watkin-Watkins's voice.

Arfon had never endured such pain. This was far worse than the many thrashings he had had at school. The first stings were the worst: they made him bite into the mat to stifle his cries. He almost swooned away. Then gradually the stings seemed to lose their awful bites. Now they became quite different, warm and shuddering. He began to wait for them with a quickening of his blood. The minister's voice had become a mutter of abuse and curses. Arfon couldn't recollect feeling the devil slip out of him. Quite suddenly Mr. Watkin-Watkins ceased and sank with a groan upon the sofa. And Arfon lay in a kind of half-swoon on the mat. His body was both cold and hot, his flesh aching in a strange torment.

He turned his head and peered round the room. Mr. Watkin-Watkins had collapsed in a big heap and was breathing heavily. The sight of his ugly fat shape heaving and snorting was frightening. Arfon felt that the dark room was besieged with devils. They had big jaws, fat bodies, and paws that tore and mangled; they rose out of the earth in the darkness and hid waiting among shadows, prowling. He suddenly sprang up, startling Mr. Watkin-Watkins, who swore at him.

'Put the light on!' screamed Arfon.

The minister, frightened of Arfon's cry, obeyed. Arfon quickly dressed, and Mr. Watkin-Watkins, his underlip shaking, fetched cakes and lemonade and told Arfon that he ought to be grateful to the end of his days for what had been done to him that evening.

'Cured you are now,' he added with unction, 'and don't you go behaving funny in the future. Soon you will be a young man, and you must not allow the devil to have you in his power again.'

But Arfon went home with terror still vague in his mind. It laid a shadow over him like a menace. His hatred of the world grew. He would like to do something to have his own back. He would like to see people crying and full of rage at something he had done. He would be proud then. When he got home he stared at his mother and father with a vicious hostility. They saw a fresh light woken in his face. They examined the weals on their son's body and decided the result was worth them. For Arfon's manner did change. He answered back with impudence sometimes and could snarl like his father. He seemed more awake.

But he turned to his drawings with greater persistence. He began to draw ordinary things like old boots, pails of rubbish, a dirty shirt thrown over a washtub, and also fanciful things out of the Bible—the tablets of Moses, the does of Solomon, and the strange beasts of St. John the Divine. But his pictures of these things were so queer that he made people either laugh or ill-tempered. A shirt dripping over the side of a washtub seemed to brood in such dejection that it wept, and the weary boots waited for death like old, sad women. Arfon loved his drawings with a fierce, protective love. They appeased a hunger that nothing else could satisfy.

He wouldn't grow beyond the stature of a young boy. Mr. and Mrs. Edwards continued to lament their lot; they didn't know what to do with Arfon, now he had left school. He was too fragile for the mines, and because of his strange look no tradesman would employ him.

'What you want to do?' bellowed his father. 'What d'you think you've got talent for?'

'I want to make drawings,' sulked Arfon.

'What d'you want to *work* at?' continued his father impatiently. 'To earn money. Think we're going to keep you? And dead we'll be soon. What'll you do then?'

Arfon wished his father would die. 'Draw pictures for papers I can,' he muttered.

'The only thing left,' moaned his mother, who would have liked him to be a preacher, if there had been money for his training, 'is for him to help you sell your things in the streets. A hawker he must be, like you.'

'Don't you call me a hawker, Mrs. Edwards,' snapped her husband. 'I am a respectable tradesman of twenty years' standing.'

So Arfon followed his father and the cart in the streets and sold oil and oddments. He did his work with the uncomplaining delicacy of a saintly martyr; he deftly measured out the oil with his thin fingers and counted threepennyworth of clothes pegs in a manner that made the transaction memorable to the women customers. His old-world courtesy, his large eyes slowly looking at them, his darling small body, tickled the women and girls. Sometimes they did their best to flirt with him.

But Arfon became a very grave youth. His mind was always occupied with visions. He still imagined a different race of beings in the world. These fanciful persons were always tall, vigorous, and gentle in a proud way. He made pictures of them: walking, sitting, lying, naked or draped idly; and though their behaviour was earthly, their beauty was not the beauty of this world as we know it. Every evening he sat at his drawings, lifting the brass oil lamp to the kitchen table and sitting down in an alert and serious way,

22

indifferent to any interruptions in the room. Once, his mother, who sat watching him for some time, got up and began to examine the drawing on the table. A flush came to her worn, dried cheeks.

'What are these, boy?' she cried shrilly.

'Men and women,' he said, without raising his head.

He saw her thin, spotted hand, gone sharp and clutching, snatch up the drawings. His head jerked up. She was about to tear the papers, and he uttered a cry, fierce and dangerous. The mother looked at him, her action withheld. The fury in his eyes burned her, but it was not that that prevented her from destroying the drawings. Seeing his agonised face, her heart warned her of the damage she would have done him.

'You do pictures,' she cried, dropping them, 'like that in my house!'

'They are good,' he cried indignantly, and sighed with relief that they were out of her hands.

'Good!' she muttered, moving away. 'There's awful your mind must be.' She crouched over the fire. There was no doubt he was daft. She had never seen such evil things put on paper. His mind was horrible. Ach, she had been an unfortunate woman. But all the time her heart was aching with pity and sorrow. She dreaded what the world could do to him.

He was very lonely. Other youths would have no truck with him because of his queer look and reputation, and though there were girls who were ready enough to be approached, interested in his oddness, he was at the age when, to some sensitive natures, living young women are more fearsome than horned and tailed devils that have brimstone shining under their skin.

A small, fragile figure in a neat black suit, he was often to be seen making his way with a slow, dwarfish dignity to the coal-dusty lanes that led down to the river or to the large cemetery among the yew trees on the hillside. The river was dirty and weary as it wandered among rust-coloured rushes and hungry, unkempt alders; and the cemetery beyond its borders of yew trees was raw with cut stones and white pebbly paths among the rows of graves. Yet he experienced a mournful satisfaction in these places. In the hush of the cemetery his senses seemed to open like delicate bells of flowers, and the sound of the dusty, crawling river, as he squatted at evening beneath a tree, lulled him into a mysterious trance in which he saw strange figures and landscapes. Then he would go home and draw what he had seen, in the light of the oil lamp.

Mockery hurt him as though death gripped his senses in an icy clutch, though he seldom showed what wounds it tore. He would only become impassive as a stone. He was mocked at enough. Children called rude things after him because of his little stature; acquaintances jeeringly asked him if he still saw angels climbing under women's skirts and up men's legs; groups of girls tittered as he passed; and the uncouth gangs of youths that go about the lanes tried to tear his trousers down. Often the world seemed to be nothing but malice and meanness and shame; he wanted to get away from the place. His father said roughly:

'What you going to do and where's the money to come from? At a disadvantage you are. A boy such as you can't go out into the world like ordinary, well-grown chaps. Stay here you've got to and take my cart round yourself when I'm too far gone in my rheumatics to move.'

He was a very dejected figure sitting high on his father's piled-up cart, the reins in his thin hands and stoniness in his grey, large face, while the aged horse ambled through the bleak rows of dwellings. Since Arfon could do the work thoroughly, the father took to grumbling about pains in his limbs, staying in bed.

Never once had Arfon been to the world beyond the hills of the valley. Newspapers were read, but the behaviour of that outside world might have belonged to another age or to a book. The knowledge that had been taught him in school was used up in dreams; there was no need to apply it to the simple living of the valley. Far countries and different customs were the substances of visions that he tried to place in his drawings. And so people laughed at his fantastic pictures, or angrily denounced them, or were upset at some, though no one ever forgot the power of their curious lines and completed designs. They had a life of their own and were not related to civilisation; they had the virginity of pure creation, like the art of savages on cave walls or in carved wood.

At last, late, he began to long for girls, being seventeen. He forced himself to court one or two in the traditional manner: winking at the favoured across the gallery of the chapel and approaching them after the service for a walk. Some went with him. But he did not like their amusement. They seemed to treat him as a joke and he suffered deeply when they tittered at his high, romantic love-making, that was courteous and poetic. They were strong, well-fleshed girls and sometimes he had an impulse to maul them. But he was too proud, and so the girls laughed at him, getting their own back in dissatisfaction.

Then he became passionately enamoured of Dilys Roberts. He had seen her accidentally one warm summer day coming down the garden from the back door of her aunt's cottage. She was wearing nothing but a gay pale green undergarment and, unconscious that he stood behind a lilac bush, she half-waltzed down the path, with beautiful young movements, her heavy gold hair dripping in the shine of the sun. She uttered a little scream when she saw him, but stood her ground and began to abuse him.

'A Peeping Tom, that's what you are,' she said indignantly.

'I come here,' he protested, 'every day to see if there's any oil wanted. Look you at my cart outside.'

His face was gleaming with homage.

She looked at him consideringly and he flushed, becoming very aware of physical oddness. She had a slight, thin face that yet was very decided in its contours, her red mouth wilful and her eyes dark blue and calculating. Her nude thighs were alive and vidid, her breasts were the size of full-grown pears. She was about eighteen. He drew breath and said in a deep, slow way:

'Fine you looked coming down the path. I couldn't turn away or do anything.'

And a slight breeze rippled the silk of her garment. His eyes were warm and full of light. She looked at him and recognised his homage. Now she was very self-possessed and haughty in her undergarment.

'You knock the door first next time,' she told him. 'You got no right to come in people's private property.'

He had never seen her before. Later he found that she had arrived to live with her aunt in the cottage. She came from Swansea and so was a town young lady. She was an orphan and failed to find favour with the people of the place. They said she was flighty. She hadn't been in the valley a week and already she was walking out with a young collier, a handsome lout who drank and ran whippet races. She had been seen smoking a cigarette. She was common.

Her beauty was a new world to him. When he thought of the delicate slope of her thighs his muscles would clench in a new quick ecstasy, and the fact that she walked the earth, that she went through the same streets, that she breathed the same air, was so exciting and extraordinary that he was willing to believe anything, that dragons and fairies and magicians and dog-faced human beings lived in the world. He would have laid down his life fighting for her.

She wore a lot of jewellery: large pearls and sparkling red stones at her throat, dainty rings on her fine fingers. He was a little cold about her display of these ornate things when he saw her walking in the streets. He wondered if they were costly. He saw the collier boy with her and stood in a numb, staring trance. They went past him. She saw Arfon and smiled at him subtly, her eyes coquettish and full of enjoyment. He woke into a world of jealousy and torture.

When next he called at the house she came to the door and looked at his haggard face with the same smile, her wilful mouth curled in pleasure. He always let her have oil, soap, candles, anything he had on the cart for nothing now. The money her aunt gave her for the purchases she kept for herself, of course, since it was her beauty that got them free. And, looking at him, she basked in his intense homage and hunger for her. Her eyes encouraged him to stammer:

'You—you will walk out with me one evening?'

She nodded her head gaily, watching the excitement that inflamed his face. She had never roused such passion before, and she liked it. Her blue eyes were wicked and calculating.

'Where,' he breathed, 'shall I see you then?'

'In some quiet spot,' she said, 'where there are no people.'

He understood that was because of her collier boy. He was content, though how proud he would have been to display her in the streets! They arranged to meet on the hillside beyond the school. And the couple of days that elapsed before the meeting were like a dream. The hills cried and the valleys murmured her name. He stole roses from back gardens because in their perfume she was nearer to him; he bathed in the sheep pond in the hills because the coolness was like her skin against his; and the warm sun, shaking off its red glow as it lifted over the rim of the far vale, saw him at his bedroom window waiting for the day.

He was at the appointed place long before the proper time. He wore his best black suit and a bowler hat that gave a bit of height to his dwarfish stature. He stood beneath a mulberry bush and never took his eyes from the bend in the road. That hour's wait for the assignation opened up all the wells of suffering in him. Would she come, would she come? Or had she teased him? She was thirty-five minutes late.

She came slowly up the hill, glancing back now and again. The pale evening dusk was behind her, and his heart sang; they would have a lovely evening together in the mystery of the night. She wore a red tam-o'-shanter, a dark bit of a frock, and silken stockings. She looked impudent and larkish. The ordinary, careless way in which she greeted him filled him with acute chagrin. But she had come at last.

'Shall we,' he asked meekly, 'go up the hill, then?'

She peered up the grey slope of mountain.

'There's no one about,' he said petulantly.

'Lonely the hill looks,' she said. She looked at him consideringly and decided it would be safe to go. Too safe perhaps, she thought, and with a little gay movement took his arm.

'You're a funny little thing,' she said.

That hurt him, because he hated any talk that might be applied to his body, that was miniature in stature but adult in perception. But the hurt was almost a pleasure. She was with him and holding his arm.

'Why,' he suddenly asked with difficulty, 'do you go about with that chap I saw you with?'

'Since when,' she enquired coolly, 'must I ask you to choose my friends?'

He was silent. He looked at her intently. And though she was with him and holding his arm she seemed so mysterious and inaccessible he thought that never would he have the courage to press her to the ground and kiss her. Yet he was burning to do it. He felt that he could never rest or sleep again until he had felt her body and kissed her mouth.

She became coy. She was fond of a bit of joking and a bit of lewdness. She began to give her views on things. She didn't believe in God, and the Bible was full of silly lies. Presently she asked him if he knew any limericks.

'No,' he said. 'You tell me some.'

She shook her head. 'I don't mind *listening* to them,' she said.

Intently he kept his eyes open for a suitable hollow to which he might lead her. The ones he saw were already occupied with silent, loving couples; the hill was not so lonely as it looked. All the hollows of the hills were filled with happy embracing lovers. He began to be irritated and impatient at his failure to find an empty one. Dilys kept on chattering.

'Won't you ever get bigger than you are now?' she asked suddenly.

He did not answer. She laughed in a teasing way.

'I bet you make up for it enough in other ways,' she said flatteringly.

Anger began to stir in him. But then he spied an empty hollow and sighed with relief.

'Let's go there,' he said in a shaking voice.

She held back a moment, looking consideringly at the bracken in the cosy dip. But she laughed daringly and pinched his arm.

'You behave yourself, then,' she whimpered.

They went into the hollow and sat amid the bracken. He could not wait. Anger and irritation and hunger and homage were mingled in a rising fume of passion. He pulled her down. She uttered a cry at his sharp clasp.

'Let go of me, you brute!' she said indignantly.

He loosened her, thereby making an error. She appeared to be tidying herself.

'You mustn't be *bossy*,' she said.

He sulked. Then she began to tickle him, subtly, with her lewd hands. His passion burned up and he began to handle her. But she lost her temper again and denounced him, calling him a ruffian and a rude, ill-bred boy. He subsided in a fret of pain and submission. Then again she began to play about with him, as though he were a baby or a doll.

'You funny little thing,' she cooed. 'Darling little thing.'

And because he was so hungry for her touch he lay still and let her fondle him. That was all she wanted, he said to himself bitterly; and, even so, there was an ecstasy as she touched him. But presently she tired of it and got up.

'I mustn't be late,' she said. 'Not tonight.'

In pain he watched the beautiful grace of her movements as she shook the bits of bracken from her dress. Ah, she was so lovely, he could have died with her. Her cruelty was something he could not understand; it was part of that vast implacable brutality that he had always endured from the world.

'Come on,' she said, 'my dear.'

Her affectionate tone soothed his dissatisfaction. They descended the hill in the half-light of the summer night. She announced at length:

'I have a birthday next week. Fancy, I'm eighteen then! Soon I'll be a woman.' She pressed his arm. 'When is your birthday, dear? You must tell me.'

'Not for a long time yet,' he answered. 'But you tell me now what you would like for your birthday.'

'Oh, no, no!' she cried. 'You mustn't give me presents.'

'I got a bit of money,' he said, 'and there is nothing else to spend it on.'

'Are you rich?' she asked. 'Very well off you must be, doing a big trade with the cart. You can make plenty of money by yourself. But that's no business of mine.'

'What would you like?' he asked.

After a while she gave way and admitted she had a fondness for some amber beads she had seen in the jeweller's window. But he wasn't to buy them, they were much too expensive, she wouldn't take them. And she became lovingly well-disposed as they walked along the road at the back of the school. She even called him a sweet darling.

Then he felt he would do and get anything for her. He listened in a desperate joy to her affectionate talk; he must keep this precious thing that had come into his life, he must not let it go.

She stopped in the shadow of a wall to leave him before they came to the streets. And suddenly she bent her head and lightly, sweetly, as though a cold flower touched him, he felt her lips on his. As quickly she drew back and, whispering, 'Monday, at the same time and place,' she left him.

He leant back against the wall, his eyes closed; and his soul opened within him. The sudden cool, sweet kiss seemed beautiful beyond all meaning. It cleansed out of him all the bitterness and dissatisfaction of what had gone before.

From then he lived in a quickened world. His confidence was like the strong full shine of that summer's sun. The next day he trotted down to the local jeweller's. He had a little sum of his own, hidden away in a cocoa tin up the chimney of his bedroom. The beads, however, were eight shillings more than his savings; he was startled to see them priced at two pounds. But he went into the shop and asked that they should be reserved for him, paying what he had. Money was nothing but a collection of ridiculous round pieces. Dilys must have her beads.

He took the eight shillings out of the takings of the cart, and since his father still ran the business and took all the profits, giving Arfon pocket money, it was dishonesty. Arfon decided that he would make it up by giving short measure with the paraffin. Nothing mattered except Dilys's pleasure.

And with a fiercer spurt of inspiration he began some new drawings. Of Dilys, clothed and unclothed, as he imagined her. He worked with quick, nervous energy, a heat in his limbs, his mind warmed through. It was as though he was possessing her as he drew.

His inflamed vision did not see what came through in the drawings. In spite of the untamed rough beauty of his line there was a sinister ugliness in the portraiture of the young girl. A cruel meanness hovered in her face. Had he been aloof from his personal reactions to the living girl even he would have seen the masterly vulgarity his strange talent had worked into the drawings. The cruelty of that ugliness emerged in a desperately triumphant way from the luminous beauty of her physical form. And he treasured these drawings as though they were an inseparable part of the loveliness she had brought into his life.

His mother watched this new intense industry with narrowed eyes. Her anger with him now was always mingled with grief. She could not loosen her love for him, she could scarcely touch him, and sometimes she wished him safe in death. She saw one or two of the drawings and jumped.

'Who is this?' she cried, wrinkling her brow, that was brownish and spotted like an old lemon.

'Someone,' he said, working on, 'someone.'

She peered at them closer.

'It is that Dilys Roberts, the flighty slut from Swansea!' she exclaimed. 'Ho, ho, she is the one you are interested in, is it? Fine pictures of her too! Angry she's made you? And let me tell you, boy, she's—'

'Leave them alone and don't you talk about her!' he shouted in such a rage that she drew back as though from thunder. And gathering his things he hurried out of the room. He could not bear her voice intruding in his dream.

He dare not think too much of the young collier whom Dilys walked about with quite openly. At the barest thought of him he wanted to do violence to the ruffian, fight him, maim him, assert his mastery in a high, vigorous way. But he knew himself helpless. When he looked at his own fragile boy's body he was filled with shame and anger. Why had he been born thus and what could he blame? At such moments he felt murderous with hostility and malignancy against the world. And he knew that Dilys's familiarity with the collier boy was still another grin of mockery from that world.

Again on Monday night he was quivering with apprehension that she would not come. The beads were in his pocket. When he saw her saunter out of the turning in the road, late, his sinews tightened and all his nerves were alert in an exquisite torture of shyness. He would have prostrated himself at her approach and set his mouth to the earth that her feet would touch. She smiled gaily and expectantly. She had sewn a long tassel on her red tam-o'-shanter, which hung rakishly on the back of her head. Her eyes were full of a wicked and pleased amusement and he wondered why.

'Happy you look,' he remarked in his sensitive voice.

'Next time I'll come looking sulky,' she said. 'Perhaps you prefer me that way.' They began to climb the hill.

He said tentatively, 'Never am I sure what people are thinking when I see laughing in their face.'

'Oh, go on, you silly thing,' she said, and took his arm familiarly.

He brightened. 'I have brought the beads,' he announced proudly.

She uttered an excited cry. 'Really? No, you haven't! You weren't so extravagant and silly as to go and buy them? Teasing me you are. I shan't take them! Indeed, I never meant—'

He drew the beads out of his pocket. The shiny yellow marbles gleamed in the evening dimness. She was silenced and, loosening his arm, she held out her hands excitedly.

'Oh, aren't they lovely! Are they for me? Oh, I shan't take them. I never meant you to buy me things.' She flushed in gratification and eagerness. He dropped the beads on the tissue paper and gave them to her. He felt the eager warmth of her blood and the gift was nothing as payment. His veins began to burn.

'I shall wear them!' she cried proudly. She turned to him and said generously, 'You must put them on me the first time.'

They stopped, and he took the beads. But his fingers trembled so much at her nearness that he couldn't fix the clasp properly. His fingers at her neck, while she laughed at him, he felt a sudden strange impulse to handle her slim throat in a rough, passionate grip. His heart beat like a hammer as the dark impulse leapt out of the unknown, his fingers at her slim, fine neck, her

30

unbearably beautiful body so near to his own. He drew away, his chest as though filled with breath that couldn't be released, his face rigid. His fingers had mechanically fastened the clasp.

'There!' she cried, still quite absorbed in the gift, 'aren't they lovely! Oh, I'm proud of them, I am really.'

'Nice they look,' he breathed.

'But I shan't be able to sleep, thinking what they cost,' she said, fingering them.

'That's all right, then,' he said, beginning to be vexed at her complete absorption in the stupid beads. 'Come on, now.'

She was very nice to him as they climbed the hill looking for a hollow, asking him about his home life, his mother, and his school life, and she seemed to be very interested in his short and abrupt replies, musing on them commentingly. But she kept on glancing at her string of beads.

When they had found a hollow and had sat there a little time she complained of a headache, saying the strong air of the hills affected her.

'Indeed, not very well I've been the last few days,' she sighed. 'So be nice and gentle with me, Arfon, and pet me. My aunt has been very trying, working me to death, unwell as I've been too. She takes advantage of me because I'm an orphan.' Her voice appealed to him not to be rough with her.

He was disappointed. He thought she looked well and happy enough when she had greeted him earlier. Still, he had heard that girls had strange bouts of moody sickness sometimes. His yearning arms half embraced her, but she lay as if asleep and, mortified, he had to be content with stroking her neck.

From that time she did as she liked with him. They made an arrangement to meet secretly once a week. He complained about her open familiarity with the collier, but she lost her temper and told him *that* was something he did not understand, afterwards, in pity at his distress, adding that it was he she was fonder of but she was afraid of the collier, what he would do if she finished with him. 'He's so big and bad-tempered,' she said, 'and he's got a hold on me now.'

She often kissed Arfon in a sweet, delicious way. Within a month she had received from him the amber beads, a gold-plated watch, and some ear-rings. He cunningly cheated his customers and stole out of the takings and lied to his father about the value of the goods that remained in stock. Nothing mattered but Dilys's pleasure.

But there came a time when he could steal and cheat no more and he was left with only his few shillings of pocket money. October came, and Dilys was fancying a little fur to put round her neck; it was getting chilly on the hills, she complained.

'A darling little fur I saw in Lewis's window,' she said, 'just like real fox it looked.'

'How much was it?' he asked, beginning to be angry.

'Only forty-five shillings.' She sighed again. 'I wish I wasn't so poor. I don't get a chance to save a shilling a week. My aunt is so miserly.'

He felt, like a mutter deep within him, a revulsion from her rise up, dark and strange. And he thought bitterly how mean she was with herself. When they could have had such lovely times together. Her meanness, when she possessed such beauty of form, touch, and glance, kept him always at an intense pitch of half-angry and half-suppliant desire. He began to realise it, deep within him, like a submerged mutter.

'I don't know if I can buy it,' he said, angrily kicking some stones away from the path they walked on.

'Oh, Arfon, I didn't expect you to!' she cried as though in pain at the very thought.

He looked over the stock of the cart to see if he could possibly sell more without his father suspecting it. He dare not risk it; his father had been examining the stock only a day or two ago. But that he was unable to get the fur nagged him into irritation and anger and hatred of the world. Why couldn't he ever get what he wanted, why couldn't he be happy? He was only really happy when he was working at his drawings, in a kind of dream state. But he wanted to be happy in the world and with real people; he hated all the mockery and the harshness and the misunderstanding he met with.

Then because he had not managed to get the fur, he decided to take Dilys his drawings of her when they met next. These drawing were his most treasured possessions, but he would give them to her; she had not seen them. There were fourteen, and as he looked at them his pulses took fire from the strange, perverted beauty he had given them. Lately he had been unable to do any more drawings of her. Even at the thought of trying to design her on paper his desire would reach a pitch of intensification that made all work impossible; he could only lay his head on his arms and moan.

When they met she glanced at the thin, flat parcel inquisitively. He knew she expected to see the fur. After a while he said nervously:

'I have been doing some pictures of you.'

'Are those them in the parcel?' she asked.

'Yes.'

She said nothing. They climbed the ancient hill. It was almost dark. The landscape looked old and wrinkled. He said, with a throb of suffering in his voice:

'You must take them, because they belong to you.'

'How do they belong to me,' she said, 'when you did them?'

She spoke in a voice of indifference. Again a spasm of anger contracted his heart for a moment. If it had been the fur! But her face was so beautiful in the dim light, her slim throat so white, like the soft throat of a great pale bird.

'Well,' he answered, 'I couldn't have done them at all if I hadn't met you. You must see them, indeed you must.'

'All right,' she said.

She did not brighten at all that evening. Her manner was so cold and aloof he dared not even touch her with his hand. They took a short walk over the hill and then she said she'd have to be going back. She felt icy, she said. As they descended the hill he told her that he'd like to buy her that fur she had spoken about.

'Oh, don't you bother,' she answered. But she visibly softened. 'No, indeed you mustn't.'

But as a threat she didn't kiss him, and she was about to leave him without taking the drawings. He thrust the parcel into her hand. 'You be alone when you look at them,' he said.

And all the following days he was in a fume of excitement, now that the drawings were in her hands. Now she had seen his real worship of her; now she knew how beautiful he thought her. All he dared not tell her was in the pictures, and all that he imagined her like. She would admire him now, because he could make such pictures. He knew they were good.

Impatient to receive her admiration, he called at the house the third day, with the cart at the back door. He called out, and after keeping him waiting some time, Dilys appeared.

She came slowly down the garden path. He looked at her intently. Something had upset her, he said to himself. Perhaps her aunt had been bossing her again.

'Two dozen candles,' she rapped out, 'and three bars of carbolic soap.' Her hand held the money for the goods, which she would have for nothing, in her pocket.

He fetched the articles. Her face was pinched and pale with anger. As he laid the candles and soap in her hands she looked at him in a direct stare, with the terrifying fury of a female who is seldom stirred to her depths. She said, slowly and evenly:

'You do drawings like that of me again and it'll be the worse for you.'

He stared. Then her voice began to flame up.

'What do you think I am, low and dirty-minded creature that you are! Been showing those pictures to people, have you?'

He stared at her. Something in him shrank back from her as though from an evil. Never had he received such a blow as this. He could not speak.

She became truculent. 'You dare do drawings of me like that again and I'll tell the police. You ought to be put under lock and key.' Seeing his strained numbness she added brutally, 'Those you gave me I put in the fire.'

His faculties started into life at that. But it was a raw, quivering life of anguish. She had burned them!

'You burned them!' he whispered.

She was dignified and superior now, eased by his suffering.

'You learn to respect me, you nasty-minded boy. People like you think that because a girl is nice to you she's what-not. There's no one can say a word about me. Even though I *do* walk out with one or two boys, they might be girls for all the harm that's done—'

But he had turned and gone. He climbed into the cart and laid whip on the mare. The unaccustomed lash roused the animal into a quick trot.

The day passed slow in a merciless and taunting misery. He wanted the night and sleep. At last he crawled into the darkness of his bedroom. It was like the lair of a wounded beast. He did not understand the hurt that had been done him. Only it seemed that he must suffer for ever now. The last loveliness had been taken from him. There remained nothing but contempt in the world.

He could not sleep. And, strangely, though he tried not to think of her and what she had done, Dilys was nearer to him now than she had ever been. Before, she had been a beautiful girl who escaped his eager touch. Now, she seemed to be deep in him. She held his nerves and shadowed his blood and spoke in his mind like a ghost. And again in the grief of that night he longed to have her body clenched with his, to caress her sides, her breasts, her slim white neck . . . When at last he slept, at dawn, his face was lined and exhausted as an old man's.

He had no peace from her. From his nerves and his blood and his mind she sang a low, urging song of mockery and passion. He felt goaded on to some unknown fulfilment. He could not live without her. The next day but one he called again at the house. She came out to him with displeasure held in her face in aloof elegance. He was dirt. She smelled of violets and she wore his amber beads. He looked at her and she saw his new fixed gaze.

'You will come and meet me the same as usual?' he asked in a low voice.

And she was fascinated. His miniature body was so firm and his ridiculous large head was held high.

'I wonder,' she began, 'you got the cheek to ask. But if you promise to

34

respect me and stop doing those drawings, I don't mind seeing you for a little while.'

'I will bring that fur,' he said.

A gleam crossed her eyes. 'Indeed,' she said, 'I think you ought to make up for the insults you've done me.'

There were two days in which to find the forty-five shillings for the fur. Trade was poor that day and the next. He searched the house for money. He failed to scrape even thirty shillings. But he would get it for her the next week. Surely she wouldn't mind waiting another week.

His desire for her became desperate. He would like to bear her away to some far vale among the lonely hills and there serve her and love her in lawless passion, far from the ugliness of other people. The evening when, waiting, he saw her come round the turning of the road behind the school he could have cried out with relief. He was so obsessed with her that he forgot to apologise for the absence of the fur.

She was cold and aloof. But his senses were so quickened he did not notice it. They went up the hill. But she resolutely refused to sit in a hollow.

'I'm cold,' she said. 'I must go back soon.'

'No, no,' he muttered.

And he flung himself upon her with a sob. She was knocked over. He had not meant to do that, unaware of his strength. She bounced up, and the back of her hand caught him viciously across the eyes.

'Take that!' she cried savagely.

The blow went deep into him. He, too, reeled. And then the desire utterly to crush her came to him. He fell to his knees, his head whirling in a drunken darkness. The world was reeling and falling about him as the desire to crush her utterly rose up strong and triumphant. He remained on his knees, his slight body bent over, swaying his head in the darkness. Her blow had been nothing. But he had realised at last her miserly use of him.

'What's the matter with you?' she cried, a little frightened that he had risen from his curious swaying prostration.

He rose slowly, averting his face from her.

'Go,' he whispered; 'go away from me.'

She backed from him, and he remained with his head dropped on his chest. He had no sight in the new mad swirl of desire that was beating through his body to his hands, which were stretched rigidly against his thighs. The darkness came out of his consciousness like the endless dark of death, and his old self was obliterated. When he slowly moved his face up, the girl was gone. With the slow, plodding step of a man who has doom in him he descended the hill in the silent night.

35

The next few days he transacted the business of living in a fixed and unbreakable silence. He spent hours staring into space, greatly irritating his mother and father. Then one evening he came home from his hawking and entered to a loud, furious shout from his father.

'Here comes the thief!'

His mother looked at him with anger and contempt.

'Found out we have how you been stealing from the takings for that bitch!' continued his father, his face mottled blue.

His mother put in accusingly, 'You been buying her things. I been told. And boasting she is about it.'

'Gold watches!' shouted his father frantically. 'Out of my goods. A criminal thief, that's what we've brought up, Lizzie Edwards. In a reformatory he ought to be put. Ha, if I wasn't lying here bent up with rheumatics I'd put the whip about him. The whip he ought to have. A good whipping. The pounds he must have stolen. Gold watches and what not!'

He subsided into a whining groan. He had always been miserly.

Arfon did not lose his sullen silence. Only his eyes took on a deeper and more luminous gleam.

'Shame on you,' his mother said in disgust. 'And she going about boasting of what she's had out of you. A laughing-stock you'll be. A slut of a girl like that!'

'Out of my sight, you sulky b——!' roared his father anew, from his bed chair by the fire. And turning to his wife he said, 'Oh, what are we do to with our business now, Lizzie Edwards, for a criminal thief can't have it. He must be turned out.'

'Hush now,' said Mrs. Edwards, looking from Arfon to him.

Arfon had said not a word. Their denunciations meant very little. But that his high, lovely passion should come to this! He suffered with the fierce, uncontrolled suffering of adolescence, that is like no other in its depth and misery. Silently he went out of the house. His mother wanted to follow him, out of the instinct of a subterranean hurt in her being. But she didn't. She couldn't forgive the gods their sport in giving her such an eccentric and deformed child. Let him come to his conclusion alone.

He wandered through the evening streets, not knowing where to go. At last, almost unconsciously, he got to the cemetery, where in his childhood he had spent such hours of pensive meditation. He had known serenity in this graveyard among the yew trees. He crawled in through a hedge at the back. The white stones were mysterious in the darkness and there was a sweet damp odour, as though loads of chrysanthemums were scattered over the ground.

36

The yew trees dropped their dim robes of shadow. This was the land of the dead.

Squatting against the back of a firm, sharp cross of marble he stared fixedly into the quiet dark. And almost he was soothed as he sat thoughtless and abstracted in the slow throbbing of misery. A silence rose out of the earth and laid upon him its pure cold hands of peace. For long he remained thus. He did not know that he should have clung in desperation to that source of silence that had been offered to him. Even in these moments he began to long for Dilys. He would forgive her all if he could have her touch him then. All that she had done to him. How wonderful it would be if she laid her head on his knees and, his hands in the thick drip of her hair, she listened to his voice telling her that he would love her for ever. He shut his eyes in ecstasy at the thought, his head leaning against the marble of the icy cross.

But she was not there. Again he remembered, and misery rose up full and undiminished in a new force and beat in his nerves again.

Christ, she was lost to him. She had cast him off now. She could boast of what she had got out of him! Christ, she was a slut, as his mother had said. Somebody ought to do damage to her. She ought to be made to suffer.

Rage began to burn up in him. His small chest seemed to swell to massive proportions, the muscles of his arms and legs tightened to an iron strength. His breast moved convulsively as he panted for air. He had risen to his feet, but he fell again and lay in the narrow space between two graves. His mouth bit into the earth. He lay there until the fury had subsided into a numbed pain clenched in the pit of his stomach. His limbs were stiff and aching and damp. A blackness had come over his mind. He rose and began to walk out of the cemetery. But his gait seemed a crouch, as though his mind was in dread of some doom. His face was mute and cold.

It was night now, and the main street was noisy with young girls and fellows courting and flirting. Everybody seemed gay and happy. Guffaws of laughter, feminine titters, and teasing remarks emerged from the shop doorways. The world was enjoying itself.

Arfon did not see a young man detach himself from a group of his companions and follow him up the main street. He turned to take the longer way home, down by the river beyond the houses. He did not want to reach home until his father and mother had gone to bed.

Down by the lonely river, that was shallow and dirty amid its stones and alders, he became aware of the young man following him. Suddenly the fellow strode up, caught him roughly by his coat collar, and growled:

'Now I got you, you little monkey.'

Arfon glared at him in the faint light. But instantly he knew it was the

young collier Dilys walked out with. He tried to squirm out of the grasp. It
was useless. The collier's other hand caught him by his trousers over the belly
and he was completely helpless. He began to shout and curse. The collier
thrust his jowl upon Arfon's face and said:

'You touch or speak to my girl again and I'll half kill you, you little bastard.
See!'

Arfon exerted all his new-found strength. He managed to kick the collier
on the shin. Swearing, the collier lifted him bodily, carried him to the river
bank, and threw him into a pool.

'Cool off, you bloody little ape-face.'

He floundered to his knees in the shallow pool. His bruised body was full
of murder. If he had a knife! He caught a huge stone and blindly hurled it at
the collier. It missed. He took another and ran through the water to the low
bank where the other stood.

'Ha!' cried the collier derisively, and leapt quickly on a mound in the river,
caught Arfon, knocked the stone out of his hand, and ducked him smartly
into the nearby pool, holding him face downwards in the water. Then he
lifted him out and cast him contemptuously on a shallow reach of the stream.

Arfon could scarcely draw breath. He thought he was dying. His limbs
twitched convulsively. Consciousness of the world had gone out of him. Then
gradually he became aware of the soft, cold flow of water beneath him, and its
gentle noise among the stones. His heart began to pound. He opened his eyes
and saw the vast arch of the sky. And now he had entered another kingdom,
he was of the old world no longer. He was conscious of a dark, sinister force
in every movement, every attribute, and every manifestation of this kingdom,
a cold urge of determined cruelty.

In this new awareness he rose and was indifferent to the bruises and
discomfort of his body, even to his soaked clothes, which were clammy and
cold. He felt a desire to laugh, loudly and brutally, laugh until the granite hills
cracked and were shattered in the grand upheaval that he could see at the back
of his mind. He was greater than the hills, their massive power was as nothing
compared to the power of destruction that was in his own mind and hands.
They should see, they should see.

He went home in a kind of delirious ecstasy. That night he slept soundly a
deep, dark sleep in which he went down into the very heart of silence and
annihilation. Now he had entrance into that kingdom of the underworld that
he had sensed for some days, and he tasted of its sleep. When he woke,
refreshed and warm, he lay for long in meditation.

He called at Dilys's house during the day. She came out to the back garden

38

and looked at him curiously. His manner was deferential and his voice pleading as he said:

'Please forgive me for that night. A bad fit of temper it was.'

'You can't be trusted at all,' she said curtly.

His expression became humble. 'You forget it now,' he appealed to her in thorough dejection, 'and I will be polite and respecting to you always. Oh, Dilys, don't you turn from me now. I will look after you well, indeed I will, I will do anything for you.'

She began to relent. She still wore his amber beads, and her fingers, as she considered the matter with queenly dignity, played with them. Her face was aloof and dignified, her neck stiffened as she decided the issue. He watched her from beneath drooped eyelids. At last she said:

'Very well, then. You behave properly in the future and we will walk together.'

'Thank you indeed, very much,' he said with exaggerated politeness. And he added in a brisk, businesslike fashion, 'That fur you want now? I shall be pleased to buy it.'

She rewarded him with a pleasant smile. 'Well, you have promised it to me,' she said.

'That you shall have and much more,' he said royally.

'We will take a little walk then tommorrow evening, shall we say?' she granted him with equal generosity.

'Thanks now, thank you,' he said, out of his throat, as though he were moved to tears at the reconciliation. But he would not lift his eyelids and look at her fully. Without losing his deferential manner he muttered more thanks and left her. The blood in his veins sang.

He bought the fur, stealing, with careless indifference, the money from the next day's takings. His father thought that he would not dare steal again, after the discovery of his previous dishonesty. His mother watched him narrowly as he prepared to go out, aware of the subtle change in his features and expression. She began to be afraid of him, and that night she prayed on her knees that he would become a good, God-fearing young man. Lately he had refused to go to chapel and she thought he would become a disordered atheist. She prayed long and simply for his safety, going to God with the confidences and fears she couldn't bring herself to utter to her son.

It was a cold, windless night. The hills, under the high, dark blue sky, had the stillness of eternity. Their stretches of tawny earthy and granite, that had been trod by the Druids in their secret sacrifices, swept up in terrific repose to the silence of that immaculate sky. So far, far away seemed the heavens, withdrawn and aloof from the trival human habitations in the valley. Only the granite shoulders of the hills yearned, in their magnificent dignity and silence, to the sky that was so supremely high and apart. Humanity seemed nothing. Arfon, a tiny figure climbing the lowest slope of one of the hills, beyond the raw cemented school dwelling, looked like an insect crawling over their immense sleeping limbs.

He was glad it was such a still night. There was nothing to distract him. He felt the loneliness of the hills. No one came to them when the cold weather set in; there would be plenty of unoccupied hollows tonight. In his hand he carried a parcel: the fur.

As usual Dilys was late. But tonight he was not impatient. He waited in the shadow of a naked shrub like an image of stone, his large head scarcely moving even when he saw her come slowly round the bend beyond the school. But, as she approached, his veins tightened until they seemed like knotted whips over his body. In a spasm of delight he listened to the little tap, tap of her feet, and for him the sound rang to the high skies.

They greeted each other politely.

'Oof!' she said, 'there's a rush I've had to get here. And I can't stay long this time. Such a cat for watching me my aunt is now. Is that the fur you're carrying, Arfon dear?'

'Yes,' he said.

'Oh, that's nice of you. Let me see it at once. I want to wear it now. My throat is cold.' She stretched her hand for the parcel eagerly.

He gave her a teasing little smile. 'I will put it round your throat presently,' he said. 'You will be nice now and let me have the pleasure of putting it on you? Wait until we get to the top of this hill though. A bit of light there is on the hilltops and we can see it better.'

'Oh,' she pouted, 'let me have it now.'

'I like to tease you,' he said, smiling. 'You shan't have it until you have been a little walk with me. There, shut up now and say no more.' He pretended to be very bossy, like a young man courting a girl properly.

She peered at him. 'Indeed,' she said doubtfully, 'I don't know if I can trust you so far away from the houses.' She looked towards the aloof hilltop in apprehension. Then she remembered his frail-looking stature and how she had clouted him the last time. And the fur excited her, though she did not like Arfon's demeanour, that had a touch of jeering.

'Come on, then,' she said impatiently, beginning to hurry up the hill.

She went on a step or two before him. He kept his eyes on her dim shape. The path was narrow and ascended in a winding fashion. Above, the slope spread deserted under the great nave of the sky. No moon or star had appeared but still there was a dim grey light. He was no longer aware of the beautiful

40

shape and movements of her body. He saw her now as a symbol he could desecrate in a last triumphant act of power and contempt.

'Very quiet you are,' she called back to him.

'A lot to tell you I have when we get to the top,' he said.

They walked together when they reached the brow of the hill, where granite boulders were scattered like prehistoric monsters asleep. The grey light was still and cold under the dark blue of the sky. Arfon peered about.

'We can't stay long,' she said. 'A little walk and then I must go. Give me the fur now, you funny boy.'

'We must rest,' he said, 'before we part.'

And coaxingly he led her to a dip in the upland, untying the string of the parcel as they walked to it.

'There's a a lovely soft fur!' he cried, rippling the length of the garment before her.

She stretched her eager hands to catch it. He ran into the hollow of the dip, flying the fur. The bracken was withered and dead. He flung himself into the lap of the hollow and rolled over, caressing the fur and laughing. She had followed him and stood appealing for the garment.

'I don't think you shall have it!' he cried, smoothing the hair with his hands. 'I like it myself. Indeed I'd like to sleep with it. So soft and nice it feels, to keep me warm in the winter.' And he rolled over again, putting his face in the fur and uttering strange laughter in his throat.

She dropped on her knees at his side, stretching out her arms, her face pouting and greedy. She wore a green satin frock that shone. From its bodice her neck emerged naked and white.

'Give it to me!' she cried, reaching her hand and trying to pull the fur away.

He lay stretched with his face buried in the hair of the garment, his hands gripping it fast.

'Give it to me!' she pouted.

He lifted his head and saw her leaning to him, her face stretched beseechingly, her eyes shining with greed, her neck long and bare.

'Come, then!' he said.

She leaned further to him, on her knees. He lifted himself and with slow gestures placed the fur over her shoulders. She went very still, staring at him.

'Let me place it,' he whispered.

He gripped each end of the fur and, crossing them, pulled them tight, at the same moment rising to his feet and thrusting her on her back. He knelt on her, never losing his firm grip of the fur. Her choking cries were strange and awful. He had never heard their like. His own voice uttered quick, deep sighs, that were like groans, while his chest heaved and sank. Tighter and tighter he

41

pulled the fur. And she went silent, though her body continued to throb beneath his legs.

Then at last, when his own nerves were ready to snap in the terrible desire that beat through his body and his hands, he gave way and fell on her in exquisite relief. He swooned away into depths of unknown consciousness that became like great seas covering him. And he wanted to die, he wanted to die in that bliss of unfathomable depth, he never wanted to rise again to the world. He lay still. And in a soft passion of relief he thought that death was coming to him. His being seemed to flutter in the depth where it lay so far from the world, his shut eyes became firm, and all feeling went from his limbs. The soft rise and fall of thought in his mind told him he was dying, and he was filled with a gentle gratitude. Then at last he fell into deep, serene slumber.

He lay there for a couple of hours, and woke with a start,. He was shuddering with cold. He wondered what strange, soft substance his face lay in. His eyes still closed, he put up his hands and felt the fur.

He drew away from the girl in deathly fear, his voice crying out. And then he lay groaning in the withered bracken at her side. When at last he lifted himself and, in that cold mountain radiance of the night-blue sky, saw her face gone still in death, he went rigid with terror.

Yet he remembered and knew it had to be done. Only now it was so awful. His belly was icy with sickness and horror, his shoulders swayed, his legs grew limp. He fell again to the ground and clawed at the bracken.

When he lifted himself his shrunken face was contracted in tearless weeping. All his body was contracted in pain. He saw her face stretched out as it gazed at the sky in dark, statuesque suffering, and he cried out that he might die. He could not stand the sight of her. He began to stumble away from her stretched, still figure staring up in death. And he could not bear the silence, which his broken sobs deepened, he could not bear the awful height of sky and stretch of barren upland, with the dim outlines of the greater hills so cold and dead against the dark blue. He stumbled on. He must cry it out, he must tell, the earth must know what lay staring up so silently to the sky. He must tell, he must tell.

He began to crawl down the steep hillside, not waiting to find the path. He saw the dim rows of dwellings far below in the valley. He did not think of the consequences his tale would have for him. He could be hurt no more. Only he must escape and tell what lay stretched in death up in the hills. She must not lie there in her awful staring.

This was the end. His heart knew it was the end, and if only he could forget her face lying up there he thought he would know peace. He did not want to live any more. He had had enough of all that was done under the sky. Yet he continued to weep and sob, stumbling down. The hills lay in silence all about him. They looked magnificent in their eternal tawny sleep under the high arch of the far skies. Such strength of silence and eternity they had, Arfon should have been eased as he stumbled and crawled in disordered weeping, down to the houses of the people.

A WOMAN

I

Her father, one of those stony primitive Christians whose grim memorials are the chapels of Wales, discerned the impulse of evil in every action of the flesh; the pleasure he himself had frequently taken therein was always followed by periods of fanatic penance, aided by his wife, who thought of her body as a great sow that had imprisoned her soul. God would free them one day from the slimy walls of flesh that held their pure souls: until then one's only desire was to battle in fury with the horrid pleasure that was enacted in the body.

Jane was their only child. She was conceived in the silence of forbidden processes: there was no divine sanction in this symbol of the sin the father and mother had exchanged.

'She must be taught to subdue the flesh,' said the father, 'so that she may attain a lasting cleanliness.'

The child grew, startled and lost, in a home where repentance was bread and sacrifice drink. At fourteen she was a scraggy little girl with a misty face and a precise wintry manner. Her narrow white brow was smooth as an egg, her eyes liquid and profound as a dog's. Gaunt, black-clothed and lean, her father faithfully taught her the Scriptures, his great voice booming into her as though it were the very voice of God issuing from a mountainous altitude of rock and snow: while her mother, withered and bleared in stern sacrifice, watched and slew every manifestation of frivolous interest.

'Tonight I will read the story of Lazarus,' the father announced. He cleared his throat and with accurate aim spat fully into the centre of the red coals. 'Out of St. John.'

Wide-eyed and grave, Jane listened. She saw the dead rise and come forth from the tomb, a napkin about his face. *Lord, by this time he stinketh.* Flesh was terrible, a thing of decay and death . . . Yet, she did not want to believe it of her own body: and she thought of her thin white skin. Her bosom issued from her narrow waist, like a slim hyacinth breaking from its sheath, her white legs, freed of her flannel petticoats, she loved to stretch and kick with a nervous joy.

'Let no boys,' her mother warned her fiercely, 'play about with you. At a disadvantage a female is with her loose clothes.'

As she got older, her flesh thickened a little, her eyes corroded into a lovely animal glitter: she was not without her father's sublimated passion. Twenty, she was a still, brooding creature with sudden vitriolic outbursts of anger and long wounded moods of pitiable fear. But her father pursued her with an ascetic fury that became more intense as, a young woman, she found coigns of pride and silence in which she could shelter from him.

She stayed out one night beyond the nine o'clock limit.

Moreover, her mother had been told by a neighbour that she had been seen with a man. She arrived home at a quarter to ten and her eyes were starry, her movements easy.

Her father's belly tightened.

'So,' he said slowly, 'taken to flightiness you have!' Her slight body, swaying half fearfully, half proudly from the hips, filled him with a hate, and he shot out, 'A man you been with!'

'Yes,' said Jane, with sudden spear-like haughtiness. She thought of the fierce courage she had felt in her lover's arms.

Her new pride drove him to madness. 'That lout Samuel Evans!' he shouted.

'Well—' said she, defiantly, 'courting me he is.'

He suddenly reached forward and slapped her sweepingly across the mouth. His eyes were black and sightless. 'Been seen with him on the mountain!' he hissed. 'Lying on the grass!'

She had reeled back. But her gaze, fixed on him unswervingly, was thin and searing. He felt it like a blade in his heart and he could have done her endless cruelty. The lucid loveliness of her face made all his blood rigid. She was terribly alive to him, a thousand times more alive than his wife, who nodded her head, that was bound with black flannel, watching and silent in a corner of the room.

'You . . .' Jane muttered, as her mouth bled, '. . . sorry you'll be for that.'

'Pah!' he spat out. But he drew back, eased at the sight of the red blood on the luminous white of her face.

She moved out of the room, passing her mother, who cried at last:

'And let me tell you now that many's the slut that has passed through Samuel Evans's hands!'

II

The one day of absolute freedom was the Sunday-school outing. Under the patronage and shepherding of the preacher and his wife, the pupils and teachers of the school were allowed to air themselves for a day at a seaside place.

It was a June day this year. Early in the morning the local station seethed with excited shiny faces and bulging bags and baskets, which contained joints of meat, loaves of bread, Caerphilly cheeses, fruit and bottles of a smoky-coloured liquid, cold tea. Slowly, with a subdued and frightened air, the train drew in amid the screeching voices of the multitude and, pulling up with a bawling mass of blue, white, and red draperies, perspiring and frantic faces, tense legs and yellow straw hats. The prolonged wails of babies clawed protectively to hot breasts mingled with the abusive complaints of angry older women who could find no seats and the loud sexual cries of girls tickled advantageously in the crowd. After a long period, the engine moved in a shocked start and, as though continually in indecision, stopped, ambled forward, retreated, and finally crawled out of the district like a refractory beast at last deciding to make the best of its burden.

In the compartment where Jane had a corner seat there were ten people standing, crushed against each other. Nevertheless, once the train began to move, everyone forgot the discomfort, eating apples and nuts and taking difficult swigs out of their bottles of cold tea. Jane, however, wore a hostile and sulky expression, diminutive but very watchful in her corner.

At the other end of the compartment Samuel stood joking with Bronwen Price, a big handsome girl who at intervals opened her fat mouth and loosened into the carriage peals of abandoned laughter. Jane had had cause to fear Bronwen Price before, for Samuel seemed to waver uncertainly between them, and now, arriving late, she had forced her way into their compartment and stood next to Samuel. The day had become cold and drab for Jane. Would the girl attach herself to them all the time? She was spiteful enough. Besides, Samuel himself seemed to encourage her.

'Jane,' called Bronwen over the people, 'quiet you are down there. Asleep you are?'

Jane quivered; the voice was like a snake striking her.

'Darro,' said one of the men, 'there's hardly room for her to find her voice. Pressed flat as a pancake she is.'

'Pass her these nuts,' Samuel's voice came. 'No, wait you, I will crack them for her. Little and dainty are her teeth.'

People laughed. But Jane had a momentary gleam of happiness. She took the nuts as an offering of propitiation, though even as she ate them she could hear Samuel and Bronwen joking again.

They arrived at the seaside at last and there were ecstatic cries as bits of the sea were seen between the sandhills; everybody was going to enjoy the day. Jane's face was shut and long, like a snowdrop. Bronwen had become more unbearably flirtatious as the journey went on. She and Samuel got out of the compartment first and Jane, gathering herself together with miniature dignity,

46

was the last. The fold of her flowered muslin skirt dropped chastely to her feet. Out on the platform Bronwen stood vulgar and loud in a puce satiny dress, beneath which her body seemed to expand with healthy success. She had a lovely complexion, and as the pale Jane stepped on the platform her bright eyes began to roll in mockery. Samuel stood at her side, his hands in his pockets, waiting. Jane hesitated a moment and peered about her as though searching for someone; her heart was plunging in fear. Then, gloriously, Samuel advanced to her and said loudly:

'Here I am, Jane.'

Bronwen advanced too and stood brightly beside them, smiling. There was a short silence. Then Samuel said, tilting his straw hat to the back of his red head:

'Well, Jane, what about that little visit you have to make to your cousin? Now we will go?'

'A relation you have living here!' Bronwen exclaimed.

'Yes,' said Jane, aloofly.

The smile had died from Bronwen's face, which became heavy and seemed very big and fleshy. The three began to move down the platform.

'Perhaps later we'll see you,' Samuel murmured to Bronwen. His hand played nervously with his watch-chain. Bronwen exuded an atmosphere of female anger that was very evident in the air. If she exploded, here in the station, it would be uncomfortable. He mumbled:

'Very likely we'll be on the beach this afternoon for tea, Bronwen.'

Bronwen did not answer: the sun caught the glass beads on her moving bosom and made them quiver like lightning. Samuel went on hurriedly:

'The excursion is always lucky for weather.'

Jane's dignity was obvious. In her white muslin, with its sprigs of rosebuds, she moved like a lady, silent and remote, down the platform. There was a moment's indecision as the three paused outside the station. Beads of perspiration stood on Samuel's shiny forehead. Then Bronwen said rudely:

'You want to get rid of me now, Samuel?'

Samuel's mouth dropped open. He muttered something under his breath.

'Good-bye, Bronwen,' said Jane coldly and indifferently, moving off. Samuel hastily followed her, leaving Bronwen standing high and dry in the middle of the road.

'Ach,' he snorted, 'ach, stupid as a jelly-fish she was. Not enough were our hints.'

'Encouraged her you did in the train,' Jane declared angrily.

Samuel's face wore a pained expression.

'Always the same you are with women,' Jane complained. Then she laughed. 'A teaser you are.' Under the flappy hat she glanced up at him in adoration. He was the beau of the chapel.

He squeezed her arm. 'A good day we are going to have,' he whispered down to her.

She trembled. Her love for him was like a dreadful fear clutching at her heart. She was afraid of the world that could separate them, marry him to someone else, kill him. There was evil in the vast darkness of the world, and God could lean from the sky any moment and crush Samuel into His hand of death. Worse, perhaps, the chapel was full of attractive females who might by their various wiles annexe the susceptible darling . . . Continually she brooded how best she could keep him steadfast to her.

And she wanted that day to be important. Not often was she so free of her parents. They did not come to the outing, for the tickets would have to be purchased, whereas Jane, not being twenty-one, went at the expense of the chapel. It was her only holiday, and there was no other opportunity to have such long hours with Samuel.

They walked to the esplanade. Far away, beyond the desolate flats of mud, the sea crawled, a sheet of dirty-looking liquid under the glassy sky. On the narrow stony beach family parties set up their households for the day. The air stank of manure. Bright ice-cream barrows were everywhere, and along the esplanade were rows of rusty horse-drawn vehicles. The women stepped along in their sweeping skirts and high small waists, their big hats burdened with bouquets of lovely flowers, bunches of grapes, pears and apples—for the fashionable also came to the place. The men looked austere and tight in their narrow trousers and with their staid well-behaved expressions. At the end of the parade a stout woman with a group of donkeys bawled for customers; her face was burnt to a rich gravy brown. Samuel tentatively asked Jane if she would like a ride, but Jane refused and glanced at a barouche. Samuel said they would hire a vehicle in the afternoon.

'I know a place, said he, 'where there is quiet. Out of the town.'

Jane had brought a packet of sandwiches in her little bag, but Samuel insisted on going to a restaurant for some food. They had fish and chips, apple dumplings and tea; and all through the meal Samuel held her legs between his knees and grinned, so that she was ashamed and afraid that people would see what was going on under the table. Someone kept on putting pennies in a slot, which made a piano begin playing, though no one sat at it; and at the next table, where there was a family feeding, a noisy and terrible child in a sailor suit indignantly shot a plate of prunes into the lap of his well-dressed mother.

After the meal they visited the Fair. They went on the roundabouts and

Samuel tried to win a purse for her at the houp-la stall. *Secrets of Paris. Adults only.* was announced on a board outside a small dark tent. Jane hung back from this, but Samuel insisted, and inside they peeped into little lanterns and saw extraordinarily life-like pictures of ladies in corsets with pairs of gleaming legs issuing from frothy underwear. Jane was bored, for they were all the same, except that some of the ladies stood and some sat. She waited for Samuel at the entrance and wondered what he could see in such foolish pictures. He studied each one, bending his body to peer in the lanterns, his hands on his knees, but came to her at last, smiling.

'You didn't see them all!' he exclaimed.

'Dull they seemed to me,' she said pettishly.

'Ach,' he laughed in delight, 'like stronger meat than those you do!'

He put his arm about her and jovially pressed her narrow waist.

'Now we will go to some quiet spot,' he said.

He hailed a barouche and they were borne along in comfort over the crowded common. There was not a cloud in the brilliant blue of the sky, and the sea was nearer, thrusting an edge of foam along the muddy shore. It was like heaven. Samuel's eyes were on her continually and then, laughing, he thrust his hand under her leg.

'Now, Samuel,' she whispered, 'not in the carriage—!'

They dismissed the barouche where the road ended near a little bay, and they set out through the fields. Samuel kept on teasing her. He was very good-looking in his navy serge suit, his nice teeth gleaming out, and his hand was so warm and sure when he touched her. Gone were all thoughts of home. She was aware only of a rich bliss in her heart and a delicious excitement under her skin. This was the first time she had really been alone with Samuel. He lifted her over a stile and smacked her behind in a most adorable fashion . . . But she thought it proper to remonstrate with him when he went too far, much as she enjoyed his antics.

'Tired you are getting, my darling?' he asked.

'Very lonely this place is,' she remarked.

Samuel looked at his watch, then up to the sky. There was plenty of time.

'Let us have a small nap here among these bushes,' he said, glancing for the nicest place.

From the secluded cliff-top they could view the sea, now rolling in handsomely. And they were alone.

Jane thought how beautiful it was to be alone with Samuel. His kiss was better than she had ever imagined kisses could be under the same circumstances. It was all like a dream. Surely she would wake up soon and find herself in her narrow bed . . . But no, this was different, this was a new joy mingled with a bright fear.

'Jane . . .' Samuel whispered, sighing and sighing.

She felt so secure and proud in his arms. She was herself. Nothing else mattered but this strange pleasure of love that was opening her nerves as though they were flowers. Her father, her mother, who were they? This was her own joy, her own creation, her own business . . . She saw the flowing high-waved sea coming to her and it gave her strength.

His arm lightly lying across her breasts, Samuel slept. Jane lay gazing over the sea. Presently she carefully moved from Samuel and went away. When she returned, her face looked prim and unchanged. She allowed Samuel to sleep for half an hour or so and then she roused him.

'I want a cup of tea,' she said.

He grunted and then laughed up at her. He was a collier in the pit and earned good money. Jane decided she would marry him as soon as he asked her.

He did not ask her, oddly enough, that day. Jane was surprised and piqued. In the train going back home he treated her with deference and great politeness but to the last moment, even though he accompanied her to the end of her street, he remained silent about marriage.

'Well, Jane darling,' he said in parting, 'in chapel you'll be on Sunday as usual, I suppose . . .'

III

In September her mother took her apart one evening. The woman's eyes bulged out like a toad's and her knees shook. In a voice that sank back upon itself breathlessly, she demanded a question of her daughter. Jane shrank and for a while was silent and still. But in that silence she was born anew. Her pallid face took on a proud strength and became defiant. She trod down her fear, she answered:

'Yes.'

The mother became rigid as a corpse. The tick-tocking of the parlour clock measured three minutes before she gained her voice. Then she shrieked:

'Ooh, that I should have borne such a slut!'

She darted out of the room and called to her husband, who was making spills out of newspapers in the kitchen:

'Shones, Shones, come you quick.'

And then she collapsed in the passage-way.

The man emptied a jar of cold water over her head and, her voice gurgling out of her foaming mouth, the woman recovered and darted up like one possessed. She pointed to the parlour.

'The slut is with child,' she panted.

After the first rigidity of the shock had passed Shones seemed to swell. The hollows of his grey face burned, his breathing became like the suspiration of a powerful and lustful beast. Evil had come to the girl at last. He strode into the parlour.

In the light of the hanging oil-lamp he saw his daughter, her white face lifted with a sinister pride. She sat like a young queen in the best oak chair of the parlour. Her sloping shoulders were set in stiffened strength, her white hands clasped the sides of the chair.

Madness came upon the father. Her look blasted him with fury. And a man had rifled her: she had discovered the secrets of the flesh: a man had possessed her . . . The father's sinews tightened, his blood ran in madness. The girl's shut snowdrop face, that was closed and turned from him, so fulfilled in itself, made him groan. There flared in him a pure fury.

'True this is . . .?' he breathed.

Her eyes were sparkling like a mad girl's. She answered: 'This is not of your business—'

She could have said nothing more drastic. That reply, putting him beyond her consideration, tightened his fury. If she had opened herself to his wrath, been all soft and swooning, if she had wept in contrition and shame, he would have been appeased . . . His hands moved to his waist, to the buckle of his leather belt. His eyes were half-closed, his nostrils quivered, his face was contracted as though a pain rippled him.

Jane started out of the chair with a cry and ran to the door. Instinct for the budding thing within her put her to this shameful flight. But she was too late. She felt an unbearable sting curl round her face and the shock numbed her, so that she stumbled. She saw her mother crouch back in the passage-way, she heard her father cry a name again and again, she felt the belt on her shoulders, her back, her belly . . . She had fallen to her knees, her arms on a chair, but when that last sting came to her belly she leapt up and in one sweeping gesture lifted a vase off the table and hurled it at her father's head. She heard it smash and knew she had been accurate in her aim. Then with a wild flutter of skirts she rushed headlong out of the room, past her screaming mother, into the kitchen and down the back garden.

Her flight was wild and thoughtless, for there was no outlet to the long wild garden, which abutted on the railway. She raced frantically to the railings and then drew up sharply. The railings were too high to climb. So she plunged into the mass of lilac bushes at the end of the garden and crouched down in their dusk.

Yet there was no pursuit of her. She crouched in startled agony beneath the bushes, and the earth seemed to rock drunkenly under her. She pressed her hands to her breasts and between her panting her moaning voice broke from her lips. Ah, she could have died, there, in those moments. She did not want to live, she would have her life finished completely. An unutterable despair came upon her. She felt that life had crushed her down at last.

She crawled further into the tangled wildness of the garden, for there was no room to lie beneath the lilac bushes. The evening was cool and still. There was not a sound from the house. She lay on cold leaves, her head beneath a huge coarse rhubarb leaf. Her eyes were closed and her fingers were stretched over her belly. How long she lay there she did not know. For a time her heart beat like a hammer on an anvil. Then she seemed to sleep. When she opened her eyes again the moon was riding high in the sky.

Jane gazed up in wonder. She lifted her hand and bent aside the rhubarb leaves so that she could see better. How magnificently the moon rode, proud and clear and eternal in the spacious heavens! And she seemed to be aware of Jane down there among the rhubarb leaves, she seemed to say: 'Lift your head; take courage into your blood'; she seemed to pour a yellow warmth down, so that Jane lay all receptive and quivering, her belly lifted to the lovely white flare of light.

Already she felt a new strength in her joints, a new supple determination in her flesh. She rose and tossed back her loosened hair. She saw the great sunflowers, that came out in their untended luxuriance year after year, and their tall stalks and the pointed gold petals of the enormous flowers gave her strength too.

With unfaltering steps she went back into the house.

As she expected, her mother and father had taken their trouble to God. They knelt either side of a chair, upon which rested the big family Bible. A piece of rag was tied round her father's head; the vase had inflicted damage then. So intent were they on reaching the Lord that they did not hear Jane enter the kitchen. Jane listened to their mingled gabbling for forgiveness, she heard their request that a suitable punishment might be visited on her.

And a pity filled her heart. It seemed to her that her father and mother had had a mischief done to their minds, it seemed to her that they had not entered into realisation of the marvellous things that were under the sun. She broke into their lamentations:

'Don't you pray for me, please, I shall go without any praying . . .'

52

They looked up. Her father's tight-lipped mouth gathered to spit some word, her mother babbled incoherent abuse. Jane raised her voice proudly:

'. . . I am leaving you now. I do not want to live in this sad old house any more. And when I have time, I will pray hard enough for you.'

Her simple dignity, that was like a star on her brow, subdued them, for she turned and went out in silence.

IV

Though she was certain of no place to which she could go for shelter, she had no qualms at her decision to leave her home for ever. All her life she had felt that she never really belonged there, and all her instinct had been urged to the flowering of this moment. Ah, she breathed in relief as she realised that moment had come at last. She was free. Her life was her own.

She went directly to the house where Samuel lodged. Her brow was set in a straight clear line of determination.

Samuel was preparing to go to bed. Working on the day-shift, he rose in the morning at five o'clock. He had just finished a glass of beer with the man of the house and his candle was lit in his hand when Jane was announced by the woman of the house, an inquisitive and childless female of mature years, fond of her glass too.

'Samuel,' she called, 'Jane Jones is here to see you. Shall I call her in then or will you come out to her on the pavement just?'

'Put her in the parlour,' came Samuel's surprised voice . . . and then he appeared, peering at Jane in amazement. 'Well, well, Jane . . .'

'I must talk with you alone,' said Jane resolutely, as the landlady hovered about, straightening the mats with her foot and glancing with a suspecting eye at Jane.

Samuel had lit the parlour lamp. His large good-natured face was a little peevish. Later in life he would become very stout. The landlady left them, after cautioning Samuel about extinguishing the light properly, when the conference was over.

'I have left my home for ever—' began Jane, fixing her steady and lit eyes on him.

Samuel's jaw dropped. The round astonished aperture of his mouth issuing no sound, she continued—and her voice had an edge and point in it that gave added vigour to her determined words: 'Come has the time, Samuel, for plain facts to be spoken. With child by you I am. And the time for dillying and dallying is past. Married we must be. Surprised I have been ever since the

Sunday-school outing that you have not spoken on this matter. A respectable man I thought you and not a lout doing mischief with a trusting girl. Respectable you are at heart, perhaps, but flighty your ways are, Samuel, and melancholy enough you have made me. But now you must deal with serious business and finish with these mischievous ways. Not a colt you are any more and unnatural it is for a strong and healthy man like you to live in lodgings so long . . . Married we must be, Samuel.'

Samuel stared and stared, his nose and mouth betraying a deepening peevishness. He was not prepared for marriage, had not contemplated such an ending to his many pranks . . . But it was true he respected Jane and admired her trim little body. If he was to be married, better have Jane than one of the others. But he loved his freedom and did not want the constriction of marriage. He was thirty and had not been faced with such a dilemma before. He muttered:

'Well, Jane, there's foolish you must have been. A shock you have given me. Forgotten all about the old outing I had nearly just—' Seeing the look of hot fury come to Jane's face, he added, 'except for a dear five minutes in it, of course, Jane fach. Mean I do that no worry have I had over it. But, darro me, a big thing it is you ask me. An important step it is to marry a woman . . .' He suddenly cocked an eye at her examiningly. 'Sure you are about this affair?'

Jane bent her pale face to him. Her eyes were fierce. 'Sure that I am with child or sure of the father?' she asked dangerously.

His face became sullen.

'Well, now,' he mumbled, 'I know how it is with women—'

She lapsed back into her chair with a queer little sound in her throat. At last she gauged his flighty nature. She was disgusted and shocked. An element of militant righteousness entered her love for him. After a moment or two of silence, she announced:

'Samuel Evans, an awful insulting question you have asked me. Lowered in my respect you have gone . . . But neither here nor there is that. Married we must be, and very soon. An honest woman I am and an honest woman I must be kept . . . and nasty habits must you be kept from too. A strong and hardworking person I have always been and will be. A good cook I am and can turn out anything from a little Welsh-cake to a full-sized dinner. Thrifty and a good shopper I am too. A right I have to boast of these things, for well enough I know the silly and giddy ways of young women nowadays. Samuel, married we must be soon . . .'

And she smiled at him . . . a hesitating smile dainty with her old charm. Samuel looked at her and shifted uneasily in his chair.

'Not prepared for marriage am I yet,' he mumbled.

Jane's brow became threatening.

'Samuel, Samuel, disgraced through the valley you want to be? People to point at you you want, saying, "Ach, there's an old lout and a ruffian for you." Warn you I do that I will not rest until justice is done by me . . . Oh, Samuel, Samuel, don't say such paltry excuses to me, for awful it is to me to have you sinking in my respect.'

And without further ado she burst into a howl, accompanied by a pitiable sobbing that was heart-rending to hear. Samuel writhed in his chair, got up, and began to pace the room. He was not a bad character in the district and did not desire to become one, even though of late he had been dodging the chapel's claims on him and frequenting public houses more. And, in spite of his knowledge of women, he did not really suspect Jane of freedom with other men. At last he shouted:

'Stop your grizzling, Jane. A nasty noise it is this time of night. A silly wench you are . . . Well, well, all right then. Married we'll be.'

Jane dried her eyes.

'How much money have you got in the bank?' she asked, her eyes lit again.

'Fifty pounds just. But for my old age that is. Live in lodgings we'll have to for a bit . . .'

'Go on, Samuel,' she cried indignantly, 'a mockery you want to make our wedding? . . . A house to let there is in Craig Ddu. A bedroom set and a parlour set of my own I must have. And a tea set of best white china and a black sofa of horse-hair . . . See to it I will that good value we'll get for the fifty pounds . . . And now where am I to sleep tonight? A good rest I want after all that I have suffered this evening.'

Gruntingly, Samuel called his landlady, who, having learned the facts of the affair and being one of the few local women not allied to a chapel, sheltered the sinner by allowing Samuel and Jane to sleep together. And Jane went to bed that night as proud, forgiving and triumphant as any angel . . .

V

The houses of Craig Ddu crouched together in a little hollow of the hill, some distance away from the bed of the valley, where the long, long rows of dwellings are. Rough steps of loose stones led up to the plateau of the hollow. The houses were worn and old, and, isolated in their shadowy recess, they seemed to lean towards each other like a lot of lean black birds forlorn in a bleak captivity.

November winds and rain were hurtling in Craig Ddu when Samuel and

Jane took up abode there. It had taken Jane a month to dispose of her old life and begin the new. On her twenty-first birthday she married Samuel in the chapel and felt herself at last a liberated, independent and full-sized woman. It was a quiet wedding. Samuel seemed not to possess any parents and Jane's declined an invitation to attend. Samuel, indeed, had wanted to be married in a registry-office, thinking it in better taste, since he had been friendly with nearly all the girls of the chapel and was not in very good odour with the deacons. But Jane insisted that a registry-office contract was irreligious and would never make her feel married. She desired no honeymoon, preferring that the money should be spent on household goods.

She became an admirable wife. In spite of her advancing pregnancy she papered and painted the six tiny rooms of her cottage herself, she scrubbed, worked in her kitchen with ecstatic energy, tended the little garden and made garments for herself and the coming child. Not a day passed but she made pancakes, Welsh cakes, scones or tart for tea. She rose before it was light, to prepare Samuel for his day in the pit, and from that beginning she scarcely rested for the day. She often had a stitch in her side.

Samuel appeared to enjoy married life, so that even his work in the pit did not prevent his body from developing ample curves. He ate hugely and slept vigorously. He stayed at home during the evenings. Since the home was in another part of the valley, they were able to go to another chapel, to Jane's delight, for she did not want to attend the edifice where her parents worshipped. She felt she worshipped a different God from theirs.

And now that she was married and settled she too had a profound esteem for sacred matters. The Might that governed human affairs had given her a respectacle position with good prospects and it was only just that she should be properly thankful. She rented half a pew in chapel and tried to coax in Samuel a revival of his religious interests. And though Samuel did not put much heart into it, now that he was married, he accompanied his devout wife now and again and sat in the pew with a roving but subdued eye.

The child was born on a shining late March day that was all lovely with the delicate strength of spring. The valley was invaded with a sudden and unusual sunlight, and the grey flanks of the hills became a most tender green. Jane heard the soft trembling cries of the new lambs on the hillside at the back of the cottage and, turning to her own child, wonderfully and lingeringly fingered its petalled face. It was of the sex she wanted, a girl.

Samuel nodded on hearing the news when he arrived home from the pit. The midwife had prepared his meal. After eating he washed his face and hands and went up to the bedroom.

'Like you she is, Samuel,' complained Jane.

'Like nothing on earth she is yet,' Samuel grunted, peering at the object in his wife's arm. 'Pity she's not a boy. A toss-up a girl is always, but a boy you can put out in the world and blow your nose in comfort.'

The mother looked at the child. 'I will see to it,' she said with a fresh determination in her voice, 'that she will be reared into a respectable girl. Not my fault will it be if she comes to disgrace. She shall be brought up religious and proper.'

At that moment the child opened her eyes and began to cry in a lusty manner. Her eyes were blue and living and healthy.

REVELATION

I

The men of the day shift were threading their way out of the colliery. The cage had just clanked up into the daylight, the tightly packed men had poured out and deposited their lamps, the cage swishing down again for the next lot, and, hitching their belts and shaking themselves in the sunlight, these released workers of the underworld began their journey over the hill down to the squat grey town that was in the bed of the Valley. As he was passing the power-house, just before depositing his lamp, one of these colliers heard his name called from its doorway:

'Gomer Vaughan. A moment, please.'

Gomer went over to the man who called him.

'You live near my house, don't you, Vaughan? I wonder would you mind calling there to tell my wife I won't be home until about eight this evening? I've got a job on here, tell her, and I can't leave it. You see, she's expecting me now . . . Hope it's no trouble?'

Of course it wasn't. Gomer was glad to take the chief engineer's message. Montague was liked by all the miners: a chief engineer with sympathetic principles, though an Englishman. Gomer nodded and resumed his way, soon regaining the particular companions with whom he always walked home. They were all young men.

'What the blighter want?' asked one.

Gomer told him.

'She's a beauty, she is,' said another, meaning Mrs. Montague. 'Proud of herself, too, strutting about and looking as though the world's no more than ninepence to her, whatever.'

'Got something to be proud of she has,' returned a short terrier-looking fellow, perking himself to have his say. 'A sprightlier bird never trod on two legs. Half French they say. Ach, she makes our lot look like a crowd of wet and pannicky hens. Got something our skirts don't seem to have.'

'I wouldn't,' said the eldest of them critically, 'swop her for my old 'ooman. Too much opinion of herself she has, by the look on her. A spirited mare she is in the house, I bet.'

Gomer said nothing. He was the latest married of the company. He did not want to say anything on this subject of women. Though he could say a lot, by

God he could. He could let flow some language—a lot of language. But he held himself tight, his eye glittering, while the others went on as men will, saying what they'd up and do if any woman had too much lip and bossiness. He had been married a year: and he was all raw and fiery from his encounters with Blodwen. God, he never thought a woman could be so contrary. Soft and simpering as she was before they married . . . Well, he'd show her yet . . . And as the colliers swung along together Gomer planked his huge nailed boots down on the pavement with a vicious firmness.

They had descended the hill, and as they reached the long dismal rows of dwellings that constituted the town they separated to climb to their different homes. Gomer lived in the last row reaching up the side of the greyish-green hill. At the end of this row was a detached house, where the engineer and his wife lived. The lonely bare hill swept up above it. Gomer had to pass his own cottage to climb to the villa.

It was a warm sunny summer's afternoon. There was a clear soft mist in the still air. Gomer wished there was a country lane of shady trees with a clean stream running near, in this part of Wales. He would have liked to stroll there in peace that evening. But no—after his meal and bath there would be nowhere to go but the street corners, the miserable pub, or the bare uninviting hills. Ah, what a life! Gomer sighed. The same thing day after day. Down to the pit, up again, food, bath, quarrel with Blodwen, slam the door and then a miserable couple of hours trying to jaw to the fellows on the street corner, and back home to see Blodwen's face with the jibe on it still.

He cleared his throat and spat before opening the gate of the garden. Ach, he had had enough of her tantrums, and if she wanted a fight he was ready for her. Trying to dictate to him, just as her mother had tried it on him. Save up to buy a piano indeed! And no one in the house who could play it. He'd give her piano! . . . He knocked the shining brass image on the villa door and glanced about. Natty house. Bright little garden—a rose garden. There were bushes and bushes of them: he'd never seen such big red and white roses. And such a smell! He almost snorted as he breathed in and emitted the perfume.

No one had answered his knock. He turned and knocked again. Where was the servant? Keeping him hanging about like this. He wanted his dinner. He knocked again. Then there came sounds of steps, upstairs it seemed, and as the steps sounded nearer, hurrying downstairs, a shrill voice called:

'Can't you wait a minute, darling!'

It was Mrs. Montague, of course, Gomer said to himself. She thought her husband was at the door. And there was laughter and excitement in her voice. Ah, that was the way to greet a tired husband coming home from work. An excited voice calling 'darling'. Made a man think a woman was worthy to be a wife. . . . The door was flung wide open.

Gomer's tongue clave in astonishment to his mouth. The gaping silence lasted several moments. A naked woman stood before him, and then slowly, slowly retreated, her fist clenched in the cleft between her breasts.

'Mr. . . . Mr. . . . Montague asked me . . .' stammered Gomer, and could not switch his rigid gaze from the apparition.

How lovely she was!

'. . . told me . . .' he went on humbly, '. . . said . . .' His voice dropped and he stared at her like one possessed.

She turned at the foot of the stairs . . . fled up: and it was like the flutter of some great white bird to heaven.

'. . . told me to tell you he couldn't come home at all until eight o'clock just . . .' suddenly bawled Gomer into the empty passage-way.

He waited a few seconds, wondering if she would answer. He heard her hurry about upstairs. Then she appeared again, wrapped now in a loose blue garment. Her face was flushed as she came down the stairs, but as she advanced to him she laughed. By God, how she laughed! Gomer felt his blood run. She wasn't ashamed, not she. And still her white feet were bare. They were bare and flawless and like lilies pressed on the floor.

'What is that about my husband?' she asked easily.

Gomer told her. Under the pit-dirt his cheeks burned.

She thanked him very prettily; and then she said:

'I thought it was he at the door. I'm sure you'll understand. I was having a bath. You are married, I expect?'

Gomer nodded. She looked up at his gazing eyes again in a queer laughing way and said in dismissal:

'Oh, well. Thank you very much for the message.'

He turned at last, and the door closed. He stepped out of the porch and, his eyes lifted in thoughtful amazement, made his way slowly to the gate. Never before had he seen a naked woman. Not a live one. Only in pictures. Respectable women—it had always been understood—kept themselves a mystery to men. But was that quite right? Ought they to keep themselves such a mystery? When they were so beautiful. Surely Mrs. Montague was respectable enough! Her husband was a fine respected man too. He wouldn't have things done that weren't right . . . Gomer suddenly made a decision that it was quite natural for a woman to meet her husband naked. It was lovely too.

As he opened the gate he saw a rose-bush stretched up the wall. There were several curled pink-flushed roses. One bloom wouldn't be missed. His hand

60

immediately snatched a flower, and, when he got outside the gate, he laid it in his food-tin.

Gomer's shoulders seemed squared and defiant as he went down at a quickened pace to his cottage. He was going to make his peace with Blodwen. But he was not going to be a namby-pamby fool either. After all, she was his wife: and he was not an unreasonable man. He had been quite fond of her too: and there were times when he thought her handsome enough for any man.

II

'You're late,' she said accusingly. And before waiting for him to reply she went on shrilly, 'Don't you blame me if the dinner's spoilt.'

'Which means it is, I suppose!' he said. But he smiled at her, his good white teeth shining out in his blackened face.

'Come in at your proper time then,' she rapped out, prodding the meat viciously.

He leaned forward and playfully slapped her on the back. She uttered a scream and the meat slid off its plate, hesitated on the edge of the table and fell on the floor. His action and the ensuing accident had an exaggerated effect on Blodwen. She arched up her long neck in a tight rigid fashion, her face flamed, and she darted out into the little scullery like an infuriated turkey.

'I've had enough,' she screamed, 'and more than enough.'

And she banged some crockery about.

'Now then,' Gomer called to her soothingly, 'now *then*, my pet. What's the damage! A bit of dust on the old meat! Look, it's all right. Now, Blod, behave yourself. Where's the taters? I'm hungry.'

He knew she'd find his gentle coaxing astonishing. Another time he would have hurled abuse at her. But she remained in the scullery. He sighed and went in there. She turned her back on him and went to the tap. He followed her and whispered in her pink ear.

'Now, now, what's got you, my darling! There's a way to treat a tired man who's been working hard as he can to get you a bit of dough! Turn about, Blod—and show me your chops laughing, the same as you used to! Look, look what I've got you—' He lifted his hidden hand and tickled her ear with the rose, then reached it to her nose. 'Smell! Put it in your blouse.'

She turned and said angrily: 'What do I want with a rose in my working blouse! Where did you get it whatever?' She was relenting.

'Ah, my secret that is.'

'Oh, well,' she said, tossing her head, 'put it in a cup on the table.'

During the meal she reverted again to the piano controversy. 'A catalogue came today from Jones & Evans. Cheaper they seem than anyone else. There's one that works out at seven-and-six a week.'

His brows were drawn in wrathfully for a moment. He did not speak. She went on talking, and at last he dropped in:

'We'll see, we'll see.'

The meal finished, a big wooden tub was dragged in to the place before the fire, the mat rolled up. Blodwen, sturdy enough, lifted the huge pan of boiling water from the fire and poured it in the tub. Gomer stripped. The pit-dirt covered his body. Blodwen added cold water and Gomer stepped into the tub. While he washed she cleared away the dinner things. She was quick and deft enough in her work, and the house was bright and neat.

'I'm ready for my back,' Gomer called.

'Wait a minute,' she said coldly, taking the remainder of the dishes into the scullery.

So he had to wait standing in the tub with the patch of coal-dust beneath his shoulders glaring on the whiteness of the rest of his body. He knew she was exercising her own contrary will again. He might have yelled at her, but today he didn't want to. He was holding himself tight in glowing anticipation. When she came at last to rub the hand cloth over his back and swill him down, he said nothing. Only grunted when she had finished:

'Not much respect have you got for a man's naked skin, Blod. You rub me as though I'm a bit of old leather.'

'Bah!' said Blodwen— 'a nice little powder-puff I'll get for you.'

He laughed, lingeringly and good-temperedly. He wanted to get her in a good mood. 'Ach,' he said with affection, 'one of these days, Blod fach, perhaps you'll come to know what a nice skin your husband's got on him.'

'Conceit!' she said, and would not look as he vigorously towelled himself.

Early that evening, when he sat comfortable and easy by the fire, he said to her, as she was about to go upstairs and change:

'You're not going out this evening, are you, Blod?'

'Yes. I'm going to the chapel.'

'Don't you go this evening, if you please,' he said.

Amazement was now evident on her face. This politeness and interference with her arrangements was quite unusual. 'Oh, indeed!' she began, ready for a battle.

He cocked his tight-skinned sturdy young head up at her. His eyes gleamed, there was an odd smile on his lips. 'Well, go and change first,' he said.

She shrugged her shoulders and went upstairs.

He sat waiting for her. She appeared in a peach-coloured silky dress. Her face shone clean. She was prepared for the women's meeting in the chapel. He looked at her appraisingly and said softly:

'Come here, Blod.'

'What d'you want now?' she demanded, withheld in spite of her coldness. She moved near to his chair—but apparently to the mantel-shelf looking for something.

'You're looking nice to-night,' he said. And he suddenly leaned out of his chair and caught her. She cried out, disliking this horse-play in her best silk dress. But he held her and she had to keep still. Then he whispered a few words in her ear.

She suddenly wrenched herself free and slapped his face. He sprang up. Her face and slender tightened neck were mottled.

'Indeed,' she breathed, 'indeed! You rude ruffian. What d'you take me for, indeed? Please to remember I'm your wife, will you? I'll teach you to respect me, Gomer Vaughan.' Yet there was an undercurrent of fear in her breathed words of contempt and horror.

But he had caught fire. His head lurched towards her, his eyes like flame-lit glass, he shouted:

'That's just it, my fine lady. Remember you are my wife I'm doing. Look here, you. Enough of your silly airs and graces I've had. A lodger in this house I might be. You do what I tell you to, now.'

'Never!' she screamed. 'Such rudeness I've never heard of.'

'What's in it?' he demanded furiously. 'You see *me*, don't you, when I wash?'

She was retreating from him in obvious fear now.

'Never have I heard of such a thing!' she exclaimed. Her face was contracted, her eyes were strange and hunted. 'Never. A woman is different from a man . . . And never do I look at you . . . not in that way.'

He was advancing to her. She saw the clear determination burning in his eye. With a sudden quick movement she darted out of the room and he sprang too late. She was out of the house. He heard the front door slam.

III

He knew where she had fled to. Twice before, after their more furious clashings, she had hurried off to her mother's—Mrs. Hopkins, a widow, who kept a sweet-shop. Mrs. Hopkins had come up 'to see him about it' afterwards. No doubt she would come this evening. He hated her.

She arrived half an hour later. Directly Gomer saw her pale, large aggressive face, he buckled in his belt and thrust out his chin.

'What's this I hear from my Blodwen, Gomer Vaughan?' she began with shocked asperity. She looked startled this time too.

He uttered an exclamation of contemptuous ire.

'That daughter of yours got no right to be a wife at all, Lizzie Hopkins,' he fumed. 'Running to her mother like a little filly! And don't *you* come here poking your nose in this business either. You go back and tell your silly daughter to return at once to the man she's married. See?' And he turned his back on her abruptly.

'Well you might look ashamed'—Mrs. Hopkins replied in a rising voice— 'well you might. Scandalous is the thing I have heard from Blodwen now just. Advice she has asked me. Gomer Vaughan, a respectable man I thought you. Please you remember that my daughter is a religious girl, brought up in a good family that's never had a breath of scandal said about them. And now you want her to be a party to these goings-on.' Her voice reached a dangerous pitch. 'Dreadful is this thing I have heard. Surely not fit to be married to a respectable girl you are! Shame on you man, shame on you. What my poor dead Rowland would have said I can imagine. Why, Gomer Vaughan, for forty years I was married to him, and never once was I obliged to show myself in that awful way! Don't you fear the wrath of God, man, don't you think of His eye watching!

Gomer retained an admirable silence through this tirade. His thumbs stuck in his belt, he spat in the fire and said:

'Pah, you narrow-minded old bigot, you.'

Mrs. Hopkins began to breathe heavily.

'Insult and rudeness! Would my poor Rowland was here! And would my dear girl was single again!'

Gomer lost his balance then. He turned and shouted:

'You be quiet, jealous old cat! What do you understand about young married people today? Interfering! Turning Blodwen's ideas the wrong way. A girl she is, isn't she then? Nothing extraordinary was it that I asked her. Only today was it I saw such a thing.'

Mrs. Hopkins said quickly: 'Who?'

In his ire Gomer incautiously answered, as though to strengthen his case, 'Mr. Montague's wife. I—'

But Mrs. Hopkins broke in with a loud exclamation:

'Ha! So that's it then. Ha, now I understand well enough. *She* is the one, is it? Long have I had my feelings about her . . . Very well, Gomer Vaughan, very well—' And she began to back out of the room, her heavy head nodding with hidden menace, her pale eyes fixed on him triumphantly.

Gomer shouted at her:

'You send Blodwen back here at once.'

Mrs. Hopkins whisked her bulky figure out of the doorway in a surprisingly swift way. 'We'll see, young man,' she darted back over her shoulder, 'we'll see.'

But Gomer had no doubts that Blodwen would return.

IV

And so she came back—sooner than he expected. Mrs. Hopkins scarcely had time to reach home and impart whatever she had to say, and Blodwen was dashing into the room where her husband sat in brooding wrath.

'You,' she panted— 'you been seeing that woman!'

She looked as though she wanted to leap on him. But like an enraged hound on leash she stood prancing and glaring wildly. 'That's where you been, when you came home late! That's your monkey's game, is it—'

'Now, *now*, Blodwen—' he began. Then he was silent, and he did not attempt to deny her accusation. There was a wolfish grin about his mouth. Blodwen continued to heap vituperation upon him. She became wilder and wilder. Her mouth began to froth, her eyes to protrude. And he liked her fierce, savage beauty. She had a splendour thus. His cunning wolfish grin widened. She became desperate.

'Not another night will I spend in this house! Gladly will my mother welcome me back—'

He decided she had reached the pinnacle of fear. He got up and went to her. She shrunk away and he followed. He took her arms firmly and with power.

'Long enough I've listened to your insults, Blod. Where did you get that idea from that I've been running loose? Eh? Has that old bitch been lying to you then?'

'You told her you been seeing Mrs. Montague naked—'

'Well, well, and so I have—'

Blodwen struggled to be free. 'Oh, oh!' she cried aloud.

'Some women there are,' he said, 'who are not so mean as you about their prettiness! Mrs. Montague's got very good ideas how to make her husband happy. Listen, my silly little pet . . .' and he told her of the afternoon's event.

She became quiet. Surprise, astonishment, and amazement leaped successively to her wild-coloured face. And, also, there came a slow and wondering dawn in her eyes . . .

'There now,' Gomer finished. 'See how ready you are to think evil of me. And here I came home wishing to see a better sight than Mrs. Montague could give me. And well I could have it too, only you been brought up wrong. That's where the mischief is. Too much shame you have been taught, by half.'

Blodwen's head was a little low. The curve of her healthy red-gold cheek filled him with tenderness. And magnanimity. He said softly:

'I tell you what, Blod. We'll strike a bargain. You want the piano bad, don't you? Well, say, now, we'll give way to one another—'

She hung her head lower. Some threads of her rust-brown hair touched his lips. He quivered. His hand slipped over her shoulder. But she would not speak.

'—And be nice to each other,' he continued, 'not always squabbering as your mother and father used to do! Live in our own way we must, Blod . . . There now, isn't she a sweet one . . . there, ah! sweet as a rose, my darling, a better pink and white than any rose's! . . . there, my pet, my angel!'

DEATH IN THE FAMILY

When Eli Prichard's son and daughters heard that their father was dying they hastened in all speed to the old home. Though, as the four of them lived in the Valley, it was only a tram-ride to Bwlch, that part of the vale where old Prichard lived—he was widower—with his one unmarried child, a woman of thirty with a hare-lip, Dilys. Prichard, an obstinate and obstreperous man, had always refused to make a will. 'Next to nothing is there to leave,' he insisted. The children knew there was no money. But there was the furniture. Good mahogany and oak articles, Welsh and substantial, including a fine, heavy piano: and none of the married children had been able to afford a piano as yet.

Eli Prichard lay dying. No one would have thought it of him a week ago. He looked such a hale man: spare with it though, and given to bouts of hard drinking. And it was drink that had brought him to his end. When returning home one stormy night he had slipped on a swaying unrailed bridge and fallen into the swollen river, which carried him to a shallow reach, where he lay and slept until morning. He was sixty: and all that week he swore—during his intervals of coherent consciousness—that he wouldn't die. But he sank and sank, and then on the Sunday the doctor announced he wouldn't last out the night.

All the children arrived towards evening. They came in their best clothes, for death is an important event. And they wanted to lay immediate claim to those pieces of furniture they fancied. Three daughters: Beth, Cassie and Aga, and the son, Jenkin, who was accompanied by his beak-nosed wife Mary Jane.

They tramped up to the father's chamber first. Each was shocked at his swelled appearance and remarked at the delicate and musty plum shade that had spread over his puffed-out face.

'Hard he lived, and hard he's dying,' Beth said.

'Now let bygones be bygones at his hour,' Aga observed, for at every opportunity Beth would rake up the bitter family altercations.

'There's comfortable he might have been in his old age!' Beth insisted. 'Now there's not a penny of his own to bury him.'

'You been paying in to insurance,' Aga said tartly. 'That'll bury him.'

'My rightful share I'll give,' Beth said, who was the most prosperous of the sisters.

'He shall be buried proper,' Jenkin said, 'with a hearse and all.' At which his wife, Mary Jane, put in her word:

67

'Surely enough friends he's got to carry him on a bier? Always drinking and spending pounds on that crowd in the Black Rock. A fine funeral it will be! All the drunkards in the place.' She finished with a subdued but acrid titter.

For at one time there had been money in the Prichard family. Before the death of the mother. *She* had kept Prichard in the bounds of moderation—and died early with the strain of it. From then Prichard had gone his own splendid way. The mother's money had gone, and with it the savings that came from his well-paid job as a fireman in the colliery. He should have been one of the most prosperous men in the place. When his children came to expostulate with him, he sent them flying with oaths and insults.

'A pack of thieving apes, that's what I put in the world,' he would shout.

Often, too, he could not abide the sight of the ugly and hare-lipped Dilys and more than once the woman had taken a job as servant elsewhere. Always to return, however, for, though simple in mind, she had a habit of stealing any odd money that was left about, with which she would buy either a canary or a quantity of boiled sweets.

They assembled downstairs. At intervals of a few minutes one of them would run up to the death-chamber to see if any change had taken place in the unconscious man. The disposal of Dilys was the first problem.

'An eye open you've been keeping, Dilys,' began Cassie in a bullying voice, 'for a job?'

'No,' said Dilys, who seldom had anything to say. Her great bald eyes accepted this family conclave without comment.

'Well,' continued Cassie, 'after the funeral, going to share out the furniture of this house we are. And no money you've got to pay the rent, have you? No? well then, a job you must find quick. And no daft tricks and dishonesty this time, for no home will you have to skulk back to. Understand that? No home will you have.' The sister raised her voice menacingly.

'Yes indeed, Dilys,' put in Aga, 'for no right have you to come and live on our backs.'

Jenkin, the son, began to mutter something, but at the sound of his voice Mary Jane, his wife, lifted her bold angry nose and insisted on her say:

'Shame it is that she can't keep a place. A big hulking woman like Dilys! Never let her skulk back to me. No dishonest woman will I shelter behind *my* doors. Warn her sufficiently now.'

Dilys's face remained bald.

'A place far out in the country she ought to take,' said Beth, 'far out. I will write to a friend in Cardigan about her. On a farm she should be put.'

The other women agreed that Dilys should be sent to the depths of the country. Then any disgrace she might incur would not be known locally. The matter of Dilys thus disposed of, they began to wrangle over the furniture, crockery and kitchen utensils. The piano came first.

Beth, being the eldest, considered she had the right to first choice of all the furniture.

'Mine the piano is,' she began, looking round suspiciously. 'Already my little Megan has been having lessons for it.'

'Indeed, indeed,' put in Jenkin's wife in a silky voice, 'and what room for a big piano have you got in your funny little house, then? And what about my Fannie, who has got *talent* for the piano?'

Beth flushed arrogantly and furiously. She began to shout:

'Who are you, woman, to talk! Don't *you* poke that nose of yours where it's got no business. Jenkin it is who should speak. An outsider you are.'

Jenkin had always been alarmed of his big, hefty sisters. Cowed he looked, and cowed he was, sitting between them and his dominant-nosed wife. And it was she who now brought out the trump card:

'Well now, *ladies*, know you do, I suppose, that my Jenkin can make claim on *all* property, since it was the wish of your poor dead mother, who owned it.'

This pronouncement caused an uproar that would have subdued a more courageous man than Jenkin. The sisters seemed to become twice their normal size as they rose and swelled in wrath. Beth actually shook her fist under Mary Jane's excitedly twitching beaked nose. Then she, Cassie and Aga turned to the agitated Jenkin.

'Threats or no threats,' Mary Jane's voice shrilled above the din, 'you cannot go against the wishes of your dead mother.'

'Shame on you, woman, shame on you,' shrieked Aga— 'that you can say such a thing with our dear father dying in the house. Out with you—turn her out, sisters. Low-minded and cunning old serpent as she is. Coming here, where she got no right. Out with her.' And Aga advanced to her sister-in-law with arms ready for violence.

'You lay your hand on me, Mrs. Aga Evan,' hissed Mary Jane, 'and a summons I'll have taken out on you this very hour.'

Jenkin at last raised a despairing voice:

'Women, women,' shocking this is. No robber do I want to be. Listen you to me now. An idea I have. Lots we will draw. Out of my old hat—'

'No lot will I draw for the parlour chairs of red plush,' Cassie cried, 'Mam said when she bought them, "Cassie," she said, "you take them when the time comes".'

'And no lot will *I* draw,' took up Beth, 'for my father's bed. I will be the one to treasure the bed he died in.'

69

'And mine is the mahogany chest of drawers in the back room,' Aga contributed.

'Tut, tut,' said the unquelled Mary Jane, who had moved to a secure corner behind the table, 'a few sticks and a jug or two there'll be left for you, Jenkin. Speak up for yourself, man, and don't you be robbed of what you've got a right to.' There was a bitter warning in her voice.

'A serious matter this is getting,' moaned Jenkin. 'For why didn't the old man leave a will!'

Just then Dilys, who had gone upstairs during the altercation, put her head in at the door and announced excitedly:

'Opened one eye he has!'

'Ha!' exclaimed Jenkin in relief, 'perhaps he is coming to. Good that is. Then he shall decide about the furniture. Come, people, let us hurry.'

They trooped upstairs.

Eli Prichard lay, a stiff and stark shape, in his candle-lit chamber. They thronged about the bed. But both his eyes were closed again. Dilys assured the others that one eyelid had lifted itself. Beth placed her head over her father's chest and said, as though she was listening to a clock:

'It's going all right.'

'A pity we didn't catch him,' said Jenkin, 'so that he could settle this business.' He leaned over the bed close to the still head. 'Perhaps not too far gone he is.' And he raised his voice: 'Dad . . . Eli Prichard . . . ho there . . . open your eyes now . . . Eli, Eli . . .'

There was no movement. The darkened face lay stern and majestic. It had an austere mien, and the mouth was set in a sharp and self-willed downward curve. And all his shape seemed carved and stony. He would have his religious bouts, too, in his varied life, and could sing a hymn as lustily as any Welshman. He looked now an old stern prophet out of the Bible. The bed-clothes fell in statuesque folds from his long, fine shape.

'Black he's going,' said Aga, peering into his face watchfully. 'Not much use is it to call him, surely. And if he came round, angry he'll be if we bother him. Well enough you know his temper.'

'Dad . . . Eli Prichard . . .' shouted Jenkin, 'ho there . . .'

Cassie, who imagined herself the favourite daughter, began to aid her brother. She put a wheedle into her voice too. For some minutes they laboured to bring their father from the shades of the dead. And at last they were rewarded by a slight twitch of the rigid eyelids . . . only for them to slip into absolute rigidity again. Jenkin put his ear to the chest and raised a despairing and perspiring face.

'Beating well it is too,' he said.

Beth had an idea then. 'Let us sing to him all together his favourite hymn,' she said. '*Cwm Rhondda* he liked best and it always was a hymn to rouse him and make him religious after he had been on the booze.'

'Ach,' Jenkin protested, 'don't speak of such things now when he is in God's hands. Fancy talking about his booze when a man is half-way across Jordan!'

But he agreed that the singing of *Cwm Rhondda* might bring Eli round. And so it did. They pressed about the bed and raised their voices together in the hymn that is the glory of Wales. The lovely lamenting music swelled and sank in the customary Welsh way, with all the ecstasy and the mourning of an old and religious people. Eli hearkened and turned his face from the other bank of Jordan. His eyelids trembled, a slight hiss came from his lips, and the rigid shape of his body moved . . . Jenkin made a motion to the others to keep singing . . . And so, Eli's eyes shone out on them, his mouth opened, and they saw again his long, sharp, foxy teeth . . . Jenkin held up his hand for silence.

Eli did not speak. His pale, pale shining eyes rolled slowly from one face to another. Then Jenkin began;

'Ho now, father, glad we are you have come back for a while. A little matter we want to settle, because no agreement can we come to amongst ourselves. A will you ought to have made—but there now, no good is it to quarrel about that at this moment. Say you first who is to have the piano.'

The dying purple lips moved. The women leaned over the bed to catch the decisive words. But all they heard was, slow and sighing as a breath of autumn wind:

'*My kingdom is not of this world.*'

'Darro me,' said Jenkin, anxiety hurrying his protesting words, 'hold you now and be nice at this hour! Let our misunderstandings be forgotten now. Your own children it is who are about you, and bury you well they will. Don't you be obstinate now, Dad bach. Help me in this matter. Come you now! A lot of quarrelling and temper there'll be about the furniture unless you say now how it is to be divided. Say you whether the piano is for Beth, or Aga, or Cassie, or for my own little Fannie, your grandchild, who is very musical.'

'There's nonsense,' Beth exclaimed; 'it's my little Megan it is who is most talented—'

But the father's lips were moving again.

'*I go,*' they sighed, '*where neither moth nor rust do corrupt.*'

'Provoking this is,' said Cassie. 'He is not having sense of what we are saying.'

The glazed eyes turned on her. Cassie moved back an inch. And she felt she had lost her chance of the piano . . .

Then the eyes turned from her and fixed their gaze on nothing.

'Gone he is,' shrieked Aga, who was the most excitable of the sisters. 'My father is dead!' And she fell into peculiar lamentation, working her face frenziedly, though no tears fell.

'A waste of time it was,' Mary Jane remarked, 'to bother him. His mind was set on the other world, as was only proper. Jenkin it is who must see to the disposal of the furniture.'

Beth, outraged and denunciatory, turned on her sister-in-law:

'A wicked woman you are. Please to remember that my father is dead and this is not the time or the place to talk of what he has left.'

'Yes, indeed, Mary Jane,' her husband protested, 'we must wait now until after the funeral.'

Mary Jane opened her mouth again, but they turned their backs on her and in the fuss of the moments that followed she was ignored. The blinds had to be lowered, and the neighbours informed of the event, the doctor and the layer-out had to be fetched. Mary Jane took advantage of these moments and slipped quietly out of the house with a pair of vases she had always admired. In half an hour news of the death had travelled over the place. The mourning daughters of Eli Prichard received the condolences of the many visitors that evening. Jenkin went off to the undertaker. The sisters wept at intervals: they experienced grief. 'Religious he died,' they would say to a visitor. 'With holy words in his mouth.' And they were glad they were able to say that truthfully, for they were ashamed of their father's reputation as a drunkard, and at one time theirs had been a most respected family.

After the funeral the controversy of the disposal of the furniture was resumed. They gathered together again. Jenkin looked pale and haggard. Mary Jane sitting boldly at his side, he announced to his sisters that by law he was entitled to the piano and, indeed, everything else. He did not want to be hard, however, and had taken into consideration the fact that the sisters had contributed towards the expenses of the funeral. So he and Mary Jane would be content with the piano, the bed linen, the parlour jug, the wardrobe, the sewing machine and his father's shirts of Welsh flannel. His recital was followed by a violent scene. Beth laid hands on her sister-in-law and a fierce struggle ensued. Cassie attacked her brother with hideous words and a couple of slaps on the face. Aga swooned, and Dilys came in from the kitchen to attend to her. The uproar caused neighbours to intrude. A small crowd collected outside the house. At last the sisters, their faces saturnine and pinched with defeat, departed, vowing dreadful vengeance from their husbands.

And from that day an eternal feud was maintained in the family.

The hare-lipped Dilys was dispatched to a remote village in Cardiganshire. The day of the journey, she carried secretly on her person a sum of fifty pounds, eleven shillings and sixpence. He had awakened that day before he died and told her the money was in a stocking that was hidden in the bedroom chimney, and that she was to tell Jenkin it was for his funeral . . . Dilys had in her box, too, her father's old wooden pipe, his photo in a frame of shells, and his hymn-book, which objects she had begged of her brother. In Swansea she had to change trains. She went out into the town and bought a large box of confectionery and a handsome parrot in a cage. She arrived at her destination in happy spirits and set about her work on the farm with great diligence. Her parrot was her beloved companion.

CONFLICT IN MORFA

I

Priscilla Edwards was a woman of some consequence in the village of Morfa. A Christian soul and deeply religious, she possessed a prosperous farm and was rich from a family inheritance. She remained single (after rejecting many suitors), she worked and governed her farm with an energy and art equal to any male's, she owned many of the village cottages, employed many men and girls, and at Christmas gave everyone a pair of boots—nailed for the men and buttoned at the sides for women.

At the time of this tale Priscilla was gone forty and had a tall and tight body whose members never ailed or tired, and a lean face with angrily defined features. She was a woman with a Will and a Way, and she contributed largely to the expenses of Soar, the little Methodist chapel of Morfa. There, however, she had lately come into conflict with the new minister.

Mr. Vincent Thomas-Thomas was not admired in Morfa. He was not a man of the district and his sermons were of a cold and calculating kind, quite unlike those of his deceased predecessor, the fiery and native Mr. Noah Williams. His nature, too, was bossy, and he thought Priscilla interfered too much in the chapel affairs. But because of her contributions to Soar, he allowed her much licence. It was only when Priscilla desired to bring her pet cow Alice to chapel for the Sunday-evening service that their enmity became active.

II

All the creatures of Priscilla's farm held their mistress in esteem. The swine grunted at her affectionately, the geese stretched excited necks for her caress, the hens gurgled blissfully when she was near, the two horses twitched and quivered at her voice, the cows and bulls looked at her with eternal worship in their luminous eyes. Priscilla, going among her stock, changed her personality according to the creature she addressed, and she had the happy and rare knack of successfully establishing contact with these different forms of low life. When she clucked amid her hens she became of their mentality, and indeed as she fed them she would excitedly hop about in their fashion and dart her neck hither and thither, uttering a cluck that was not to be distinguished from a hen's. Her imitation of a pig's snort was successful too. Sometimes, at some entertainment in the village, Priscilla could be induced to give a recital of farmyard noises, and she was often told she could earn a fortune in a circus.

Priscilla's favourite creature was the cow Alice. Alice was an old member of the family and had lovely patches of a rich burnt-umber on her ivory coat. Her teats were large and vigorous and she had been a wealthy creature in her time, of great financial value to Priscilla. Milk produce apart, though, a deep affection and understanding existed between the two. There was a special and sincere caressive quality in Priscilla's behaviour towards Alice, and the cow showed its sense of the honour by returning a firm but respectful love for her mistress. Her melancholy cry when Priscilla would leave her field or shed told more than any lament of poet separated from his mistress. Her perfect repose when Priscilla milked her or stood near her had something eternal and mystic about it, her eyes then becoming soft-coloured like dog-roses. But she never took any liberties: throughout their long association Alice never once attempted to touch her mistress with head or foot—never once played a naughty prank. She behaved with respect and consideration whenever Priscilla was near.

Lately, however, Alice had begun to develop idiosyncrasies. She would follow Priscilla from field to field, she would utter her grieving cry often and often, especially when the mistress went among the other creatures of the farm. She came up to the farm one day and put her head in the doorway, crying piteously. She was getting old.

'Let her,' said Priscilla to Job, one of her men, 'to roam where she is pleased. Only no place is there for her in the house. Small are the rooms and a nuisance she'd be indoors.'

'Indeed now,' said Job, 'satisfied with the shed she's been up till now and sociable enough with the other cows. But yesterday she did put her old head low and shout at them. Peevish she's getting.'

'Don't you say such a thing,' exclaimed Priscilla, suddenly angry. 'If my men and 'ooman servants served me as well as Alice has done, a rich lady would I be today.'

Priscilla was fond of elevating the animal kindgom to the disadvantage of man.

Then it was that Alice followed her mistress to chapel. The service had progressed beyond the first hymn and Mr. Thomas-Thomas was on his knees praying when Alice's mooing plaint was heard in the porch. Throughout the prayer—for no one would move while the preacher was on his knees—the cow continued her call to her beloved. Priscilla left her pew, after Mr. Thomas-Thomas had risen with an indignant face, and went out to the beast.

How Alice knew her mistress was in the chapel only a cow can tell. But when Priscilla appeared, the beast immediately lay down in the porch and was prepared to be at peace with the world.

Priscilla looked at the cow.

'It shall not be for me to deny you the Word of God,' she said to Alice.

And she took a chair and sat by the cow's side, there in the porch of Soar, for the remainder of the service, which they both could hear distinctly enough through the wooden partition. When the service was over and the people came out, Priscilla said to them:

'Look now, people of Morfa, there's an example for you! My Alice has come to chapel though never was she taught to! There's real Christian feeling for you, there's extraordinary! One converted cow is worth six dozen converted humans, surely?'

III

The following Sunday Alice repeated her visit to the chapel, and again Priscilla was obliged to leave her pew and comfort the cow in the porch. But after the service Priscilla waited for the minister and announced to him:

'Mr. Thomas-Thomas, a place we must find in the chapel for my cow Alice. No pleasure is it for me to sit out here in the porch with her, especially with the cold weather coming on now, indeed.'

Mr. Thomas-Thomas stood back a little way and gazed at Priscilla, his whiskers twitching. His green and righteous eyes protruded angrily. He held himself in leash, however, and said to the rich Priscilla:

'Come you, Miss Edwards, a surprising thing to ask is this. Tie Alice up you must, indeed, on Sundays. No business has she to come to chapel. Soar was not built for cattle at all. Well, well, you be reasonable now, whatever—'

Priscilla stepped up to him, while Alice waited outside the chapel door, watching but amiable.

'Deny the Gospel to her you will then?' she demanded in shocked amazement. 'Know you do how she has come to chapel of her own will on two Sundays. The first to welcome this miracle you should be, Mr. Thomas-Thomas. There's a lot of preachers would be proud if they could convert a cow! Surprise me you do.' Cat-like she watched the angry, turtling minister.

'I am not licensed to preach to cows—' began Mr. Thomas-Thomas.

'Very well,' snapped Priscilla. 'Not ashamed of my cattle, am I. And a respectable well-behaved cow Alice has always been. Where I am there she has a right to be. Quite convenient would it be for her to rest in the space that is near the back-window of the chapel, and no nuisance would she be there. But you must say what is to be done in this matter . . .'

Mr. Thomas-Thomas understood. It meant a large drop in his already meagre stipend to lose Priscilla. His neck swelled, his hair moved, and he said:

'I will call a meeting of the deacons to discuss the matter, dear Miss Edwards. Too important it is for me to judge it alone.'

Priscilla tightened the purple sash at her waist and turned away. The cow, after glancing at the red-flushed preacher, followed her mistress contentedly. Priscilla called at many of the cottages as she made her way to her farm, Alice waiting at the gates with benign patience. Priscilla talked to the cottagers, many of whom she employed, and hinted at the extra gifts she intended distributing next Christmas. Over the matter of the cow Alice she received much sympathy. And it was agreed that the new minister was a stern and bullying man, not fit to preach to good country people and quite unable to understand the ways of cattle.

IV

Mr. Vincent Thomas-Thomas paid a visit to Priscilla a few days later. He wore his best frock coat and top hat and he carried an umbrella and white woollen gloves. Lowering himself carefully into the arm-chair in Priscilla's parlour, his chin was held up fashionably by a high and clean white collar. Priscilla felt the importance of this visit and, after giving the preacher a glass of small-beer, appeared in a scarlet silk blouse and a skirt of crêpe. The weather and other small subjects disposed of, Mr. Thomas-Thomas opened:

'Well now, Miss Edwards, the deacons met on the matter of your cow Alice last night—'

Priscilla smoothed out her skirt and waited with pursed-up mouth. The preacher sighed and continued;

'Never before has a problem like this come into my chapel life. No consideration for cattle has there been in my knowledge—' Again he stopped and looked at Priscilla with a sad hope in his eye, but seeing the gathered firmness of her mouth's aperture, he mopped his brow and went on, 'Odd it has seemed to me, and lacking in Christian feeling, but a man I am after all and liable to err in judgment. Respect I have got for you, dear Miss Edwards, and in much respect do the deacons hold you. Willing they are that you can have the cow Alice in the space at the back of the chapel and willing am I. But it has not seemed proven to me that Alice has been converted and wishes truly to hear God's Word as it is spoken in Soar. So shall I ask you, dear Miss Edwards, for a small proof of the cow's religious feelings?'

Priscilla stood up. Her hands firmly clasped over her stomach, she answered with dignified unction:

'Mr. Thomas-Thomas, a little surprising you are, but not my business is it to dispute the wisdom of a preacher. Not for me is it to remind you that the Lord Himself created cattle such as Alice and saw that it was good, not for me is it to talk of Noah, who worshipped the Lord amid the beasts in the Sacred Ark, not for me is it to remind you that the little Jesus was born in a shed of cattle. Not ashamed of these nice beasts were the good holy people of olden days . . . Ha, rather would I go to Heaven riding on a cow's back than as a 'ooman wedded to many a Christian man of today!' She paused to draw breath, and went on smoothly, 'Yet, perhaps wise in your doubt you are. But the proof that you ask shall be given you whatever. Alice is resting now, for she has been milked, and drowsy she'd be. But come you up tomorrow afternoon and the proof that you ask shall be given, indeed.'

Mr. Thomas-Thomas lifted himself out of the chair.

'Very much thanks to you, Miss Edwards fach,' he said with perfect politeness. 'Well now, if the cow is taken to religion, as no doubt will be proved tomorrow, who am I to dispute it? . . . Good-bye now then, and let me say how glad I am that you are so zealous in sacred matters. A pleasure it is to know such a woman.'

Priscilla acknowledged the compliment with a righteous inclination of the head. And the preacher left the farm with a stately step.

In the village, however, he met a crony to whom with anger and denunciation he related the conference, concluding;

'But triumph yet I will. Not thus will I be insulted for long, and not long will the old cow be allowed her way.'

'A difficult and a crafty woman to handle is Miss Edwards,' said the crony, 'and very fond of Alice she is.'

'Tut, how is she to prove the dirty beast is religious!' said, with great contempt, Mr. Thomas-Thomas.

V

Priscilla, Mr. Thomas-Thomas and Llew Lewis, a deacon, made their way to the field where Alice lay the next afternoon.

As they approached, Alice politely rose to her feet and held her head low as though in pious modesty, turning her eyes humbly to her mistress. Her tail lay still and submissive.

Priscilla had declared that the cow would kneel at sound of any prayer. She stood with her hand laid affectionately on the beast's flank and said confidently:

'Recite you a little prayer, Mr. Thomas-Thomas. Go you on your knees as you do in Soar and speak you to the Lord. Alice will join you.'

The preacher placed his handkerchief on the turf and knelt, and Llew Lewis did likewise. Mr. Thomas-Thomas began a prayer, thanking God for health and the sunny weather. Priscilla's hand tightened on Alice's flank. And lo! the beast bent her forelegs and remained on her knees, her head hanging down in an attitude of devotion. Priscilla followed. Mr. Thomas-Thomas's prayer shook, he lost the thread of what he was saying and ended in a mumbling voice. He got up, his eyes fixed savagely on Alice, and when Priscilla rose, the cow lifted herself too. Llew Lewis exclaimed;

'Indeed, indeed now, remarkable this is. The cow is a wonder! And glory be to God that I have witnessed such a miracle! Who can tell but that a new time is come upon us? Jesus Christ was on the earth to save mankind, and perhaps the sacred beast who will save *her* kind is Alice. For surely she is a most pious creature and is behaving remarkable. There's a godly example she'll be to other cattle.'

Mr. Thomas-Thomas's Adam's-apple rose and fell as he tried to master his rage, and at last he said, with a sinister glance at Priscilla:

'An extraordinary doing is this for a cow. In olden days said it would be that a witch has been at work here in black behaviour. But surely a spell is on the beast right enough.'

'A spell from the Lord!' Priscilla said sharply. 'As anyone with a pious mind can see.'

VI

So Alice accompanied the triumphant Priscilla to Soar. Every inhabitant of Morfa waited before the chapel for the arrival of the two. They came quietly down the road from the farm like any other peaceful worshippers making their way to their weekly devotions. But for the Sabbath Priscilla had tied a bow of purple silk ribbon on each of the cow's forelegs and a length of the same rich material round her neck: and everyone felt it was right and proper that the beast also should have suitable array for attending chapel. Priscilla was congratulated on her good taste and thought. The two entered Soar with quiet and reverential step, Alice glancing at her mistress for the initiative. A quantity of bright yellow straw had been laid down in the space at the back of the chapel, where the pews terminated: and there was a chair for Priscilla, for she wanted to sit near her companion. Priscilla knelt for a moment's silent prayer and the cow did likewise. They rose almost simultaneously, and a sigh of awe and surprise went over the chapel.

Throughout the service Alice conducred herself with a grave deportment proper in any Calvinistic Methodist. She lowered herself and rose with diligent activity. During the sermon she reposed on the straw, but kept her head lifted in wakeful patience. Her entire conduct was above reproach. Priscilla was quite correct when she declared that Alice's manners in public were equal to any human being's.

Mr. Thomas-Thomas made no reference, in his sermon, to the miraculous conversion. Indeed he never as much as glanced to the corner where the beast lay. But he preached a sermon of rigid and austere dignity, his face opulent with condemnation, distaste and wounded vanity. And more than ever the people disliked his preaching. There was no hwyl or spirit in his sermons at all. Even a miracle had failed to stir him.

VII

It was not many months before Mr. Thomas-Thomas, unable to bear the criticism of Morfa and mortified at the triumph of Priscilla, resigned from Soar. His successor was a preacher after the heart of the people, a man who had been born and bred among them and was of their nature, and who had a proper reverence for Priscilla and her religious cow.

To the day of her death Alice remained a respected member of Soar. She died of a pneumonic complaint, having taken cold one bitter November day. Priscilla, happily, is still with us.

BLODWEN

'Pugh Jibbons is at the back door,' cried Blodwen's mother from upstairs. 'Go and get four pounds of peas.'

A sulky look came to Blodwen's face for a moment. She hated going out to Pugh Jibbons to buy vegetables, she couldn't bear his insolent looks. Nevertheless, after glancing in the kitchen mirror, she walked down the little back garden and opened the door that led into the waste land behind the row of houses.

A small cart, with a donkey in the shafts, stood there piled high with vegetables. Pugh Jibbons—the son of old Pugh Jibbons, so called because he always declared that jibbons (that being the local name for spring onions) cured every common ailment in man—leaned against the cart waiting for her. This was almost a daily occurrence.

He did not greet her. He looked at her steadily, as she stood under the lintel of the door, a slight flush in her cheeks, and ordered, in a harsh voice of contempt;

'Four pounds of peas!'

Pugh Jibbons grinned. He was a funny-looking fellow. A funny fellow. Perhaps there was a gipsy strain in him. He was of the Welsh who have not submitted to industrialism, Nonconformity or imitation of the English. He looked as though he had issued from a cave in the mountains. He was swarthy and thick-set, with rounded, powerful limbs and strong dark tufts of hair everywhere. Winter and summer he bathed in the river and lived in a tiny house away up on the mountainside, near to the lower slope where his allotment of vegetables was. His father, with whom he lived, was now old and vague and useless; the jibbons had not kept him his senses; and his mother was dead. They had always lived a semi-wild life on the mountainside, earning a bit of money selling their vegetables, which were good and healthy, in the Valley below.

'Fourpence a pound they are today,' he informed Blodwen. And all his browny-red face went on grinning. He looked right down into her eyes. His were dark and clear and mocking, hers were dark blue and inflamed with anger.

She shrugged her shoulders, though she was indignant at the doubling of the price since yesterday.

'Coming to an end they are now,' he said, weighing the peas, but keeping

81

his eye on her, which he winked whenever her disdainful glance came round to him. But she would look into the distance beyond him.

There was usually a box of flowers on the cart. Today there were bunches of pinks in it. He took one out. She held out her apron for the peas and he shovelled them into it, placing the bunch of pinks on the top.

'But I'll chuck those in for the price,' he said.

Though nearly always he would thrust a bunch of flowers on her. Usually she took them. But today she didn't want to. She wanted to tell him something. She said;

'Take those flowers back.' Her colour came up, she arched her beautiful thin neck, her eyes blazed out on him. 'And if you keep on following me about the streets at night I'll set the police on you, I warn you. Where's your decency, man?' And then she wanted to slam the door in his face and hurry away. But she waited, looking at him menacingly.

His mouth remained open for a moment or two after her outburst, comically, his eyes looking at her with startled examination. Then he pushed his cap to the back of his head, thrust out his head aggressively, and demanded:

'Is that bloke that goes about with you your fellow, then?'

Her disdainful face lifted, she rapped out, 'Something unpleasant to say to you that fellow will have if you don't watch out, you rude lout.'

Then he became mocking and teasing again, his eyes sharp with wickedness. 'He's not a bloke for you, well you know that,' he said daringly. 'Toff as he is and tall and elegant, he's not a bloke for you. I know him and I know the family out of what he comes. There's no guts to any of his lot. Haw-haw and behave politely and freeze yourself all up. There's no juice and no seed and no marrow and no bones to him. Oswald Vaughan! Haw-haw.' And screwing up his face to a caricature of a toff's expression, he stood before her undismayed and mocking, his short thick legs apart and almost bandy.

'You . . .' she muttered, raging '. . . You wait. You'll be sorry for this.' She slammed the door and hurried to the kitchen.

The unspeakable ruffian! What right had he to talk of Oswald like that! And 'He's not a bloke for you, well you know that!' Impudence. Pugh Jibbons, someone they bought vegetables from! Why, however had it happened? To have a ruffian of a stranger talk of her affairs like that.

She threw the peas out of her apron on to the table. The bunch of pinks was among them. She trembled with anger. She had intended throwing them back at him. She ought never to have accepted flowers from him before. He was always shoving a bunch of flowers in her hands or sticking them among the vegetables. Never again. She'd throw his flowers back at him. These pinks she had a good mind to put in the fire.

But they smelled so sweet and they were so delicate, she couldn't throw them away. She lifted her arm for a vase. Her shape was splendid. She was a fine, handsome young woman of twenty-five, all her body graceful and well-jointed, with fine movements, unconsciously proud and vehement. Her face, when she was silent and alone, was often sullen. But always it had a glow. She was a virgin. Her sister was married, her father was checkweight man in the colliery, her mother was always urging her to wed.

Oswald Vaughan, the son of the local solicitor, had been courting her for some months now. He was in his father's office. His family was one of the most respected in the place, big chapel people. Mrs. Vaughan had been put away in an asylum at one time. Even now there was a strange dead look about her. But Oswald was quite normal, he was all right and all there. He was the smartest man in the Valley, with his London clothes and little knick-knacks. Both father and son read big books, and indeed they were very clever, in their minds. Very brainy.

Oswald courted Blodwen with great devotion. He came to her as though to a meal. He himself said he was hungry for women. He would sit with her in the parlour of her home and hold her hands tightly or hug her shoulders with a lingering pressure. He respected her and, believing her to be intelligent, he brought books on verse and read her Wordsworth and Tennyson, especially the latter's *In Memoriam*, of which he had a profound admiration. When he left her he was refreshed and walked home in an ecstasy. Blodwen would go to the kitchen for supper and, oddly enough, something would be sure to irritate her, always, either something wrong with the food or she took offence at some observation of her mother or father. She was a difficult girl, really.

Her anger against Pugh Jibbons persisted as she went about the duties of the day, fuming continually not only in her mind but in her blood. If there had been a stick near as he had mocked at her that morning she would have laid it about him. It was the only way to treat a man of his kind. She was quite capable of giving him a good sound beating with a strong stick. The low-down ruffian. And her anger had not abated even by the time Oswald called that evening. She went into the parlour, her eyes glittering with bad temper.

Oswald sat opposite her and laid his clean yellow gloves on his knee. His face was pale and narrow, with a frugal nose and pale, steady eyes. Dull his face was, Blodwen suddenly decided, looking at him with a new gaze, dull and unredeemed by any exceptional expression. And what he said, as he neatly pulled up his fine creased trousers at the knees and then sat back with his hands clasped in an attitude of prayer, made her want to slap him.

'You're looking very wicked and naughty this evening, my dear. That's no way to receive your young man.'

Her face became inscrutable: she stared through the window. He went on:

'You know, I always think a woman should never be anything but bright and happy when her men-folk are about. That's her duty in life.' He leant towards her and took her hand. 'When you're my wife, my dear—'

'Let's go out,' Blodwen suddenly interjected. 'I feel I must have some fresh air this evening. I've been in all day.' Her voice had become even and calm.

He drew back, a bit stiffly. He sighed. But he was submissive, much as he wanted to stay in the parlour and caress her. He began to draw on his gloves.

'We'll go to the pictures if you like,' he said. He was very fond of going to the cinema with her. Nothing he liked better than sitting in the warm, florid atmosphere of the cinema, pressing Blodwen's hand and watching a love film.

'I'd rather go for a walk,' she answered, turning her sparkling eyes on him fully.

'There's so few walks about here,' he sighed.

'There's the mountains,' she said.

She liked going up the mountains. He didn't. Not many people climbed the mountains: they had been there all their lives and seemed not of much account, and dull to walk on. Great bare flanks of hills.

'All right,' he said, getting up and looking in the mirror over the mantel to put his tie straight. Blodwen went out to put on her hat.

As they went down the street the neighbours looked at them appraisingly. Everybody said what a picture they looked, the picture of a happy couple. He with his tall, slim elegance and she with her healthy, wholesome-looking body, her well-coloured face, they seemed so suitably matched to wed. His fine superiority and breeding wed to her wild fecund strength. They looked such a picture walking down the street, it did the heart good to see it.

They crossed the brook that ran, black with coal-dust, beneath some grubby unkempt alders, and climbed a straggling path at the rocky base of the hills. Presently Oswald remarked:

'You're very quiet this evening.'

Then there came to her eyes a little malicious gleam. He had taken her arm and was gazing down at her fondly—even though, as the path became steeper, he began to breathe heavily, almost in a snort. She said;

'I've been upset today.'

'Oh! What was it?'

'You know that man called Pugh Jibbons, the son of old Jibbons, who sells vegetables in a donkey-cart?'

'Yes, of course. Everybody knows him. They're a fine rough lot, that family. Half-wild.'

'Well, he molests me.'

'Molests you1' Oswald exclaimed. 'He has attacked you, you mean?' His mouth remained open in astonishment and horror.

'Oh no. Not attacked me. But he bothers me and follows me about. And this morning I was buying vetetables from him at our back door and he said— oh, he said some rude things.'

'Does he follow you about in the streets, make himself a nuisance to you?' Oswald demanded alertly, the young solicitor.

'Yes, he does,' she said angrily.

'Then,' said Oswald, 'we'll send him a warning letter. I can't have you being bothered like this. The rapscallion. I'll put a stop to him. I'll have a letter sent him tomorrow.'

'Will you?' she said mechanically, looking up to the hills.

'Of course. That's where I come in useful for you. A solicitor's letter will frighten him, you'll see.'

'Perhaps,' she said after a moment or two, 'you'd better leave it for a time. Nothing serious is there to complain of. And I told him myself this morning, I warned him. So we'll wait perhaps.'

She persuaded him, after some debate, that it would be better to postpone the sending of the letter: but as he argued she became angrier and nearly lost her temper. Then he became very gentle with her, endeavouring to soothe her, realising she had had a trying day. But her eyes remained hard.

Not until they got to the mountain-top did she seem to regain her good spirits. She loved the swift open spaces of the mountain-tops. They sat beneath a huge grey stone that crouched like an elephant in a dip of the uplands, which billowed out beneath them in long, lithe declivities. They could see all the far-flung valley between the massive different hills. Some of those hills were tall and suave and immaculate, having escaped the desecration of the coal-mines, others were rounded and squat like the wind-blown skirt of a gigantic woman, some were shapeless with great excrescences of the mines, heaps of waste matter piled up black and forbidding, others were small and young and helpless, crouching between their bulked brothers. Blodwen felt eased, gazing at the massed hills stretched along the fourteen miles of the Valley. She felt eased and almost at peace again. Oswald glanced at her and saw she wanted to be quiet, though the storm had left her brow. He sat back against the rock and musingly fingered his gold ring. He did not care for the mountain-tops himself. It was dull up there: and he seemed to be lost in the ample space.

He couldn't bear the silence for very long. He had to say something. He couldn't bear her looking away so entranced in some world of her own.

'A penny for them,' he said, touching her shoulder lightly.

She gave a sudden start and turned wondering eyes to him. And her eyes were strange to him, as though she did not know him. They were blue and deep as the sea, and old and heavy, as though with the memory of lost countries. She did not speak, only looked at him in startled wonder. One would have thought a stranger had touched her and spoken.

'Why d'you look at me like that?' he said at last, uneasy and hating her staring.

Her expression changed. She almost became his familiar Blodwen again. She smiled a little.

'You're a funny little woman,' he said, sliding his arm round her waist.

'It's fine up here,' she said.

But still she was different and not the human Blodwen that he knew in the parlour or the cinema. He couldn't warm himself with her at all. Her body seemed rigid and unyielding in his caress. She was hard and profitless as these mountain-tops. Almost he began to dislike her, and something inside him stirred in dark anger against her. But all the time his manner and tactics became gentler and more coaxing and more submissive to her whim. His face was appealing and submissive. But she persisted in her odd aloof withdrawal, and at last he decided she couldn't be well, that she was suffering from some esoteric feminine complaint that he must not intrude upon. So he abandoned his love-making and sat back against the rock and became deliberately meditative himself. He did not see the shade of impatience that crossed her face.

He considered the evening wasted and a failure as they descended the mountain in the grey-blue light. And something had happened to Blodwen, something curious and beyond his understanding. Yet for all his secret dissatisfaction he became more anxious in his behaviour towards her, more gentle and tremulous in his approaches. But she spoke to him and treated him as though she were another man: they might have been men together instead of lovers. He was hungry to hold her, to feel the strong living substance of her body. But somehow he could not penetrate the subtle atmosphere of aloofness that she wrapped herself in. He kept on sighing, in the hope that she would notice it. Women were very funny.

She did not ask him into the house, but lifted her lips to him, her eyes shut, inside the gateway of the garden. In a sudden spurt of anger he pecked quickly at her mouth and withdrew. She opened her eyes and they seemed unfathomable as the night sky. They both waited in silence for a few moments and then, lowering her head, she said calmly:

'Good night, Oswald.'

'Good night, Blodwen.'

He lifted his bowler hat and turned resolutely away.

She went in, slowly and meditatively. Her face was calm and thoughtful now. But she was aware of Oswald and his dissatisfaction. She couldn't help it. There were times now and again when his limp and clumsy love-making affronted her, as there were times when it amused her and when it roused her to gentle tenderness. After all, he was young: only twenty-five. Married, she would soon change him and mould him, surely she would? She wondered. Married, things would be different. She'd have to settle down. Surely Oswald was the ideal husband to settle down with. She would have a well-ordered life with no worries of money or work. Oswald would have his father's practice and become a moderately wealthy man: and his family had position. Had always been of the best class in the place. Different from her family, for her grandfather had been an ordinary collier and even now they were neither working- nor upper-class. Her mother was so proud of the step-up marriage to Oswald would mean: she had already bought several things on the strength of it—a new parlour set of furniture, a fur coat and odd things like a coffee-set and silver napkin-rings and encyclopaedias and leather books of poetry. It would be a lovely showy wedding too.

But she wished she didn't have that curious empty feeling in her when she thought of it all, sometimes. Not always. Sometimes she realised Oswald's virtues and deeply respected him for them: good manners, breeding, smartness, a knowledge of international affairs and languages, a liking for verse. Yet she knew and feared that void of emptiness in her when she thought of all that marriage with him implied.

When she went to bed a little perplexed frown had gathered on her brow. She rose early in the morning feeling very discontented and melancholy. She had a cold bath. In a kind of anguish of bliss she shuddered in the water, sluicing it between her pink-white breasts so that it rippled down her fine length like a quick, cool hand. Her wild fair hair glistening as though with dew, her limbs tautened by the cold bath, she strode downstairs and ate a good breakfast of bacon and eggs, stewed apples, toast and tea. Then she felt somewhat better, though she was far from being content.

She remembered Pugh Jibbons and how angry she had been with him yesterday. What he wanted now was a good rude snub and she'd give it him that morning. And thinking of him, her blood began to run faster again. She'd never heard of such impudence. Anybody would think she had encouraged him at some time or other. That riff-raff!

When she heard his shout in the back lane she asked her mother what vegetables they wanted and sauntered up the garden to the door.

'Morning,' said Pugh, looking at her with just a suspicion of mockery in his face. 'And how's the world using you today, then?'

Statuesque, with that insulting ignoring of a person that a woman can assume, she did not hear his greeting and ordererd peremptorily:

'Three pounds of beans and six of potatoes.'

'Proud we are this morning,' he observed.

He stood before her and looked at her directly, unmoving. She began to flush and arch her neck; she looked beyond him, to the right, to the left, and then her glance came back to him. His smile was subtle and profound, the light in his gleaming dark eyes was shrewd. She wanted to turn and hurry away, slam the door on him. But she didn't. His swarthy face, with its dark gipsy strains, was full of knowledge that she sensed rather than saw. His head rested deliberately and aggressively on his powerful neck.

Suddenly she ejaculated furiously:

'Don't stare at me like that! D'you hear! Where's your manners? What right have you to stand there staring at me!'

'You know what right I have,' he answered slowly. And the smile had left his face and given way completely to the hard determination of desire.

She hadn't expected all this, she had meant to coldly snub him and depart. And how strange she had gone, how still and waiting her body, as though absorbed in expectant fear for what would happen next. And she was amazed, when she answered, unable to bear the silence, that her voice faltered in her beating throat:

'I know, do I? I warn you, Pugh Jibbons, not to molest me.'

'Suppose,' he answered, a thin, wry grin coming to his face, 'that Oswald Vaughan would have something to say and do about it?'

Her anger flowed up again. 'What right have you,' she demanded again, 'to interfere with me? Never have I encouraged you. Haven't you any decency, man? You're nothing to me.' And then she was angry with herself for submitting to his advances to the point of discussion, instead of maintaining a haughty aloofness. She couldn't understand why she had given way to him so easily.

He looked at her. All his body and face seemed tense, gathered up to impose themselves on her.

'I figure it out,' he said, 'that I've got a right to *try* and have you. Because I want you. You're a woman for me. And I think I'm a man for you. That's what I think. I could do for you what you want and I want. That's what I feel.'

She stared at him. She had got control of herself. But she couldn't snub him in the harsh final way she had intended. She said haughtily:

'I don't want to hear any more about this. Give me the beans and potatoes, please.'

Pugh Jibbons came a step nearer to her, and she became acutely conscious of his body and face.

'You come to me one evening,' he said. 'You come to me one evening and a talk we'll have over this. I promise to respect you. I've got more to tell you about yourself than you think.'

She drew back. 'Ha,' she exclaimed with fine derision, 'what a hope you've got! Are you going to give me the beans and potatoes or not?'

He looked her over and then immediately became the vegetable man. He weighed out the beans and potatoes. Aloofly she watched him, her face stern. Today there were bunches of wide flat marguerites in the flower-box at the front of the cart. He took out a bunch.

'I don't want the flowers, thank you,' she said coldly.

'Nay,' he said, 'you must take them. You're one of my best regular customers.'

'I don't want the flowers,' she repeated, looking at him stonily.

He tossed the bunch back in the box.

'Silly wench,' he said.

'Don't you call me names!' she turtled up again.

'You deserve them,' he said. Then he looked her over with desiring appreciation. 'But a handsome beauty you are, by God, a handsome beauty. Different from the chits of today. Pah, but your mind is stupid, because you won't be what you want to be.'

She quivered: and her anger had become strange in her blood, rather like fear. She could find nothing to say to him; she turned, slammed the door and hurried with the vegetables to the kitchen. All her blood seemed to run cold, fear seemed to sink down in her body, and suddenly she felt desperately anxious. Desperately because something was withering within her being, some living thing she should have cherished. Beyond the anger and irritation of her mind she knew a fear and anxiety like a touch of icy death in her being.

The day became cold and drab to her. She went about the house shut in a sullen resentful silence. Her mother looked at her with ill-temper. The mother was a tall, vigorous woman. But her face had gone tart and charmless with the disillusion frequent in working women whose lives have been nothing but a process of mechanical toil and efforts to go one better than their neighbours. She, too, in her day had had her violences. But her strength had gone to sinew and hard muscle. Even now she cracked brazil nuts with her teeth, heaved a hundredweight of coal from cellar to kitchen and could tramp twenty miles over the hills on bank-holidays. And now she distrusted the world and wanted security for herself and her daughters.

'What's the matter with you, girl?' she demanded irritably as Blodwen sat silent over the midday meal. 'Shift that sulky look off your face.'

Blodwen did not answer. But her mouth sneered unpleasantly.

'You look at me like that, you shifty slut,' the mother exclaimed angrily, 'you'll leave this table.'

The daughter got up and swept out of the room. Her head was turtled up fearless as an enraged turkey.

'Ha,' shouted the mother after her, 'don't you dare show that ugly face to me again, or, grown-up or not, you'll feel the weight of my hand. Out with you.'

But Blodwen had dignity, sweeping out of the room, and her silence was powerful with contempt.

'Bringing a girl up,' muttered the mother to herself, 'to snarl and insult one, as though she's what-not or the Queen of England. Ach, that she was ten years younger. I'd give her what for on that b.t.m. of hers. The stuck-up insulting girl that she is.'

Blodwen stayed in her bedroom for the rest of the day, knitting. At six-thirty Oswald called. She came down to the parlour, still a little sulky. There was anxiety on Oswald's face as he greeted her. She had frightened him last night. And now he couldn't live without her: she was the sole reality in his life.

'My dear,' he murmured, pressing her hand, 'my own dear.'

She actually smiled up at him.

'Are you better?' he asked gently.

'I haven't been ill,' she said.

'Nothing physical, perhaps,' he said, primly, 'but out-of-sorts mentally, I should think.'

She sat beside him on the sofa.

'Oswald,' she said, 'when shall we get married?'

He started excitedly. Before, he had never been able to make her decide anything definite about their marriage. She had always dismissed the subject, declaring there was plenty of time yet. He wanted to get married quickly, so that he could proceed to entire happiness with this fine woman: he wanted it quickly.

'My darling,' he cried gratefully, 'my sweet, as soon as you like. I could be ready in a month. There's a house going on Salem Hill and I've got the money for furniture. We could begin buying at once. I saw a lovely walnut bedroom suite in a shop in Cardiff last week; I wanted to reserve it there and then. I'll phone for it tomorrow. And all the other things we could choose together.

We'll go down to Cardiff tomorrow. I'll get the day off.' His face began to shine excitedly.

She looked at him.

'Not a month though,' she said slowly; 'perhaps we want more than a month to prepare.'

'Six weeks, then,' he said.

'Soon,' she said, in a curious kind of surging voice, 'soon. Let it be soon. Six weeks, then. That will be soon enough.' Her hand crept up his arm. 'That will give us time to prepare and not too much time to change our minds. Six weeks. Oh, you do want to marry, don't you, Oswald?'

'My dear,' he cried in pain. 'How strange you are!'

But she put her face to his to be kissed. Their mouths met. She clung to him desperately.

She would not go out to buy vegetables off Pugh Jibbons again. She told her mother how he molested her. The mother went to the back door and roundly denounced the young hawker. Pugh had laughed at her. And Oswald again offered to have a letter sent him.

The weeks went by: autumn came on. There were endless preparations for the wedding. Blodwen, it was true, took little interest in them. She allowed Oswald to arrange and buy everything. She was very calm; and her manner and behaviour changed. She lost her high-flown demeanour, she never lost her temper, and her face went a little wan. Now her dark blue eyes seemed deeper and more remote beneath her long brows, and her mouth was flower-soft, red as geranium, but drooped.

The week before the wedding there was a touch of winter in the air. Blodwen liked the winter. She was as strong as a bear amid the harsh winds and the wild snow and the whips of rain that winter brings to the vales of the hills. She took on added strength in the winter, like a bear.

One early evening as the wind lashed down through the serried rows of houses huddled in the vale she stood looking out at the hills from an upstairs window of her home. The grey sky was moving and violent over the brown mountains, and the light of evening was flung out. Her face was lifted like an eager white bird to the hills. She would have to go, she could not stay in the house any longer. She entirely forgot that Oswald was due in a few minutes.

She wound a heavy woollen scarf round her neck and, unknown to her mother and father, who were in the kitchen, she let herself out. And blindly, seeing no one and nothing in the streets, she went on towards the base of the lonely mountains. Slowly the light died into the early wintry evening, the heavens were misted and darkened, moved slower, though in the west a dim exultance of coppery light still loitered.

Her nostrils dilated in the sharp air, but her limbs thrilled with warmth. Her feet sank in the withering mignonette-coloured grass of the lower slopes, and she climbed lithely and easily the steep pathless little first hill. She was conscious of Pugh Jibbons' allotments surrounding his ramshackle stone house to the left, but she did not look at them. He, however, saw her, rising from his hoeing of potatoes.

The night would soon come. She cared nothing. She wanted to be on the dominant mountain tops, she wanted to see the distant hills ride like great horses through the darkening misty air. She quickened her steps and her breasts began to heave with the exertion. She had crossed the smaller first hill and was ascending the mountain behind it. She was quite alone on the hills.

The black jagged rocks jutting out on the brow of the mountains were like a menace. She began to laugh, shaking out her wild hair; she unwound her scarf and bared her throat to the sharp slap of the wind. She would like to dance on the mountain-top, she would like to shake her limbs and breasts until they were hard and lusty as the wintry earth. She forgot her destination in the world below.

She had reached the top. Night was not yet; and out of the grey seas of mist the distant hills rode like horses. She saw thick, massive limbs, gigantic flanks and long ribbed sides of hills. She saw plunging heads with foam at their mouths. She saw the great bodies of the hills, and in her own body she knew them.

Oswald sat in the parlour with Blodwen's mother. The gas had been lit and a tiny fire burned in the paltry grate. Oswald looked distracted. He had been waiting for over an hour already. It was most strange. It had been a definite arrangement for him to see Blodwen that evening. There were important things to discuss for the wedding on Saturday. Her mother could offer no explanation but kept on repeating angrily:

'Why didn't she say she was going out! The provoking girl.'

'Can't you think where she has gone to?' Oswald asked more than once.

'No. Most secretive she's been lately. Secretive and funny. I've put it down to the fuss of preparing. A serious job it is for a girl to prepare for marriage. Some it makes hysterical, some silly and others secretive and funny, like Blodwen.' She tried her best to keep the conversation going with the distracted young man. Inside, she was fuming. She suspected that Blodwen had gone out with the deliberate intention of escaping Oswald. What madness! She'd give the girl a good talking-to when she returned.

'Have you noticed it too?' exclaimed Oswald. 'I've wondered what's the matter with her. But, as you say, it's such a big change for a girl to get married, she must lose her balance now and again.'

'Especially a highly strung girl like Blodwen,' said her mother. 'For highly strung she is, though in health as strong as a horse. No trouble of ailments have I had with her. From a baby she has trotted about frisky as can be.' And to try and soothe him she added gravely, 'Do you well she will, Oswald, a big satisfaction you'll have out of her. And in house matters she can work like a black and cook like a Frenchie, she can make quilts and eider-downs and wine, and she can cure boils and gripe and other things by herbs as I have cured them in my own husband. Taught her all my knowledge I have. A girl she is such as you don't see often nowadays. Highly strung she might be, but, handled properly, docile enough she'll be.'

'I think we'll get on all right,' said Oswald nervously, 'though no doubt we'll have our ups and downs.'

'Aye,' said the mother.

The clock ticked away. Oswald kept on glancing at it mournfully, then at his watch, to make sure that *was* the time. The mother looked at him with a sort of admiring bliss in her eyes. He was such a toff and belonged to such a family. Fancy her Blodwen marrying into the Vaughan family! No wonder she was an envied mother and people were deferential to her now. She had been a cook at one time.

'Wherever can she be?' he repeated, sighing.

'I can't think at all,' said Blodwen's mother, sharpening her voice to sympathise with his agitation. 'But I'll tell her of this tonight, I'll tell her, never fear.'

'Oh, don't please,' he begged. 'We must be gentle with her the next few days, we must put up with her whims.' He looked at her appealingly and added, 'No doubt she'll have a reasonable explanation when she arrives back.'

But Pugh Jibbons, in his old stony house on the hillside, was laying a flower on the white hillock of her belly, with tender exquisite touch a wide, flat, white marguerite flower, its stalk bitten off, his mouth pressing it into her rose-white belly, laughing.

THE JOURNEY

I had got on the train at Ventimiglia and to Cannes I was alone in the compartment; few people seemed to favour this train to Paris. I felt depressed at the thought of the seventeen hours' journey alone: an empty train for a long journey is as melancholy as an empty theatre, and though, alone, I would be able to rest stretched along the seat, it was preferable to have one or two persons—even if only to look at, or to hate, to sneer at, or derive, perhaps, a secret amusement.

A woman entered my compartment at Cannes. I glanced at her, a little disappointed. She was a middle-aged Frenchwoman loaded with small parcels and a hatbox; a wispy porter followed her, borne down with two large suitcases. Dropping her parcels everywhere, she sat in turn on the three corner seats at her disposal and finally selected the one opposite to me, but kept another one reserved by depositing a coat on it. 'Someone will join her at Marseilles,' I thought, 'she is keeping a seat for a friend.' But smiling at me brilliantly and displaying a short row of perfectly matched but false teeth she opened conversation by saying it was pleasant to change seats on a long journey and also one didn't want the compartment full.

In my stilted and careful French I politely agreed. Her black, black eyes looked at me with that shrewd, quick glance of the alert Frenchwoman and, after a few tentative observations, she put her head on one side and asked if Monsieur had liked the Riviera.

We drew out of Cannes. The train was cutting along the narrow, brown-yellow *plage*. It was afternoon and early spring. The air was thick and warm with yellow sunlight, so yellow you felt it was silk on which you could wipe your hands. And there was the blue sea, with its slow, lazy curls of little waves like white ostrich feathers as they fell on the sand. The other side of the train, the gardens of the villas and the near hillside were foamy with almond-blossom and mimosa and, beyond, the rocky hills of the inland valleys were cool in their blue-grey silence. Northwards, it would be cold and wet and the trees would still be shriven; it still would be winter, a few hours hence.

I told her I admired the Riviera, in spite of its eczema of villas and its ridiculous millionaire hotels, palaces and casinos. She differed from me in her tastes, I gathered, as, adroitly smiling her small, glittering smile, she chattered in a pleasant and lively manner. She liked the smart hotels and the fashionable towns of the Côte d'Azur. It had been a change for her. Apparently she lived a

94

suburban family life outside Paris and had been enjoying a three weeks' holiday with her sister, who kept a *pension* in Cannes. I had been dawdling along the coast into Italy, living in villages, for five months. She sat smiling at me and listened attentively when I spoke, nodding her head, now sagaciously, now with an agreeable vivacity, in the politely self-assured manner of French women. She seemed very alive and of happy but mature temperament.

'I like gaiety when I am on holiday,' she told me. 'In Paris I work at my home like thousands of other women. Here I have been among the select and the fashionable of the world!' She sighed, with an excessive melancholy. 'Tomorrow I will be back in my home.'

She had wanted to be gay, I could see, she had wanted romance. Perhaps the Riviera had given it to her. Her face for three or four moments had become pensive and sad. She was middle-aged and married. But she was charming. I liked her, aloofly. I could have exchanged jokes with her, a discreet train flirtation. Her highly-decorated face amused me, but I gave her credit, too, for taste and artistry. Her red was not too red, her eye-black thin and delicate, and her cream-pinkish skin was smooth as vellum, freshly powdered. Such mastery of cosmetics I had not seen for some time. My glance rendered her homage, which she received accurately and graciously. Again she smiled. 'Monsieur's French is very good indeed,' she lied. I was almost offended at this offering and decided she was clumsy. With disarming intuition she looked at me wistfully and added, 'Everyone must be encouraged in their efforts to speak French; one must not be impatient or laugh at them.'

Soon, soon, we would be leaving that warmly-tinted coast. All my five months became like a single drowsy afternoon spent in lazy dreaming, and I held it in my memory as though I were carrying a sun-warmed apricot in my hand. A single afternoon of indolence and soft, warm colour. And it was past. The grey rain and the windy streets of the north awaited me. Between the palms and over the red rocks of Théoule the sea spread like soft blue velvet dropped from the shoulders of goddesses who had gone up into the hills to bathe in the sunlight. I had seen beautiful women in the villages: they had been mellowed by the sun and they moved slowly and gracefully, as though they had a contented stillness within them. And the train was rushing away with gathering speed, towards the city.

Sighing, I looked away from the window. Madame, opposite to me, was still gazing out. Her face had become sober. She too, I thought, she too is protesting that there are such things as duty and work, cities with all their horrors of factories and giant cliffs of stone where people creep or hurry like insects. Age broke through the careful cosmetics of her face. Perhaps she had been enjoying a romantic episode on this southern coast, perhaps nothing had happened to her, perhaps she disliked her husband in Paris. Now she was returning with a sad acceptance in her dreaming heart.

Knowing my gaze, she turned and looked at me, a prepared expression of faintly wistful interest in her face. I suppose she had heard my sigh.

'Monsieur has regrets at leaving the Côte d'Azur,' she suggested with a hesitating smile. Assuring her I had many, she added, 'Ah, but you are young, very young yet, and perhaps you can return many, many times. This, I think, will be my last visit.' She looked at me with her bright black eyes, that had contradictions of temperament in them, and I could see that she decided I was young enough for her to feel nothing but a maternal interest in me. 'I cannot come here very often. But *you* have everything before you.'

In a little while she had extracted from me a few personal details, and from her I learned that she had two young sons who were going to cost a great deal to educate: that was why she would never be able to afford a Riviera holiday again. She said not a word about her husband; perhaps he was dead. Her face, I decided, had a jaunty bravery in it. She wanted to keep young, gleaming, alert—and I admired the pretty art of her face with a renewed approval.

We swept into Marseilles. Now I thought, we shall be invaded by passengers and we shall have a full compartment for the remaining thirteen hours' journey to Paris. But again few favoured the train. A man of forty or so put his head inside our door and, after glancing at Madame and then at me, took possession of the corner seat on her side. Since Madame did not remove her coat from the remaining corner seat, it was not taken, though never once did she use it herself, in spite of her statement that she liked to change seats on a long journey.

The newcomer, I judged, was a commercial traveller. He carried with him a business-like portfolio, and he was respectably dressed, neat and subdued, except for a glittering tie-pin in his spotted puce cravat. He had the half-weary, half-efficient face of the French businessman, and it was thinnish and pallid. He was like ten thousand other men, hard-working in routine and commercial honesty. His thin hands in their movements were decisive and crisp. But he looked bloodless.

Madame, I saw, examined him too. I felt that he met with her favour, as far as one's judgments are affected by fellow-passengers on a long train journey. It was not long before they were talking. He had examined her in return, and when she wanted to make sure that there was a dining-car on the train, he was able to inform her definitely. From that they proceeded in a quick, bitten kind of French that tested my knowledge severely.

Evening was approaching and the sky was lilac-coloured over the glimpses of sea one saw beyond Marseilles, the last glimpses. But there was still the

Provençal countryside to look at, the tidy vineyards, and the silver-green olive groves, the tiny crouched collections of rust-brown and rose-plastered cottages perched here and there on hilltop or in hollow. It would be dark when the formal, uneventful landscapes of the Rhône began. After dinner perhaps my two fellow-passengers would cease their lively talking and I might sleep. It was a curse that one could not afford a *wagon-lit*—and doubtless every chink of a ventilation would be closed by my typical fellow-passengers. Their chattering French began to annoy me.

Madame looked at me once or twice again and nodded her head as though in recognition or greeting. But I was really ousted from her interest, I could see. She had her own kind and her own age to talk to now. And the commercial traveller had no use for me at all.

Madame had come to occupy his full attention. He paid her, with gesture, glance and the occasional words I picked up, polite flattery; once he leant to her and patted her arm with a gentle reverence. They passed, I gathered, from a discussion of the Paris shops to the prices of *appartements* in the different districts. She placed a gracious intensity into her manner. Her plumpness and her brave rouged face pleased him, I saw. And she opened her shining eyes, that seemed so passionately dark, in delicious surprise at some of his statements.

Of course they dined together. I sat at an opposite table. His deference and solicitation were admirable; I could guess that he wanted her to make a good meal—the waiter returning for those who wanted second helpings, he chose for her with graceful flourishes some select piece on the outstretched platter. They did not share wine—each had a half-bottle, and she, I saw, with that watching forgivable on a weary train journey, paid her own bill. He gave her cigarettes with her coffee and chatted with renewed fervour. Madame, who had taken a very good meal, was a little more subdued. Her rouge had become flaming.

They left the dining-car before me and I thoughtfully lingered over my cognac. We had passed Avignon: the train was rushing into a soft blue night. The shadows over the dim meadows were beautiful to watch, and the trees flying past were mysterious in the gowns of pale evening mist that still clung to them. I ordered another cognac and hoped I would sleep when the gloom of night had fully come. Surely Madame and the commercial traveller would exhaust conversation soon.

I was mistaken. They talked until midnight. He sat closer to her now. Madame was a little less animated than she had been in the early evening, but the arch coyness of her manner was still manifest and she still gazed at the commercial traveller with her sultry dark eyes. 'She is having a last little fling,' I thought, 'before she returns to her strict home in the suburbs.' Her pleasure

97

in being able to interest this man to veiled love-making was obvious. She had not yet grown too *passée*.

When at last she decided to rest, he became beautifully anxious for her comfort. He shook out the pillow she had hired, he saw no draught caught her and, with reverential and soothing touch, he took possession of the carpet slippers she had taken out of her bag and, after she had removed her shoes, held them out, one in each hand, to her small and rather shapely feet. She thanked him prettily and then he lifted her feet and placed them gently on the seat, so that she curled up, a little plumply but attractively, to settle herself for the night. He loved achieving these little attentions, he gave a little shake of delight like a terrier, and smiled again at her . . . and patted her ankle. Then, after demanding if I were agreeable, he switched off the white light and turned on the dim blue. There were nine more hours until we reached Paris.

I slept intermittently in that train crashing and swaying through the night, but the mournful noises of the journey penetrated those snatches of slumber. The grind of wheels, the hiss of steam, the sound of the torn air, mingled with the fragmentary dreams that came to me. Drowsily I saw that journey as a crossing between the extreme periods of life. The fresh gaily-tinted charm of the south was passed and already the train had entered the bare cold regions where it was winter. I hated it that I was being rushed on in this night. Sometimes I rubbed my eyes and peered out of the window, but the darkness was vast and impenetrable. Madame, opposite me, dozed with her head fallen on her chest, and the commercial traveller seemed to be sleeping with ease and comfort, his pale face lapsed into the immobility of a man calmly dead.

Twice, almost overcome by the stuffiness of the compartment, I stumbled out into the deserted corridor and, in a stupor, walked up and down. How the train swayed as it screeched and ground its way through the thick darkness! It seemed to have a downward plunge and writhing steam hissed up from beneath the coaches and shrouded the windows. It was as though we were crashing into an inferno.

Again I slept. When I fully awoke it was late morning. In an hour we would be in Paris. I felt dirty and dazed and went to wash myself. Madame and the commercial traveller were both awake—she sat hunched in her corner, with averted face gazing out of the window, and he, I think, was waiting for her to turn to him again.

I had a scrappy wash and returned to the compartment: there was no breakfast to be obtained on that train. The atmosphere of the compartment, I sensed, had become forlorn and, in spite of the stuffiness, cold. Cold. Madame still sat averted and hunched, her face hidden from us. Through the dirtied windows one could dimly see the wintry countryside, the shriven trees, the wet grey fields, and a grey, hostile sky. I did not want to look out too long.

What was wrong with Madame, why did she crouch there hiding herself, unmoving, in an untidy lump? I could see part of her face, since I was opposite her. Her charming colour seemed gone. Why did she not go out and freshen herself, apply more cosmetic? Huddled and still, she continued to stare out of the window, the collar of her coat turned up. The commercial traveller still waited in his corner, quiet but watchful, his brown eyes a little hurt.

Only once did she stir for a few moments out of that dazed stillness—and that was when the commercial traveller left the compartment for a while. She merely shook herself a little, turned, looked at me for a moment, and then moved back to her huddled and averted staring out of the window. And when she looked at me, in a single blind glance, colourless, I almost averted my face too.

She was changed almost out of recognition. Not so much because of the colouring that had disappeared in the night, but because of the almost saturnine despair in her face. She, who had been so gay and lively. I went out to the corridor. Perhaps she wanted to be left quite alone for a few minutes.

But she had done nothing to revive her former appearance when I returned to the compartment a little while after the commercial traveller. She still sat in her almost sinister brooding at the window. And he still waited for her to turn to him, looking hurt and pathetic and at a loss. The grey light of the morning made the skin of his face into a kind of oyster-grey, too. But he awaited her pleasure watchfully, his arms folded, his hair watered and plastered down freshly.

Paris at last. A light brownish fog hung over the suburbs. How disconsolate and weary those suburbs looked, shrinking under the dirty brown shawls of fog. And I thought of the fluttering naked pink almond-blossom in the warm spring breeze of the south, and the yellow air that was like silk. Cities, cities, why were they necessary?

I was afraid to look across openly at Madame. I knew her sorrow and her despair. But I wanted to render her some service, or I should have liked to have seen her smile a little. And I was sad now that the journey was passed. To the last she ignored the commercial traveller, and I was glad that I managed to forestall him in lifting down her bags from the rack. Not once did she turn her face to him as the train drew into the Gare de Lyon and we prepared to part. He began to look indignant, those last few moments. When the train stopped in the station he hesitated, to give her another opportunity, and then, flashing me a sulky glance, hurried away disappointed.

I did not care to intrude on the privacy she obviously desired, so I allowed her to wait until a porter would come to help her with her bags. I saw her once more, on the platform, a porter hurrying after her with her two heavy suitcases. She passed quite near to me. Her face was heavy and resentful, but shut in a kind of blind determination. She hurried out quickly. It seemed as though she had some bitter duty she was determined at all costs to perform. But I was glad to see that her despair had given place to this strength of motive, sullen as it seemed. And I wondered at her destination.

Outside the station, the morning air smelt of the nearby fog. The sky was a waste of grey ice. It was very cold. I would go to bed for a comfortable sleep when I reached the hotel. Then it would be evening, and the warm lights would shine out, white in the streets, but in my favourite café, among the tarnished mirrors, the cupids, the faded plush and the tinted glasses, yellow.

THE BARD

I

When Gwyn brought home another Prize Chair from the Eisteddfod, his wife Bronwen could no longer restrain herself. She eyed the massive oak object with a mixture of enmity and despair.

'Where can it go?' she demanded. 'There is one of these chairs in all our rooms, with three in the parlour. This is more than a joke.' Their cottage was very small and poky.

Gwyn had placed it on the mat before the fire and was now walking round and round the tall angular Prize with a justifiable look of self-congratulation and esteem.

'Fifty bards tried for it,' he said.

'It's not,' continued Bronwen callously, 'as though we ever sat in them. They have no more comfort than sitting in a soapbox.'

Gwyn ran his finger appraisingly along the highly varnished wood.

'It is a chair,' he cried raptly, 'fit for a coronation.'

'Sometimes,' Bronwen said, a dark glinting look in her eye, 'when we are short of firewood I am tempted to chop up a chair or two.' She lifted the gaunt scrag-end of mutton from the saucepan on the fire and pushed it with contempt on the supper table. 'A pity,' she added disagreeably, 'they don't let you have the value of a chair in money, instead.'

Gwyn pulled his wild auburn hair with the authentic poet's rage. His face, that had been flaccid with gratification, contracted in wrath.

'You chop up one of my chairs,' he cried, 'and I'll . . . I'll chop you up.'

She was unimpressed. 'There's your supper,' she snapped. 'Not much of a banquet is it, true enough, for a bard that's brought home the chair.'

Gwyn's face had passed from divinely flaming anger to a sombre sulkiness. But he moaned:

'Banquets! Who wants banquets? You talk vulgarly, Bronwen. I am content with simple food. Bread and a bit of Caerphilly cheese. Greater men than I have fed on less.'

'And many more,' she said aggravatingly, 'have had poultry, green peas, and champagne.'

'Such food and drink,' he answered, becoming dignified in turn, 'are also my ambition.'

'Well, well,' said Bronwen comfortably, with an air of giving way to him, 'you are young yet, and if you go on winning chairs you'll be able to open a nice big shop for selling them.'

He clutched his ears.

'Stop now, stop now,' he groaned. 'You shall have the last word.'

'I dare say I will,' she said, undiminished.

During supper—for he was a creature of swiftly changing moods—Gwyn became vivacious.

'You ought to have been there to see me chaired, Bronwen,' he chirruped. 'There was a crowd; the chapel was packed. When the sword was sheathed over my head and they all shouted "Peace!" my pleasure would have been a thousand times greater if you had been present. Dan Evans said, "Where is your wife? A proud moment this should be for her".'

Bronwen, steadily cutting slices of bread and butter for him, said, 'I've seen it often enough. It's boring after a while. And I had jobs to do in the house.'

'Baba Price came up to me,' he continued happily, 'and said, "Let me recite some of your poem at our next concert, Gwyn".'

'Did she!' Bronwen said. And added carefully. 'What was she wearing? Something new and grand, I expect.'

He waved his fork impatiently in the air. 'I didn't look,' he protested. 'I don't look to see what women are wearing.'

'No, indeed,' she agreed, 'you don't.'

'She asked me,' he swept on, 'to take a copy of it up to her house tomorrow afternoon. She'll recite it for me first to see if I approve.'

'So very likely you won't be home to tea,' Bronwen remarked.

'Nothing was said about tea.'

'Oh yes,' Bronwen said coolly, 'you'll have tea together all right. And pretty little cakes and watercress and chocolates. You stay to tea and enjoy yourself for once.'

He made an arch and tittering sound through his teeth.

'You are narrow-minded, Bronwen. Out in the world no one takes notice of such things.'

But Bronwen said grimly, 'I know Baba Price. She gets her funny little thrills in funny little ways.'

'Ho, ho,' chortled Gwyn, pleased, 'jealous are you?' He smacked his chest in a virile manner. 'Well now, every poet has his fancy woman.'

'You encourage that woman,' Bronwen declared with sudden high temper, 'and it'll be the worse for you. I'll have no scandal.'

'Baba Price is a lady,' he began to thunder bardically. 'A lady of good substantial stock and position.'

102

'She is a crank,' said Bronwen contemptuously.

'You have no tact or taste!' And once more his hands ravaged the wealth of his hair.

'I wonder why you married me,' she said with a faint sneer.

'Indeed!' he groaned.

Her little inheritance of five hundred pounds had been spent long ago. Now there was never enough food in the house. She had no clothes that could be called clothes (Gwyn had pronounced, 'Your apparel is decent and respectable'): and now she never went to the cinema or concerts or even chapel. It was all very well for Gwyn to come home with a chair and crowned with bardic glory. Poems were very nice in their place, but they neither fed nor clothed. Well she knew it.

II

He had always been a little queer. Never able to master a job properly. In the old, old days he would have been a minstrel and a teller of tales, wandering from village to village over the countryside and earning his meals and a bed by recitals in cottage and farm. Those men are no more, but the spring of song still flows in their modern descendants—torrentially, as a rule, undiminished by the discouragement of a busier age. The Eisteddfod is the only arena where they are welcomed, and there they disport themselves with a few remnants of their former glee: colliers, farm-labourers, butchers, ministers of the gospel, insurance agents, each with a thick wad of manuscript, fruit of spare hours after the ordinary day's work is respectably achieved.

But Gwyn lusted after a full-time glory. He wanted to sing all day long. As a youth, his father and mother forced him into, in turn, office, shop, pit, farm, religious revival, council work on the road, house-building, and the manufacture of mineral waters. But if it wasn't the sack, he would lie in bed one Monday morning and declare he would go into decline if he persisted at the particular job. And indeed he was a half-wit at all mundane labour. True, when he married Bronwen, at twenty-five, he had been in a job for six months, reading gas-meters for the Council, but a month or two after the wedding he was dismissed because of a series of incorrect readings—really due to his mental absorption in a long saga on Tristan and Isolde, portions of which he would declaim in those friendly houses he visited (though it was said that Gwyn, in his frenzies of poetic generosity, deliberately mis-read the gas-meters if asked to recite). But he never allowed himself to be overcome with pessimism at his inability to grapple with work.

Bronwen had pleased him a great deal. Docile in her first adoration of his visionary mobile face, handsome hair and unusual conversation—for he had made love to her in a style founded on some of the luscious episodes of the Mabinogion—she ran away with him to Swansea and they married in a registry office. She had been a school-teacher. For some time, spending her five hundred pounds, they had been happy. And a few months after the loss of the gas-meter job Gwyn had found another as haulier to a grocer, delivering goods from a cart up and down the Valley. But that too he had lost because whenever he was visited by an idea for an ode—which was frequently—he would walk off over the hills to compose it, leaving people waiting for their butter and bacon: literature came first with him.

Since the haulier job, they had existed on the meagre proceeds of a 'tally-trade' Gwyn erratically worked at, securing all kinds of household goods from blankets to saucepans at a wholesale price from a firm in the North of England, and selling them for weekly payments to local wives, who were equally erratic with their shillings. But already he possessed a large trunk full of manuscript poems, and he gave Bronwen permission to roam among them at will. She still pleased him to a certain extent. He only wished she were more romantic. He would like to see her arrayed in a long robe of yellow velvet, a chaplet of leaves and flowers on her hair. But, as he had often told himself, he kept his good-humour. Life was chock-full of stuff for poetry. Who could dare to be unhappy and idle amid such plenty!

His Welsh poems were long and enormous with mystic exaltations, fanciful pictures of bygone ages, stormy combats between the powers of good and evil, taking place amid strange landscapes that bore no resemblance to anything known to the five senses. Their very size and heroic squandering of words made eisteddfod adjudicators blench with a kind of respectful fear. Bronwen complained bitterly at his refusal to write on both sides of his manuscript paper, declaring she would be able to buy a 'proper joint' for Sundays if only he would oblige; but he refused, firmly and indignantly.

Since the age did not favour volumes of poetry in the Welsh language, he depended on eisteddfodau for the human homage due—and indeed necessary—to a poet. Throughout Wales not many of these annual festivals lacked a contribution from Gwyn. He had not yet been successful at the great National Meeting, though he knew he would achieve that grandeur in the near future. Meanwhile he had gained eight bardic chairs in the minor festivals: fine pieces of varnished oak strongly nailed together and substantial enough to hold the stoutest person. Anyone would be proud of the chairs.

Except, of course, Bronwen. Bronwen seemed to have gone a little sour of late. Occasionally he devoted a minute or two of heavy thought to her. But

104

even those minutes gave him a few lines to insert in his latest epic. 'Women,' his mind chanted dolorously, 'oh ye daughters of the fallen Eve, women haunt my senses in sinful (or *sick?*) meditations.' *Sick* would be the safer word he decided. And Bronwen would not be likely to apply the words to herself, even if she ever read the poem. Sweet Bronwen! A good girl she was. Would never let him down. Well, well, it was only natural that a girl should pout sometimes. They did not have the busy interests that a man possessed.

III

The next day, after the midday meal, he went up to Baba Price's house, a copy of the poem under his arm. He slipped out of the house quietly, without telling Bronwen that he was going. But she heard him from the kitchen and splashed her hands angrily into the washing-up water. Wasting his time with that ludicrous old woman.

Baba Price was a well-to-do woman who fussed at various functions in the Valley. She particularly liked being chosen as the judge of literature in an eisteddfod, and she herself wrote what she called 'Visions'—lofty and very short prose-pieces which were, apparently, variations on a spiritual theme. She wore highly-decorated gowns, tightly-fitting but usually with triangles of lace here and there from which beads and objects hung very brightly: when she walked she tinkled, though not unmelodiously. To be invited to tea at her house was considered a compliment. Miss Price had also at various times put musical young men of the district on the road to success: some of them had sung in concerts at Cardiff and Swansea. Bronwen disliked her and thought her unreal. *False*, she thought again, clattering the plates in the greasy water.

Gwyn wasting his time up in her house! She'd bet anything he would stay to tea. Why couldn't Baba Price invite them both one evening? Taking a man away from his work in the afternoon! Gwyn ought to be out canvassing for orders for blankets, now that winter was approaching. Oh, he was useless, useless.

A fool! That's what he was. As she said it to herself, she left the washing-up, sat on a chair, and cried. She had married a good-for-nothing fool. She cried for ten minutes. When would he take himself in hand and live and work properly like other men? She was sick to death of it.

At half-past four she made a cup of tea. Gwyn did not return. And as the time wore on she felt herself becoming fierce. Lolling up in that house, reading poetry while Baba Price purred every now and again, 'Charming, charming.' Ha! And at half-past five a customer called wanting towels.

Bronwen took her into the front room, that had once been the parlour and was now transformed into a kind of shop. It was very untidy.

'A couple of the two-shilling ones, Mrs. Roberts,' said the customer, a slack-bodied and pallid miner's wife. 'And perhaps a pair of pillow-slips I'll have too, now I've come. But I've forgot my book. Your husband knows how much I owe.' She spoke wheedlingly and complainingly, as though she were not long for his world. Probably she owed Gwyn a lot already, Bronwen thought.

And the room was in such confusion. She couldn't find the beastly towels. Piles of blankets and rolls of calico and American oil-cloth and sheets and rugs, all mixed up and chucked anywhere. When at last she came to the bundle of towels lying under a table draped with cretonne, drops of perspiration were running down her nose. The customer kept on sighing and condoling.

'You are paying something?' demanded Bronwen so sharply that the customer, who had not intended such an action, handed a shilling to her.

'I'll put it down in our book,' said Bronwen. Fortunately the ledger was visible. She hunted in it for the customer's name. But the ledger was not to be understood. Indeed, lines for poems played hide-and-seek with the business entries. And when she did come across a customer's name, she found a comment attached, such as, 'Mrs. A. P. Adams: Her countenance is like desert, but where her mouth is, there also is an oasis,' and 'Mr. Evans: Honest John Evans, of such are the mighty sinews of our country.' Bronwen, after searching for some time, flung the book away, in a real fury now.

Back in the living-room, she tried to subdue her anger by cleaning the cutlery. But it continued to rise in sharp and urgent waves, right to the top of her head, where it seethed like boiling pitch. A fool and a waster! They'd never have five pounds in the bank. More likely, Gwyn would find himself in trouble, customers not paying for goods that did not belong to them. There'd be a warrant out for him one day. And they'd be sold up. She'd be cast out into the world. Why, oh why, had she let him have her five hundred pounds! The scoundrel.

Seven o'clock! Was he in that house still? Of course he was. Preening and enjoying himself, sitting back among silk cushions. They were having a glass of sherry together. Baba would play the piano. Her eyes, with their peculiar kind of glitter, were smiling at him, telling him to remain if he would like to.

At eight o'clock Bronwen swept the cutlery into a drawer and, with a pale and determined face, came to a decision. She dragged one of the high Prize chairs into the scullery and, taking a hatchet, braced herself into chopping it into firewood. It was a hard task, smiting the slabs of wood apart, but at the end of half an hour she had made a big pile of useful pieces. Firewood was really needed, and it was too late to go to the shops. Then she sat in the living-room, her knees pressed together, and did some knitting.

IV

Gwyn appeared at ten o'clock, looking very pleased with himself and the world. He seemed to have a puffed-out appearance, as though he had suddenly become stouter. Baba Price had been turning his head with flattery, it was obvious. He called to Bronwen quite jovially:

'Baba Price made me stay to supper, after all.'

Bronwen's clicking knitting needles were working at an exaggerated speed.

'You've been enjoying yourself, have you?' she asked.

'Yes. Talking about poetry.' He flopped into a chair as if he was now a little exhausted by the experience. 'A very intelligent woman,' he added, sighing.

'Yes,' Bronwen agreed, 'she looks that.'

He peeped out of her, from beneath his auburn hair, that so poetically flaunted itself.

'You been at home all the evening?' he asked.

'I have,' she said, staring at the swiftly moving thread of blue wool.

Presently he rose from the chair, a little restlessly, drummed his fingers on the table, glanced indecisively at a row of stout books, and finally went into the scullery and lit the gas-burner. She heard him brushing his teeth. He wanted to go to bed, did he! After a while he came striding quickly into the living-room.

'What's that pile of wood in the scullery?' he barked shrilly.

'One of your chairs,' she said immediately. 'There was no firewood left for the morning.'

'You chopped up one of my chairs!' he screamed in a feminine wail.

'I told you I was going to,' she said, as if the information justified the action. The blue thread of wool moved like flashes of lightning over her small hands.

'Oh, oh!' he foamed. His fingers went to his hair, he seemed about to swoon. To come back from Aspasia to these hateful matrimonial squabbles. 'You . . . you wicked woman,' he wailed, and banged the table.

'You don't think those chairs are a decoration to a house, do you?' she demanded. 'They're depressing to look at. And there are seven more of them.' She finished with a note of gloating in her voice.

He began to stride across the room. 'I . . . I've a good mind to *strike* you,' he cried, venom becoming active among his foam. He crossed to her and raised his arm menacingly. 'You hear me. I could strike you.'

'Why don't you, then!' she cried, bending her head to her knitting as if to receive the blow on her neck.

'That,' he said, distending his nostrils proudly, 'I will not do. Much as you deserve it.'

'Ha!' she exclaimed.

He left her, drew a chair to the table, sat down and laid his head on the table among his arms.

'Why did I marry you!' he wailed. 'Nothing but strife and bickering in the house. Nagging and spite. I get no peace of mind. My work is being ruined.'

'What work?' she asked. 'The tally-trade or the poems?'

He moaned in despair. It seemed to him very typical of her vulgar mind that she should ask that question. He hated to be reminded of the tally-business. Nevertheless he answered sweepingly:

'Everything, everything.'

She laid down her knitting, stood up, and looked at him with cold and hard eyes.

'Yes,' she said, 'everything *is* being ruined. And the ruin is in yourself. Because you're a natural clown. Because you can't get to grips with life. Because you're lazy. Because you ought to be a kept man. Because you ought to have married such as Baba Price. And because, God help me, I won't be blind to what you are and pander to your conceit.' Her mind had been working with clear rapidity over the knitting.

He had lifted his head and was looking at her with horror. It was as if he was being forced to listen to harsh iron bells ringing in a place of grey desolation, a prison with high, blank walls. Bronwen, facing him in cold judgment, was like the incarnate spirit of that place. He couldn't bear it, or the sight of her. His inside felt sick. His mouth worked.

'What . . . what was all that you said?' he demanded, in hysteria.

'You heard,' she said.

Gwyn had. But her words had already gone out of him, washed away in the foaming tide of his own dramatic suffering. Only the spirit of the words remained before him, implacable and harsh. And he didn't quite know what to do about it and how best to close his eyes to that spirit. He felt like giving vent to a soliloquy, like Hamlet. But his mind seemed unable to find a suitable beginning.

'Go away from me,' he cried at last, and averted his face again. 'You don't understand me, you never have, and you never will.'

And Bronwen was struck dumb. She stood staring at him. Her denunciation, that she had delivered out of a high sense of justification, was as naught. It meant nothing to him. She knew that he would triumph, that he would always triumph. He had for ever the shield of his belief in himself, closely buckled to his hand. He would for ever do battle for the Muse that he worshipped.

Suddenly she began to laugh. She sat in her chair again and laughed, loud and long. Tears ran down her cheeks: she dabbed them away with her little pink-frilled apron, that Gwyn had given her on her birthday, a pretty thing that she wore in the evenings. Her laughter bubbled and rippled, with now and again deeper and darker notes running in her throat. She had married a clown. And she would get her share of fun out of him.

After a while, glad that the disgusting squabble had passed, Gwyn even joined her, contributing a delighted smile. For he too had a sense of humour, peculiar to himself. And after all, he told himself, married life was bound to be a little dramatic, and even unpleasant sometimes.

THE TWO FRIENDS

Out of the dark back lane that ran between twin rows of decrepit dwellings two women, shawled about the head and aproned respectably, appeared and passed under the corner gas-lamp, that slanted up from the earth like a long-stemmed yellow flower. The sky crackled with stars, but the November night was rough and blowy.

'Cold, Eunice,' said one, stopping for a moment to pull up a cotton stocking. 'I forgot my garters.'

'Nowadays,' said the other bleakly, 'string I use. It keeps 'em up even though it cuts into the flesh and raises the veins.'

'Garters don't cost much, Eunice,' protested her friend, shocked.

'The price of a bottle of stout they cost,' said Eunice flatly. 'And I know which I prefer.' She added defensively, 'It's all that keeps me from pitching into the grave nowadays.'

Gwyneth answered with a kind of affectionate whine to this, squeezing her friend's arm. 'Don't you think of going before me, Eunice. Awful it would be here without you. Especially now.'

'Aye,' grunted Eunice in response, 'aye.' She was of harder, dourer disposition than Gwyneth, possessing a long, austere nose that had a constant amethystine drip. Her sharp eyes seemed always crouched in readiness to attack a dishonourable world.

Friends since they were children, reared next door to each other in a pastoral offshoot of the valley, the two had sallied forth during their girlhood to the nearby coal-mining district and got married to colliers. Those were new, exciting days, with snatches of prosperity. Now in disaster, with the pits closed and no money anywhere, they clung to each other as if in a foreign and hostile land. They had doleful conferences, in which they went over their advantages and grievances. Gwyneth had a tidy chapel-going husband, but a houseful of growing brats that she didn't know what to do with; Eunice was childless, but had a shifty, good-for-nothing husband. Over both women the common local spectre of unemployment had hovered for several ill-natured years.

Tonight they were taking another of their nocturnal excursions. There were few people about. Soon they were climbing beyond the inhabited places, leaving the lean rows of houses for paths that wound up the broad lower sweeps of the mountains. From the upper ridges a cold wind swept down gustily. Sometimes the two women stumbled as they climbed higher and higher. But both knew the path. The valley night seemed full of mystery and stealth. Gwyneth shivered.

'We could be taken for burglars, Eunice.'

Both women carried under their shawls a canvas bag and a stumpy pick-axe. Also candles and matches. Eunice carried, in addition, a packet of cake and a small bottle of cold tea.

'Or they'd say that a grave we were going to dig,' she answered grimly.

Gwyneth moaned, as if biliously. 'The last year or two, Eunice,' she whined, 'always wanting to shove a grave under my eyes you are.'

'It's what we're making for smart nowadays,' Eunice replied, ascending with sudden brisk energy.

Gwyneth, clambering behind, bleated anxiously, 'You mustn't leave me behind, Eunice! In the dark!'

Presently they reached a small plateau, jutted out into the swirling dark space like a craggy chin of the mountain. Here the wind sprang friskily, sometimes changing into a great sudden mouthful blown insolently from above. The women's skirts billowed, their shawls flapped. The valley far below, winking with lights, seemed in another country.

'Don't cling to me, gal,' Eunice croaked, not unkindly. In these remote dark heights even she felt a little insecure. 'We'll have the candles going in a jiffy.'

At the back of the plateau, cut in the mountain, was a ragged hole like the opening of a cave. The women stooped to enter, feeling their way cautiously. Inside they each lit a candle. And there was disclosed a roughly hewn passage-way, the roof sparsely propped with timber. Large stones bulged loosely from the sides. There was a damp earthy smell.

'When I think of the rest of the hill pressing on top,' quavered Gwyneth, 'and what we're risking—'

Eunice swiped her hand with an habitual movement under her nose. 'Didn't the men work this level for months during the big strike!' she said. 'It's safe as anything is in this rotten world. Get your pick ready, gal.' She advanced down the passageway, stooping. Presently she was obliged to bend and almost crawl along. Gwyneth followed, feeling her way like a wary crab. The candle-light was wrapped close round their gauntly stooping figures. Ahead and behind them the thick, silent blackness seemed as though it had body.

'Here it is,' Eunice muttered. Dropping pick and bag from under one arm and setting her candle on a stone, she squatted on her haunches.

Gwyneth panted after her. 'We mustn't be long,' she breathed. 'Bad for my chest the air is here.'

But Eunice was already at work. Before her, low in the cave wall, a thick

111

vein of coal glittered brilliantly, black, blue, and silver, wedged among stone and earth. She set her pick smashingly into the brilliance and presently a small shower of the precious mineral fell crisply at her feet.

Gwyneth was slower in setting to. She had to fold her shawl neatly and turn her grey canvas apron. Then she knelt. There was not enough room to turn round easily.

'Keep your pick away from me!' cried Eunice irritably. But she herself, squatting, heaved her pick dangerously.

'What we're risking,' Gwyneth panted again, 'for a few handfuls of coal.'

'It saves us half a crown a week,' Eunice pointed out.

'Oh dear,' lamented Gwyneth bitterly. 'Half a crown! Oh dear.'

'We'll have a swig of tea presently,' Eunice promised impatiently.

It was not long before there was enough coal to fill their bags; the vein was easy and gernerous. 'Good coal,' Eunice remarked with satisfaction, as she stuffed her bag. 'Full of life; almost out of your hands it jumps.'

'And bright as the stars it burns,' sighed Gwyneth.

They heaved the filled bags to the entrance of the tunnel, dropping them there. Outside, the night had become rougher. Clouds were now blowing over the stars. Gwyneth went to the edge of the plateau and peered into the abyss of heaving darkness beneath her.

'I don't know how we'll get down with those sacks,' she wailed. The fists of the wind were pounding against the mountains.

'Oh, don't worry,' called Eunice from the entrance. 'We'll get blown down.' She was opening the packet of cake.

Gwyneth returned to the cave. Just inside, out of the wind, the candle-light gave it a cosy look. It seemed a peaceful habitation, remote from the world.

'A fire shall we light this time?' she suggested softly. 'And stay awhile? We left some sticks and paper.'

Eunice nodded. She would not have minded staying up there all night, being of a more adventurous disposition than her friend. And she had no particular affection for her home below, which, indeed, had done nothing but annoy and harass her ever since she married.

Gwyneth took from a shelf in the wall some thin sticks and paper. She laid the fire in the centre of the floor a couple of yards from the entrance, using small pieces of coal from the bags. Soon a crisp red shooting of flame lit up the cave. The two women squatted on the ground beside it.

'We might be gipsies,' Eunice said, satisfaction whipped into her voice.

'Always you wanted to be one, didn't you, dear?' remarked Gwyneth. 'A pity you didn't go off with that roundabouts man that time. The one who asked you to have a look into his caravan in the fair—you remember?'

'Only three months I had been married then,' Eunice said, with a certain amount of savage regret. She passed the bottle of cold tea to her friend. 'I wish he'd come back now.'

Gwyneth appeared shocked. 'You couldn't go off now, at forty-one,' she said severely. She surveyed her friend's worry-raddled face for a while in silence. Then she said in a hushed voice, 'No good it is, Eunice dear, us expecting more from life. Our day is over.' And she added lamentably, 'Look what we've got to do to get a bob's worth of coal!' Her pale, puffed eyes seemed about to weep.

Eunice munched the plain currant cake before replying, and took another swig of tea out of the bottle. Lean and taut, she seemed as though her flame of life was only half choked yet. Her small berry eyes darted restlessly, though her cheeks hung down slack and wrinkled and her breast was woefully scraggy. 'I'd like to go to jail,' she said suddenly.

Shock quivered plainly in Gwyneth then. 'You always had *cravings*,' she quavered. She stared about her, particularly at the sacks of coal, resentfully for a while. She was annoyed. In a careful voice she went on to praise the cake. 'I can't make it so light,' she said tactfully.

'Yes, jail,' repeated Eunice with grim insistence.

'What d'you want to go to jail for?' wailed Gwyneth. She had always known there were dark, obscure reaches in her friend's temperament, and sometimes she had been frightened of her savage outbursts against her destiny. And yet Eunice had always remained a respectable married woman, like herself. Battered, but still respectable.

'Because,' croaked Eunice, with gaunt hopelessness, 'because the only exciting thing it is that can happen to me now.'

Two tears rolled down Gwyneth's smudged cheeks, and half a one remained pendent at the corner of her weary eye. Behind her fear, she understood. She crawled across to her friend, the other side of the red-sparkling fire, and laid an arm along her shoulder. 'Why don't you let yourself cry, Eunice?' she whispered rockingly. 'Have a good cry. It washes things out.'

But Eunice remained stark in her friend's sentimental embrace. 'My tears,' she said hardly, 'won't come out. Behind they are, but they won't run out.'

'A pity,' sighed Gwyneth, trying to believe. 'They're meant to come out.'

The tea and cake were finished, and both women sat silent for a while, gazing broodingly into the soft red of the fire-glow. The candles dripped, the wind hurried past the entrance with much muttering and exclamation. But, inside, the buried silence remained undisturbed. There was a strangely soothing touch in that silence, and now that the women did not talk, it entered their hearts like a promise of perfect peace.

113

'Nice here,' murmured Gwyneth at last. 'Makes you feel you don't want to go back. No men, no children, no squabbling. No cooking scraps, and washtubs, and patching of old clothes.' She sighed, bliss mingling with unlovely memories. 'Let's come up here often,' she suggested, 'and forget the world for a bit.'

'What's the good, Gwyneth, what's the good? Back we've got to go and live in that world, lousy as it is. Don't whine, gal.'

But her friend knew that she, too, felt comforted and somewhere nearer to peace; she was never one to make a *show* of joy. Leaning against Eunice, slowly Gwyneth began to sing.

She sang 'Watching the Ripening Wheat'. The song about summer days and the doomed lovers among the golden corn. Her voice was a shabby, hoarse contralto now. But at one time she had secured a silver medal in a chapel eisteddfod. The voice sank wornly to the melancholy ending. 'Now you sing, Eunice,' she asked. 'Something sad.'

'It's bound to be,' said Eunice with a bitter grin. And she launched into a slow, weird rendering of 'All Through the Night,' musicless and raucous. Nevertheless, Gwyneth was enchanted.

'Sweet that was,' she said, stroking her friend's arm. And she began a soft singing of a Welsh hymn. Eunice joined in. They sang quietly, affected by the buried silence of the tomb-like space. They swayed together, arms entwined. Suddenly, Gwyneth broke into a piercing scream and with a wild flurry of skirts darted up and plunged down into the cave. Framed in the black entrance was the tall and corpulent figure of a policeman.

'Don't go down there, you fool,' Eunice called after her friend calmly; 'you can't get out that way.' She turned her head to the advancing constable. 'Now what do you want, P.C. Price?' she asked severely. 'Frightening my friend!'

'Very cosy you are up here!' exclaimed P.C. Price in his turkey-cock voice. 'Aren't you now! Well, well. Singing hymns, were you?'

Down in the dark cave Gwyneth was still wailing and weeping. Eunice rose, saying: 'Enough it is to frighten the life out of any poor woman,' as she flung the P.C. an angry glance. She went to fetch Gwyneth, taking a candle.

'Why now, missus,' P.C. Price called out helpfully, 'not going to swallow you up I am. Come now.' He sat on a stone, took off his helmet, and leaned towards the fire. Presently the two women reappeared out of the dark, Eunice urging her stumbling friend, whose eyes stared in dread.

'There now,' cried the policeman; 'don't be afraid, missus.'

But to Gwyneth, whose heart was sitting up like a roused hare, his exclaimed comfortings held a menacing quality; she leaned totteringly against Eunice's shoulder. And her fears were justified. Placing his helmet on his head,

114

and speaking soullessly as a schoolmaster announcing something about the habits of caterpillars, the policeman said:

'Now, now. Four times you two women have been up here taking coal. Very well you know the Company that owns this property. They are going to prosecute. Others have been at this game. In broad daylight too. It is stealing. You'll be summonsed.' He nodded portentously, lifted his bulk like a horse, and went over to the bags of coal and peered inside them.

Gwyneth suddenly loosened a shrill torrent of hysterical complaint. How were poor women to live? Were her five children to go to bed cold? How was she to boil a kettle to fill their little cold stomachs with tea? Who did the coal in the mountain belong to? Why, God, of course. Finally, she buried her weeping face in Eunice's dusty neck.

'Shut up,' muttered Eunice proudly. 'What's the good?'

P.C. Price had taken out his notebook and, very slowly, was tracing words in it. He repeated them with his lips; now and again his pinkish-blue tongue leaped out as if to lick them away again. 'Two canvas bags containing, roughly, sixty pounds of coal each . . . Women are sitting round fire singing hymns. . . . Roberts complained of poverty and said her children had no food or clothes.' He closed the book. 'There you are, gals. Duty's got to be done.' He looked out towards the black, windy night, frowning.

'What'll it be?' Eunice asked whippingly,

'Oh, very light they'll let you off. Ten bob fine each, I expect. But a summons there must be. The Company got to put a stop to this pinching of coal in the mountains.'

'I shan't pay it,' said Eunice decisively. 'Not ten bob nor ten pence.'

'You don't want seven days, do you? Perhaps fourteen.'

Gwyneth clutched in anguish at Eunice's arm. Prison! But Eunice took no notice. Her head was lifted in exultation, her face shone. Gwyneth stared at her. What was she like? Yes, like that red-gowned woman in the stained-glass window in church, the one who had been given the torments and was about to go up to Heaven.

'Eunice,' whispered Gwyneth. 'Eunice, I'll come with you. We'll suffer together.'

'You've got your children,' answered Eunice dramatically, as if she were on a stage. 'They mustn't be disgraced.'

The policeman prepared to go. 'You don't want my old company down, do you?' he said slyly. After some further cheerful observations he disappeared into the smudge of black at the cave mouth.

'He means,' whispered Gwyneth, 'we can take the coal as long as he doesn't see us.'

One of the candles was guttering and the fire was no more than a plateful of glowing ash. Again Gwyneth anxiously took her friend's arm. The cave oppressed her now; its aloof peace had been ruined for ever. 'Let's go, Eunice, let's go. Come home with me and I'll make some chips.'

Eunice's lean body was still taut in exultation, and her nose, raw but proud, was tilted upwards. 'Fourteen days!' she said with sombre triumph. 'Peace. Shut away. Fed with somebody's else's food.'

'Oh, Eunice,' wailed Gwyneth distractedly, 'prison it is, after all.'

Eunice's voice rose until it rang in scorn against the cave walls. 'What has our life been the last few years? Prison. Prison at our own expense. Every day dull as a pan of stale dishwater. No decent money and no faith in anything—'

Once more Gwyneth began to drop tears on her friend's meagre but stiffened breast. 'Yes, yes,' she wept, 'I understand, Eunice. A pity it isn't a hospital, though. Myself, I've longed many a day to go in and have a serious operation.'

Eunice half pushed Gwyneth away. 'Well,' she said, with a touch of malice, 'enjoy ouselves we will, stepping into the box at court. Better it'll be than going to the pictures. Acting oneself.' She shook out her shawl like a whip. 'And I shan't whine, either. I'm going to be haughty and grand as that Greta Garbo. I've got my say to say, I can tell you.'

Gwyneth allowed herself to be heartened a little by her friend's proud wrath. She dried her tears, but continued to sigh and wheeze. They decided to take the coal they had broken out of the mountain; they might as well keep what they were being prosecuted for. Eunice fixed her shawl, and, with help from Gwyneth, the lumpy sack was slung across her bony but sinewy shoulders.

'I'll drag my bag,' Gwyneth said. 'Not so sure am I on my feet as you are.'

Outside the cave the dark wind sprang on them like monkeys. The mountain night had a look of eternity. Light would never break in such a place. The stars were quenched. From the plateau the women could smell the damp, writhing clouds. Eunice found the path instinctively and began to tread its winding length with unafraid feet, her arms raised to the load on her shoulders. Gwyneth followed untidily and insecurely, dragging her sack. The wind scrambled after them like a gang of small hissing furies.

THE CONTRAPTION

The Almshouses were of old-bruised stone, knowing two centuries' wear. They were sheltered among the elms like things forgotten of this world, with that air of idealistic peace one still comes upon occasionally in the country. Nine women of the district inhabited them, their characters having been thoroughly vouched for and poked into by a local committee presided over by the Rector. And tranquil the small grey houses had been for many a long year, until Mrs. Hope-Cary decided that improvements were needed.

Pushing out a dramatic face over the huge nigger teapot, old Sarah Crump declared ungratefully at supper one night:

'And who's she, then? Been in the village ten years—pah, five minutes. I for one don't want her contraption. What say you, girls?'

Ida Neate, eighty and always trembling like a brown leaf, wet her lips with a tongue narrow as a lily-pistil. 'She step into my room and says: "Winder never opened," and when I says opened winder always gives me croup, she says: "Nonsense, good 'ooman, the very reason why you has it."' Ida tittered. 'I lay she'll never live to be eighty, with her winders open and never knowing how to sit her body down and let it take a mike. She fusses about till you can see steam coming out of her trap.'

'That was a wig she 'ad on,' declared Susie Eighteeen dourly.

With bated breath, Ena Tulk asked for details of the contraption the lady was suggesting for installation. Frail as smoke, her hands fluttered over her eyes as she giggled modestly: ''Taint wanted here, surely!' she gasped. 'The old way has done us all our lives and no harm's come of it.'

The other women voiced their criticism too. Mrs. Hope-Cary was not liked. Sarah Crump, indignantly pouring herself another cup of strong tea, cried:

'If Committee's got all that brass to spend, we'd lief have it turned into what's good for our *insides*. What do what *she* says we ought to have matter? Ena's right. The old way's done our families since time was, and no harm's come of it . . . Beer's thin and sloppy for dinner. The money ought to be spent on something with more body to it. And the penn'orth of boiled fruit-drops on Saturday!' She leaned over the teapot angrily. 'Across in the houses at Milchester,' she whispered dramatically, 'they get *quarter-pound* of liquorice allsorts *or* black-currant gums, which you like.'

The company made suitable exclamations of surprised envy. They wore

117

black serge gowns and bibbed white aprons; a white frill clasped half their heads. None except Sarah Crump had much hair. And whether it was by virtue of her great twist of iron-grey hair, or her busy tongue, or the bright swing of her cherry-dark eyes, Sarah was acknowledged boss of the bunch. She it was who spoke up when the women were invited to do so by the visiting members of the Committee; she it was who had obtained tins of salmon for Sunday-night supper, instead of cold cod pie; she it was who obtained official permission for the wearing of stockings in bed. She hissed now:

'Girls, don't let's have it. I'll lay my gold hoops that her it was that stopped the Sunday papers and got us these silly frills for our heads. Rector, he's in her power and don't come here now. Don't let's have what she says we're to have!'

'You can't stop her putting it in,' Lizzie Payne quavered.

Sarah, with a very meaning glance round the company, quoted an adage: 'You can take a donkey to the well, but can't make him drink.'

'We'll have to go *somewhere*,' Rachel Burch croaked, meditatively stroking her pinched nostrils.

'We'll find a way,' Sarah said mysterious;ly. 'We'll teach her not to bring her awful newfangled contraptions where they're not welcome.' She began again, snorting fresh anger over the massive teapot. 'Didn't we ought to have been *asked* first, didn't . . .'

Elderly Nancy Sheet made her comment too. No one knew what it was, for she always spoke deep down in her chest, like a rumble, and the words never managed to come out. But Sarah said, nodding her head, 'Yes, Nancy, that's right.' Some of the women called Nancy 'Grannie,' she was so old—over a hundred, it was believed. Her photo had been in a newspaper.

II

The contraption was installed, amid silence from the women. It took some days to build and was attached to the back of one of the houses: the one shared by Ida Neate and Susie Eighteen. Also a patch of sward was torn up to carry a pipe and Ida's bed of double stocks ruined, greatly vexing her. Ida it was who broke the women's malign silence by leaning out of her little trellised window like an infuriated Judy and shouting to the workmen:

'Donkey you take to the well, but can't make him drink.'

Sunning themselves in their porches or on the little squares of lawn, the women sent each other meaning glances. One or two of them dug peaceably into their flower-patches, tending marigolds, sweet williams and pansies. Sarah, who could stretch herself and mount a ladder without getting giddy, was clipping the rose that clambered so thickly, showering a myriad pink blossoms, over Nancy's house. Except for the clatter of the workmen behind, the afternoon quiet seemed to purr like a drowsy cat.

It was disturbed just before tea-time by Mrs. Hope-Cary, who lifted the latch of the gate with a decisive click and swept up the gravel. Tall, well-dressed and painted bright as a barber's pole, she was full of undiminished energy, though sixty. Wife of an architect over in the city, she had been childless. No one rose to greet her, though the lady lifted her hand like a queen acknowledging huzzas.

'Well,' she said briskly, 'how is the work proceeding?' She swung to the back of Ida's house, but only glanced at the contraption for one discreet moment. Returned to the lawns, she said, loudly, since she was speaking to the old, 'It is time you women received the benefits of modern methods.'

Silence—except for the clip-clip of Sarah's shears among the climber. But Mrs. Hope-Cary was busy examining the flower-borders. She hovered near Lizzie Payne, who was crouched doubtfully in a kind of half-stoop, neither up nor down, trowel in hand.

'The violas are charming,' Mrs. Hope-Cary told her graciously. 'But all your flowers are charming. You have green fingers, Mrs. Payne.'

Startled-looking, Lizzie peered at her hands. 'Black, mum,' she mumbled, very innocently, 'begging your pardon. It's the dirt—'

'Oh come, come,' the lady smiled, 'I don't mean literally. In the country, we say of a successful gardener that he has green fingers. Surely you were reared in the country? Otherwise you wouldn't be in our Almshouses.'

'Seventy-six years in this same village, mum,' Lizzie said mildly. 'I was married here and 'ad—'

Sarah had climbed down quickly from the ladder and gone into her house. A lattice was flung back with a bang, Sarah popped out an arm and shrilly rang the tea-bell.

'Ah, there goes your tea-bell,' Mrs. Hope-Cary murmured.

'Yes, mum,' said Lizzie, her gaze wide and innocent.

'I do hope you women,' said Mrs. Hope-Cary in dismissal, 'don't still drink your tea black?'

'No, mum.' The lady had already given them a talk on the evils of strong tea.

'So bad for your digestion,' she murmured, peering to examine a clump of very gay poppies.

The old ladies took tea all together. Mrs. Hope-Cary had departed, with a brisk slam of the gate. Lizzie Payne rocked with frail laughter. She was the most easily amused of the bunch. Shuddering giggles shook her. 'Green fingers,' she gasped, 'green fingers! Lawk a'day, it's a mercy I haven't got a green mind.'

'You didn't ought to have gossiped with her,' said Sarah severely. 'Haughty, that's what we've got to be now.' She pressed the cosy down tightly and smotheringly over the pot. 'Haughty and proud.'

And though her face still retained its sweet old-woman's look, she croaked to them in sinister warning. 'Horrible contraption will be ready come Saturday.'

III

One afternoon three weeks later Sarah, surrounded by all the other ladies, stood carefully arraying herself in her best. They were black clothes with a dash of puce here and there, and voluminous. Her face was already very austere in preparation, though a misty patch of colour glowed in her cheeks.

'My locket, Ena,' she asked. Ena passed over Sarah's head the long gold chain with its heavy pendant. Sarah tucked the pendant, which contained a photo of her late husband's head and a shred of his hair, into her satin waistband.

'Don't you break down now,' quavered Jane King, who was nearly always in a state of fear and whining. 'Don't you let 'em fret you.'

'I'm not likely to be fretted,' answered Sarah, indignantly— 'no, not if they was a lot of Red Indians.'

'It'll be best to keep your temper and be a lady,' advised Cissie Stand, who had been a lady's maid in her time.

Lizzie Payne tied the bonnet strings firmly under Sarah's roused chin. 'Not so tight, Lizzie,' she grunted, 'I won't be able to move my jaw properly to them.' A bunch of ancient artificial violets bobbed under the poke.

She set out in good time, accompanied to the gate by all the women, who twittered further advice and encouragement: two wept. Remind the Committee of this and that scandalous deprivation. Remember how Cissie Inge had asked for gin the day she died and was denied it. Sarah planted her umbrella firmly before her and began her auspicious walk to the village hall. The sun shone brightly on the rusty black satin. She looked neither to left nor right, but kept on like an old war-horse roused once again by the sound of cannon. She reached the village hall a little out of wind.

120

The members of the Committee sat in a long line at the table, all facing her.

'Come in, come in, Mrs. Crump,' called the Rector kindly. 'Please be seated there.' He pointed to a chair.

She lowered herself with careful dignity to the cane chair. All the six ladies of the Committee were present, and four men. Mrs. Hope-Cary sat next to the Rector and had before her a pile of papers, which she was sharply looking through: she hadn't even glanced up. When later she did look up, Sarah caught instantly her hostile stare.

'We . . . we'll attend to your little matter in a moment, Mrs. Crump,' said the Rector. And for a while they talked of accounts. Sarah felt rather dashed. But she had time to get back her wind and cool down. She gazed admiringly now and again at smart Colonel Cole, who wore an eyeglass: since she was a girl he had always been her idea of a man and her secret beau. She used to go hot when he galloped past her on his horse, going to barracks. She experienced no such trouble now, but felt his equal in experience of the goings-on of this world.

'Ah, now, Mrs. Crump,' said the Rector at last.

'Yes, sir,' she spoke up, neither too bold nor too meek.

'Perhaps Mrs. Crump would like a glass of water,' said Colonel Cole, pointing to the flask on the table.

She declined, but the Colonel's thought warmed her through, as if she'd drunk a glass of whisky. She wondered if she ought to stand. There seemed a great deal of clearing of throats and uttering of ahs and m'ms among the Committee: the Rector was rubbing his nose as though in perplexity. Mrs. Hope-Cary tapped her pencil against the pile of papers and looked cold. At last the Rector adjusted his pince-nez more firmly and began:

'We have asked you to come here, Mrs. Crump, because we know that you are . . . um . . . shall we say, the uncrowned queen of the ladies of our Almshouses—'

'You were the May Queen in '75, if I remember rightly, Sarah Crump?' asked elderly Sam Lime, grinning in his beard.

Sarah flushed with pleasure and nodded prettily. Fancy old Sam Lime remembering after all these years! Really, all the men looked pleasantly disposed towards her. But Mrs. Hope-Cary did not. A quick glance at the lady's frowning face kept Sarah from weakening. The other ladies looked as though they had withdrawn all expression from their faces, even nice Mrs. Gascoyne, who sent pots of bramble jelly to the Almshouses.

'And I'm sure,' added the Rector gallantly, 'that Mrs. Crump even now could dance round the maypole as friskily as any of our young lassies.'

'Hear, hear,' said the other men.

She began to feel a little uncomfortable. Were they buttering her up because some dreadful punishment hung in the offing? But she would not allow her little say to go unsaid, whatever they threatened. She waited in a determined calm. The Rector quickly whisked back into seriousness and began again:

'Well, Mrs. Crump, we have asked you to come here in the hope that you will be able to give us some explanation of this, this . . . recent behaviour in the Almshouses over the . . . ah . . . matter of the recent installation.' In this difficulty he turned to the lady next to him, 'Mrs. Hope-Cary, I understand there is an unanimous decision in the Almshouses about this—'

'A peculiar obstinacy,' said Mrs. Hope-Cary sharply. 'Mrs. Crump, I'm sorry to say, is the ringleader and all the women treat the installation as though it were not there.' She was silent for a moment, then could not resist adding, 'Wicked, wicked and foolish!'

Sarah began to burn again. She had an impulse to loosen herself and let go. But she felt her neck go stiff. Once a princess had passed through the village and bowed her head at Sarah Crump as she passed. Sarah bowed hers now in imitation towards Mrs. Hope-Cary and said:

'Thank you, mum, for speaking so plain.'

The Rector began again, more hastily, 'You must realise, Mrs. Crump, that the installation has meant a great deal of expense. It is up-to-date. The Committee is at a loss to understand why the Almshouses ladies . . . ah . . . scorn it.'

'Well, sir, it's because me and the ladies can't bring ourselves to sit over water.'

There was a silence in the room. No one seemed to know what to say. But Sarah was pleased to notice that Mrs. Hope-Cary reddened with annoyance. Sarah gave them quite a time to reply and then began again, gazing meekly at the Rector:

'You see, sir, if I'm so allowed to speak, us women are all old, as you know, sir, and got set in our ways. We never had truck with such as this contraption. We are well satisfied with the old place and want to use it always, with your kind permission'—she swept her look across the row of faces— 'sirs and ma'ams. Newfangled notions don't suit us, and the ladies was upset already by having our brown stout changed for that mild dinner ale with no body to it, and having the Sunday papers took from us too in the middle of the serial that Mrs. Ida Neate was reading out to us. Begging your pardon for speaking and since we have many comforts in the Almshouses.' And she sat down quietly, perspiring a little.

The Rector still seemed overcome. Mrs. Hope-Cary had screwed up her eyes and the ginger powder on her face looked cracked. 'But, my good woman, this is nonsense,' she snapped. And she added ruthlessly: 'The old place will be taken away.'

She repeated with a stubbornness that made the words solid as rock, 'The ladies won't sit over water.'

Mrs. Flower then said something about modern hygiene and afterwards Colonel Cole and Mrs. Gascoyne tried to coax Sarah. But to no avail. Old age gleamed with obstinate pride in Sarah's eye. She repeated again and again that the ladies were set in their ways and meekly she implied that to interfere with the habits of their very long lives was the direst cruelty. But what would they do, bravely enquired a member at last, if the old place was taken away? With equal bravery Sarah replied that they would then use the hedges betwixt the fields. It became quite a long, exhausting meeting.

An hour after her entrance Sarah made her exit, knowing in her bones that triumph was hers, though the Committee made such a show of being vexed. The old place would never be taken away. And she had left in the village hall a cunning suggestion that Mrs. Hope-Cary's so-called 'improvements' only made the women unwell. Opinions varied about 'improvements'. Perhaps, Sarah thought, as she hurried home, longing for a nice strong cup of good black tea, Mrs. Hope-Cary would now resign.

All the women were waiting in the garden for Sarah's return. Slowly they followed her in procession into her house. Tea was laid ready. 'Make it strong, Ida,' panted Sarah, as Ida lifted the lid of the teapot, 'I been talking heavy.' Sympathetic hands removed her bonnet and shoes. When all was ready, the women seated about Sarah in expectant silence, she, after taking three quick saucers of tea, launched into a minute word-for-word description of her ordeal. Her listeners breathed excitedly as the tale rose. At last, in anguish, Lizzie Payne could contain herself no longer: she quavered entreatingly:

'Tell us now, Sarah, if they're going to let us keep the old place! We been waiting so long all the afternoon.'

'Yes, tell us,' cried the others.

Sarah eyed the plateful of cake, which was fast diminishing. She had had no opportunity to eat. So she brought her recital drastically to a close.

'Yes,' she said, flatly and confidently, 'we'll keep it.'

The ladies sighed in relief. Each thought affectionately of the old place, cosy and familiar, with its seat tacked over with rabbit-fur.

'And what's more,' added Sarah clairvoyantly, 'I'll lay all I got that *Madame* Hope-Cary will resign.'

She was right. The lady withdrew from the Committee shortly afterwards, going in more for politics: it was rumoured that she would be the Tory candidate at the next election. The women of the Almshouses are often malicious about her in a sweet kind of way, to visitors. And if you are a liked visitor, they will point out to you the famous unused contraption, now derelict.

WRATH

I

Before Matthew at last decided to marry her, Alice had sat for long, long years in a large box, giving out shilling tickets at the entrance lobby of the local cinema. At one time she possessed bright auburn hair of lively texture, and then quite suddenly, in a few weeks, a lot fell out in masses and what was left became drab. She was often in a state of roused indignation, and would then deny entrance to the cinema of many a collier if he appeared to be tipsy. She had joined the local women's Conservative Society for a couple of seasons, and the amiable lines of her well-knit body became slack and loose. And at the Pleasant Monday afternoon meetings in chapel she spoke with heat of this and that, denouncing things. But after a while, dissatisfied, she chucked all connection with such affairs and turned her gaze inwards, becoming morose and moody.

Cross as two sticks she went out for Sunday afternoon walks with Matthew and endeavoured to rouse him to awareness of her mind. Dutifully, on leaving her at evening, he pecked at her lips, and once, after a Boxing Day performance of a Mendelssohn cantata, he had lingered at her bosom, sighing. After twelve years of such friendship they had married. She had never been pretty, and by that time she was plain. But there were always points like sparks, somewhere behind her eyes, and often her slack body would turtle up, swell, and she seemed to thresh the air as if with wings, like a roused swan. Perhaps she never quite forgave Matthew for keeping her waiting so long.

He had never really wanted to marry and had kept the business at bay as long as possible. True, he thought of her desiringly at times, off and on between his passion for motor-bikes, toy-engines and wireless-sets. Then his mother had died and for a few months a succession of landladies had made life very uncomfortable. One morning, feeling a little aggrieved, he had taken Alice off to a registry office on the back of his motor-bike: he wanted no fuss, he said, being shy.

He had a round, plump face and his round, tight body always wore navy-blue serge suits and grey pin-spot ties. And he spoke in a tight, thin-lipped way, very smug. He had no male friends, but everybody recognised him as he went through the valleys on his collecting rounds: he was an insurance agent with quite a good book. His solid and safe demeanour persuaded people into the wisdom of taking policies. His favourite opening remark to a prospective client was:

125

'Life can be very cushy if you've a mind to make it so.'

Soon he would be forty and the thought of it gave him satisfaction. To be middle-aged, with safe work, no worries and everybody convinced of their prudence in taking insurance policies, seemed to him the acme of comfort. In an upstairs back room of his house he made and repaired wireless-sets and now nearly all his spare time he spent closeted with valves and batteries. Alice would call him, angrily, to a meal or bed. She had a habit, when she called him thus, of hissing between her words. Hissing like a roused swan. Presently he would call out:

'All right, old girl, I shan't be long.'

A steady, respectable chap, he could sleep like a hog, going to bed late from the intricacies of his wireless-sets.

II

He took to the pleasures of the table. But Alice was not really a satisfactory cook, or rather she was not interested in a gas-stove. He complained: she stiffened with anger. Then, one day three years after their marriage, Matthew, with astonished satisfaction, said at the dinner-table.

'This is a beautiful piece of steak. Lloyd's meat is improving.'

Alice scooped more cabbage on to his plate. 'More of these greens, dear,' she murmured, 'they'll do you good. I was going to give you beans today,' she went on chattily and oddly good-humoured, 'but the greens looked so fresh.' Smoothly she continued to talk about vegetables. But Matthew, struck with the exceptionally quality of the meat, kept talking of the butcher.

'Lloyd is pulling himself together again,' he declared. 'Very poor his stuff got after his wife died. Didn't care, I suppose, about his trade—went to pieces for a time.'

Alice rose from the table, sniffing and saying that the rhubarb-pie was burning: she hastened into the scullery, where the gas-stove stood, and remained there several minutes. After banging the oven-door, she looked into the mirror over the sink, vaguely patting her hair. Her skin was yellowish, her mouth slack—she noted other details with a swift impatience. Only yesterday she had moved the mirror to a different position, but her appearance was no more flattering. However, before leaving the mirror she smiled at herself, a sprig of a smile, lean and secret. Then she pulled out the rhubarb-pie. It looked good. Undoubtedly she had produced a well-made dinner today: everything had gone delightfully.

Matthew thought it was a good meal too. He complimented Alice, saying that she was improving. After the meal he went, for the remainder of his dinner-session, to the back room where the wireless things were kept. At two-thirty he jumped on his motor-bike and went off on his collecting rounds. Alice took a short, sweet nap, which seemed to do her a lot of good, for her mouth was smiling when she woke.

And on Sunday Matthew sliced the joint with anticipatory pleasure. It was a leg of mutton, golden and russet and richly odorous. 'Seems a rare piece,' he remarked. Eating confirmed his judgment. The meat was excellent.

'I cooked the joint slower this time,' Alice said, 'and basted it more.'

'I must run in and tell Lloyd,' Matthew said, taking another slice. 'I want to see him about a life-policy on his mother, too. He did all right on his wife's. Who would have thought she'd have gone off like that, so young, poor woman.' He shook his head. 'More meat, Alice, another slice? It's good, isn't it?'

'Give him time,' Alice said. 'It wouldn't be decent to go worrying him about polices so soon.'

'A chap told me that he didn't seem to be grieving much. Been seen down at the dogs, and in the bus the other night he was fizzy as a glass of health-salts.'

Alice said: 'I wish you'd take a look at that mangle some time today, Matthew. The handle's all loose again.'

He nodded, though usually he resented any effort to take him away from the wireless-room. And all day he was benign and willing. Once or twice he actually cocked an amorous glance across to Alice, aware of her. Vaguely he knew that she was different. Not that she had brushed her hair back, instead of parting it at the side, and that it was smarter. Nor the delicate scented powder that lay like a bloom on her skin—which until lately she had not bothered to conceal or adorn. He arrived at a conclusion. She was More Cheerful. But he did not attempt to discover the reason. He accepted the conclusion with satisfaction and mended the mangle. It had been bought secondhand the week they were married and during the five years following it had broken down every month or so.

Once again that week, Matthew referred, over some veal, to the new delights of Lloyd's meat. He rose to a flight of imagination. 'The calf that this came from,' he vowed, 'chewed cuds in Paradise.' Alice told him not to be silly: the meat was only what it ought to be. Matthew remonstrated and she was obliged to admit that for a time Lloyd had not been a good butcher. Matthew reminded her that at one time they had almost decided to transfer their custom elsewhere. Only the hope that Lloyd might be persuaded to take out another insurance policy prevented them.

'Alice,' he said suddenly, 'you've took your eyebrows out!'

'Oh,' she said offhandedly, 'I made them a bit thinner, that's all.'

'I liked them better bushy. It's no good,' he went on, half jocular, half severe, 'you trying to look like a jane off the pictures. You keep steady, old girl. I don't want you to go looking like a prize in a raffle. See!'

At the same time he was rather fascinated by her new oddness. That night he made love to her. He did not know why. But she spread a different warmth about her. True, he still scrambled through the business too hastily; and she dug her elbows painfully into his ribs, whether accidentally or deliberately he could not tell. And for days following he was aware of her new warmth, though the fact did not penetrate to his mind. He merely found her more attractive to himself and acted accordingly, and blindly.

As for Alice, she bore with him inscrutably. She watched his plump face become plumper, she noticed his air of self-satisfaction becoming more complacent, more pronounced. Once or twice he tore himself from the wireless things and took her to the cinema. Sometimes he jovially tweaked her cheeks during the day, a new gesture from him.

III

Basket on arm, she went down to the butcher's. It was a corner shop and old-established. Bert Lloyd had succeeded to his father's business. He had put in a new facade and slabs of marble. Behind the shop, with an entrance in a lane, was an out-building which had been used as a slaughterhouse in the bad old days: neighbours used often to hear from there the dying bellows of bulls, the hysterical shrieks of stuck pigs. Now the slaughterhouse contained odd bits of furniture, thrown out of the Lloyd household above the shop: a chest of drawers, chairs, trunks and an old-fashioned horse-hair sofa, black, large and commodious. One day, after the death of his wife, Lloyd had put up a notice on his cash-desk: *Secondhand Sofa for Sale*. Alice had asked to see the sofa, thinking of a blank wall in her back parlour, and Lloyd had taken her into the slaughterhouse to see it.

Today she wore pearl-drop ear-rings as she entered the shop and carefully examined the tray of lamb chops. Lloyd was serving Mrs. Baptist Evans, the chapel minister's wife: she bought scrag of mutton and complained that the liver he had sent her the day before was stringy. 'Very bad,' she said threateningly and loud enough for Alice to hear: she did not quite like Lloyd.

He grinned. Lloyd usually gave a grin to almost everything that was said to him. Perhaps it was a nervous grin. But he did not look nervous. Muscular and broad-beamed, he looked like a bantam boxer, and he had red cheeks, coarse hair and rolling eyes. A gaping youth of sheepish mien assisted in the shop.

Whistling cheerily as Mrs. Baptist Evans went out of the shop, he grinned at Alice.

'These chops—' she said in a severe voice.

'Call 'em chops!' he sang. 'They're bits of my old boots.'

Thus he bantered with Alice. Occasionally, years ago, he used to flirt with her through the slot of the cinema pay-box, and at one time she had fancied he would go further. She had noticed his gross good looks, and she found his impudent manner offensive one day, attractive another. But he had married May Roberts, a frail girl who, one would have said, was quite unsuited to him.

'Now then, George,' he said to the boy breezily, 'nip off to the bank and get five bobs' worth of coppers.'

A collier's wife was hovering round the window outside, gazing shrewdly at the cheap meat. Lloyd began sharpening a knife, his powerful short arms dexterosuly wielding carver and steel. 'Steak all right yesterday?' he grinned. Alice had to admit he owned dazzling teeth. She nodded.

'Made up your mind about the sofa yet?' he asked enjoyably.

Alice caught sight of her face in a mirror set in the marble between two dripping flanks of beef and decided she had dabbed on too much rouge. 'No.' she said.

'Want to see it again?'

The collier's wife was joined by a friend, and they stood gossiping on the pavement. George returned with the coppers and stood gazing into space, mouth open: he suffered from adenoids. Alice took two chops specially cut for her from a piece hanging in an unseen corner: with a flourish Lloyd entered the item in the ledger, grinning. She left the shop, hesitated on the corner, and then vaguely made her way towards the lane behind which was also a short cut to her home.

The boy George served the collier's wife. She wanted a pound and a half of the pieces of cheap steak. They were spread bloodily over a tray in bluish-red disorder.

'Where's the boss?' she demanded, scowling.

'Back soon, expect.' George grunted. He plunged a raw hand deep into the mass of meat and tossed a great fistful upon greaseproof paper.

'Meat he calls his stuff,' she said dourly. 'You tell him, George, that Mrs. Evans said the kidneys was bad she had on Tuesday. A fork there is for using, too, boy,' she grumbled.

'Hand's clean!' George replied in gaping surprise. He would never learn to use the fork. He placed the meat on the scales and lifted one chunk away, his red fingers closing on the grisly piece and then chucking it back on to the tray among the other sodden lumps.

'T't, t't, t't,' clicked the collier's wife through her gums. She wore a scrap of old flannel across her shoulders and her used white face seemed already beyond the pleasures and torments of this world. 'Treats the meat as if it was dirt,' she scolded on wearily.

'Ow's Gwenny?' asked George suddenly, alluding to her daughter who had gone into service in London.

For some reason or other she took anger at his enquiry. 'My daughter Miss Evans you mean? Now then, boy, hurry up. No time to waste I have.'

When she had gone, George vaguely tidied the tray of steak, stuck in the price-ticket, and then stood, arms akimbo, staring out vacantly into the street.

IV

For two or three months affairs in the home continued to go smoothly. A wife who had suddenly blossomed like a rose, though with a mysterious air about her that was nevertheless oddly attractive; no more complaints about the time he spent in the wireless-room; contenting dinners. The clean-faced clock on the living-room mantelshelf, which had been a wedding-present, ticked out its seconds with a spick-and-span orderliness. Alice wore soft new poplin dresses at tea-time.

Matthew had induced many more people to take insurance policies. One of these was Lloyd. Matthew tackled him one afternoon, going into the butcher's shop with a complimentary smile and beginning by praising the quality of the meat. But to his surprise Lloyd, whom he had imagined to be a happy-go-lucky chap about such things, put up no resistance, and bought a policy on his widow mother's life. But after all, Matthew thought, Lloyd had obtained a welcome sum on his late wife's policy and must have been convinced of the luck they brought.

So things were rosy. Prospering, Matthew bought expensive additions to his own complicated wireless-set and listened-in to exotic stations denied to ordinary sets. As Alice said, it would not be long before he reached Heaven itself and heard the voice of God thundering its judgments. She herself bought a gramophone with records that included fox-trots and sweet Chopin nocturnes: the jazz she played while washing the breakfast dishes, the Chopin in the quiet of her drowsy afternoons.

Matthew came to her more frequently still. Ambling to her side, he bristled with well-fed pleasure. She remained inscrutable concerning this development: she had the look of one reserving her mind. Sometimes she picked up his head off her chest by the ears and held it before her, like Salome, gazing with aloof mysteriousness into his stupid eyes.

One evening in September, just after they had sat down to supper, Matthew, exchanging the gossip of the day with Alice, inserted into his contributions, as he dabbed mustard on a cold sausage:

'Lloyd the butcher hasn't been long in taking a second helping, so I hear.'

Alice sat like stone: Matthew was bent over his plate and, not receiving comment, went on:

'The barmaid of the Horse-shoe it's to be, they tell me. He's marrying her in time for the Christmas trade . . . I wonder if he'll take a policy on her—'

Alice quivered into life. So *that's* what it was! Only yesterday she had had forebodings. Matthew was greedily taking another cold sausage: as usual, when stirred, she went into the scullery, stayed there a few minutes, and came back with a jelly. Redly rotund, Matthew's face beamed at her. Affectionately he called her 'old girl' twice during the remainder of the meal.

But things began to go wrong in the home. To begin with, Alice changed. Matthew became puzzled and, after a while, really vexed. Having accustomed himself to the new warmth he had sensed in her, he now found her withdrawn in a dour isolation. And if that was not enough, the dinners began to be uneatable. Particularly the meat. Back to the old tough pieces they went, stringy, flavourless and drab. Matthew began to roar about this, while he sulked about the other.

'What's this stuff? I'm not a horse. Why don't you roast a piece of oak tomorrow? What you given me a knife for! An axe I want.'

'I can't help it,' Alice snapped. 'That's the meat I get.'

'If this goes on, Lloyd will lose our custom,' he warned.

Which, as she knew, Lloyd desired. But daily she went to the shop. Lloyd grinned and, with astonishing sangfroid, treated her like any other customer, jauntily. She was just a name in his ledger. But by the bad pieces of meat he would recommend to her she knew he was stealthy and wanted to see her no more. And the youth George never left the shop while she was there. She became pale and fixed Lloyd with her glittering eyes: he vivaciously hacked a carcass, whistling. Happy in his new love for the barmaid, he was strong and merry as a coarse old ballad or a tankard of XXX ale. His bland wiliness made her thin with rage.

Matthew, his eyes popping, asked her if she was unwell.

'Yes, I am,' she snapped. 'I'm sick of this world.'

'It's the only one we've got,' he reminded her.

And sick she was. She had long recognised the desire for vengeance that was in her. She looked at him with hatred: she locked her door to him. Some days he was actively hostile and ordered her about as if she were a slovenly domestic; others he hid himself in his tight flesh and moved about the house as if she did not exist.

One Sunday he began carving the meat. It was a piece of beef. All that week the meat had been deplorable: Matthew had commanded Alice to shift her custom from Lloyd and buy the weekend joint elsewhere.

'Where did you get this piece?' he demanded suspiciously as he jabbed the fork into the beef.

'Lloyd's.' She seemed to hurl the name at him like a clod of dirt.

'What did I tell you? Do you think I've got money to waste on stuff we can't eat!'

'Don't worry so much about your stomach,' she said contemptuously.

He tasted a piece of the beef, grinding his jaws. The meat resisted his teeth. And because he wanted to blame her for other things, he said to her accusingly: 'You must have done something to annoy Lloyd. What is it? He's a client of mine, and you should have kept in his good books.'

Alice had not sat down at the table. She was going about the room with jerking movements, her elbows angular, her hands outstretched, the fingers quivering. Now she was silent, but her face burned. Incensed by her silence, he went on blaming her.

'You put on airs and annoy people. That's what it is. What d'you think you are? A lady? You're the wife of a working man and, by God, I'll keep you one.' And in a crude effort to threaten her with humiliation, he promised: 'I'll go to see that butcher tomorrow and ask if you've offended him. There must be something wrong for him to keep on sending us such meat.'

He was seated now, bending over his plate. Arched and taut she crept behind him, snatched up the hot joint and brought it down on his head with majestic force. He yelped in surprise, then roared as the red and brown blood trickled over his face. But before he had time to rise from his chair she had swung the tough lump flat into his face.

She did not scream. But in a low agonised voice she hissed: 'Take that. And that. And perhaps from now on you'll never talk of meat again.' Then she threw the joint in grand contempt on to the table.

Matthew, blinded and sore from the hot impacts, clawed at his face. He stumbled into the scullery for a towel. By the time he had ragingly swerved back, Alice was upstairs locking the door of her room. Roaring, he thumped on the door. He heard her draw her suitcase from under the bed, he heard the wardrobe door flung back. He roared again. But his roars and thumps had no real body to them. He was wilting from the sacred and awful wrath that spread from Alice, through the door, the walls, down the stairs, through the whole Sunday afternoon silence of the house.

CHERRY-BLOSSOM ON THE RHINE

After dinner the river was drab and the balcony cool. On the opposite bank the steep vineyards bristled with poles, the *Schloss* crowning the hill was black and suitably romantic, man's picturesque addition to the already imposing hills. But how softly flowed the Rhine, so unassertive in its wide ease—Louie stood on the balcony and her heavy eyelids seemed to lose their weariness, watching the water. The flowing evening river was an ablution. Masses of fleshy food, and people who moved with awful solidity—she had revolted against eating and she was tired of looking at the people heaving their way about the place. Louie was thin and delicate: too thin. Her large eyes, spreading their searching but weary blue light over her pale cheeks, seemed as if some penance were continually at work behind them. Perhaps she envied the Germans their complacent treading of the earth, their smacking appetites, their so serious and unimaginative acceptance of natural phenomena.

She wanted to be quiet for a while and away from hotels, large platters of *Schweinekoteletten*, excursions and the pouncing on a particularly attractive arrangement of river and hills. If only her mother, who was renewing acquaintance with the river after twenty years, would keep still for a few days! She had the shocking energy of the physically healthy middle-aged on holiday, feeding on sightseeing with insatiable lust. They had come to rest a night here, at St. Goar, after a long day's boat journey through large pieces of ambitious landscape. But for a whole week Louie had been bullied and hustled and overwhelmed by grand scenic effects.

The cool drab grey of this last evening light was pleasant. She hoped the night would be black, with no moon. Last night there had been an enormously full moon, bursting with gold, crawling like a fat yellow crab over the sky. The river, the hills and the orchards had become more romantic, more 'worth coming to see.' It had been too much, that moon, after all the sights of the day. Altogether too much for the peace of what Louie considered were her nerves.

What she would like now was a talk with the four *Wandervögel* who had been on the boat, particularly the very blond one with the wide healthy smile. Get in touch with young people not of her own nation. She remembered that she had always felt a wish to marry a foreigner, to grapple with a mentality and a love that wasn't British—at the same time suspecting that fundamentally, as it were, aliens were no different from Billy Hawkins and Jack Sanders and the

134

others who had taken her to dances in the Assembly Rooms. A kiss, the usual misunderstandings and raptures, and bourgeois marriage after a while. There were Turks, of course, and blacks—but they were far beyond even the alien category and not to be thought about at all.

All the same, she had felt her blood cantering a little in her veins when she had noticed that her very blond one was cautiously following her about on the steamer. At last she had given him an opportunity to sit with her in the draughty stern, where there were no people, out of the sun. He was a student from Munich, and twenty, like herself. She laughed at his young warrior look; and his thick bare knees, as he sat beside her, had a determined thrust that amused her—she very much wanted to touch them, particularly the golden hairs springing out of the hardened flesh. In a curt black corduroy jacket and shorts, and blue-and-yellow-striped stockings, he looked like someone off a poster in a railway station, too handsome to be true. But he was there beside her, with his gold knees and flamingly healthy face. Telling her he had an English friend in Hammersmith. She said she liked his song while one of his companions played the guitar: what was it?

'A poem by Heine,' he said. 'But I sing like a cat.' When he spoke, his harshly red lips were drawn back from the vigorous teeth in a way she had never noticed in anyone before.

How pale and die-away she must have looked beside him, who was so muscular, outdoor and ruddy-gold! Then, the boat passing an orchard on the flat under the vineyards, he said:

'The cherry-blossom, you are like it.'

And there had been a threat of the national sentimentality in his voice. But no one had talked to her like that before. And probably it was accurate that she suggested the cherry-blossom, pale, frail, fluttering. However, her mother, suddenly swooping round on them in the stern, had called with automatic severity:

'Louie, why are you sitting there, in the cold?'

'Improving my German,' she had answered smartly.

'Which is good enough already for all ordinary purposes,' retaliated the mother, Louie having gained a certificate for the language at school.

So they had parted. She knew he had watched them enter the hotel. Then she had heard his big iron-clamped boots, and those of his three companions, pound away. Perhaps they had gone into one of those secret villages among the dark pine-hairy inner hills. The thousands of *Wandervögel* she had seen that week, disappearing among trees and up roads, singing their songs! Almost it seemed as though the hills and forests ate them: they vanished and were never seen again.

Ah well, let him go. Already she had come to realise that life's best things were but snatches out of a long dreariness. Perhaps some day she, too, would be only too glad to feed on scenery. Almost she burst out laughing as she reflected that the student's gold knees and his moist red mouth had given her one of those brief keen moments of pleasure so rare in life. She was being sticky. Let him go. She'd be peaceful and easy, like the evening river, tonight.

All the same, her heart jumped when she heard the ring of heavy nailed boots on the miniature promenade below. The feet of large men who trod a hundred hills in a day. Cautiously she peered over: the *Wandervögel* clattered on the little stone quay before the hotel and sat down with their legs dangling over the water. And they had brought the guitar.

The light was already a dark grey-blue. Along the river the white yachts were deserted for the night, poised like great still birds on the grey water. Crushed under the night sky the hills were losing their stark loud grandeur. The place was dim and still when the guitar began to sound. Louie felt she could now approve of the land: it was no longer clamorous and militantly picturesque.

'Ich weiss nicht, was soll es bedeuten,
Dass ich so traurig bin;
Ein Märchen aus uralten Zeiten,
Das kommt mir nicht aus dem Sinn.
Die Luft ist kühl und es dunkelt
Und ruhig fliesst der Rhein:
Der Gipfel des Berges funkelt
Im Abendsonnenschein.'

That voice. What was in it? Its yearning startled her. But there was something else, too. Something implacable, demanding, almost peremptory, attacking through the melody. Louise became critical. There were absolutely no clothes on that voice. How could he do it, in public, as it were, though it was night and only one or two loafers about? She hid against the door of the balcony, her heart alive. She listened to other verses, reflecting how very male was the sound of the muscular language, compared to the airy femininity of French.

She would have to go down to them, she wanted to be with them. Or at least with the blond one who was singing. She had not come to this foreign country merely to look on its land and water, to eat its monster food, to sleep in its corpulent beds. Going back into the room she slipped on a light coat and went downstairs. In the stuffy lounge that was open to the hotel lobby her mother sat with a strange woman: she called to Louie as the daughter was making an effort to skulk away unseen.

136

'Louie, here's a lady, Mrs. Seed, who knows Mildred Wright in Bristol. Isn't it strange? All this way from home and —'

Louie had once spent a fortnight with Mildred Wright, a friend of her mother's, in Bristol. Memory of it offended her now. So she refused to appear either surprised or pleased to greet the lady, who looked more tourist than one would have believed possible.

'I was just saying,' her mother went on, animated and impressed by the oddness of meeting one who had lived in a villa opposite Mildred's, 'the world *is* a small place. I must send a postcard to Bristol tomorrow. Sit down, Louie, what keeps you standing there—'

'I'm going out for a walk.'

'A walk in the dark! There's nothing to see by night, it's only a village. You didn't have any coffee; call the waiter. Mrs. Seed tells me that Mildred's father-in-law died of kidney trouble in January.'

'On New Year's Day,' Mrs. Seed added. 'And only taken ill the day before Christmas.'

'I'm surprised that Mildred didn't let me know—'

Louie wandered up to the little bookstall in the lobby and stood turning over picture-postcards. She saw the two women digging deeper into Mildred's life and slipped away quietly. Her mother would want to come out if she decided there was something to be seen.

The guitar was still being plucked at the waterside. Standing on the hotel steps, she saw the four black shapes of the young men: they had become part of the peaceful easy night. She wished there would be no more singing; the guitar was enough and suited the night. One of the shapes rose and was coming towards her. In the lights of the hotel she saw his bright blond hair and the big sportive grin of his red mouth.

'We came to serenade you,' he said, bowing. 'And I have had a good wash. I was dirty on the boat.'

'Yes,' she said, 'you wanted a wash.'

Her matter-of-fact agreement surprised him, it seemed. But immediately the fond, yearning look returned to his grave eyes. His eyes remained serious even when he smiled. She perceived now that only half of his being really laughed.

'You will take a walk with me?' he asked, bowing again.

'I shall be pleased.'

His three companions had been discreetly watching. But as Louie walked off with their friend, the one with the guitar began to play an approving sentimental tune.

'What is your name?' Louie asked.

137

'Siegfried. Siegfried Bichler.'

Impossible, when she had been thinking of him as Siegfried! But she was pleased. 'As in Wagner,' she said.

'You have had a good meal?' he asked, politely.

'I don't each much,' she said.

'You ought to eat plenty,' he said, solicitously.

They walked along the river. Soon they came to an ornamental garden. It was deserted. They sat on a seat. There was no sound from the dark river, the hills opposite were black, for night had arrived now.

'Why did you want to talk to me?' she asked curiously.

'Because you are thin,' he said.

Louie wondered if she ought to be offended. She searched in herself for a trace of indignation. But there was none. Young Herr Bichler seemed honest and simple: she liked that.

'You said I ought to eat plenty. I should get fat.'

'No. Your bones are small, your frame, you are a sylph.'

Something was beating up in his voice again, like a froth. So she placed repulsion in her own voice:

'I don't want to be a sylph. Or a fairy. Or something out of the water or swinging on a crocus. I wish I was substantial, like your Gretchens.'

After a minute or two of silence he said, oddly, 'Love is international.'

She began to wonder if he understood her German. And he seemed to be choosing his words stiltedly.

'It ought to be,' she agreed. 'But your nation is not helping.'

'I would like to marry an Englishwoman,' he said.

'A thin one?' she laughed.

'Love is international,' he said again.

She looked at his knees, dimly looming beside her. She felt it would eat up too much of the time if she tried to make him develop the statement about love, that seemed like a battle-cry with him. She waited. He put his arms round her: she shivered: he drew her close.

'If we married,' he said, 'you must let your hair grow long and not put red on your lips and powder on your face.'

'Rubbish!' she said. All the same, she was interested in the insistence, the *ordering*, in his voice.

'It's not rubbish,' he said, 'it's our belief now.'

Louie thought it better to remain silent.

'You would like that?' he asked.

'What?'

'For us to marry.'

'Do you ask that of every girl you meet on the wayside?'

He began to laugh again then, and she was glad. Serious, he was ominous. She drew away from him. At that moment the rim of the yellow moon appeared on top of a hill.

'The moon,' she said, disappointed.

'It will make the river valley very beautiful,' he said.

'I didn't want it to appear tonight,' she wailed.

'The moon is coming,' he said.

'No more moonlight,' she cried. 'And no more scenery and no more legends.'

'Soon the moon will shine on the Lorelei Rock,' he said with satisfaction.

'Maidens combing their golden hair,' she protested, 'and luring sailors. Bah, I'm sick of nymphs that sit combing their hair and expect men to die for them.'

'Shall I sing you the Lorelei song?' he asked gravely.

'No, no.'

'You are tired,' he said then, solicitously.

The rich red moon wheeled into the full sky. The river valley rose out of the night. Siegfried's face was lifted to the Lorelei Rock in admiration.

'Does she still sit up there, the lovely maiden?' Louie asked.

'A maiden,' he answered, 'ought to be placed there. Certainly on a night like this.'

'It would attract thousands,' she agreed. 'And she could wear a wig with hair down to her feet.'

'Not a wig,' he said.

'And when there's no moonlight, coloured electric lamps around the rock.'

The moon being safely out on her journey, he turned back to Louie. 'You do not like our legends?'

'They're no worse than ours.'

'A nation is glorified by its history and legends,' he said, and Louie began to notice the parrot in his voice. 'We are building a new Germany now, but we do not forget the red blood of our old warriors.'

Louie's pale thin young face was bent meditatively towards the flowing water. 'The past,' she said, 'seems sickening to me. I never want to think of it. The old warriors ought to be forgotten in their graves. And how much glory is in the past? Much more slaughter and thieving and . . .' She sought for a word in German . . . 'and swinishness.'

'We must overlook their shortcomings,' he said obstinately. 'They did many patriotic things, they were always willing to die for their ideals.' Still his arm

139

lay along her shoulder. But she felt it as a hard dead weight on her while he talked.

'Why do you say that love is international?' she asked curiously at last, thinking how fiercely national his countrymen had become.

'I meant among the pure white people,' he answered briskly. 'Not yellow and not black and not Jews—those are not allowed. When I saw you I knew you were pure white. Like the cherry-blossom,' he added again.

'Not *quite* pure white,' she answered slowly. 'My great-grandfather married a Jewess.'

He took a minute to arrive at a decision. 'Your *great*-grandfather! Ah, that was a long time ago. Only once a Jew in your family?' he added anxiously.

'Only once,' she agreed and began to look again with great weariness at the heavy golden scene roused in the moonlight: lumps of hills, black castles and steep guts of ravines. Obese, menacing scenery.

'You are white and delicate,' he decided, love-making beginning to tramp back into his voice like a battalion on the march. 'You are wholesome, like all our girls are becoming. I take no notice that your hair is cut and there is cosmetic on your face. I love you,' he finished triumphantly.

Louie laughed quietly, but suppressed the malice she felt. 'You are very kind.'

'You will come to Munich?' he asked gravely. 'And your mother will visit my mother? My father is a jewellery-dealer.'

'And mine is a miller,' she said, watching him.

'A miller?' he repeated, disappointed.

'Not a village one,' she said. 'A big one. He employs a hundred and twenty men.'

'Ah! A merchant.'

She nodded. 'He is very busy.'

'When will you arrive at Munich?' he asked, eagerly now. 'I will arrive on the same day. I shall be proud to take you and your mother to my home.'

His arm tightened on her shoulder. His mouth was near her cheek-bone: she felt its warmth. The moonlight lit his gold knees; Louie lifted her hand and touched one of them. Then she withdrew out of his embrace and stood up.

'We are going to Berlin,' she said. 'Not Munich.'

The big handsome blond head had looked princely in the moonlight. Louie turned and glanced along the river: she did not want to give him the chance of perceiving her despair. Or her liking. Or her boredom. There had been a wounded bewilderment in his own face.

'You will not come to Munich then?' he asked, his voice fallen.

140

'Not to Munich,' she said slowly.

He stood up too, disconsolate. She stood remote and abstracted. But though thin and delicate, her body seemed to be poised with a fine quick strength: she looked as though at any moment she might surge away, like a seagull, a creature of cold fire and the sharp strength of the brine. The youth was broad and heavy-muscled, his limbs were hewn out of stone, his shoulders of rock, beside her, in the moonlight. He stood weighed down with the sense of failure. The confusion in his face had deepened. At last she turned. Her smile was like the gleam of a thin blade, and cold as crystal.

'I am sorry if I have disappointed you,' she said. 'But I do not care for the way you carry a banner about women.'

'A banner?' he stammered.

'Yes, a banner. All that scrawled on it about face-powder and hair and wholesomesness. It's insulting, it's . . . it's oafish.'

He was silent for a minute. Then he said, and his voice had become sturdy again: 'But we believe in it, it's a belief, a religion . . . And the women like it.'

'It might amuse them for a time,' she answered. The steel-cold smile was still on her lips. 'But in some way or other, later, they'll have their vengeance on you, for laying down the law to them, for putting them in bondage again. You see,' she went on, with a kind of gay contempt, 'women are much more international than men. They have only one belief—that a man shall understand them. Then it doesn't matter what colour he is or what creed.' She paused a moment because she was surprised at herself, then resumed, 'By understanding them, I mean that men are expected to make love for the sake of making love, not because they have certain beliefs about women. How can you talk to me about being wholesome! When your own mind is in such a fever.'

Louie herself wondered at her long speech. But she saw now that behind her long weariness, in her hours of boring travel through this tragic land, her opinions had been forming only half known to herself. This nationalised youth had brought them forth. And she still liked him, she would have liked an hour of love-making with him, beside the river. What a pity he couldn't throw his banner into the water!

'Ho,' he exclaimed with some haughtiness, 'ho, my mind is not in a fever. I belong to Hitler Jugend, I am strong and live with orderly cleanliness, I have ideals.'

'I dare say,' she said. 'But they're a nuisance, those ideals, from what I've heard about them.'

'Why have you come to our land?' he demanded, with some angriness in his voice.

'Why do women travel?' she countered ironically, but laughing now. 'To search for love.'

'I offered it to you,' he said. And his big, harshly red lips pouted.

'You made a mistake. I'm not wholesome. Not at all like cherry-blossom really.'

'You do not like me now?' he asked. And suddenly he was simple again: the attractive blond head was bent a little, in humility.

'Not much,' she answered. And she refused to be attracted again by his sudden humility and simplicity.

He brought his heels together at her reply and lifted his head proudly.

'You will return to your hotel now, Mees?' he asked.

'Thank you, Herr Bichler, I shall be pleased.'

They walked out of the little garden. The moon was rosy and idle in the high sky, the river was violet. They passed a bush of yellow jasmine in flower. Louie sighed. Moonlight, a tree of yellow flower, and a handsome young man beside her. What more should a girl want! But she was becoming colder and colder. With a little scream in her mind she remembered that she would be twenty-one in August. And she had not fallen in love yet. She supposed she was becoming a terror at home, with her tantrums. Well, travelling abroad hadn't so far achieved any good.

Before leaving Herr Bichler near the hotel she touched his hand with her finger-tips. 'Good night, Siegfried,' she murmured. 'I am sorry I'm not what you expected. Some day perhaps I will be.'

He bowed. But he said, grievously, 'I told my companions on the steamer, there is an English Mees I would like to marry.'

Louie touched his hand again. 'No, no,' she said. 'You would not like me.'

'How do you know?' he asked urgently, and gripped her fingers.

'I'm not wholesome,' she mocked, dragging her fingers away from him. 'And I like my clothes from Paris, not cut out of a banner on the Rhine. And in the morning I shall always use rose-red lipstick, and in the evening magenta. And your love is *not* international.'

From the hotel steps she turned and waved him a regretful farewell. The poor young man. Calling her wholesome! As though she might be a cup of cocoa or a dish of spring greens. And the sergeant-major in his voice! Betrothed to him, he would expect her to march through the streets under the flags, wearing solemn serges—as she had seen the young women in the towns, following the young men in procession and singing with such desperate seriousness of their new national glory. Well, she supposed it would have to be Billy Hawkins. At the same time, despairingly, she remembered that Billy talked incessantly, according to season, of rugger or cricket, and merely glanced at the outside world from between wickets or goal-posts. More than once in his company she had felt herself hypnotically turned into a football or a bat. How distressingly unsatisfactory young men were as lovers!

And Louie, feeling severe and disagreeable, refused to give her mother an explanation of her disappearance from the hotel for an hour, at night. 'Am I a child?' she demanded crossly. 'Do you think I am incapable of taking care of myself, even in this mad country?'

In the morning, under a charming blue sky, they set off for Wiesbaden. But all along the river there were the same elephantine hills, and pork chops were served for lunch on the steamer.

GLIMPSES OF THE MOON

For some reason or other, Joe always told people that Ellen was his sister. He had settled with her in the foliage-buried cottage since he had left the Army at fifty years of age, having served in Africa and become shrivelled and scant and burnt-looking, though a demon still lurked, half drowsy, in his eye.

Ellen was older; after ten years with him in the cottage she was now sixty-five, her face a mass of curled wrinkles and on her head thousands of diminutive silver curls of wonderful vitality. Her eyes were of the colour and freshness of harebells, and she spoke in a voice that always contained an odd raucous chuckle. Common as any wayside herb she had been, and now with age she possessed a kind of astringent strength that broke often into claps of laughter that could hide the church-bell or into a bawdy observation that her age chastened. Ellen smelt of walnuts, Joe of damp bark; their cottage was only moderately clean, their front garden striped and lurid with clotted masses of flowers. When I remarked on their agile profusion, Ellen said:

'It was the same in my garden in Aldershot.'

From where she had hailed. The villagers said she had been a soldiers' favourite there, and, indeed, her conversation, her vitality, and lack of interest in the village wives pointed to an attractive amount of truth in the gossip.

Joe turned his hand to most jobs about the farms and the village and, fancying himself a gardener, he would come begging for work, though likely as not he would pull up new three-a-shilling shoots for weeds: he would begin: 'My sister Ellen, she hollered to me this morning, "There's no dough in the house, go and ask Mister if he got a job for you." Poor girl, she's getting on in years and wants one or two comforts now—'

Not that he seemed sentimental or gallant concerning Ellen. He swore at her and blackened her eye on occasion. Screech and roar often sped up with the smoke through their chimney; crockery was smashed. Some old, old nervous conflict found utterance at almost regular intervals.

Sometimes Ellen would look very unsettled: she would stand at the top of the rise behind the cottage and gaze fixedly across the downs to the horizon. Once she noticed me at my window—for their cottage was swaddled in bushes at the end of my garden, looking no bigger than an ornament for a mantelpiece—and called out from the eminence where she was brooding and gazing into the sky:

'Those swallows got wings, but us poor women be buried like beetroot.'

144

'Where do you want to fly, Ellen?' I called.

'Ah!' She looked mysterious. 'Ah!' At the moment, her silver hair and crinkled face gave her a look of excessive respectability earned through long blameless years of country labour: her dun flannel skirt swirled blowsily out of her securely laced and still shapely bodice. Descending the slope towards her back door, she added: 'Summer coming makes my heart pine for a journey.'

That same evening there was a row in the cottage. Ellen's shrieks and Joe's barks seemed of extra intensity; they rose to crescendo and there was a grand final crash of symphonic depth. A minute or two afterwards Joe was banging at my front door.

'Mister, Mister,' he yelled impatiently through the letter-box, 'my sister Ellen has done a fit and I can't get her round.' Opening the door, he added, demonish in the eye and his hands still fisted: 'She fell into the fender and must have hit herself in the fit. You got something to bring her round, sir?' he enquired, a certain amount of fear popping in his voice.

After snatching a flask of brandy I broke with him through the hedge that divided our properties and, treading on young marrows, reached the cottage in a few moments. It seemed struck into awed silence after those thunders. Had Joe killed the sweet Ellen, I wondered, shivering in that silence. I hurried after him into the oil-light of the living-room, and was just in time to see Ellen's venerable head pop up swiftly from behind the settle.

Directly Joe entered she aimed a tea-caddy at him. But from her silver hair dripped a long scarlet stain. The tea-caddy hit him on the chin and brought from him a trooper's oath. He began to rush towards her, then turned snapping back to me. 'Many's the time,' he said hoarsely, 'that I've been tempted to give her a hiding. If she wasn't my sister—'

'Ah, ah, ah!' mocked Ellen. For some reason she was very dirty, her face wrinkled as if shreds of tobacco were sprinkled over it. She seemed to be in a state of high ecstasy, uttering her throaty exclamation that was neither laugh nor sob, and reared up behind the settle.

'She's bleeding,' I murmured.

'Hit herself on the fender,' Joe said, scowling in his impotence now. 'She must have come to while I was with you.'

'That wound should be bathed,' I said.

'She's as hard as a mule,' he growled.

'Ah, ah, ah!' screamed Ellen. 'I'll tell him. I'll tell Mister—'

I took a step or two towards the door. One the other hand, Joe's burning eye boded no good for Ellen, if he were left alone with her. Ellen was charming, she was a good hearty vegetable of the old earth, a product that had a certain sturdy grandeur: I respected her. The flask of brandy in my hand gave me an idea. I turned back.

'What you two want,' I said, 'is a drop of this.'

Ellen stepped out from behind the settle, and Joe immediately went to the cupboard insert beside the fireplace and brought out glasses. Irritating lack of sustenance had probably caused their row, I thought, remembering it was Thursday—a bad moneyless day for Joe. Ellen wiped her hand across her mouth and grinned.

'Wipe yer head,' Joe shouted, showing off a bit now. 'And yer face is black.'

'Mister don't mind,' smiled Ellen knowingly. All the same, she went to a broken segment of mirror stuck behind the pipe above the water-tap and swilled her face, uttering strenuous gasps the while. Joe had a look at the wound under the spun silver hair. 'Not much,' he growled. He licked a finger into a tin of vaseline and rubbed it on the bruise. 'Lucky you didn't hit yourself dead,' he barked at her.

'Ho, ho, ho!' she bawled, in a different key now, and raising her hands above her head she snapped her fingers, castanet fashion. 'I'm not dying yet.' She winked at me. The row had obviously exhilarated her.

The brandy mellowed them somewhat. Joe sank into a reverie: I could see he was turning something over in his mind, turning and turning it over. Ellen declared that she was 'minded of Old Vic's Jubilee' when she got drunk on brandy at Aldershot, amid the celebrations, falling down and taking with her a big tray full of china. Joe raised his small, hard, bullet head and looked at me sombrely. But there was a pathetic appeal in his voice, as if he was asking me to submit judgment:

'Ellen,' he said, 'wants ter go back to Aldershot to live.'

'There,' said Ellen loudly, 'I c'n see a bit of life. Here I'm like a spud under the ground.' She fixed me with her surprisingly vital eyes, that were yet of such a tender and frail blue. 'I got a mate there,' she added.

'Mate!' cried Joe contemptuously. 'Queenie Parrot. She's no mate for a good woman—'

'Queenie's got a new house,' Ellen announced.

'She keeps on moving,' said Joe, with malevolence. 'Got to, I lay.'

I turned to Joe. 'Don't you like Aldershot?' I asked, imagining that because he was an old soldier he would have some roots in the military town. I surmised that their squabble had been caused by Ellen's desire to move.

'Lousy,' he said.

'What's he come here for?' cried Ellen of me, but pointing threateningly at Joe, who began to glower again. 'Hiding—'

Shiftily but pathetically, Joe rose and stood with his back to Ellen,

146

obliterating her and facing me. 'Mister,' he said, 'a bit of hot stuff like the brandy goes up straight to her head.'

I prepared to go. Ellen tossed off the remainder of her brandy. She began to sing 'Her golden hair was hanging down her back.' Joe accompanied me to the door.

'Tootle-oo,' called Ellen in farewell. 'When the blackberries come I'll make you a dozen pots of jam, Mister.'

'She's a handful,' whispered Joe. 'No sense has old age brought her. Sometimes I wish I was back with the Hussars.'

But for a week afterwards I heard almost unceasing squabbling, Ellen all raucous threats and Joe yelping with oaths. At last he accosted me on the road and asked despairingly:

'What would you do with her if she was yours, Mister?'

'My sister?' I asked.

He blinked his lizard eyelids, under which dark fire lurked yet. 'In a manner of speaking,' he answered vaguely.

I shook my head. 'I don't know.'

He scratched his hair, a harassed scowl on his face. 'I been thinking,' he said, 'I'd let her have a bit of a run in Aldershot. A holiday,' he said strictly. 'She can jaw over old times with her mate, Queenie Parrot.'

'That's all she wants, I expect,' I said. 'A little holiday.'

'If you had a job for me, Mister, to pay her fare—'

So one morning Ellen, voluminously arrayed in a thick and oddly shaped red overcoat—though it was warm summer—a sprigged green cotton gown, well-skewered hat stuck rakishly far back on her silver curls, brilliantly polished boots, and a faded old parasol pushed inside the strap of her plaited straw suitcase, waited for the bus outside her cottage. She waved to me at my gate, a blush of the most delicate pink in either crinkled cheek.

'Good-bye, Mister,' she cried, 'I'm off to Aldershot.'

'Take care of yourself,' I called.

'Ah, ah!' she chuckled in her odd raucous way. Her eyes were shining and hard in excitement, their blue deepened into indigo.

'Come back soon,' I added, as the bus grunted towards her up the hill.

She grinned widely, lifted her hand to feel if her unaccustomed hat was still on her head, then, advancing to the middle of the road, waved to the bus-driver an enormous bandanna handkerchief like a flag.

The first week of her holiday Joe was quite amiable and bright. Philosophically, he said: 'She's getting on, and it'll be her last holiday, most likely, and it's a change to have no ranting woman shouting at me if I stay in the pub till closing time.' Then after the granted seven days had elapsed, he brought me a note from her, his brows sombre. 'See what they get up to,' he said, 'if you let 'em loose for a bit.'

Dear Joe (she wrote in a neat and careful hand),

I wish you was here but its no place for you now that the mates of your regiment are dead or gone somewhere. I met Corporal Cox that used to be Queenie's intended before she married Archie in the old days, he has rheumatics very bad now, but I took him to Queenie's and made them kiss each other and forget and he brought whisky and we had a party, Queenie says I can have her old collapsing harmonnium for eight shillings, see if Mister will give you work and if the buss will take it if I will bring it.

Yours truly, Ellen Banks.

'No word to say when she's coming,' he began to storm. 'Drinking and parties and knocking round with old soldiers. Harmonium be hanged—when I get hold of her I'll make her squeal better than any harmonium—' The half somnolent demon began to bristle into life. He declared that he was going to order her instant return. Perhaps I smiled dimly, for he finished: 'A chap's got to look after his sister when she's got to Ellen's age, and she's a bit on the misbehaving side, like she is—'

'I don't suppose your sister will come to any harm,' I tried to soothe him.

Darkly thrusting his fierce glance at me, he muttered: 'You don't know her, Mister, like I do.'

Another week passed and still there was no sign of a returning Ellen. Joe swore and drank and had bouts of queer hysteria during which his fingers seemed to itch and bristle for action. He kept on complaining to me across the hedge and became extremely malignant concerning the whole female sex. Ellen sent him a postcard the third week; on one side was a picture of some barracks, on the other merely: *This is where the dragoons are now Joe, Yours truly, Ellen Banks.*

'She's going to keep there, the . . . the . . .' he splattered. 'That's what it is.'

'Well,' I said, 'why don't you fetch her back?'

He started. Then he scowled. 'If she don't want to come back,' he muttered, 'I can't make her, can I? I can't put the whip to her, at her age.'

'You talk about her,' I said at last suspiciously, 'as if she was your wife, Joe.'

His hollowed and burnt face became inscrutable. I think he took offence. After a moment or two he turned and walked strictly away. The fourth week of Ellen's holiday, however, he came ceremoniously to my door carrying a small box. In the sitting-room he opened the box and drew forth a long old-fashioned gold watch-chain, a heavy silver watch and a cameo brooch.

'Mister,' he said earnestly, 'how would you like to buy these at bargain prices or have them as pledge on a loan of money?'

148

'Now, Joe,' I said, 'what are you after?'

He looked at me furtively, twitching his burnt but strong brows. 'I'm going to fetch her,' he said in a determined voice.

'Well, your fare won't cost you the price of one of these, Joe.'

'I'm going to take a cart,' he said.

'A cart!'

'Farmer Jeffries will hire me his cattle-cart and horse for a quid and a half for the day. I don't trust her in trains and buses, Mister. How am I going to get her to the station, to begin with?'

'Well, you've got to get her into the cart.'

'I can,' he said sombrely, 'chase after her with the cart all over Aldershot. I'm going,' he continued, a cunning gleam in his eye, 'to take the cattle-net with me and tie her inside as if she was a porker.'

'Come now, Joe—'

He looked at me then with great solemnity, and suddenly he seemed very pathetic. 'I won't get her back at all, Mister, unless I do something the likes of this.'

'It looks,' I said hesitatingly, 'as if your sister *wants* to stay away.'

'She isn't my sister!' his dramatic overwrought voice declared ringingly.

'Joe, Joe,' I said reprovingly.

He grinned for a moment or two, then as suddenly looked frightened. He asked, subduedly, if I had a thimbleful of brandy I could spare. After tossing off the nip he sat down and whispered across the room:

'I got another wife!'

'Oh?'

'A black one,' he added. And again he grinned and again he looked frightened.

'I married her in Africa,' he continued, 'where it's hot and you see millions of 'em.'

I nodded.

'She turned Christian,' he said, doleful now, 'for my sake. And I married her and left her in the lurch when the regiment left Africa. Yes, Mister,' he agreed, 'it was a tyke's thing to do, but a young soldier with hot blood in him and bad mates and the drink and those tropics—Oh, I was worn to a shadow after a bit, and I lost sense of what's right and wrong.'

Rather at a loss, I shook my head.

'You and me,' he went on appealingly, 'been mates almost, and you being fond of Ellen, I can tell you this, that no one knows hereabouts . . . You see, after the regiment was in Aldershot for a bit, them missionaries wrote to the Colonel about my case, and I did a bunk, thinking I'd be put in clink or else sent back to Africa, or perhaps have a black woman on my hands in Aldershot and everybody'd laugh. And Ellen followed me after a bit—I used to run about with her in Aldershot. She used to be fond of the Dragoons,' he added parenthetically, 'but I took her off 'em, after a fight or two. I was in the Hussars.'

I poured him some more brandy.

'I dust not marry Ellen, and setting up here in a proper cottage, it was cleaner to say we was brother and sister,' he continued. 'Folks don't give you work in their gardens if they think you're living loose with a dame.' He began to look quite cross and irritable. 'A worrying time it's been for me, but Ellen, she don't care and chews the rag about my "black pudding," as she calls her, and asks if we was both cannibals and tried to eat each other after we got married.'

He seemed to wait for comment, fixing me with his smouldering eye. 'Oh well,' I said, 'it happened so long ago, I expect it's all forgotten now in Aldershot, so no doubt it will be safe for you to go there.'

'That's what I'm wondering, but I know if I don't fetch Ellen, she'll slip back to her old ways there.'

I suppose I must have looked at him enquiringly. He gave a quick and shifty glance past me, then looked up again with a deliberately stolid mien.

'The drink it is that's her trouble,' he said.

'But she can't afford to drink much,' I said defendingly. The phrase about revisiting the glimpses of the moon was passing through my head. 'I expect she's just enjoying herself seeing her old friends,' I added. 'Tea-parties and such like, Joe.'

'You don't know Queenie Parrot, Mister,' he growled. 'She's one of those dames that never grow old. Dragoons, Hussars and Lancers, they all know Queenie down in Aldershot. She's no mate for my Ellen.'

However, he gave her still another week's grace. And still no intimation of her return arrived. On Saturday morning he drove past my cottage in one of those carts in which the smaller cattle are taken to market. A fixed scowl was on his face, and one could see he had a professional handling of a horse. It was twenty miles to Aldershot. He stood up in the cart, alert and straight, and made one think of a Roman soldier in a chariot: the horse was young and brisk.

The cart had not returned at midnight. I was preparing to go to bed half an hour later, closing *The Anatomy of Melancholy*, when I heard the wheels crunch down the hill. Lamp in hand I went to the door.

'Mister,' called Joe out of the blackness, 'give us a hand, for the love of God.'

Out in the lane he was turning the light of one of the cart-lamps on the inside of the cart. Ellen lay fast asleep on the straw-covered floor. A net was stretched over the top of the cart. Beside Ellen lay a couple of empty beer-bottles.

'Oh, Mister,' lamented Joe, 'I had to give her them flagons to keep her quiet, though she was under the influence when I found her.'

He began to loosen the net. He seemed to be snorting with exhaustion. Ellen lay in disorder; she looked very far gone into slumber. Nevertheless, the dignity of age prevented her from looking laughable. Joe took her shoulders, I her feet, and we hoisted her into the cottage without her blinking an eyelid. There was a look of gentle satisfaction round her nose and mouth. We laid her on the settle.

'I told you,' panted Joe, 'I wouldn't get her back unless I netted her inside a cart. There she was enjoying herself like a lady, drinking port and stout mixed together, in Queenie Parrot's house along with a lot of riff-raff. Quite a party, it was, I stayed for a bit till Ellen took so much she lay on her back like a flat-fish.' He glistened with kindling triumph. 'I had paid a boy to look after the hoss outside the house, and there it was all ready when I heaved her up and took her out, what was my rightful belonging, though that Queenie Parrot screamed like mad.' The triumph shot into his eyes. 'I galloped through Aldershot like I was back in the Hussars and with my old hoss Sparkle.'

He was swelling his chest extravagantly, warrior-like. 'And didn't she wake up and shout?' I asked.

'Not till we got outside Aldershot. Then she began to holler, crying and scratching. So I had to buy her the flagons and afterwards she went to sleep again.'

Ellen, lying on the settle, looked quite cosy now. There was a youthful bloom on her wrinkled face, like a bright pink of a wild rose, and her lips pouted. The mass of silver curls shone with a lively gleam. Joe, his hands on his hips, looked at her lordlily. Then he lowered his voice to an intimate whisper:

'She looks a pretty little dame lying there, don't she, Mister? Innocent-like and what men lay down their lives for. A pity they're not always like that.' And going back to the lane to take away the horse and cart, he added, with satisfaction: 'A chap's got to act smart if he wants to keep 'em, he's got to act smart . . .'

151

THE FUNERAL

Already the November afternoon was vaguely tinted with brown. There was a faint odour of fog too. The fogs liked to steal down into this bowl of a London suburb and stay there lazily; the window-curtains of the serried villas always smelt of them this time of year, those that were of white lace becoming a slack damp grey. And the chrysanthemums that nearly every garden wore had the same grey bitter odour as the fog, the ragged flowers of white, yellow and brown, haggard with a weary look. Those residents who could do so moved as soon as possible, to a house up on the hill perhaps, from where, if you cared to look that way, you could see the Alexandra Palace.

With a solemnity suitable to the occasion, the two young girls walked about their narrow slice of back-garden. They were looking for a site in which they could dig a grave. Enid, the younger, whose peach-like fatness shone a golden warmth over her efforts to look lugubrious, called out shrilly, pointing:

'There, under the chrysanthemums. They'll give him shelter from the rain.'

'Hush!' Celia hissed once more, 'hush! The relations don't shout on the day of the funeral.'

'But we're grave-diggers now,' Enid protested.

Celia was suddenly cross at her sister's lack of acting finesse. 'If you were a real grave-digger,' she said, 'you wouldn't shout. They never do. They whisper. Because nearly all day they're *down in a grave themselves*.' She sounded threatening, as if she wanted to frighten Enid into the necessary demeanour.

'Oh, all right,' Enid said, carelessly.

Celia meditated, gazing round. 'I think,' she said very mournfully, 'I think that we'll have it where the asters were, in that border over there.'

'I saw Mrs. Wright's cat scratching there this morning,' Enid said. 'It's too near the railings.'

'If we bury him under the chrysanthemums,' Celia said, 'Daddy will tread over him when he goes to tie up the bushes.'

'Well, there are plenty of other places,' Enid said, rather heartlessly. 'Make up your mind.' Her sister was stretching out her grief-stricken search too long, she thought.

'You don't seem to care very much,' Celia complained. 'Perhaps you don't want to bury him at all?' she asked, acidly. 'Perhaps you'd like to *burn* him, or leave him to rot in the dust-bin?' Finishing quite in the manner of their severe English mistress, 'You wicked girl.'

'It'll be dark,' Enid warned, 'before we start the funeral.'

Thin mists were crowding into the end of the garden, stealthily, their grey patched with smoky brown. Like pale snakes, they hung and trailed from the bare dark branches of the apple-tree, and they billowed along the ground in soiled snowy waves. Already the chimneys of the next row of villas had disappeared: the sky was leaning down in a swollen woolly mass. Enid was right, Celia thought, it would soon be dark. A damp creeping dark that would become thick as blackberry jam.

'Here,' she announced at last, 'where he'll be near the house.' She had chosen a curved little border under the scullery wall, where the black earth was destitute of flower and plant. Enid objected to its nakedness, but gave way. They could plant flowers there in the spring.

With trowel and spade they dug into the sombre soil. Celia, thin and determined in her nervous energy, dug the most. Between hair swinging like a bunch of amber candles her face was serious as a sermon: her skin was wax-white, but water-colour-blue eyes distributed a delicately lovely colour out of the thin length of her face. Already her body moved in the rhythm of nerve-dictation, while Enid, beside her, looked easy and undisturbed in a physical richness. This burial was Celia's idea, something new in an afternoon when they had been left alone. Perhaps the grey mourning look of the day had suggested it: perhaps something else . . . It was not long before a rough oblong was torn in the earth.

'Oh, it looks black and cold,' exclaimed Enid, squatted stoutly beside the grave.

Celia straightened her aching body with a jerk. She was entered fully into the passionate drama now. 'Come on, Enid,' she cried in a melodramatic wail. '*His time has come.* We must prepare. The hearse is at the door.'

Then it suddenly occurred to her that they had no really suitable hearse. There was only the garden barrow, which was dirty and undignified. Her mind quickly snatched at various things they might use instead. Then she remembered about Jack Blake's toy-cart: she had seen it in the glass-house over the railings only a couple of days ago. It was painted a bright red and blue, but at least it looked a little more ceremonious than the garden-barrow. And quick as the thought she nipped through the broken gap in the fence which Jack himself used when he came over to play with them.

Arrived in next-door's garden, a queer feeling came over her. Was she doing right, at such a time? With Jack sick in bed. Mum had said last week that he was very ill. 'Will he die?' she had asked, and her mother had been shocked and told her sharply to take a spoonful of cod-liver oil. And now they were playing at funerals. Why had she thought of a funeral at such a time? But

153

Jack wouldn't mind. He had always been ready to play at anything and he never rudely pulled her hair like the boys in Number Six. She darted over to the glass-house at the end of the garden.

Besides, he was better now. Only on Monday Mum had said he was sitting up in bed and he'd soon be out again. You couldn't keep Jack down for very long. She pulled the toy-cart out of the misty glass-house. Keeping a sharp eye on the house though. But the house had a very still look, as if nobody was in. And the garden had masses of chrysanthemum-bushes, among which she bent, wheeling the gay cart like a crooked old country-woman gathering kindling.

Enid was peering through the railing-gap. 'I've got Jack's cart for hearse,' Celia hissed. 'It'll just hold the coffin.'

'He hasn't used it since last Christmas,' Enid said. She helped to manipulate it through the gap. 'Come on, Celia, hurry up. Do you want to bury him in the middle of the night?'

The day was fast hastening out of the gardens. 'I've picked the flowers,' Enid added, and pointed to a tangled heap of weary chrysanthemums. 'A pity there's no time to make a proper wreath.' Even her solid contours were being blurred in the thin fog, though seeds of moisture glittered on her hair and eyelashes. As she walked towards the house, her matter-of-fact proportions became almost frail, the trailing heap of chrysanthemums she now carried going into mist. Then, even she became mist too.

Trundling the cart, Celia followed between the clumps of grey-green leaves and the flowers that crouched under the fingers of the fog as if in horror. The day would just last, she calculated. Only there would be neither time nor light enough to read the proper burial service out of the prayer-book. A little prayer perhaps, no more.

She parked the cart outside the french-window of the dining-room and sped inside. On the table lay the open coffin. It was a long tin of someone's delicious toffee assortment. Inside it was Carrots, a made doll whose skull under his wild red hair was smashed beyond repair. Enid was giving him a single flower, tucking it under his limp blue melton arm.

'Go and fetch the mourning,' Celia whined.

Enid peered up at her. 'Are you crying? she asked, enviously.

'Nearly,' answered Celia, in a voice of strain.

'You didn't cry that time when Uncle Fred had his funeral,' Enid remarked jealously.

Soon they had gathered a few black things: a tattered lace scarf, a fur, a skirt, a toque, a beret, an old ostrich feather. They arrayed themselves, Enid taking the fur because Celia snatched the ostrich feather, sticking it in a pleat of the toque. And with the long skirt trailing on the floor she looked dramatically

154

a mourner. She held her waxen face high, as though she were a tragedienne of the Comédie Française.

'Close the coffin,' she ordered sepulchrally, 'and toll the bell.'

Enid, swathed heavily in the fur, shut down the coffin-lid and then went into the passage, where she continued to strike the Indian brass dinner-gong which Dad had bought at an auction and which was never used. Called back, Celia and she carried the coffin with impressive slowness out to the cart and heaped the flowers all over it. Celia took the shafts and Enid formed the procession behind. And Celia said, 'Now.'

'What?' Enid enquired.

'Why, start crying.'

'You start first,' Enid said sulkily. 'I can't cry not even if I pinch myself or stop my breath.'

'You ought to be ashamed. Little girls should always cry.' Celia began to push the cart. 'Well, I'll begin.' And she set up a soft doleful wail while her skirts swept over the concrete ground in gushing black waves.

'Oh, Carrots,' she wailed.

'Oh, Carrots,' sang Enid, stoutly at first.

'Oh, oh, Carrots, my dear, my dear.'

'Poor Carrots, sweet Carrots, oh, oh.'

'He was only six,' wept Celia, now thoroughly gone into grief.

'Only six,' bawled Enid, so that Celia turned round and pointed warningly towards Jack Blake's house.

'He died of a wound in the head, our poor, poor Carrots,' whined Celia.

'—a wound in the head, our dear Carrots,' Enid mourned faithfully.

Dusk met them in the garden, like another lament. The fog had thickened. What light there was had turned yellowish, pushing its way through the clouds of fog. But the grave yawned distinctly enough. Celia, shaken and tear-stained now, told Enid to bury Carrots herself. She could only watch and mourn. She would not admit that the funeral had begun to make her feel queer.

'He's so light,' murmured Enid pityingly, lifting from among the chrysanthemums the bright casket. 'He went very thin after he was taken ill.'

Celia shivered. She had gone cold. All the garden was mysterious and silent. She felt her cheeks icy and damp. She was visited by the fancy that people from another world swam and billowed through the mist, their grey gowns flicking: one in a cloak heavy and woolly as a sheep-skin shrouded half the bare lilac-tree. Then she heard the back-door of the next house open and close, and she crouched apprehensively over the toy-cart. Perhaps Jack had asked for it, being better now and able to play again; perhaps his mother was going to the glass-house. She bent over Enid and whispered: 'Keep quiet, Mrs. Blake has come out.'

Enid was shovelling black earth into the grave. And suddenly Celia felt sick, her head turned giddy. She straightened herself and leaned back against the scullery wall. In her nostrils was the damp bitter odour of the earth, mingled with the bitter sting of the fog. Her eyes were caught by something moving against the railings. Fear sprang to her throat. Mrs. Blake had seen the cart! But it was only Jack himself, pushing his way through the foggy gap, as he had done hundreds of times.

Celia made a sudden movement towards him, instinctively. Enid, scrambled on the floor, was still busy closing the grave. And for some reason or other Celia felt terribly ashamed. 'Oh, Jack,' she whispered, very softly, 'we were only having a game. We borrowed your cart—' She stopped and her whisper trailed away. Jack stood looking at her, frowning and nervously rubbing his fingers along his navy-blue jersey. She made another effort. 'I hope you don't mind . . . I'm glad to see you are better,' she added formally. His frown distressed her. Her voice was like something lame in her throat: it didn't seem to come out properly.

He did not answer. She remembered there were times when he would sulk. Mum said it was because he wasn't well. This time he carried his sulks further. Instead of demanding possession of his cart, he turned abruptly and went back through the gap. Yet, before he turned, she caught such a hostile look on his face that her knees shook. What was the matter with him! Yet she did not run towards the gap to demand explanation, she stood quite still, breathing the bitter odour of fog and earth.

'There!' murmured Enid, from far away.

There was no need now for Celia to whine and bully herself into crying. The tears ran easily down her cheeks, though not for long. The electric light was switched on in the dining-room window: Mum had returned. Enid saw it too and jumped up. Her hands were filthy.

'Strew the flowers,' Celia breathed. Shivering, she bent and lifted handfuls of the chill chrysanthemums, thrust them obliteratingly over the grave.

'In heaven,' said Enid comfortingly, 'he'll have a new head.'

'Take the cart back, Enid, will you?' Celia whispered. 'I fetched it.'

Enid didn't mind: she disappeared into the moving fog. Celia, still feeling disturbed at Jack's untimely discovery of them *playing that game*, shrank back from the gap, through which she had helped to push the cart. And without waiting for Enid, she hurried through the shifting grey shapes towards the gold light of the dining-room, the ostrich feather in her toque whisking through the mist like a plume of black smoke. Back in the dining-room, amid the exclamations of Mum, who at first was shocked into silence when she knew what they had been doing, Celia waited palely for the door-bell to ring. Mrs. Blake would surely come in and complain of this impudent borrowing of the cart without permission.

Mum was looking at her peculiarly, in between getting the tea-things out. Enid was in the scullery washing her hands and cheerfully singing 'Daisy Bell'. But Mum kept on looking worried and quiet. At last Celia, her hands still feeling as though they were shivering inside themselves, forced herself to burst out:

'I went into Mrs. Blake's glass-house and took Jack's little cart to use as a hearse.'

She saw Mum's eye widen, staring at her. There was a silence. Celia felt herself go small and afraid. Mum lifted the teapot from the hearth and Celia noticed that the pot shook a little She wet her dry lips; she did not know why she was feeling so funny. At last Mum said:

'Mrs. Blake didn't see you playing that game, did she?'

In a small tight voice Celia said, 'No—' She was going to say something else, but she felt too frightened.

A look of relief passed through Mum's eyes. But her voice was unsteady when she said:

'You see, Celia, poor Jack died this afternoon.'

Celia stood quite still. She heard herself whisper protestingly that Mum had said Jack was better and Mum said something about Jack getting worse again. She heard Enid come bursting into the dining-room and saw her, far away, proudly holding out her white spotless hands. What was it, what was it? She felt herself go smaller and smaller. The fog was coiling round her again, the grey mist . . . And in her nostrils was its bitter odour, mingled with the odour of the black earth and the wet bitter smell of chrysanthemums . . .

CALEB'S ARK

Caleb was a gaunt, middle-aged bachelor of thrifty habits, who lived in a shabby old cottage beside the river and under the frown of the black-browed hill of Llan Powis. Though peculiar, a few women, in a roundabout way, had proposed marriage to him—he had been left a few hundred pounds by his father, who had been a cockle dealer—but Caleb shook his swarthy head and turned back to the interpretation of prophecies in the Book of Revelations and other picturesque scripture. His nose was always running, his gaze insecure and nervous, but he was heavy and strong. And this world seemed to him created solely for the purpose of being destroyed again, malignantly. God was a pirate roaming the skies with cannons and other destructive ammunition.

He did not work. What was the use of labouring when it was certain this world was doomed to destruction? Yet there were times when Caleb liked the world: he did not wish to leave it. He often paused to admire the flaring gold and red of his cockerel who strutted proud among his seven silver-spangled Hamburg hens; and the gross fat energy of the sow and boar he kept behind the cottage also roused him to admiration. He could see that the world moved and had being in certain attractive ways. But, nevertheless, a curse remained on it; Caleb was certain that sooner or later in his lifetime it was to be demolished. Did he not often in dreams see it gobbled up like a fowl in the mouth of a wolf?

The great sea lay two miles down the river from the cottage. From that, too, destruction could come. Mighty waves. Outside the cottage the river was quite narrow. Often Caleb felt he ought to move to some position high on the hill. But the cottage seemed to depend on him like an affectionate animal; he liked the look of it waiting for him as he returned from a brooding walk. Sometimes Margiad Jenkins, who had been postwoman for twenty years, said to him such as this:

'Caleb, Caleb, your old pants want darning, indeed. There's a disgrace on the line! Let me have them now.' She looked in horror at the flapping garment which he had washed and hung out.

'I can patch and I can sew,' Caleb muttered distrustfully.

Margiad was continually offering her domestic services. She was a dumpy, slack-bodied woman of fifty, who kept secret her bad varicose veins, in case her job would be taken from her: she tramped many miles a day delivering her letters in scattered farms and cottages. She said to Caleb then, unable to suppress the little fund of malice in her:

158

'Not a handsome sight you'll be in a ragged pair of pants if the bad old world got drownded and you was thrown up on the seashore of Heaven.'

'You mock, woman,' Caleb replied menacingly; 'you mock where wise men would shiver.'

'Here's a letter for you,' she said. 'Ha'penny stamp, a circular it is from the Socialist candidate. I wish I was bringing you a love letter instead.' And, cackling, she made off, down between the nodding flowers.

According to his reading of the Scriptures, a catastrophe was due very soon. Men flew through the air, and, in London, he was told, they also travelled in trains under the earth; such perversities were omens; proud and vain in their shocking accomplishments, men were to be brought to their original simplicity. The process would be painful. It had been given to him to see the vanity of these wicked men; he had stood apart and watched their ridiculous antics. They would pay. Every Monday morning Caleb washed his mass of rudely cut hair and bathed in expectation of disaster, for somehow he felt he would escape.

November brought a battalion of storms. Winds roared, the sea snarled, clouds ran out of the sky and burst over Llan Powis: the terrible rains of that winter began. Caleb, his insecure eyes popping with excitement, had very little sleep, and each early morning he stood at the door of his cottage and searched for signs of the world's débâcle. The charging clouds, the whipped water of the river, the savage winds gnawing at the hilltop—they were ominous enough in their fierce strength, but as yet there was no majestic damage visible.

Yet how startling were the nights! Then the howling winds and the thrashing rain tossed the world like a child's rubber ball through the very clouds. Caleb became quite certain that the world had been torn out of its usual orbit and chucked into a desolate grey place where the elements were wilder than wild beasts. Quite soon now the truth of its position would be fully revealed. Such rain had never fallen on the earth before. It hissed and beat madly; it stamped on his garden and jumped through his thatch; it ate up the light of day and tore the night to shreds. Caleb began to foresee it was through the rain that the end would come.

He watched the river with a smile of excitement. Yes, it was rising. And the roar of the sea could be heard: the sea was swollen. The waters of the world were rising. Caleb removed his clothes and walked seven times in the rain round his cottage, to become accustomed to the unheated wet. Nevertheless, he had a plan. He believed that if he imitated a previous example, God would see that a man who took warnings seriously was still left in the earth and forgive accordingly. He would make himself an ark.

Or, rather, buy one—a boat which could be used as an ark. Tom Prosser had been unable to sell his boat, and it now lay rotting not far from the cottage, so it ought to be cheap. The day of his decision Margiad arrived with a letter, screaming through the door.

'Let me in, Caleb, let me in. I'm drowning fast and I can't swim at all.' When Caleb unwillingly opened the door, she panted: 'If I was only a duck! If I was only a black duck, I wouldn't mind now, not a bit.' Dripping over the sanded stone flags, she pushed her way into the kitchen. 'Let me have five minutes by your fire, Caleb, and if you have a spoonful of hot broth, I wouldn't say no. Here is a letter for you. Ha'penny stamp and from the seed merchants.'

'I want no letters,' Caleb announced with the mien of a prophet. 'And can seeds be sown in water?'

'Well,' said Margiad literally, 'there's lilies that grow in water, and cress, and—'

'Not in the waters that are about to cover the earth!' he thundered.

Margiad, perceiving his ecstasy, immediately became respectful. She dropped the petticoats she had been holding up before the fire, and likewise her eyelids; she looked pious and humble. He continued, powerful in his belief now:

'Listen now to me, woman, and you spread my warning as you take letters on the round. Disaster is about to come on us. Take warning and double warning. But I know they will not listen. As for me, I shall take my ark to the top of Llan Powis, together with my cockerel, hens, and my pigs. A store of victuals, too, and a barrel of drinking water and a dove. My ark will float over all the world!' His loosened eyes became brilliant with triumph, his voice rose. 'And then when all else is dead and the water is subsided, if God sees fit to rescue me I shall step out into a clean Land, yea, a fresh Land. Even as Noah in a time before.'

Margiad gently lifted her eyelids. 'And what about a Mrs. Noah, Caleb? There will have to be a Mrs. Noah. Come now! The fowls and the pigs will be all right, and you will not lack for eggs and bacon, indeed. But what about a wife in the ark, for things to be proper?'

Caleb roamed round the kitchen, clapping his hands, behind his back. Taking a wife had not occurred to him, having proceeded in life so long without one. Then he decided he couldn't stop now and choose one, there was no time. He announced definitely:

'Heaven will provide, if it is seen fit that I shall be rescued.'

'Now, now, make sure, Caleb,' she cried anxiously. 'Very cold and wet and lonely will the ark be up there. And a wife can keep watch for the dove coming back while you sleep.'

'You go out from the kitchen now!' Caleb shouted. 'I know what I know.'

When he had driven her away he made his final preparations, taking some of his money from the earth under the lilac beside the door. Swathing himself in old canvas, he walked out to Tom Prosser's house that sat on another lap of the hill. The howling wind and the lashing tails of rain kept his exaltation continually on the boil. He had neither eyes nor ears for mockery. Prosser was only too glad to be rid of his derelict old boat, for which Caleb handed cash. Caleb then found the village, which was concealed in another angry cloudburst, and interviewed eight farm labourers idle because of the prolonged wet. In exchange for a fee of ten shillings each they were to drag the boat up the side of Llan Powis. The men, steady members of the chapel, eyed Caleb with a mixture of respect and good-humour. But one said thoughtfully:

'All drowned except you we are going to be. What use then ten shillings? No shops or banks are there in Heaven, surely now.'

Caleb saw the heaving world from the inn window. 'Don't you stop me with vain arguments,' he raved, hostile. 'A new spotless shroud you can buy with the ten shillings. Lay yourself in it on the sixth day from now. Doom is on us.'

Had God put prophetic fire in Caleb's tongue? And there were scarlet stars in his cheeks. No man remembered the like of these storms that followed one after the other. Even as they searched for ropes and poles awful thunder rushed out of the sky like a legion of bellowing black angels, and great white-hot silver cracks split the clouds and ran hissing across the whole world. If it was true that the earth was being demolished, it could not be done in better style. Far away under their minds the men half-believed and began to think secretly of the caves in the hills, where their forefathers had crouched on similar occasions.

That afternoon the *Nansi,* black and leaky in the mud beside the river, was pulled and pushed with much secret swearing up Llan Powis's sodden side. Half-way up, the men, wet to the skin, struck and demanded their money threateningly. Caleb paid out. The men announced that they would finish the job in the morning. 'What if the Flood comes during the night!' Caleb shouted between claps of appropriate thunder. The men, longing for cups of steaming tea, left him gesticulating on the icy hillside. But that night, it was said, several of them were visited by dreams of terrible woes to come.

Margiad paid an unofficial visit to Caleb the next morning. She wept, she cajoled, she threatened. And even the Postmaster-General, she declared, would not expect her to deliver letters to an ark on top of a wet hill, so Caleb would be cut off entirely from the warmth of human beings. He remained unmoved. Then she implored him to take with him plenty of flannel under-things, an oil stove, and a bottle of cough mixture. At last he said angrily:

'Get behind me, woman: I see horns on your forehead.'

Wearing black oilskins, the chapel minister called, too, frowning at Caleb's presumption in meddling with sacred matters. But, denunciatory, Caleb was more than a match for him. Afire again, Caleb set out to rouse the hired men, for the river had risen several inches and there were menacing sheets of water over the flat fields the other side. He had to offer another ten shillings before the men could be induced out again; in spite of their fears and bad dreams, their wives were behind them.

Before evening the *Nansi* was safe on top of Llan Powis; she rested against a rock. Caleb then employed three of the men to assist him in carrying up her cargo. The pigs made a great fuss of the journey; the fowls were carried in baskets, clucking with alarm. Pieces of wood, hammer and nails, food and water, a tub to catch the rain, bedding, a Bible, and a dove purchased in the village, these were deposited in the ark before nightfall. And all the time the wind howled and wailed, the sky broke and broke again, the rain streamed.

Caleb knelt on the deck and, large icy drops striking his face, asked for a blessing on the ark. Had he not seen that the world was full of evil? It was no place for a chaste and innocent man. If God required him to represent his kind in the new world, which was to appear when the waters subsided, he would promise to live without corruption. Let the foul old cities disappear; their stink was everywhere. Let men and women be drowned; they were of no more account than frogs. He had seen the bestiality of people too long; let the world be made into a sink of dirty water. And he would release a dove that would find the white hilltop; and when the waters subsided, would there not be a wonderful new orchard? And underneath a blossoming apple tree a woman fresh from the hand of the Creator? Caleb was sure of it; he had faith. Concluding, he rose.

The swine he had pushed under the deck were troublesome, irritably thrusting their snouts over bare wood and squealing their dismay. Caleb turned them out on the sodden grass in the dark and they were gratified; time enough to pull them in again when the waters had risen to the hilltop. As yet the fowls were too overcome to protest against their limited space under a deck shelter; they remained huddled in a corner, even the cock. The dove was stored away in a dark corner. After much preparation, and commanding his ears to listen for the sound of the rising waters, Caleb crawled under the deck among the bedding and fell asleep.

162

The storms raged for another week. No one would have believed the sky could hold such stocks of rain and wind. In the nights Caleb could hear the screams of witches and monster birds who had been blown out of their fastnesses among the hills. Soon the churchyards would throw into the air their crackling and groaning skeletons; and afterwards would float everywhere the swollen dark-green drowned corpses of people he had known. He spent much time in prayer; he fasted; he made the swine and fowls fast too. The fourth day two fowls, looking stupefied, passed away, and on the fifth day the sow also, who had been coughing miserably since her removal to the ark. The dove remained as if petrified in its cage.

No matter. In the new world new beasts would surely appear, with better eggs and different bacon. Caleb passed the days plucking and washing the fowls in the rain and cutting the sow into pieces of pork. He went to the side of the hill to peer down into the river valley. The rain was so thick he could see nothing. But there were moaning sounds and the sounds of gurgling waters: people drowning and floods eating into their dwellings. Happy, Caleb praised Heaven for its destructive work.

The sixth day, while he was lying under the deck feeling strangely light of body, there was a loud knocking against the side of the boat. An angel! Come to warn him that tonight his ark was to float high over the world! He crawled out and stared excitedly over the boat side.

'Caleb, Caleb,' shrieked Margiad above the wind, 'or is your name Noah now? But there is a letter for Caleb. From your brother in America, that hasn't wrote for a year . . . How are you, man? Speak, and don't stare at me like that! Speak now!'

'You go away!' shouted Caleb, very upset. 'Tomorrow you'll be taking hot letters across Satan's land, you ugly bat.'

'Let me come into your ark,' yelled the undiminished Margiad, 'Swing down the ladder now.' And taking a packet of sweets out of her bag, she added coaxingly: 'Some Paradise Fruits I have for you here. Look.'

'Go away. Your fruits are poisoned,' he raved.

'The river,' she called, 'is in a flood over your garden. I been into your house and took up the mats. An old rat has eaten into your bag of flour and the rain is chewing your thatch.'

'The rats will live last!' he bellowed laughing. 'They will swim about and gnaw at your dead hands.'

'Your face is white,' she shrieked, staring at him through the rain. 'Pneumonia will have you and cold in the bowels. You want to die, Caleb, you want to die?'

163

'Ha, ha, ha! Jealous are the drowning. God's new fire is in my bowels. Take yourself off my ark! The ark of the Lord this is. Don't you foul it now.'

For Margiad was attempting to clamber into the boat, heaving herself up. Caleb, raving, was about to stamp on her fingers when he collapsed limply on the deck. The cockerel flew out of its shelter in noisy hysteria and ran madly over the boat. The dying male swine under the deck snored with strange, delicate snores. Margiad, with much difficulty, for she was plump, landed on deck flat and panting like a rotund fish. She dragged Caleb out of the rain into shelter.

Before the day was out she had supervised his removal, on a stretcher, back to the cottage. And that same day, with a few last clouts of rain and the wind kicking its final fury against the eternal hills, the storms abated. Except for the flooded river and a few battered fields, the world looked just the same. But Caleb, the doctor declared, had pneumonia; very likely he would die.

Margiad, however, made up her mind that he would not die. She took up abode in the cottage and became a very lively woman, a woman with a mission. Her sturdy mockery frightened Death away from the cottage door. After five weeks of clever ministrations Caleb sat up and lamented:

'Why is it the old world didn't go under? Never again a yellow or a red sun, but a black sun! For a while whatever. Now it is the same again.' He seemed dispirited, weary.

'The Big Boss changed His mind,' Margiad, knitting a new vest for him, said comfortably. 'And now clear are the intentions. Settle down like other chaps you must. No more floods for ten thousand years again. A warning to tickle us was the last. Say how you would like this vest, Caleb, with long sleeves or short sleeves? The colour you like? A blue very pretty. The colour of Hope, they always say.'

Thus she continually tried to occupy his mind with mundane things. She made herself indispensable; she showed him how fair are the ways of a woman in the house: the lamps burned brighter, the oven flourished, the sink was sweet, the bed neat as a daisy. She asked him where his money was hidden; she had used enough of her own savings. Under the lilac. She dug, counted, and kept an account. Two hundred and seventy pounds left. With her job, and when better he must work at a farm, they could manage very well. Visitors came to the house and treated her, beside his bed, as Mrs. Caleb—she had done wonders, she had rescued him from Jordan, so it was only right.

For a long time he kept mumbling of blows delivered to him that were beyond repair. He took to more visions; with a dusty broom she belaboured them. He still looked down his long icy nose at the shoddy people in the evil world; she made him golden apple-pies. She waited cunningly, and one week when he was weary, vacant, and bored, she married him. On a Thursday. And on Friday morning he was a changed man.

Margiad returned from her round and bustled into the cottage, whistling a small, pleased tune. Caleb sat in the armchair still looking astonished. She whipped off coat and hat and tied on an apron. 'Up at Magpie Farm,' she said seductively, 'a very nice job of work they have waiting for you.'

Caleb sat quiet, half awake, not quite come through.

'A new world proper for you today!' she went on amiably. 'The old one was drownded, after all.'

Caleb sat as if he still whispered, faintly like a ghost, after glories beyond the table, the dresser smelling of furniture polish and the gleaming china dogs of the kitchen. But Margiad sang. She began to dust the pictures with the new feather brush she had bought in Woolworth's on market day.

'Fifteen bob,' she said presently, 'I got for the old ark. Only firewood and such is it good for now. A bad loss on the bad side of the ledger, Caleb dear. A prank expensive, pigs and fowls in the same sum. Full stop now though, let it be forgotten. A double line under the odd business.'

Caleb wiped his weeping nose.

RESURRECTION

Half a day before the lid was to be screwed down on her, Meg rose in her coffin and faintly asked for a glass of water. Her two sisters were bustling about the room, tidying and dusting and admiring the flowers, and both, after a few moments of terrified shock, looked at the recently deceased with a bitter anger. Once again she was doing something improper.

'Water!' stuttered Bertha. 'Go on with you now. What you want with water?' Gathering strength at the sound of her own voice, she went on sternly and as if speaking to a nuisance: 'Lie back thee, lie back. Dead you are.'

'Yes, indeed,' breathed Ellen, 'dead these four days, and the mourning ordered.'

Meg, nice in a new shiny white satin nightdress, trimmed with lace, stared back. But her gaze still had something of the marbled hardness of the dead. There seemed an awful weariness in the hang of her head. Her shoulders gave little clutching jumps. Suddenly she lay back in her coffin, sighing, and without further speech.

'Ha!' cried Bertha, in relief, 'a bit of life there was left in her nerves and made her body rise up like that. Funny thing! Just like some chickens run round the yard after you've chopped off their heads.' She sat down and her face was eased again. 'But a nasty turn it gave me, Ellen. Just like her it would have been, to do a trick on us, making us spend money on mourning and that five-guinea coffin.'

'Yes, indeed,' cried Ellen, her face still very grey from retreating hysteria, but relieved too, 'and eighty-five coming to the funeral tomorrow and an announcement in the newspaper.' She turned her head away from the coffin. 'A fine disgrace it would have been for us.'

And both sisters thought of the hours that must elapse before the undertaker arrived that afternoon safely to shut up the coffin. Meg might rise again and frighten them with a bit of second-hand life. Why, the next time something awful might happen—perhaps she would be jolted back entirely into the land of the living.

'He won't come till five o'clock,' said Bertha. 'He's busy burying Samson Lewis this afternoon.'

'Can't we screw the lid down ourselves?' Ellen quavered. 'Not right, is it, for us to have shocks like this. My heart's going pitapat.'

'Talk there might be if we shut her up before the time arranged' Bertha answered, shaking her head. 'People will say we was in a hurry. You know,' she reminded her sister, 'that two or three are coming at tea-time to mourn with us while the job is being done.'

'Oh!' exclaimed Ellen, remembering at this, 'I didn't buy the cold ham at the shop this morning.'

'Sardines,' said Bertha definitely, reverting to a debate of that morning, 'will be enough, I tell you again. On toast. You can't give cold ham today *and* tomorrow.'

'When Ceinwen Roberts was buried,' Ellen, who was not quite so mean as Bertha, remarked, 'they had baron of beef, leg of pork, and veal pie. *One* meat is not enough for tomorrow, Bertha. Those there are who don't like cold ham.'

'Then the tinned salmon they must have,' Bertha grumbled. 'Haven't we spent enough on clothes! Twelve pounds fifteen in the draper's. No one can say we've stinted decent burial for her.'

'Most of it,' said Ellen, with sudden sisterly sourness, 'on our backs.' Occasionally the sisters quarrelled.

'If *we* had died,' Bertha brooded, 'as cheap as possible *she'd* have put us away.'

'Well,' Ellen said, in the manner of one generously overlooking a fault, 'she was never a one to enjoy a funeral.'

'No,' continued Bertha, with a surprising depth of bitterness, 'men and whisky was *her* bent.'

'Hush, Bertha, hush. So many years ago that was.'

'Ha, craving she had for them always. If she hadn't been obliged to take to her bed and lie there helpless, she'd have been out in the world disgracing herself and us to her dying day.'

'Well,' soothed Ellen, 'safe she is now.'

But they both glanced apprehensively towards the coffin. Bleak and raddled and wintry, the sisters, who were in the fifties, pursed their lips. They were twins. Both wore a piled-up mass of coarse, dour hair in which was jabbed small combs and tortoise-shell prongs. Their faces were puckered in, secretive, and proud. In chapel and street they liked to swank: they liked people to think they were well off and to treat them with ceremony. They were daughters of a semi-successful builder, and in a hole behind some loose bricks in the cellar was the money he had made, for he had trusted no bank; his daughters thought likewise. A widower, he had died five years ago, and since then no event of importance had happened to the twins. But now the maladies of their younger sister Meg had culminated in a death too long delayed. They had looked on her as their cross. But they told themselves that they loved her, and indeed sometimes they had brought her a baked apple with clotted cream, her favourite, and showed affection. On the day she had lain back and stiffened, they thought it was for the best, all things considered. They began to fluff and preen themselves, for death is important and brings ceremony, display, and a great going out into public.

'She,' Ellen had wept at intervals, 'wasn't bad now and again, our poor Meg. After all, she didn't ought to have gone so young.'

'No,' agreed Bertha, who at intervals had been gloomy too, 'she didn't ought to have gone before she tried to tidy up her life a bit. But now it's happened—'

'Yes,' said Ellen, 'yes indeed.'

And after an hour or so of indulgence in the magic of grief they would bestir themselves, realising that a rare opportunity had come to them. Like royalty, they would ride in a procession for two miles to the cemetery, at every corner between the rows of houses knots of people gathered, craning their heads to see.

Then, again, it seemed they were to be thwarted. An hour or so later in that afternoon Meg sat up once more and peered round with dreadful stare, her white lips pulled back and showing her naked gums—for the sisters had removed her ten-guinea set of false teeth. And again she murmured for water. Ellen was alone in the room, Bertha having gone downstairs to prepare the food for the visitors; and realising this time that something remarkable had happened to the deceased, she tottered to the door and shrieked for her sister. Bertha came bustling upstairs, a half-cut loaf still clutched in her hand. 'What now, what now?' she, demanded, her suspicious fury ready.

'Come back again she has, asking for water,' moaned Ellen. And she added despairingly, 'Not dead at all is she.'

'Rubbish now, rubbish.' Bertha stood in the doorway like a snorting roused mare. 'Hasn't the doctor signed the certificate? Dead he said she was.' But there, undoubtedly, was the starkly up-raised Meg, now looking round with vague and pathetic appeal. 'But if not dead she is,' breathed Bertha further, 'damages the doctor will have to pay us. Close on twenty pounds,' she suddenly screamed in shrill hysteria towards the menacing body, 'have we spent on you.'

The sisters advanced together towards the coffin, creeping, but angry now.

'Lie back,' Ellen also began shouting in the wrath of despair, 'lie back. Your funeral is tomorrow. At half-past two. Eighty-five are coming.'

Bertha laid her hand restrainingly on Ellen's bristling arm. She began to speak in a cunningly entreating voice, coaxing. 'Go you back, Meg, only half alive you'll be indeed if you don't. Not fit to live you are with your bladder and kidneys. And what if we go before you, who'll look after you then? The workhouse it'll be. Not worth living is life, Meg fach. A dirty business it is. Black is the future. Go you now, please, and follow soon we will, true enough. Better company in the other world than this.'

'Five guineas for your coffin alone!' Ellen took the coaxing cue from her sister, but added a whine to her voice. 'Look you how lovely it is. Polished oak. Die now, there's a nice girl, die now.'

But Meg's whitish eyes were fixed on the loaf of bread that was clutched in Bertha's hand; their dullness passed into a greedy gleam.

'Bread,' she mumbled, 'bread.' And with a pleased sigh she eagerly stretched forth her trembling hands.

Wholly convinced at last, her sisters cried out in fury and horror. The clamour brought neighbours running into the house. The foaming and stuttering twins were attended to by sympathetic women, while others stood in awe round the coffin. None attempted to lift the weak Meg out of her coffin or supply her with the refreshment she craved. Mrs. Williams, a strident and dominant woman, took charge and declared that a policeman must be informed before anything could be done. After some delay P.C. Johns appeared downstairs and in a stern, disapproving voice asked:

'What's this I hear about a corpse coming to life, Bertha Evans?'

'It's upstairs,' quavered Bertha. But at sight of the policeman she began to bounce back into energy, aware of the drama that was being offered her.

The policeman tramped heavily upstairs. Ellen had recovered some while before and was repeating over and over again how Meg had sat up twice. Exhausted with her futile demands for refreshment, Meg was now lying back amid the pleated mauve satin folds. There was no doubt, however, that life was flushing back into her features. The policeman gazed at her in the suspicious and convicting manner of his kind. At sight of him Meg gave a slight whimper, as if frightened. At one time in her young and gay days she had been arrested for drunkenness.

'A doctor must see her,' declared P. C. Johns, after ten minutes' cogitation. 'Nothing for me is there here.' And sullenly he went away.

After further delay and searching the doctor was found. It was now late evening and still Meg had not been removed from the coffin. As the news spread, people kept on trooping into the house from near and far. Bertha and Ellen, recovered, were the centre of much enquiry. Sympathy was lavished on them. What would be done with the black clothes now, and the coffin? And no ride to the cemetery tomorrow. Someone suggested that they should take a week at the seaside as recompense. Dr. Miskin himself, befuddled with whisky, as usual, glared at Meg so angrily that onlookers thought he was going to strike her. For a few moments he would not believe that she was living; he roughly pushed one of her already blinking eyelids up and down, prodded her, and spitefully gripped her limp wrist. Finally, he declared her living, told Bertha that in England such things often happened, and left instructions that Meg was to receive only milk and water for three days; he spoke as if she deserved such punishment. Bertha looked back at him malevolently.

'Dead you said she was and signed certificate. Damages I ask you. What we've spent on mourning and the oak coffin. The food for the funeral tea tomorrow I leave out.'

The doctor spat and left the house. Bertha and Ellen began to weep in rage, several women loosened their tears, too, in sympathy. The undertaker, sweating in his haste, arrived and declared that contract had been made for the funeral tomorrow—he would keep it, and at two o'clock the hearse and carriages would be outside the house; no business of his was it if the corpse was not in the coffin. He was very agitated and spoke wildly; trade had been bad all winter. Bertha and Ellen, already incensed by the doctor, screamed and threatened until he went flying down the stairs. At the front door he turned and shouted back:

'On your hands the coffin will be, however. Made for you it was and I will not take it back now.'

Bertha and Ellen had to admit defeat. A neighbour consoled them by saying that the coffin could be kept under a bed until required and would make a good cupboard for blankets and such-like.

Then once again Meg rose stark from her narrow bed and began whimpering.

'A bit of brandy,' she begged. 'And give me my teeth back, please, now.'

Bertha and Ellen looked at each other numbly. The teeth had already been sold to the pawnbroker, but this they did not want to admit before the neighbours. They went over to their sister and laid her back in the coffin.

'Hush now, Meg fach. Rest, be quiet, take time. The pump in your heart is not working proper yet. Soon it will be.'

'My teeth,' whispered Meg, 'give me my teeth—'

The twins were saved further explanation by the arrival of a reporter from the newspaper, Tommy Thomas, a frowning but brisk young man. After glancing at Meg, he took out his notebook and asked for particulars.

Bertha and Ellen began speaking together. Excitement shone from their eyes now. Never had they been in the newspapers. When Tommy asked for a photograph of Meg, Bertha declared flatly:

'No photo is there of her. But one of Ellen and myself I will give you, taken in Swansea.'

Tommy sucked his pencil. He asked the sisters if they had any special

170

comment to make on the event. Bertha's sense of grievance again got the upper hand and she answered bitterly:

'Yes, indeed. This now. What she want to come back for? A fathead she was always. In life nightmares she was always having. Peace she had a chance of. Back she is now, the fool, where a lot of worries bit at her like a plague of evil rats. Fathead twice over. *That* put in your paper, young man, and let a bit of truth be told for once. Now then, Ellen, fetch the photo.'

In her coffin Meg still whimpered, as if in weary distress. When all the visitors had gone, weakly she managed to lift her head yet again. She asked to be taken out of the coffin. The twins pursed their lips; both, now that the excitement of the drama was over, felt flat, as if something had been filched from them. Ellen looked dangerously vexed. Bertha approached the coffin and said maliciously:

'What for you want to get out? Not many people is it get a chance to spend a night in a coffin. Comfortable it is surely? Clean and dry as the inside of a nut. You stay there, Meg. Stripped your bed is, and no sheets aired. And too weak you are to be shifted. Yes, indeed. Tomorrow we'll lift you out, yes, perhaps. Settle down now and rest . . .'

171

HALF-HOLIDAY

Unlike other days, on Saturday afternoon the two o'clock train was always crowded. Clanking and groaning, it drew its rusty way through the little mountain valleys as though complaining of its burden. Clambering up inclines to villages perched like a flock of crows on the lower mountain-sides, the ancient engine puffed and blowed, coming to a standstill at the raw stations with a long disgusted shake of its tail. Out trooped some of the passengers, chattering noisily, others entered with clean, shiny faces and well-blacked shoes. All the valleys were busy, inter-changing people on Saturday afternoon.

The down platform of Nant y Mynydd station was clamorous with its contribution to this half-holiday crowd of travellers. Everybody seemed to be speaking at once, and all the voices seemed to be tenor or soprano, with a note of happy hysteria in each, often breaking into male crashes of laughter or high feminine squeals of delight. The young people teased each other, the middle-aged gossiped maliciously, and the old were mocking and boasted of past successes in eisteddfod, on concert platform or in boxing-booth.

The aristocracy of the collection was the Dramatic Society. Old-fashioned were the goings-on of singing festivals, boxing matches, football and cantata meetings. The Society, a party of a dozen or so well-dressed and important-looking people, stood in the waiting-shanty apart, listening to their producer, a very lean but intense young ironmonger, who was agonisingly reiterating some instructions. A Welsh translation of Ibsen's *Ghosts* was the play they were performing in a chapel hall early that evening. The ironmonger was the only one who knew about Ibsen. Nevertheless, the ironmonger knew that talent, passion and unafraid gusto would be declared that evening. Too much gusto was what he was afraid of now, as he spoke.

Near the door of the waiting-shanty stood Walt Matthews, the heavy-weight, with his trainer and a number of supporters. Walt was fighting Tiger Tim Thomas at Gelli. His nose was blue and flat, his face rotund as a Caerphilly cheese and his body wide as a door: while his trainer spoke of him he kept on reading a few lines of a tattered school-tale periodical.

'Those Dramatics,' angrily growled the trainer at last, 'chatter like a lot of tipsy rooks. Can't hear myself speak.'

''S'all right,' a supporter remarked wearily. 'Walt's shut up shop and don't hear. That jane's on his mind. He'll fight tonight like a slab of butter put in the oven. Can't anyone,' he asked plaintively of the others, 'can't anyone tell Walt

172

that she's been the ruin of four boxers already, the . . . the . . . Oh,' he concluded in despair, 'there's *no* word for her, all the names are compliments for *her.*' He looked round savagely, expecting to see the raffish Ellen Evans trip across to them at any moment: she attended all the boxing matches. And Walt was her latest capture.

Walt stood safely enclosed in his great mound of flesh, unseeing, unhearing, aloof as a god. His supporters knew that at times the cart-load of flesh could flash into vitality like a dry hayrick afire. But for a fortnight it had been turgid with love. His pale blue simple little eyes were hiding in his battered face now. The supporters failed to draw a spark from the majestic pile. They became more insulting, raising their voices, though they failed to overpower the 'Dramatics.' In the shanty, Blodwen Rees, who had made her money running a chain of public bake-houses, and also manufacturing sarsaparilla mineral water, was loudly declaring that this was the last time she'd play Mrs. Alving in *Ghosts.* 'Something lighter is what I'm suited for,' she cried above the protestations of the others. Really, in some psychic way, she became a remarkable person on the stage, and her performance as Mrs. Alving was grimly moving in its desolation and pathos. But always she pleaded for comic parts, saying she'd suffered enough in real life, having buried two husbands, 'wasters both of them, as everybody knows'.

The football crowd, however, yelled the most, sewn thickly among the crowd on the platform. Most of the Cwm Parc Rovers were gathered at this station, a sharp, unruly lot puffed up by their great success that season: one-time collier-boys they were, but now on the dole. They had shrill terrier voices, wiry necks and knees: they slapped each other, and when a girl passed, dressed up for the afternoon excursion, they made ceremonious way for her, pressing back and creating an aisle for the embarrassed (or tittering) young dame. A courting couple, bandy-legged Rufus Roberts and blushing Fanny Jones, were also honoured thus, someone whistling Mendelssohn's Wedding March as they advanced.

The Gosen Glee Singers, an elderly set of male vocalists, looked subdued. But, the train being late—as usual—surrounding people began to call for a song. Harris the Boot (he kept a boot-shop), the conductor and always ready to oblige, flicked his tuning-fork. And the respectful silence with which *Ar Hyd y Nos* was treated gratified for a while Harris the Boot, who was jealous of the Dramatic Society and had waxed the ends of his moustache to points as tall as darning-needles. He closed the song with a grandiose flourish. Immediately, with relieved and greater intensity, the tangled chatter of voices rose again down the platform. The Glee Singers shrank back into unimportance: they were a little out of date now.

'Sport', Harris the Boot was heard to sneer later, 'and sickly play-acting, that's all they want now. Hooligans kicking a dirty ball, and painted women and men showing off what had better be hidden.' And he glared angrily, for no apparent reason, at a smartly dressed woman who stood near and had an air of not belonging. She was an Italian and kept an ice-cream and sweet-shop with her foreign husband: the skills and furs she wore, her dusky skin and humid eyes, the supple plumpness of her handsome body—all her rather sultry appearance infuriated Harris the Boot. 'These Eyetalians that come and take our trade,' he muttered to one of the Glee Singers, 'they ought to be shoved back under their volcanoes, where they come from.'

Here and there were competitors travelling to a little eisteddfod that was opening at five o'clock in Pen Mawr, a village up under the sky and cold and quiet as the grave. These were bards, reciters, vocalists, pianists and violinists, some of the competitors being of tender age and accompanied by parents who gossiped with others of their brilliant offspring's past successes. Little Phyllis Morgans, ten and very thin and determined-looking behind immense wire spectacles, had recited those *Ingoldsby Legends* without one stumble. Eight she was then. The brush and comb she had won had not been used yet. 'Saving all her prizes I am till she's married,' her mother announced. And she gazed with disparaging malevolence at little Megan Lewis, who was to be Phyllis's competitor that evening, and who, for all her prettiness, would be undoubtedly the loser.

'Frying-pan' Williams—so called because once in his young unrepentant days he had chased his wife out of the house with a pan hot from the fire—gazed about him with suspicious dourness. Some years ago, in a 'revival,' he had turned from drink and became a kind of amateur preacher, serving up to Heaven the cold meats and small beer of these his drab last years. No one liked him. He had submitted to the eisteddfod a long poem: the subject set by the committee was 'The Fall of Babylon.' He was always angrily searching for people who called him 'Frying-pan' Williams, and thus had come to wear a dark, threatening look. But that afternoon his hostile stare was directed chiefly to Teddy Tucker.

Teddy strode ornately up and down the crowded platform, thrusting a difficult but successful way among the mob. A wide black felt hat flopped over lank red hair that dropped about his head like liquid fire: he wore, too, a scarlet shirt, yellow tie, and mildew-green corduroy trousers. He was the most successful poet in the valleys, carrying off the bardic prize chair at nearly every eisteddfod. He had once spent a long week-end in Paris, and by trade he was a wallpaper-hanger, working respectably during the week. Week-ends, however, he was the Complete Poet, dressing up and giving a touch of the picturesque to the mining valleys. Only his name worried him, depriving him of that share of dignity to which he felt his fame entitled him. He would not even nod to 'Frying-pan' Williams, his fellow-poet in Nant y Mynydd; he felt that such a man vulgarised the poetic calling.

Still there was no sign of the train. 'The engine's broke down,' a footballer cried. 'She's been threatening to do it every Saturday this winter.'

'Where's the station-master?' demanded another. 'Always he hides himself on Saturday afternoon. Jacob Watkins,' he yelled towards the booking-office the other side, 'run astray has the only train you got? Or collapsed it has? Where's the old iron gone? Look now, the eisteddfod starts at four, and the Dramatics' got to start painting their mugs soon.'

The station-master remained hidden. Pale gusts of winter sunshine brightened the air, and the day was mild. Though the train was always at least forty minutes late on Saturdays, the travellers had been waiting long before the scheduled time of departure. The Saturday meeting on the platform was not unenjoyable, and the week was drab enough, with so little money in the place nowadays. 'Retired' colliers, gaunt and wearing well-brushed old clothes, gazed remotely towards the treacherous colliery that littered the hill-side beyond the station. Not much noise and smoke came from the pits these days. Time was when their clatter and dust filled all the place.

People, however, were not to be subdued and refused to keep silent, like the pits: the clamour on the platform remained undiminished as time went on and still no train appeared. A swift and healthy humour—though at times a little malicious—darted through the chattering, clear voices like trout in a stream. Surrounding folk waited for fireworks when the parading Teddy Tucker accidentally cannoned into 'Frying-pan' Williams, stomach to stomach, but the rival poets merely glared menacingly at each other and turned back curtly into the crowd. Inside the shanty, Dick Prosser, a thick-set and hearty young engine-cleaner, who was to play Oswald Alving in *Ghosts*, winked and leered through the window at plump Harmony Davies. She was a chapel minister's daughter and she was going to perform a Dutch character dance at a concert: her clogs were in a large Gladstone bag, which she swung coyly in front of her.

At last there was a bustling sound up the line, and a few moments later the dingy engine, coughing fussily as if to excuse itself for the delay on grounds of indisposition, crawled into the station. The tail of coaches shook itself twice before coming to a frightened standstill: the worn carriages were already full from stations up the line. There were loud shoutings at doors, struggles and pushings: then the engine suddenly emitted a hoarse bellow. But everybody got into the train successfully. In a minute, except for the guard, the platform was bare as a knife.

175

At last the station-master sauntered to the platform in the sober manner of his kind; reaching the guard, simultaneously they took out their watches, looked, and returned them to their pockets. Neither spoke, but the guard cynically twirled an end of his moustache and the station-master pursed his lips. After a while the guard vaguely raised his green flag. From the train came sounds of rollicking laughter and tickled screeches.

A loud puffing and gasping through its rusty throat warned everyone that the engine was about to move. The guard gave a significant nod to the station-master and mounted: presently the engine tossed into the air a thick sniff of steam and ambled forward.

Yet still there was another delay. A high feminine scream came from the bridge connecting the two platforms. Madame Salome Jenkins, the high-class pianist, was whisking her seventy-year-old legs down the stairs. 'Stop! stop!' she shrieked. Her voice rang with fury. No one for fifty miles around could play Chopin so expertly as she. At one time, before marrying Jenkins, the flannel merchant, she had been professional. She had every right to be treated with respect.

The station-master gave a loud blast of his whistle. Madame Salome was a Power. The train had already left the platform, but it stopped, and out popped the guard's head.

'Goodness gracious me, man,' snorted the woman, 'what's the train doing almost on time! It's always forty minutes late.'

The train was backing. 'Can't trust to that always, Madame Jenkins,' said the station-master sombrely. But he was respectful.

'Nice thing if I had lost this train,' she snapped, 'when I got to play the Twenty-Four Preludes at Gilfach.'

'Two years ago,' he reminded her soothingly, 'you played them at Noddfa, our Baptist Chapel. You remember? Eleven pounds off the Building Debt we had out of that concert. Thanks to you.'

Grudgingly the train returned. Madame Salome bandied a few words with the guard, criticising the erratic behaviour of his train. It had no right to be suddenly less than forty minutes late, after numberless Saturdays of the old habit . . . Abusive, she entered a carriage crowded with Cwm Parc Rovers. Her wrinkled face steamed from her recent exertions. But she was sinewy and healthy.

After much struggling and shifting of tangled limbs, a seat was found for her. The young footballers displayed a little deference, withdrawing as much as possible in the overloaded compartment. But she patted her knees and briskly invited one of the Rovers to accommodate himself thereon: he sat there grinning widely.

'Who you're playing today?' she enquired. 'My word, you did well last Saturday with Clydach Wanderers. Oi there, stop smoking that fag, Full Back Ben Hughes, it smells as if it was cabbage. I got some better ones here . . . Golly, the train's breaking down already—'

It was true. After sundry shudderings and clankings of its under quarters, the train became dead still; it might have been a corpse.

'Ah well,' sighed Madame Salome Jenkins, settling herself as comfortably as possible with the hefty footballer on her elderly knees, 'let's have a song to pass the time. Now, boys, all together in *Sospan Fach* . . .'

THE FARM

I

The Farm had belonged to his father, but had been there, Powell would declare, since the days when the world was altogether tidy and sweet-smelling as a nut. He treasured his farm without saying too much about it. The house was of washed old stone and lay beside the recumbent body of the hill in drowsy peace. Around it three precious small pieces of respectable earth, one given to turnip, one to corn, one to barley. But cows it was that really kept the place going, their milk taken to the nearby mining valley. There was unstony pasturage for them down the lowland—not much, so that Powell's business never prospered. But all his days the number of his cows remained the same, even when the colliers' wives caught the craze for condensed milk out of tins. No other farm for miles, though within sight a tattered village was perched on the shoulder of the hill; only old people living there—the young adventured off to the mines.

True enough, the place had preserved its good looks, with its everlasting smell of morning and dew. When his daughters were children Powell would say that it was mentioned in the Bible as one of the choicer works of God. But his wife Matilda would contradict him, of course, saying he was conceited, and how did he know what the rest of the world was like? He never went further than his milk cart carried him on business. He had sorrel-like moustaches; she, daughter of the sexton up in the village, looked pliant as a willow wand, but was not.

He despised the mining valley which lay around the corner of the pushed-out purple mountain; once, in his angrier argumentative mood, he called it snot out of the nose of Satan. But they bought his milk there, which enabled him to put a tidy bit by in a bank. But to him life there seemed all roar, whiplashes, hospital, and cemetery. He was always glad to urge his horse to the return journey, coal dust on his red moustaches. Why, you couldn't leave the milk churn uncovered for a minute.

A man of the country, he was easily put out by noises that were not of nature's make; by grocer's stuff that sought to imitate true meats of the earth; by pavements that entombed roots; by a lamp-post that grew where a tree was. He had married early, snatching Matilda from the village before she could make up her mind to go where all her companions went their dusty way. Five daughters they produced, the first four alike in looks and temperament, blonde and shrill, the fifth of pale brown colouring and slimmer make, quite different. Then, after a while, Matilda died, when she was only about forty, suddenly going tired, almost in a day. She had been out of the place only once, on a visit to her sister, who had married a ship's captain in Bristol.

II

Powell became proud of his five daughters. With every reason. Healthy girls, the four having hair strong and bright as new thatch, the last one an odd and enticing contrast, they filled the farmhouse with a brilliance like perpetual sunshine. Hilda, Bella, Sue and Olwen the blonde ones, and the sultry olive-skinned youngest called Ruth.

Time was, though, when he felt annoyed about his daughters. So many of them. He wanted a son. At least one, he begged Matilda. Sometimes he accused her of deliberately preferring daughters, believing in the witchcraft of suggestion while she carried. After the birth of the fourth she wanted no more, girl or boy. No, she said, *no*. But Powell kept on urging her to one more try. The next one was sure to be a boy; it stood to reason, after four girls. She believed it to be his fault that they were always girls; she couldn't explain why, but there it was.

As a matter of fact, she had much wanted a son herself. She was not thirty after the birth of the fourth girl. She kept on saying that his children would always be girls. He sulked and said, one more try. About this time, a nasty March month, she went off to Bristol for that holiday with her married sister, who was, Powell said disparagingly, a woman of the world, and she stayed two weeks, bringing back unusual presents for everybody.

Not long afterwards, too, she told Powell that—well, he had had his way again. He rubbed his hands excitedly. Sure to be a boy this time. Yes, she said, a little feeling I have, too, that perhaps our luck has changed. But again, on Christmas Eve, a girl came. Powell at last abandoned his ambition for a son and made the best of a bad job by forcing himself to take joy in his daughters' rude vitality. So this last one, Ruth, came in for a late-flowered affection. As soon as she was old enough, he would strap her on to a seat in the milk cart and take her on his round, her good body carefully flounced in fine black-and-white flannel. Matilda took to going to chapel a great deal.

Shortly after Matilda's death, he kept on urging his daughters to get married as soon as they had opportunity, for he felt within himself a grievance against life, and he feared that he might become as sour as the butter he couldn't sell since margarine became popular.

179

'You go out to the world and find fellows,' he said sternly. 'Healthy you are, and the world turns round and customs change. Don't you stand still and wither here like last year's peas.' The responsibility of growing daughters lay heavy on him. But only the first four he urged like that, Ruth being rather young yet.

Fellows there came in abundance. In those days the four daughters rode to the mining valley in a brake from the village, going to socials and tea-parties. They each found a respectable young collier: Powell had announced that to obtain the promised hundred pounds' dowry a daughter must choose a man of decent reputation, chapel-going, and wearing a good navy-blue suit and bowler hat on Sunday. He was alarmed of their wildness at times: strong, hot-coloured girls throwing up their heads in the sun like flaming dahlias on a thick-springing bush.

Matilda the wife going off with such unreasonable suddenness had made him angry too. Only a week ill she was, beginning with a bit of a cold that would have done no harm to a day-hatched chick. It was as if she just walked off over the mountains without once looking back.

It was not right, he had muttered to himself, not right. For a time he was very suspicious and began to doubt his memory of her. Had she been false to him, concealing some woe that worried her? He had fully expected that they both would live until they were between seventy and eighty, and, having been kept warm in the family bosom of their various daughters, die almost together. His life with her had been, except for her inability to produce a son—though he had to admit she had valiantly tried to please him—as nice as eating a crust of home-baked bread with plenty of new butter on it. She was, after all, a good woman, and he never found her taste bad or tart. She worked and cooked with galloping zest, her energy, it seemed, renewed each dawn like a clock wound up.

Simple and ruddy-faced, his flesh close-knit as oak, he was one of those for whom black is still black, white white. But he knew about life and how you have to pay for joy in the world, one way or another. Health, money, and a pleasant nook had been his for too many years.

III

He soon was obliged to cease the native mourning and sombre grief that the sudden cruel blow to his comfort gave excuse. Having so much of young womankind clamouring about him on the farm, he felt important as a patriarch in the Bible. Life bustled round him. The ardour of his daughters was like a good choir singing in competition. In summer they were rich-looking as corn, in winter fresh and stinging as snow. Except, perhaps, Ruth.

Though, she, too, possessed upspringing strength and a manner dashing as a mountain brook in spring, there was on occasion a languid roll to her russet eye, a sensuous droop in her glance, which her direct, unsubtle sisters did not possess. She was the only one who liked to be abed of a morning and leave the cows go hang; she would neglect her share of work in the kitchen too.

Before they were married, her sisters, in anger, would not hesitate to assault her, exasperated by her alien indolence. In such a household as theirs it was a crime to neglect work; the farmhouse was always clean and sweet. Ruth, however, was not too bad, and as she got older she improved—which improvement the sisters declared due to their beatings. She improved because she developed a way of doing work in half the time her sisters took, owing to a different brand of sense in her.

'She got only a bit of flavour, like a marrow,' the first daughter, Hilda, declared. After her mother it was she who was female boss in the household.

'Yes,' agreed Bella, the second daughter, 'she's watery. Not so plain as a marrow, though,' she added justly. 'Sometimes like an actress she is.'

Sue, the third, put in malignly, 'Never will she have much breasts. Like hard little green sprouts they are.' Her own already swung like prize pears. 'And her behind's flat as a lily leaf on the duckpond.'

'Not so flat, though,' Olwen, the fourth, said, 'as the cake she tried to bake on Saturday. Ugh, it would have done to scotch a cart on a hill. God help the man that has her.'

Yet each knew that there was a set-apart quality in their sister that made her like a painted china ornament on the mantelpiece, while they remained usable earthenware jugs on the table.

'Sixteen in April,' the first, Hilda, began again, 'and she can't cut a flannel petticoat yet.'

'She'll never want to,' said Bella disgustedly. 'A guinea silk one from a shop is what her legs crave.'

'Hush, she's coming—'

The four were washing their hair in the little courtyard behind the house; it was a June Saturday afternoon. They washed their bright hair in a tubful of glittering suds and in a hot, splashing sunlight, shaking out the abundant threads and presently swathing their head tops in grey towels, so that they looked as if they wore helmets. This was before they were married and while their mother still lived.

Ruth was entering the gateway. And she allowed the geese to come with her: white, heavy birds with extra-fierce necks. But when with Ruth they trod the earth with a less angry step and their fans seemed to display some measure of ponderous joy, flapping heavily. Now and again she would caress their sinewy throats, liking the excitement that ran through the plumage under her fingers.

'Don't you bring those geese in here,' bawled Hilda. The grey-and-red flagstones were scrubbed daily by her.

Ruth took no notice of the fury of her eldest sister's voice. The geese trod around her; she walked among them, liking their look of attendant court women. Her skin was tawny and she refused to wear the stays her mother had bought for her. 'Keep your temper down,' she called back coolly. 'These geese never misbehave when they're with me.'

But Hilda refused to believe that. She had been suddenly roused by her sister's entrance into the courtyard, suggestive of some royalty attended by a retinue. She dashed in abusively among the geese, ready to strike Ruth. The geese shrank from her swirling skirts, squawking hysterically. Their black eyes glittered, their stiff necks swayed. Hilda's fist struck her sister a blow on the shoulder. Ruth tore off the towel from Hilda's head and took handfuls of the damp, coarse hair in her twisting hands.

An electric shudder passed over the dozen or so geese; their heavy bodies contracted and swelled. Led by a heaving gander, they attacked Hilda, thrusting rods of white anger among her clothes; the beak of one drew blood at an ankle. Hilda kicked out. The other sisters rushed to her rescue. There was a great storm of skirts, flashing arms, and terrible shrieks; the geese began to cower back.

The sisters' father, riding-whip in hand, appeared in the doorway. Behind him the roused face of his wife.

'Oi there,' he roared, 'what's this row? Oi now! Ah!' Seeing a bloody scratch on Bella's cheek and another's hair being pulled like a cow's tail, he strode over and began freely to lay his whip about, commanding a cessatoin of the battle.

Swiftly, like a hawk, the mother pounced on him and tore the whip from his hand. 'Across your own face you want it?' she screamed. 'Leave my daughters alone.'

After much panting and oaths they sorted themselves out. But Ruth had disappeared. The geese, too, were skulking out of the gateway, not hurriedly, but with offended sullenness. Only one remained, ominously crouched on the ground, as though in a swoon. Its leg was broken. Discovering this, the farmer forgot that he had been made a deacon in the chapel only three weeks since; he called his daughters several things.

Ruth hid herself among the willows down by the stream. Sometimes, truly,

182

she longed to adore her sisters. But she felt shut out from them, and she accepted their dismissal of her with a toss of the head. They shut her out from their pranks in the big bedroom and their whispered consultations. Oh, she wished she had been born a boy, so that a pair of trousers would protect her from their gross taunts and their pointing to her slim legs as evidence of her inferiority to them.

She saw them bearing down on her now from the pasture above the stream, four big girls with arms entwined, aflow hair shining like brass. They would grip her and duck her in the stream. She stood on her legs like a hare, then beautifully leapt the rocky stream and disappeared into the small tangled wood the other side. There she crawled into a secret bed among the undergrowth to which she often repaired for an afternoon sleep, liking sleep.

But though her mother teased her with distant respect, as if she were afraid and did not want to let her troubled gaze rest too much on her, she knew her father relied on her for the sweet favours of esteem and affection. She was his darling, and, as she could see already, a good comfort to him. And though she herself was vexed that she was not a boy, she was not too discontented, having early recognised that life is both a kick on the rump and a Christmas party with presents for everybody.

IV

The four daughters marrying, all within two years, widower Powell was left alone with Ruth at the farm. Declaring that only in Him was security, Powell took exclusively to God for some months, walking to chapel on week-days and, if there was no worship, dusting the pews. Then a ghostly and patient heifer died of neglect. Powell shuddered and looked around his possessions. Hedges gone slovenly, the turnip field rank with weeds. In the dairy the pans without lustre: butter unsold and smelly. He shouted at Ruth; she agreed with his complaints and suggested that he sold the farm and bought a pub in the nearby colliery district. He took a fierce offence at that and, since they were standing near it, caught her and threw her in the duckpond, greatly irritating six or seven gosling, who left in grey disorder. Ruth scrambled out and threw a stone at him, hitting an apple tree twenty yards to his left. Later, she got out of him three pounds for a new dress, so had the best of the row. She realised, however, that he worshipped the farm and urged him to get two or three hands to live in, convincing him that even the household work was too much for her.

'You get married, Ruth fach,' he said at last broodily. 'Don't you think of me.' He ended on a cunning whine, though, being a just and simple man, he really wished for her the natural lot of young people. 'My plateful I've had out of life and now I must eat of bygones. The wife, your mother, slipping off like that, so sly, has done for me.'

'I'll stay here with you and bring a husband home some day,' she said comfortingly.

'They are all gone,' he said mournfully, 'to where those coal-pits are. No young chaps hereabouts that want to work clean and old-fashioned.'

After much advertising, though, he got a couple of chaps out of Carmarthen, being obliged to pay their train fares all the way. One—who said everybody called him Nan—was offhand and scowling in manner, though he had a pretty rose-and-white face like an aristocrat; he was twenty and he soon taught the young stallion to jog his hoofs to the 'Flower Song' out of *Carmen*, which he played on a mouth organ. The other, Bandy Isaacs, had legs curving out; Ruth was stirred by his purple-black hair and sulphurous eyes, though the lanky, rude-mannered Nan, complexioned like a girl, excited her most to the bouncing display of hostility roused in her towards men at about this time, her nineteenth year.

At first she led the two young men an evil dance, being the grand young mistress, cracking the whip over them, always finding them jobs to do, insulting them for incompetence, and abusing their home district, where people couldn't speak much English, being so backward. Nastily she spoke to them in English, using words they had never heard before; she held back their wages and, if they went to the mining valley of a Saturday evening, demanded a detailed account of their doings there. First, she put them in the same bedroom, then she separated them, then said the barn was good enough for Bandy and nearly brought it off, if her father hadn't turned unexpectedly critical of this decree.

The young men bore with her. She had that hot power before which, however much it burns them, such as they like to stand. It was Nan who turned on her first. She had made him, in addition to his official farm duties, help her with the domestic labour. At mangle and with pail he worked in the house, a canvas apron round his lean waist, his complexion rose-pink. But he was not deficient in natural attributes, as Ruth found to her cost one day when they were alone in the house and he clumsily knocked over a ewer of sloe gin. She flew out at him, slapping his beautiful complexion. The young man heaved her up as if she were a small sack of potatoes and chucked her on a sofa. He shouted:

'Your backside I'll beat so as you'll never sit down again. Ugly owl of a bitch. Ach, shall I pull you by the hair and throw you to the pigs?'

184

All the time pummelling and doing damage with such wrath that her screeches ceased and she whimpered entreatingly. Suddenly he stopped and, lifting up the tipped ewer, drank the mouthful or so left unspilt. Then cruelly he went out. She rolled off the sofa and beat her fists against the floor, moaning. She did not forgive him for some weeks.

V

Every Sunday four bowler hats hung in a row on the pegs in the passage. They belonged to the husbands of the married daughters: four young colliers earning good money at this time. They and their wives swarmed over the house possessively as resident beetles. Sometimes the wives would take a picture away with them, or a vase, or a piece of brasswork off the dresser, and always a bit of farm produce. Since going to live in the mining valley, where they had neighbours, they had become greedy, ambitious, and show-off.

At this time Ruth did not mind their new habits; she seemed to have no regard for domestic possessions. Only sometimes, if she were in a temper, she would use their stealing as an excuse for denouncing them. Once she threatened to send to Bella's home a policeman, to recover a couple of pewter plates; but again the four married women, two of them extra indignant because they were about to become mothers, assaulted her.

'My daughters,' complained Powell in his prayers at last, 'trot round me like steaming mares. Manes they have, that go up in a storm. Like legs their arms, and their fists like hoofs. Male women they are and of disposition contrary to ladies'. Say to my wife Matilda, where she is up there, that I am weary of earth and my heart grizzles for accommodation in Zion. Crops bad, daughters too much, and people buying that condensed milk in grocer shops. No profit last quarter. Aye, only loss by Thy will, God, though an old man am I getting. Surely not quite fair is it. Have a look at the hairs of my head now and see how they are going white to the roots with worries.'

This was after Hilda had demanded a hundred pounds to help buy a house. The just-gone year had not been successful on the farm, the first to so behave. Powell was frightened; he had never faced failure in his life before, except the semi-failure to produce a son. Orders for milk were falling off. Lorries began to take milk to the mining valleys from distant farms, arriving hours before his yellow-and-green cart. Should he have a lorry? But he couldn't bear thought of it, though he was obliged to ask Bandy and Nan if they could or would drive one. They wouldn't answer one way or the other. At last he decided against the lorry and said quite severely to God:

185

'The lorries go over the mountains fast as deer. But ugly they are and smelly and full of noise. A horse is not ugly and is brown or white or grey or black and shining always, smelling when he drops dung only or pees as Thou made him to, and then for a short time only; and his noise goes in the ear pleasantly as the noise of a woman satisfied or a man well-off. Therefore wherefore the lorries, Almighty? Not allowed they should be. Churns of cow's milk on them is nasty to see. For condensed milk all right, which comes out of the udders of engines and tastes of wheel grease. Uch, don't You allow it for long now.'

He was pleased when he read or heard of motor-car accidents; they seemed to him evidence of the wrath of God. Around him the green-and-lilac mountains disposed themselves grandly as of old; he could forget that the far sides of them were whipped raw by the coal industry. Life was still sweet-smelling to him, in spite of cold-stomach worries. Justly he said again to Ruth, 'Marry some safe chap. One out of the world of coal, if respectable he is. Don't you think of me.' But when he spoke so he looked lonely and old and his air of wanting to do right by her was acting humbug.

She knew that he would loosen his hold on earth and go to pieces if she left him. But she was now itching to get a few slaps from life; she would enjoy a good spree. Or a fight or something. The days on the farm were too nice, too clean, like a bunch of flowers. A pub among the rough collieries now! She had begun to look twenty. But still she loved the old man.

Her shrill sisters kept their predatory eye on her. Each had cut her famous hair in the new fashion, disgusting their father, who withheld his usual money Christmas presents that year. They blamed Ruth and venomously accused her of mischief with the two farm-hands. She said, what of it? And whose body was she using, anyway? They reported to the old man, who told them to mind their own business, unbelieving.

One afternoon she sat singing and shelling beans in the front patch of garden. The roses were bad that summer, short-lived and dry and without scent. No rain at all and the earth hot like a fever. The gate opened and in came a shonny-onions, a beret on his head and on a shouldered pole four plaited strings of golden-red onions. At first the traditional hostility to intruders sprang in her and with arched neck she shouted:

'Out from here. Now then!'

The young vendor rolled dark eyes at her. She stared. There was a lightning flash between them. He said, in his careful learned-up English:

'Two shillings and sixpence one bunch. Cheap. Forty in a bunch. Best onions. Cheap.'

'You come to a farm with onions!' She thought it necessary to shout to a

186

foreigner, for him to understand. 'When we grow them! And very dear yours are.'

'From Brittany,' he said firmly, unmoved by her redness and shouting. 'Best onions. Cheap.' A faint moustache was smudged about his mouth. His thighs and torso seemed sleek and youthful in a very bright pair of striped cotton trousers and a kind of blouse, which oddly attracted her; she smiled in her mouth. She admired his slimness and delicately alert look, like a greyhound.

'Where do you come from?' she asked abruptly.

'Brittany,' he said silkily. 'You will give me please a glass of water?'

'Where is that?' she asked, fumbling among her schooldays.

'France.'

She sat aroused in interest she had never experienced before. She did not move from the stool for a quarter-hour, questioning him with direct, hungry curiosity. He with a dozen more were lodging in Cardiff; they had brought over from Brittany a boatload of onions which they stored in a warehouse, and they were now spread out in the country, taking with them small loads by train. They would stay months before returning to Brittany. He was unmarried, and no, he had never been to Paris. The sea was at the door of his home and behind, flat fields. Yes, he was a Catholic. She sat breathing of his oddness and strangeness and at last remembered the water. Or would he have milk or beer? Or a cup of tea? And some cake?

She took him into the kitchen. Her nostrils were quivering at his alien strangeness. Here was something peculiar out of a far world. She had never seen a moustache smudged down about lips like that before. Nor such smooth-looking nice legs. Ambling and heavy the gait of all she had seen before. He took a glass of beer and a thick wedge of cake.

'All of your onions,' she said, 'I'll buy. But a reduction I must have on a quantity.'

He beamed at her above the tankard. 'Thank you very much, mees,' he said softly, and stood waiting, his dark eyes full and round with wondering interest. She bustled about, stepping on her quick, small feet like a dancer.

'Surely now you are not going back to Cardiff today?' she asked abruptly, almost bad-temperedly.

'I have to fetch more onions,' he said, waiting still, in the strange house. But he had given several quick glances around, and he stood alertly listening.

'You can sleep in our barn,' she said angrily. 'And go back by bus early tomorrow.'

He nodded, suspiciously round-eyed. The heap of onions gleamed a hot gold on the floor. There was a silence; it closed about them. She bustled about again, throwing coals on the fire.

'The daughter of the house I am,' she said haughtily.

And when her father and Nan and Bandy came in for their late meat tea, she announced all particulars of the young man with a bossy confidence, daring them to criticise her determination to offer him hospitality. But Powell welcomed him, after a moment's suspicious glance, and the two talked professionally of soil and vegetables. Only Bandy's horse-long face looked malign; Nan treated the foreigner with an offhand smile.

He was merely a shonny-onions, it was true. And not much mind to him, as far as she could judge. Yet he was fine and smooth and sharp. French? Ah! It was Chinese she had always brooded on, but in the end she knew they would frighten her. What about the French? She did not ponder for long, for it was not her habit. If she pondered, she went into a fog and didn't do anything. She hated looking sideways. Always straight before her, the way she wanted to go. She came to an understanding with the Frenchie that night in the barn. Towards daybreak she got out of the eaves ten pounds, put on her best silk stockings, wrote a note to her father, and was off in a scarlet sunrise over the mountains with the foreigner. His name was André and, though he was frightened, he liked young women very much. This one was overwhelming, but her presence had a bite which was much to his taste.

As for Powell, when he read the note he bellowed and belched. Then he collapsed into a chair and whined for an hour. O Lord, how soon were the days of man over. He was done for. On his eyelids was the shadow of death. Swollen was his heart, also his feet. Let his hair be trimmed by a good barber, ready for death. He compared his soul to a brook that was there yesterday and was now dried up. Then he shouted at Bandy to take the offensive onions and fling them into the duckpond. Towards evening he forgave his daughter, the beautiful kind Ruth, and saw how the young must do something, and in their own way, to save their souls later on.

VI

His small patches of wheat had been cut the next year when she returned, on a hot August Saturday evening. Bandy and Nan had gone by bus to the cinema in the mining valley, and the woman servant returned to her home up in the village. Powell sat trying to read the English language properly in a copy of *John Bull*, which a travelling salesman had left behind. The latch clicked and Ruth stood before him, in a silvery coat and a hat pushed out boldly over her crimpled hair. Blue pearly drops swung from her ears, and in one hand she carried a small suitcase, in the other a black portable gramophone, black as sin. She smiled, though she looked very hot in her coat on a hot August evening.

'Well, well, Ruth fach,' he said suspiciously. What he had read in the periodical had confused and astonished him, and so he wondered if his sight was playing him a trick.

'There's bare the place is!' she said, glancing round, her gaze beginning to glitter as she realised that her sisters had been at their antics again.

'Aye,' he said heavily, 'bare, bare.' He tidied up his long moustaches, into which he had dribbled. But they still sprouted well and still they held their tint of sorrel-red.

She was back in the house as though she had taken an afternoon trip to the seaside. She soon had a meal going, six rashers off the frosty-looking hunk of bacon hooked to a beam, and eggs fried in the singing salty fat, very delicious and smelling of home. He finished the peculiar story in the paper and, called to the table, went. Grace was asked, the evening being so near Sunday. The coat glistened on the back of a chair.

'Nice coat!' he mumbled wonderingly. 'You bought it in that place—now, what is it called? Paris?'

'No, Bristol,' she said.

His jaw dropped. He waited cautiously, dull anger stirring in him. She asked after her sisters. Vindictively, she got out of him a long list of what they had taken from the house and from him; he saw her cheekbones harden, her eyes shine like oil. From these signs he assumed that she intended staying at home.

'France you liked very much?' he suggested at last.

Secure in her air of success, she told him presently that she had got no further than Bristol, where a rich seed merchant had wanted to marry her. 'But I had to come back,' she said flatly; 'and a big trunk full of things I have in the station for you to fetch on Monday in the milk cart.' She implied that, having seen the world and obtained her fling, she was satisfied now, and intended settling where she rightly belonged. She spoke of towns as if, for human beings of good class and wholesome tastes, they were places unfit to inhabit.

'Why for you didn't go to France?' he demanded. 'With that shonny-onions.'

She shook her head. 'Very simple he was,' she said dismissingly.

'And here was I telling people you were travelling in foreign parts!' he exclaimed. Shocking that she had been across only a troughful of water to Bristol. Misbehaving not far from the doorstep! He wanted to seize her, to throw things at her. But she was so grand and well-dressed and a lady. And his anger was not like it used to be. He felt like a tree in winter, draughty and without warmth of leaves. So he went over by the fire and sulked.

'How's the milk now?' she asked, businesslike.

He entered into a long, slow whine of his troubles. Only two churns a day now. Mothers fed their young with condensed milk and even chapel ministers ate margarine. Soon there'd be no cows left in the land, for was not margarine made out of turpentine, boiled old boots, and cast-off clothes; condensed milk out of coal and drowned corpses taken from the river in London?

'We must have a lorry,' she said decisively, 'and take the milk where it's wanted.'

He looked at her wearily, his nervous fingers feeling his paunch, that still showed round as a harvest moon. He shrank from her decision and yet was glad that she spoke so, beyond him. And for one thing he was grateful—that the grave remained as it ever was, peaceful, as created by God. He watched Ruth's swinging hips, in their bright-spotted silk. Yes, punishment was due to her. But she was grown, and he couldn't beat her.

'For this what you've been doing,' he said darkly, 'you must pay. In chapel. A lot in the collection plate, and a Sunday-school teacher you must become— very short of them we are.'

'Oh, all right,' she said.

The men arrived. Bandy pursed his lips malignly and his bandy legs went bandier with fear; she had always been like a Fury pursuing him, but since she had gone his life had been dull without battle. Nan, who had come to man's mental estate since her departure, looked her over patronisingly, as though she were an ewe in the County Show, a second-prize one, but still worthy of notice. She looked at them closely for a second or two and then set about the domestic tasks exactly as she had left off a year ago. The day woman she sacked in the morning.

So she settled down, after she had powerfully disposed of her clacking and squawking sisters, who were filled with black joy and horror at her evil . . . 'Now then, Father,' they pointed out, 'see what a bad lot she is and don't you leave her the farm.' But he, whose aspect had suddenly become mild and beneficent again, said, 'Peace now, peace for the sunset that is on my days.' Scandalised, they filed out of the house, their husbands under their bowler hats, and Ruth at the door calling, in a low, harmonious voice, 'Thief,' for stealing this, or that, meaning some Nantgarw tureen, or oak chair, or steel fender.

She chose Nan, but waylaid Bandy first, seeing that Nan was so rude. Bandy it was who must have the lorry; his nerves were substantial and he was a male man who could shave twice a day, et cetera. She gave him a book from her trunk, which he could not read, writing in it, 'Bandy, his book from Ruth his friend,' but to Nan she gave only a small bundle of picture postcards

190

depicting ships, also out of the trunk, which she kept locked. For her father she had brought two suits of pink silk underwear, which he wore when some big preacher preached in chapel or at some other festival.

But Nan was so rude, for he seemed to know she was glad of his new pushed-out chin, his assured stuck-out knees, that she saw he was a man meet for her to marry. More than once he told her that she smelt of French onions. His gaze was baldly lewd, as if she were a penny peep-show, Paris by Night, in the Fair. Before Nan's eyes she cupped her hand over Bandy's chin and drew him out into the garden at night-time, swinging her hips. When she returned, Bandy very hostile, Nan would be extra abusive, more loudly insulting, so that she was appeased a little.

Till at last, on Christmas Eve, her birthday, he gave way. She had dressed a tree, and among the dark, delicate boughs she had hung a penny matchbox, packed in brown paper and tied with cotton, his name scrawled neatly on it. Dressed in white, she lit the purple, green, and gold candles, her face sad and serious for once. All day she had been sombre and given to irritable exclamations, but now she had gone to bed, Nan unhooked his little parcel and found inside the matchbox a note, 'Ruth loves Nan.' So instead of going to his own room he went to hers, throwing off his clothes without saying a word.

And later, softly weeping with joy, she held up a cloth like a red-stained trophy. So he stayed, and the second time had nothing of hate.

VII

The mountains stay still and in the mornings say their say like trumpets and in the evenings sleep like young lions, their green hair about their shoulders. Sunday morning it is now, and nothing extraordinary is there in that. And yet extraordinary it is. Tidy is my heart, gone is my gout, and the air goes in my nostrils like the smell of apples. And the man Nan says of my daughter good things, asking for her in marriage.

Thus Powell's mind moved, as he stood on the doorstep of his farmhouse, looking around the fresh winter-cold domain. He was pleased. Master Nan was a good young farmer and had no hankerings after frivolous things. And Ruth, with native cunning, had preserved her jewel among the thieves and pawnbrokers of towns, and yet had not gone unshod, unclothed, or unfed. Virtue lost must be tolerated in a person like a wooden leg, he mused further, but virtue preserved is money hoarded in a bank that will never go bankrupt.

So no more he shouted at her, his cheeks going purple in repressed excitement. And the grave, a beautiful, beautiful bed, seemed nearer, and now he would lie in it with no worries as to who was despoiling his beloved land. He heard the snap of his closed ledger.

Bandy, bitter and baulked, handed in a month's notice when he heard, saying, 'I am going to Canada, by sea.' Farmers were wanted there, and there people were honest and one-faced. Ruth threaded new tapes in the knees of his flannel drawers and gave him, out of the trunk, a Bristol photo of herself seated on a sofa beside a Grecian temple, a bunch of roses in her hand. She urged him to take care of his weak chest in foreign winters.

The lorry was ordered. Nan took lessons. Powell said he would not ride in it. Nan could take churns to the valleys, but he would deliver milk near by in the cart, drawn by his inseparable friend, the grey mare Vic. The lorry was to be, however, his wedding present to them. And the farm was to be theirs too; a new will was drawn up.

Ruth had the pleasure of cutting two of her sisters in the main street of the mining valley, where she and Nan had gone one Saturday afternoon to buy things. 'Greediness has taken their minds,' she said to Nan indignantly, 'since they took to living here. Horrid is the place, surely. So grand are they by coming here, stuck up, always fighting their neighours for the advantage of ths and that.'

'Ugly the place is,' Nan agreed. 'But full of life.'

The place was roaring in its Saturday night, the streets were in conflagration. Men were chucked out of pubs and fought in the gutters; strike leaders shouted at some corners, roving preachers at others. As a woman stepped briskly out of a ladies' lavatory, she was set upon by a married-looking woman waiting for her beside the shadow of a doorway; and the shrill ancient accusation of harlot was mingled with scratched-out blood. Stale, smelly air was breathed out of the cinemas. The dark chapels, squat as toads, raised their faces stonily; but tomorrow there would be nice singing in them, and repentance.

'There's a bellyfull here,' Ruth remarked.

'And a belly-ache, I should say,' Nan said. Very country-bred, and refined in a queer way, he, too, was always astonished at the goings-on of industrialism, like his father-to-be.

They took the bus back. Only round the corner of the mountain, like turning the page of a picutre book, the scene changed, and there was country such as the Almighty had in mind when shifting the hills about and arranging pasture, wood, stream, and bush-clump in such manner as pleased His shrewd eye. White now with the moon.

THE SKULL

Stuffed with treasures and monuments, the stout old church, like everything else, sweltered under the burning sky. It lay cumbersome and added-to, in the old town where eighteenth-century houses still had a suave shabbiness and where there was still a village Green, with a misty cedar through which white doves flew—fanning the sultry air now. A mile away the beach bawled with trippers, the sea's blue hands slapping at innumerable pallid bathers with an incessant primeval scolding. A decrepit old harbour separated the clots of villas and hotels from the genteel parish where the church had given a last sanctuary to so many centuries of parishioners.

Millicent paused at the churchyard gate. Should she go in? Everywhere was so hot, but churches were always cool. Like a pricking sword, the sun had pursued her everywhere. She ought to be in the sea. But that afternoon, feeling grievous with a general dislike of everything, she had left the others and said, amid expressions of disbelief, that she wanted to see the well-known church—the first excuse that entered her bitter head.

Such austere and going-off behaviour was allowed her. As Alice had said, she had lately endured more trouble than a woman of thirty-two ought to be expected to bear. Only yesterday a letter had arrived at the hotel from her solicitor saying that George had finally rejected the idea of a divorce. Disreputable lout. Millicent had proudly declared that it didn't really matter, she had finished with men altogether, for the rest of her life. Alice, who had always done without them, said 'Bravo', and bought her a large bunch of white violets.

So perhaps it was natural that she should feel an inclination to go for meditation into a church. She wanted to feel peace and security—which emotions old churches managed, somehow, to supply. 'I'm feeling the same urge which drove women into convents', she told herself, 'I want the drugs of prayer and austerity.' Had the unspeakable George such power over her, after all! Driving her into convents and churches. She began to turn away from the gates.

Then she remembered about the famous windows: she liked stained-glass. And she was so very hot; and her face probably was raddled with suffering, to say nothing of the ferocious sunshine splashing on it. She entered the churchyard and sat on a lichened tombstone shaded by a yew; she took out her mirror and accessories and decked her face, swinging back into a rich bunch the damp heavy gold curls writhing down her neck. Thank God she was still more than possible, she told herself honestly. A little comforted, she strolled towards the church, vaguely aware of sounds of labour, digging, coming from the far side of the nave.

Inside there was no one and a gentle silence. It was the quiet of fading things, like a great wood at fall of leaf. Even the brilliance of the windows was of the nature of autumnal sunsets. Millicent sat in a pew. Cool it certainly was. And she would not think. Only let herself drift along on a stream of cool nothingness: like Ophelia.

But she had been married in a church. Quite as big and laden with monuments as this one, the pulpit in the same position. Always visionary, at once she saw George standing at the altar-rails, waiting, looking unnaturally sleek and terribly tailored. Even so, he still had his petulant spoilt-boy expression. Nasty little bourgeois. Though no one could deny he was handsome.

'But no brains,' Alice had warned, 'no understanding. He'll treat you like a matter-of-fact. He'll want to switch you on and off for his own benefit as if you're the electric light.'

Nag, nag, nag. Was there no peace, no escape anywhere! Millicent's mind began to whimper. Thirty-two and her life like a cheap tragedy. True, she had her talent, she could earn her fifty or so guineas often, designing her severe but pleasing country cottages. She counted her blessings. Yet all the same she slipped to her knees, on to a pad placed conveniently in the pew, and bent her whimpering head, atavistically. But almost at once, feeling foolish, she jumped back to the seat. Angrily she looked round. What submission. Bah! She rose hastily and began to examine the church. Soft thudding sounds still came from outside, like the slow muffled beat of a drum. Occasionally a man's voice called, out there. She took a sixpenny guide from a table and determinedly began inspection of the monuments.

There seemed much memorial to cruelty. For the murder of a bishop by angry sailors, a former vicar and his parishioners did penance by walking through the town with naked feet and legs, accompanied by rods to the 'conveniently bare limbs.' A duke, murdered too on the Green, had his 'boweles buried herein.' On tablets were other reminders of arson, robbery, dreadful wars, and piracy on the high seas. The church seemed like a ponderous stony lament over the sins of mankind. Millicent turned to the shiny windows, sighing.

They were scarcely more cheerful. A St. Sebastien with red rays of hair was pierced with eight arrows; he recovered from them only to be clubbed to death next door. A St. Dorothea walked prettily to her execution carrying a

194

basket of fruit and Tudor roses, though she looked extremely happy. In her prison cell at Antioch a horrid prune-coloured Satan appeared to St. Margaret and swallowed her. But she proved too much for him; he burst asunder. Yet her miraculous escape availed her nothing—she was led to the block and beheaded. In another window an azure-bodied devil with webbed white feet wheeled in a yellow barrow a bearded damned soul into the mouth of hell, the passenger, however, seeming unconcerned. Scourgings were popular with the beautiful angels in the transept. And elsewhere a frenzied woman in a ruby dress beat off from her baby Herod's brutal soldiers with their brandished swords.

The sight of so many torments, brilliantly executed in colours though they were, did not ease Millicent. Particularly she was affected by the charming baby threatened by the soldiers: he was so plump, his body stained such a tender gold. Ah, she tried to comfort herself, there had been disasters greater than hers. What was her petty trouble compared to these tortures celebrated in church windows! But they happened so long ago. And they all looked so merely physical. Hers, hers was mental, a dolour of broken faith, a funeral march of jangled resentments.

So she told herself, staring at a stone slab in the floor, under which was buried Elizabeth Cook, aged 32. Her own age, she remembered with a start. O Death—But she went on blindly, and found a model of a ship standing in a low niche: infants placed in it would never be drowned, it was said. She stared at the ship. Alas, she told herself, it seemed she at least would never be able to test the truth of the legend. And self-pity again threatened her.

Once more she sat in a pew. She had been working against the grain, that's what was wrong with her. Planning that Scottish Town Hall, harassed to death by pedantic councillors. She was run down. And a week at the seaside was not enough. She'd have to chuck things and go right away, a long voyage somewhere, over the sea. To a completely different land.

But were any lands so different, was the sea so health-giving as they said! Perhaps for ailments of the body. But wherever she went, across the purest oceans, she would take her bitter woe with her, the anger of a let-down woman, the gnawing anxiety of a mind baulked of its harmony.

Churches, after all, were bad for one. They made one brood. She was getting no peace here. In a minute she'd be going over all the sordid business again: once more she'd be hearing her own voice screaming frightful abuse. And George's taunt, 'You're too bloody clever,' he had said to her, 'for me, and you're earning too much money.' Unintelligent lout. All his kind ached for the old-style women. He couldn't bear it that she was his equal and perhaps his superior in the matter of tackling the world. She had possessed power. And he

195

had had his vengeance. She understood how with a pretty little simpering doll he would feel himself a man. But not with her.

Perhaps, after all, she told herself bitterly, women were meant to be simpering and submissive, men bossy and directive. Or had such men as George failed to catch up with the flowering of the female mentality? That was it, she decided. Pausing before another window, she looked at it sombrely. In a mediaeval garden with beds of herbs and a fountain, a seductive Eve stood beside the Tree. She was full-fleshed and heavily-bosomed, like an Edwardian comedienne. Crimson fruit hung lusciously in the Tree. Around the trunk coiled the Serpent, with the head and bust of a woman and the paws of a cat: with a paw this ironical-looking beast handed to Eve one of the fattest of the fruits. Millicent wondered if her mood had coloured the opinion she was arriving at—that the window was bestial. Perhaps it was meant to be. The Eve certainly belonged to the old hierarchy of men-bound women, who obediently puffed out their curves for the better accommodation of men: beds. . . . Scowling, she turned away from the garish window. It seemed to mock at her.

Dragging her steps towards the door, she told herself that she was destined for immolation. Gone, gone was her beautiful youth. And, looking back, it seemed the merest scrap of joy. A lot of work. And a lot of preparation for something that had never come off. Perhaps she would be a comfortable woman now had she disciplined and shut herself in a villa with George and bred. If only that dynamo had not been started going in her head!

'Perhaps,' she muttered, treacherous to herself in this moment of despair, 'it would be acts of grace if several airmen dropped bombs on all the women's colleges: Girton in particular.' Twisting the thought in her mind, she went forward into the brisk sunlight. But it was men who lagged behind, men, she added, tossing her head in the hard glare. They would not learn how to use these women for their benefit. She decided that there was some corrupt and shameful root at the bottom of this unwillingness: a decadence in men.

She paused. What was she to do with herself now? Go back to the hotel for tea? God damn those droning hotel teas. She could not face one again, unappeased. Or the dreadful ceremonious dinner, with Alice's tactful efforts to entertain her, Alice's humble entreating flattery. No. But unanchored and floating above the world like this, she supposed, women committed suicide.

Unseeing, she wandered towards the sounds of labour the other side of the nave. She was brought to a standstill by a barrier. Looking up, she saw that a slice of the churchyard was being interfered with, horribly. A large square of earth stretching from the nave wall had been dug deep and taken away, and there in the sunken place graves gasped and brick tombs yawned hollowly.

Small houses of the dead lay shattered, uncovered of their old brown earth, a peaceful little underground city broken into. Three or four men were digging among the narrow broken walls of those dwellings, and from time to time they tossed upon a heap beside them some brownish-white objects which their implements had thrown up.

Fascinated, Millicent leaned against the barrier and watched. She felt that her eyes had gone dry and old and indifferent. And she was visited by thoughts suitable to the scene before her. Not very original thoughts, she knew. Such as: Why fear and retreat from an event that has to be faced, why not look upon this ravished and helpless little town as a borough brutally without feeling and fortunate in that? Desecration there was none; a grave doesn't exist, there are no graves in the whole world. There are only omissions in the land of the living: there is a sudden hole in the air, which is immediately filled. But of places of the dead, none. The tears that undulate over grief-swollen cheeks and drop, one by one, on funeral flowers are indignant drops of water lamenting for ourselves. We have no place to rest, we will not deliciously stretch our feet, turn on an eternal pillow and take our blessed ease. We are nothing, there is nothing.

Millicent suddenly found that her mind was screaming this last observation, her fingers drumming a quick tattoo on the barrier. She quietened herself. Then, malevolently, she wanted to go down to the sunken place and meander among the shattered tombs. Her excellent eyesight detected a pale protuberance in the slice of earth nearest to her: the bald pate of a skull securely wedged. Her fingers itched to pluck the thing out; she felt that her nerves would be eased and strengthened in the act. She would have laid hands contemptuously on death . . . But what for?

What indeed? She asked herself as she turned abruptly away, unanswerably. And there would be fuss and astonishment if she asked permission to go down among the graves: very likely the foreman would refuse. What right had she to go plucking out skulls that did not belong to her! And to what end? She imagined the scandalised frown of the foreman.

Graves, graves all about her, stuck among healthy trees. Reminders to the living but of no value to their inhabitants. Rightly was the slice being raked over the other side of the nave: probably the ground was needed for transactions of the living. She read blurred inscriptions and was surprised that so many young people had been obliged to return to earth. A baker's dozen were interred hereabouts, all between the ages of twenty and thirty. What sore ailments had beset their dewy young flesh? Or had they gone from a disquiet of the spirit, unrequited of love perhaps? Millicent romantically decided that they had all died of love. And she felt herself preparing to weep, forgetting her dark cynicism of a moment before.

To prevent such a thing, she left this tragic patch of the churchyard and wandered down a flagged walk between rows of tombstones so massive that they surely protected aldermen and mayors; great chests of toad-coloured stone, clumps of withering violets sprouting out of their base. And suddenly, turning a corner of this sombre boulevard, she came abruptly on a live young man, who was seated on a wheelbarrow, smoking a cigarette.

So unexpected was this apparition, breaking into the silence of that place of death, that she drew up sharp, in a stupid flurry. She looked at him, almost angrily. He was so calm, enjoying his cigarette, half-clothed in the heat. And he stared back at her so unflinchingly that she thought him ill-mannered.

'Good afternoon. Hot,' he murmured politely.

'Yes,' she answered, dourly. Her gaze fell to the barrow. It contained three bulging canvas sacks, on which the young man was seated, comfortably it seemed. Intently she gazed at these bags. Then her eyes travelled back to the young man's sun-scorched face.

'What's in those sacks?' she enquired.

He was one of the workmen, of course. His trousers were covered with white dust and caked with earth, and he wore a dirty shirt, open to the waist, the sleeves rolled up. From him came a warm brown glow, out of his sun-burnt flesh and supple muscles: he seemed excessively, almost terribly alive in that place, good-looking. He grinned.

'You'd like to know, wouldn't you!'

Her demand had sounded peremptory to the point of vindictiveness. Again she looked at him: she felt that her gaze was being dragged out of her. Something flickered, like amusement, through his brown eyes, also glowing. He was quite young.

'They're bones,' she answered herself. To her ears her voice sounded like a croak.

The young man jumped off the barrow. 'Here,' he said, laughing, 'look at 'em.' Briskly he tipped one of the bags. A shower of bones fell into the barrow-ribs and bones of arm, leg and breast, broken and complete. They were very shrunken and as if stained with gold. He picked up an arm-bone. 'You'd think they'd smell,' he said, 'but they don't.' He pushed it towards her nostrils. It had a faint clean odour of earth.

She drew back. She felt herself go wan and weak, and for a moment, with hunted eyes, she glanced back along the avenue of the dead through which she had come. Her soul seemed to stagger within her. Then, nervously as a high-

198

strung, high-bred mare, she returned to the workman. She asked, broodingly: 'What are you doing with them?'

'Taking them to that crypt there, where I've put about a ton already.' He pointed to a miniature flight of steps descending to under the church. Watching her, he seemed very ready to chatter.

Millicent drew nearer. 'Isn't there a skull?' she asked, peering down into the barrow. 'A skull?' she repeared entreatingly.

The young man considered her, admiringly. The gold of her curled hair swung moist and heavy under his face, as she bent to the barrow, her lively thick-springing hair. Noisily he breathed its perfume. She heard him and looked up, meeting his interested gaze.

'Working here,' he said seriously, 'among these old bones, it's nice to see a young lady.'

'There *are* a lot of dead here,' she agreed croakingly.

Again he grinned. They stood talking. He told her that the graveyard was being cleared to make room for a new transept. All the graves were very old. Coffins had rotted away to pulp—except one, which had broken asunder as they came to it, revealing inside a complete skeleton with a long scarf of red silk intact round the neck and a faded old bonnet on the hairless skull. No treasure such as rings or brooches had been found in any of the graves. His old granny was buried with her gold wedding ring, he said. He sat full again on the bags of bones, partly obliterating them. Then again he restlessly stood up. He was long and loose-limbed, and brown as a spaniel: the glow of his rust-coloured eyes shone out full on her.

Millicent stood intent. She knew she had placed a strangeness in the air, and she saw it was gathered into his eyes and his smile. Now he seemed to be inviting her to partake of some celebration, looking at her seductively: it was as though the field of death on which they stood roused them to a sense of rich and passionate possessions. Again she asked: 'Where are the skulls? Show me a skull.'

'There's several in the crypt. I put two there yesterday. Like to come and see them? I'll light the candle.'

Once more, as if trapped, she glanced back down the avenue of mausoleums. The dead did not rise from their tombs; they were gone for ever. There was nothing, nothing. A kind of mournful ecstacy beat in her heart. She remembered the fearless saints in the windows, and the obese, mocking Eve. That day she had undergone a minor death, had a foretaste of the larger death. And she was still mysterious and enchanted from the anaesthetic . . . But she would like to touch some belonging of the final thing, she would like to see and handle a skull. So she told herself.

The young man preceded her down the curl of steps. A small door opened on to a dank gloom. She hesitated, stooping in the doorway, and he lit a thick stump of candle. The ring of yellow light showed two great heaps of tangled bones. He delved among them and fished out a skull. 'Here it is, a fine one,' he breathed softly. The buried place was ponderous with silence.

The skull grinned, the young man holding it out to her smiled. She still crouched in the doorway, and looked from one to the other: she could not reach to the offered skull, and the young man did not advance. Only he smiled, and looked at her with his warm living eyes. She stepped into the crypt.

'Take care of the steps,' he said. There were several more.

She took the skull. A small tuft of greenish hair still clung to the plate. 'A woman's,' she murmured. She meditated on the fact of the grin of skulls being so full of malice.

'There's nothing in handling them, is there!' the young man remarked, holding up the candle the better for her to see.

He stood above her. The candle dropped out of his hand. 'Ha!' he said, 'and I left the matches on the floor.' A scrap of grey light skulked outside the door; they were in darkness. The young man floundered round. She stood holding the skull, forgiving this clumsiness—he was so young. She began to move. They met, and instantly one arm went round her.

'Don't fall,' he murmured, breathing upon her hair.

For a moment or two she beat him away, a conventional hostility whipped up in her. The skull fell from her hand to the stone floor. 'It's smashed,' he said, as her struggles ceased. She felt her feet grind on the fragments: that grin was no more. The warmth of living flesh held her.

The young man kissed her gently. He gave her an opportunity to release herself from his embrace. But she did not go. They kicked away the pieces of the skull. And at one moment her heart cried out, with piercing joy, an inscription she had read an hour before; *O Death, where is thy sting?*

She stumbled back up the curl of the stairs. But she met the bright sun like Venus rising out of the waters, warm and gazing round on the interesting earth. The young man followed her, slowly, a little uneasy of his reception. She turned and faintly smiled. Delighted, he laughed.

'Those old skulls and bones must be jealous,' he said.

She looked about her, hesitatingly. There was an embarrassed pause. She felt him examining her, for the first time aware of her as a social person. Then, quite calmly and conventionally, he suggested that they met again. But his politeness had liking. She shook her head. 'I cannot.'

'I'm not good enough?' he said, without irony or malice.

200

'It's not that.' She began to move away a step or two, balanced lightly, easily, harmoniously, on her expensively clad feet. 'It can't be . . . my affairs being as they are,' she concluded.

'All right . . . But I'll be here for the next month or so, if you change your mind. Glad to see you any time.' He took up the handles of the wheelbarrow. 'Lucky the foreman's gone off to the office,' he laughed.

She walked back down the avenue of tombstones. She saw some violets, still fresh, and picked three or four, glad of their purple. And all her woes of the afternoon seemed foolish. She began to plan out her life for the coming season. George had no place in it. He had become a shadow. There were other men in the world, and many things to do. A touch of vindictiveness in the hang of her lips, she set her face towards the town, barely, trampling down the startled fear that threatened to overwhelm her and which was like the rush of coming awake after a particularly vivid dream. The fear of nothingness had gone, magically, her individuality was brisk within her—no more drooping willow-like over these graves, shedding futile tears . . . She'd have to begin looking around the world again: it was worth while.

THE WAGES OF LOVE

It was a wet early November evening when Olga, after twelve years' disgraceful absence, arrived home again. The rusty mountains wept, the bobbing chrysanthemums in the back gardens were running with liquid coal-dust. A wind whipped through the valley and rubbed stingingly at her silken legs. Above her ginger fur coat her sick done-in face peered like someone in awful woe.

She found no welcome. No one to meet her. Leaving her bags at the station, she climbed a steep road among sullen stony dwellings flung down like sneers on the world. At one of these, the nineteenth in a long row, she knocked timidly, her tongue licking over her dry lips. Wagons clanked under the slope below, backing out of the colliery yard. A woman in a shawl and man's cap hurried past, carrying a jug. After a long interval, the door opened and a bulky woman stood there, on her face a frown ready to develop into active hostility. The two were sisters.

'Sara,' murmured Olga timidly, 'you got my telegram?'

'Yes, I did. Telegram indeed! A fit I nearly had. Thought someone was dead. 'Stead of which,' she added in great grievance, 'you it is.' After blocking the doorway during this and narrowly scrutinising her sister and the fur coat, she stood aside grudgingly. 'I s'pose you'd better come in. But I wonder you didn't go to Mary Ann's house, not come here . . . I hope the neighbours haven't seen you,' she went on in aversion.

Falteringly Olga entered. From the ajar doorway down the dark passage came subdued murmurs. 'There's some of the family,' Sara said, adding jeeringly: 'Come to have a look at you. Go in.'

Olga shrank. But hadn't she come back to seek forgiveness? And to mortify her wicked flesh? Entering the kitchen, she made an effort to strengthen her sagging neck, that was still lovely, but once had been proud as a swan's. Around the family hearth of her childhood a ring of hostile faces looked up in the red firelight. Red angry faces.

This was the Prodigal Daughter: the Black Sheep: the Family Disgrace; whose tricks (they declared, in spite of an operation for gall-stones) had sent her mother to the grave, her father following not long afterwards. This was she who had wounded irreparably the family honour, stained its chaste history. Her sisters never sat in chapel now but with deflated seats.

'Fur coat, ha!' Blodwen, her other sister screeched. 'Come down here to show-off, has she?'

'More likely,' Sara barked, 'down and out she is, and come to live on our poor backs. They got to dress up. Strumpet!'

'Light a lamp,' called Tomos, Blodwen's husband, 'and let us see her plain.' The lamp was lit. They saw her pinched, defeated face, her sunken eyes, and their power rose.

'What you come back for?' cried Blodwen, blue with rage. 'Don't the men look at you no more?'

'Hush, the neighbours will hear,' exclaimed Sara. 'And she must be hid.'

'Only a coffin'll ever hide the same as her,' groaned Blodwen.

Sara's husband Evan, with his face like a pious goat, sharpened his two front teeth on his lip. He had never seen the famous sister before. The two men were dominated by their bellicose wives, and looked at her bleakly down their noses. She stood mute and haggard amid the jabbering abuse. It was her punishment and she accepted it. After a while she sank into a chair and bowed her head. Desolate silence was in her broken eyes. She looked like one who bled from some awful secret agony.

'What's come of that elderly brush-manufacturer that kept you?' taunted Sara. 'Left you in the gutter, no doubt.'

'And the grand foreigner with the diamonds,' sneered Blod. 'Looking for someone younger now, eh?'

'And the big stockbroker with the gouty feet, ha? And the fifty more! Hussy!' screamed Sara, forgetting the neighbours in her wrath. 'She comes back like a bag of bad old 'tatoes.'

Evan lifted his two teeth: 'Miss Olga, sloppy it is to come back here tail between legs. Foreign to us you are now.'

At last Olga whimpered: 'I want to come back and rest; I want, I want—' The hot kitchen swirled round her, she flopped off the chair to the floor. They stared at her in anger.

'Damme, ill she is,' said Tomos.

'A glass of cold water chuck in her painted face,' sang Blod.

'Put her to bed here I shall be obliged to!' wailed Sara. 'In my clean sheets! What's the matter with the duffer?'

They had planned to send her flying, after they had unloaded their opinions of her, up to Mary Ann's cottage hidden in the mountains. Mary Ann was the fourth sister and not quite right in the head. She was to keep the trollop where no one would see her. But what did the disgrace want to come back for? Was she greedily after her share of goods left by poor Mam and Dad that she had sent to the grave? She shouldn't have it, the bad one.

'Her fine feathers been plucked proper, plain it is,' declared Blod. 'Something bad's the matter with her. Best to put her to bed, Sara,' she added, gratified that the baggage wouldn't be sullying *her* house, down the valley. 'And throw her out soon as she's gor her legs back.'

It had to be done. But for some days Olga tossed in a fever. No doctor was called, and the presence of the disgrace was kept secret from the district. All the family were great members of Salem, the Baptist chapel on the hill: Blod's husband was even a deacon. Horrible if it was found that the outcast had come back. But more horrible still if she died on them, so that her sinful carcass would have to be buried from Sara's clean house. The provoked Sara nursed her with malign art, not wanting her to die and yet wanting it. She said presently to the wan, thin woman: 'Broth you want, and poultry—for out of my house you must get, quick. Haven't you got no money? Only a few shillings in your purse. Coming back here,' she began to rage, 'and expecting hard-working persons to feed your useless flesh. Ach, you bitch, get better.'

'I'm thirsty,' Olga whimpered.

'Well,' jeered Sara, 'think I've got champagne for you?'

Olga then whispered this: 'I've got over five hundred pounds in the bank.'

Sara laid down the cup of cold water she was bringing and excitedly called downstairs to the kitchen: 'Evan, put the kettle on. Poor Olga would like a cup of tea. Fetch nice cakes from the shop and a pot of bloater paste.' To Olga she said: 'There now, there now, very upset I've been, and my tongue running away with me. But nursing you I've been like a hospital. See, there's better you are! Let me comb your hair and wash your face tidy now.'

And she freshened the room. The dusty ewer on the washstand she cleaned and filled with water, brought a tablet of scented soap and a new pink towel; she plucked chrysanthemums from the back garden. Then, after feeding the trollop, she took shawl and umbrella and rushed down to her sister Blod's house.

Olga didn't get well, however. Some days she opened her empty eyes and whimpered that she wanted to go to chapel, other days she cowered down in the sheets and wouldn't speak. Something awful was consuming her. But visitors began to fill her room, including cousins and aunts and uncles from right down the valley, who used to declare that never would they go near her—no, not even to attend her funeral. Only Mary Ann, being in her head but fourteen ounces to the pound, was kept out of the news. The first visitor was Blodwen, who brought a tapioca pudding and wheedled:

'Olga, you never seen my son Ivor. Growing up he is now and wants to be a Baptist minister. But there's expensive are the college fees! "Oh dear me," I said to him, "no, Ivor, you must go and work in the pits like your father, for poor as dirt are your hard-working parents." But wouldn't it be grand for our family, Olga, if we had a chapel minister in it! Our sister Sara was saying it would wipe out a lot, indeed.'

Cousin Margaret appeared and said: 'Well, Olga! When better you are a visit you must pay me. But very poor my house is—my Willie John hasn't been working for two years. I been praying a long time for a suite of furniture for the parlour, then I could take a school-teacher lodger—'

Sara asked with loving bullying: 'Your will you've made, Olga? Better you're getting, but best it is to be on the safe side, and if you go before me I'll bury you first-class, I promise. To go on with, shall I borrow ten quid off you at once? Wages been dropping in the pit,' she groaned, 'and if I don't find money soon, bums will be knocking on the door and turn us all out.'

Aunt Gwen boldly asked for a piano and a pair of tortoise-shell glasses to replace her old pince-nez. Evan asked for a motor-bike and Tomos wanted a pair of greyhounds.

They walked in and out of her room daily, waiting till she was well enough to grant their requests. Sara gor her bags up from the station and was astonished at the silks and satins therein: she tucked them away in her cupboards. Carefully she fed Olga with broths, to keep her a while from Jordan's brink. Not that Olga would eat much. Her great hollow eyes stared emptily, her wrinkling flesh had no more life than tissue paper.

At last Sara cried out in curbed exasperation: 'What's the matter with you? Repenting too much you are. Bad you've been, but others in this world have been badder. Tell me now when you're ready for that cheque-book out of your bag.

Olga babbled strangely: 'I want to go chapel next Sunday.' She wanted to go to Salem, the chapel of her childhood, where she had been pure!

'No, no,' said Sara hurriedly, 'not yet. Very cold it is there, the heating system's broken down.' And downstairs she said to the family: 'Is she going daft like our Mary Ann? Wants to go to chapel, if you please, like we do!'

'She started to go wrong,' Blod mused, 'after Johnny Williams got killed.' Johnny had courted Olga long, long ago, till he got caught under a fall of roof in the pit. In the faraway days of her chaste girlhood.

Sara said: 'There's a lesson to us all she is! No kick in her now. Falling apart she is like a rotten old cask.'

'Yes,' Blod began to screech, 'but she's been dancing her jigs plenty in London while we stayed by here respectable and working our fingers to the bone.'

They resumed their wheedling of the ailing slut: they put pen into her yellow hand and promised visits to chapel when she was better. And before long Blod got two hundred pounds for the education of her son Ivor: the rest of the family, desirous of the glory of a minister therein, agreed she had first claim. But all the others too, except Mary Ann, got their advantages from her repentance, the purchases ranging in size from a suite of furniture down to a hymn-book in soft black leather. Sara paid off the mortgage she had raised on the house: times had been bad in the pits. Then, all this done, she went bustling upstairs one dark evening:

'Get up, Olga. Arranged we have for you to go and stay with Mary Ann. Very healthy up there in the mountains, you will get well quicker. Come now.' Olga wept and moaned. But her sister pulled her thin, shrinking body out of the bed and shoved old garments on it. In the deserted lane behind the house was Evan with his new motor-bike. Olga, shivering and dazed in the winter damp, was strapped to him behind.

Off they went. Up the valley and bumping across a naked mountain by the old Roman road: down to a vale where there was only a little pit and a couple of farms. Then up the side of a dark mountain, sour in the winter, where sheep coughed. Mary Ann's cottage clung to its side like a leech. The cottage smelt of the dozen cats that she worshipped. She squinted down dubiously at her panting sister as the bike whizzed away, and said: 'Drat me, Olga, don't know I do how there's room for you and the cats in my bed. But we'll manage.'

Mary Ann was good-hearted: her mind had never opened properly, and it purred like her cats. The damp cottage was small as a hen-house: every day she walked two miles to work at a farm, earning seven shillings a week and milk for the cats. She was strong, chewed shag, and spat on the floor like a man. Olga's past life was vague in her mind.

'Let me sleep,' whimpered Olga; 'I want to sleep. Then when I'm better we must go to chapel. I want to sing and pray.' Her quenched face had gone stiff as a dead sparrow. The cats jumped about her, frisky: some were wild as the mountain wind gnawing at the cottage.

Picking her nose, Mary Ann cogitated. 'Where's your husband?' she said at length.

Moaning, Olga wept in misery and repentance: 'I've been a bad woman.'

'All of us are bad women,' said Mary Ann comfortably, 'here below.' But her mind couldn't stay fixed for long on anything and she said: 'Let me see if I can spare a drop of milk from the cats' suppers. There's hungry the little angels are always! Cold in the face you look.' She spared a small cup of the bluish mountain milk.

Olga did not get well up in the mountain cottage. And even Mary Ann began to grumble at the tossings and weeping beside her in the bed: the cats were disturbed. Sometimes Olga cried out loud in her agony of spirit. During the day she tried to read the Bible, but there was little strength in her arms to hold up the stout book. One cat there was who became enamoured of her and leapt on her shoulders continually. Her soul began to gutter out completely. One night she panted for a minister to be brought her.

'Hush,' scolded Mary Ann gently, 'past ten o'clock it is and Mr. Isaac Rowlands is cosy in bed by the side of his wife with her red hair.'

'I want to confess,' moaned Olga.

Mary Ann soothed: 'Old he is and never climbs mountains. You tell me the confess tomorrow and I will deliver it with his milk on the way home. There now, go to sleep.'

The next day Olga, alone in the cottage, wandered out in a daze, her nightshift flapping about her bony body. All around the mountains spread gleaming white and pure as the mountains of Heaven. Crying for God's minister, she was found by a shepherd in the vale and shoved into the policeman's cottage. Delivered back to Mary Ann, in a week she was dead.

Mary Ann, excited, stayed away from the farm and walked over the mountain to Sara, who called a conference. And the purring Mary Ann was told: 'Buried from your cottage she must be, quiet by there. A grand coffin will be sent up to you, and one hearse.'

'And carriages too,' said Mary Ann placidly, 'for the mourners.' She was proud to have a funeral start from her house.

'No mourners,' shouted Sara, who was wearing a fine silk blouse. 'She don't deserve it, the life she led. Good people don't sit behind a Jezebel, alive or dead.'

The cheapest coffin in Undertaker's Jenkins's price-list arrived in Mary Ann's cottage. But she said to the bringer: 'The day of the funeral send one carriage up to follow the hearse. For me, and cost to be paid by me, Mary Ann.' The funeral day, however, Sara took it into her head to come over, in a tight ginger fur coat, and when she saw the carriage drive up with the hearse and Mary Ann ready in black, she pushed the shocking woman into a chair and hissed: 'You want to disgrace the family, you stupid rabbit!' For ten minutes she forced into Mary Ann's mind knowledge of Olga's wickedness: in the end Mary Ann sat with dropped jaw and popping eyes.

So it was that an empty carriage went behind the thin narrow coffin that had no varnish on its wood, no flower on its breast.

The disgrace safely underground, not long afterwards Blod brought up to Sara's house the first letter from her college boy and, settling her new glasses, read it out to the assembled family. He was doing fine and asked for a new black suit.

'That'll be a day,' sighed Sarah, 'when we hear his first sermon.'

Evan lifted his goat's teeth: 'Perhaps a comfort it'll be to Olga, too, where the mare is, down in the hot.'

'Do not speak disrespectful of the dead, Evan,' admonished Blod prudently. She folded the letter away into her new leather handbag. 'Poor Olga!' she mused. 'And she so pretty at one time. I used to brag about her in Sunday-school, long ago. Her face was bright as a daisy and her bosoms like spicy fairy-cakes.' She shook her new gay ear-rings. 'But too soft she was, too loving.'

'Yes, indeed,' sighed Sarah, who was altering a pink silk petticoat that was too small for her, 'and no head for business. A softie like our Mary Ann. Not a diamond ring on her finger, and there's paltry in the bank, when you come to think of all those years!'

ABRAHAM'S GLORY

When Caspar Beynon buried Elizabeth, the mother of his eighteen live children, people said: 'Come to a full stop he has now. His duty done, a sit-back he'll be. Certain it is, too, there's no woman wants to look after eighteen.' Or indeed, people felt, risk another eighteen. For Caspar was not yet fifty, his eldest daughter still under full size, and his eldest son only just begun work in the pits.

They all lived in a specially erected house, built partly on the proceeds of a chapel performance of Handel's oratorio *Samson* given in aid of the famous family. The house was up on Jack Sensation's field behind the slaughterhouse. Every window shone clean as sunlight. On its completion the key had been ceremoniously handed to Caspar by a Justice of the Peace, and a photo of the family appeared in the paper. The J.P., in a sober speech, had said: 'Caspar is our Abraham. Turn to Genesis, where the Lord said to Abraham, "Look now toward heaven and tell the stars, if thou be able to number them . . . So shall thy seed be". Our Caspar, seems like it, the same.'

It was this public ceremony that had really given Caspar his overweening pride in himself. He began to think of himself as an example and a precept to the world. In the history of Abraham he read how the Lord chose to make him exceeding fruitful and a father of nations and of kings. And was not Abraham fruitful in his hundredth year? Caspar looked at the stars. A miner, with a good place in No. 1 pit, he was tough and lithe as a whip in the body. His face was of saturnine cast, but his tongue was loquacious in a seemly way. Even down in the pit no one dared joke to him about his stalk of brussels sprouts—as, behind his back, the family was called; he was a man who would stand no nonsense.

Caspar ruled his brood with a rod of iron. He kept a register of his children, and every night at seven he would call out their names and put beside them a black or red mark. At the month's end he awarded boiled sweets out of a jar according to red marks earned; the size of the family did not allow pocket money. But in another jar, high up in a cupboard, was a collection of brownish little twists like pieces of cord, each with a tiny label. One Sunday morning those of the children who were already of sense—and Caspar did not believe in keeping them ignorant of the wonder of life—understood the significance of this mysterious jar.

Gomer, the eldest son, had promised to be a lazy young man. Twice he had

209

neglected to clean out the pigsty top of the field. Just come nineteen, on the Saturday night he had not attended the calling of the register. He had long, indolent legs, torpid eyes, and was not likely to get on in the pits, where only that week his father had learnt of his reputation.

That Sunday morning he came down to breakfast and found everybody waiting for him round the big table, staring in silence at their empty plates. At the head sat Caspar. Gomer slouched in. His place was next to his father's. On his plate was a twirl of dried brownish string. Caspar allowed the silence to reign awhile. Gomer stared at the cord. His father's voice came bleak and solemn:

'Into the world you came with only that and out of the world you will go with only that. Yours it is; take it. Nothing else will you get from me.'

He formally handed his son an empty envelope. Gomer, scowling, put his cord into it. But he looked frightened. At Caspar's sign Morfydd, the eldest daughter—for this was just after the mother's death—lifted the big teapot and poured out; by her side pretty Olwen stood with a ewer of hot water. Nothing more was said. Some of the children had their mother's stamp and were dumpy in their chairs, but most of them were of their father's darkly austere mien. All looked healthy.

Three times more Caspar had occasion to thus give warning to his children, for out of eighteen there are sure to be some that show blemish. When she was sixteen, pretty Olwen herself, supposed to be her father's favourite, found her cord on her Sunday breakfast plate. Caspar refused to overlook sloth, frivolity, and no ambition. He wanted all his children to grow up good pillars of the country. He tended their minds, and on Tuesday and Friday nights read out to them from such classics as Vicar Prichard's *Welshman's Candle* and Llwyd's *Book of the Three Birds*. Striking a tuning fork, he taught them singing, too, and made them into quite a little choir. At Easter he distributed penny chocolate eggs to them, having saved up the eighteenpence from his year's tobacco money.

Elizabeth had died not long after seeing that her eighteenth was safely on his legs. She was a woman with a large, gently clumsy body and eyes of a pondering liquid brown. During her last year she had a strange air of virginity, as if, having fully completed the circle of flesh's meaning, she had returned to a placid young freshness. Yet she went. Perhaps because her task had been done so completely and the earth knew it and whispered enticingly: 'Come back, Elizabeth. Well done, my good and faithful daughter. Come back.'

It was a blow to Caspar and it was not a blow. He had liked Elizabeth and she had never thwarted, annoyed, or disobeyed him. But facts had got to be faced. Being forty-four, her eighteenth would have been her last. This had

210

grieved him. Eighteen was an in-between, slovenly number, neither small nor large. And his own power was still full-pelt within him. Still in his dreams he saw himself populating the world, with the great Beynon family worshipping under the suns. Wherever there were children of God, there, too, would be a Beynon descendant.

The evening following Elizabeth's funeral, after calling out the register, he closed the book and said:

'Now then. A new day tomorrow, sad enough. Gone is your mother Elizabeth Ann Beynon. No more her footstep on the stairs and her hand lighting the candles. In her time like a wealthy damson tree she was; remember her with respect in your hearts. Now I am saying this to you: My mourning for the late Elizabeth Ann Beynon is great, but time is not stopping for mourning. Forty-nine I am and a lot to be done yet. And eighteen of you there are and a new mother needed. In a week or two I am going down into the country to make arrangements.'

And, deaf to the criticisms of the valley people, he went off on his search. He had connections still left in the country where, amid the clean farms, the healthy cattle, the grain, and orchards, he believed that unruined and willing women could still be found.

Within a month he wrote home to Morfydd in his bold round hand: 'Prepare my bedroom, wash the lace, beeswax the floor, and air the bed. I am marrying down by here and will come after the wedding day at once, Monday next.'

The new wife was redhead, twenty-eight, and looked healthy as a young cat; Sian by name. How he got her was a mystery, but she seemed glad to be married to Caspar. She accepted the eighteen, who were ranged up, washed, and in their best clothes for her arrival, without opinion, though later that night she bawled, bossy: 'Off to bed with you now, go on.'

Caspar looked at her with the bright, calculating eye of a young man. 'I am Abraham,' he announced to her.

She put her head on one side and smiled wheedlingly.

Everywhere, except in the connubial chamber, the house was bare, the strict furniture for use only and no decorations. But in the room where he now led her by the hand festoons of white lace draped bed, mantelpiece, window, and furniture. A fine spreading fern grew in a puce pot standing on a column of mock marble. Garlands of fat pink roses were painted on the toilet things on washstand and under the bed; this set, all to match, had been presented to Caspar by his pit manager after that performance of Handel's *Samson*. The four big engravings, each frame with its drapery of lace like a window, were of bygone preachers famed for sermons of fire. The huge bed was of brass and feathers. Sian pushed her strong arm into it and nodded satisfied. 'It is aired.'

'Your hair,' said Caspar, 'is red enough to warm the bed of old Jack Frost himself.'

'And Jack Frost you are not,' she answered solidly.

He found her behaviour was without stint and congratulated himself on his good fortune.

But a year passed without signs. Depriving himself and even the eighteen of this and that, he fed her on cream, fruit, fat slices of ham, middle cod, and young chickens. She ate all with enjoyment. But she remained flat. Another year passed and still she did not wax. Yet she flourished enough in other ways. Her manner was active and she would sing as she pegged the family washing on the long, long line out in the back. Caspar, unable to believe the suspicion in his heart, said with dangerous vexation: 'What's the matter with things now!'

'Oh,' she said, offhand, 'boss nature you cannot.'

After the third year he burst out: 'You are empty as a pod without peas. You have deceived me.'

'Eighteen you got,' she pointed out justly. 'Surely you can rest in peace now?'

'You mind your own business,' he cried in great anger. 'Don't you go sheltering behind the work of the late Elizabeth Ann Beynon. Or dodging about.' And fixing her with his sultry eye, he asked if she was barren. She tossed her head and said: 'Yes.'

His anger was awful. He cornered her and, with that power which had grown in him as a man of fame, forced explanation from her. Her history, kept from him in the country where he had judged her by the swing and dash of her fresh-looking body, was dark. An Irish fireman in a boat plying between Ireland and Pembroke had been her lover; afterwards she had gone to an old woman of the hedges, also she had fallen off a bicycle when she ought not to have fallen off a bicycle. She spoke sulkily now, and in guilt. In defence she said that with eighteen of someone else's to look after he ought to be glad of anyone, and at his age too.

But that was the last insult. Besides her main blemish, this woman was paltry and had no understanding of his heart's glory or his soul's dreams. He backed from her. The same day he told his eldest daughter to fold all the lace in the bedroom and to put away the rose-garlanded porcelain. The pillared pot of fern and the pictures were removed. Then at once he went to consult Timothy the solicitor.

'Aye, aye,' Timothy said, 'divorces there are. But it'll be a long job. And a costly. Willing she is?'

'She'll be willing,' Caspar said. 'And the money will be found.'

212

From the solicitor he went to rich old Andrew Andrews, whose love was property, and said he wished to raise a mortgage on his house. Andrew promised to accommodate him. Perspiring now, he hastened on to Parch. David Sandringham Davids, minister of the chapel where he used two pews. D.S.D. laid his hands comfortably over his paunch and listened close, his eyes beady.

'No,' he pronounced at last, 'no, certainly not. This and that would be said. The divorce I can't stop; between a man and his soul that is. But to take another woman into your bed pending is wicked. Besides,' he warned, 'go against you in the divorce it would. Timothy wasn't saying you could do that, was he?'

'I didn't mention about it,' Caspar said fretfully; and anguish for three years of waste had strangely undid him. 'Dark I was going to keep it. Three years lost—'

'You cannot,' said D.S.D. in his well-known manner, 'keep a woman in your bed dark. It is the thing above all that shouts from the housetops. It clangs louder than the town crier's bell, it is the hooter of the pits, it is the biggest noise in the market place. Why this is don't ask me. A mystery it is even I have failed to understand.'

The next few months were black ones for Caspar, even though things were on the move, including the mortgage and the first skirmishes of the divorce. He could not forget those wasted three years. He became very irritable, though Sian was no longer under his eyes. She had gone back to the country, where her eye was on someone else, and a bit of pocket money.

'Forgive you,' he had said to her, 'for playing about wastefully with me I cannot! Three years gone for nothing! Go now, go. Out of my sight.'

One evening after calling the register he said testily to the assembly: 'Growing up a lot of you are, and time for courting. Just past sixteen your mother was when she married me, and me twenty. There are those of you that are equal and more those ages and yet no signs I see that you are doing what you are on the earth to do. Now then! Fretting me you are. Don't you stint yourselves where marriage is concerned. You, Gomer, and you, Morfydd, and you, Olwen. Let me see three weddings of you this year and then in short time a rising in you, my daughters, and in you, Gomer, a proper conceit.'

'A bachelor I want to be,' called Gomer rawly. It was as if his father's fertility had given him horror.

'A bachelor!' And Caspar's scorn was biting. 'There is no such thing as a bachelor. Live he doesn't. A shadow he is. He folds up early and mopes in death's corner. Death takes him and says: "Hollow seed this is, no good to the earth, chuck him away". Into thin air he goes and is not remembered.'

Caspar's face became darkly ferocious. 'Don't you be disgracing me, Gomer. You go out this very evening and set about your true business. There's good and solid young ladies waiting this very minute for what I've given you. Be off,' he thumped the table irritably, 'and lay your head in the sensible comfort of a woman's breast. You have the look of one in want.'

In all the children's characters, wayward though some of them were, there was a natural obedience to their father's force. Gomer put on his cap with a sulky look. Morfydd and Olwen went upstairs and, before the mirror, whispered and plotted with sisterly confidences; Caspar had already given them permission to go dancing. The younger children had listened to their father's homily with looks of close concentration; he had that way.

But this whipping up of his children did not really console him. He felt the angry dread which comes to an ambitious man when obstacles and setbacks appear undeserved on his path. He became more dejected and even cadaverous of face. He knew that the valley people were mocking him now, for though everybody had bought tickets for that performance of *Samson* in aid of him, people never really forgive a man who sits above them in any natural advantage, and their pleasure when he is brought low is extreme. Women said he was a bad example and had deserved that country redhead.

It was the dark night of his soul. He felt his life had come to a stop. There was no pleasure in the day's unroll. Yet, rousing himself, he took to attending—for Sian's perfidy had given him a distrust of the country parts— where people gather in the converse of local life, his roaming eye alert, his ear pricked. But the valley men had no information for him of ready young widow or spinster, and the women turned their faces from him. Besides, a man who divorces is not of best odour in the valley.

The year went by and the law still sat brooding over his divorce. His anguish grew; his sunken eye burned. Those three wasted years were going into four. Must he come to a full stop, as people expected? No, no. He prayed in fierce language, but as week followed week and still no woman appeared on the horizon he began to shiver in the atheistic thoughts assailing him.

Taking a restless walk one Saturday afternoon, he found that his feet had brought him to where the trams stop and turn round, about three miles from his home. The cemetery gates were just above on the hillside. He stood on the kerb wondering why he had arrived here, where he hadn't been since burying Elizabeth. Was Elizabeth calling to him? He had walked here in his heavy grief without knowing where his feet led. Did she want to comfort him?

A tram clanked noisily to a standstill. A bunch of flowers in pink tissue paper rolled to his feet. Clumsily descending from the tram was a thick-set young woman in black; she was carrying two green tin vases, a little trowel,

214

and a bag of bulbs. Her tidy round face was comfortably serious. And as Caspar handed her the flowers there was that in the look of their eyes which takes people back to when they were lizards without words. They went up into the cemetery together. The fine day was turning into November red.

Caspar's voice was famished and anxious: 'My wife, the late Elizabeth Ann Beynon, is buried here.' A young widow is she, he thought, her husband killed perhaps in that explosion in the pits down this district?

A flush ran in and out of her cheeks. She agitatedly dropped the tin vases. Looking at him sideways, her eyes were thick and soft as oil.

'You have buried your dear?' he urged at last, bold but sympathetic.

'My father,' she breathed. Little bubbles appeared at the corners of her lips, which were cleft like a ripe peach.

They reached her father's grave. He leaned on the glistening marble headstone and, stooping, gazed into her drooped face. The strong red autumn sun was behind him like an ally. And though his gaze was vehement, the assault of his voice was smooth and subtle:

'Eighteen children I've got, by my late lying over by there. Eighteen, and all healthy and strong as new barrels. Likewise myself. Likewise you, if you are not minding these words. We are full. Living we are. Feel my hand! The hand of a young man it is.' He stooped lower and saw how her rich bosom was swelling in pain. 'Think on this miracle! You and me, met together we have in this place of death, and one hour ago strangers! Surely a promise it is? Carrying bulbs you are? Fit and proper. Present moment we are as them. But in spring shall not a champion tulip bloom from us?'

Swaying lower, she would have fallen on the grave had not his strong arm held her, the tumult in her face was such. For he had accurately realised her dormant soul. He knew what he was about when he mentioned his previous eighteen. She, too, wanted abundance. Not for her the fear, the paltriness, and the niggard quarter-living of present day. Was that why she was still single?

'I,' she said at last—and her voice was as if it had remained in long vigil deep inside her— 'I have been waiting.'

The sun's red cheek lay on the shoulder of old Iau Mountain when, at the keeper's bell, they came down among the thousand white stones. Caspar knew then that there is no more successful place for courting than a cemetery. Her name was Enid, aged twenty-six, and her late father, whom she had worshipped, had been carpenter in the Bwlch pits. Her mother was now wanting to go back to the country parts where she came from. Enid had no money, only herself, and Caspar preferred her without money.

Every Saturday until the divorce was granted they met safe in the cemetery. Alleys of yews and expensive tombstones hid them. She was not a talker. But

215

he was, and, sitting by her father's grave, she listened with her full cleft lips parted moist. One Saturday he swept his arm towards the great crop of headstones, the crosses, the broken columns, the marble angels in doldrum attitudes, and said: 'Concerned with such as these we are not. Stone we are? Angels that have done with the earth? Bones and a cup of dust? No! My late, lying over by there, is approving; sense she had and testify she would for me, could she. First-class condition I am in. And you?'

Her habit of blushing made her round face more sumptuous. 'A doctor,' she said shyly, 'I have never had. There's nothing the matter with me.'

'All the same,' he said honestly, remembering the redhead, 'a gamble you are.'

The wind was howling loud through the darkening December afternoon, pushing the yews and bumping against the headstones. They were the only people there. They did not hear the keeper's bell. And at the end of January she met him with a deeper blush on her face.

'It is done,' she said, her drooped gaze on the young bulb blades in her father's grave.

In February the divorce was granted and the very next day Caspar led Enid by the hand into his home, she already in soft swell as he wanted her, and he a proud lesson to all slothful malingerers, dodgers, and bad characters. The eighteen, washed and in best clothes, were ranged up. Enid's round eyes were oily with emotion. She kissed the daughters and shook hands with the sons.

'The tea is ready,' Morfydd said, stolid. 'Shall I pour out or will you?'

They were married in a fortnight. Once more the newly washed lace festooned the bedroom and the shining rose-garlanded porcelain stood in its places, and the big shooting fern on its marble pillar. And down in No. 1 pit Caspar earned a new respect and those men who were of grave turn began to wonder if he really was Abraham born again.

He worked on the day shift. On an afternoon in the early autumn the telephone rang at the shaft bottom and the groundsman who answered called quick to a stableboy: 'Go and find Caspar Beynon in the Wern drift. Tell him he's got to go home at once and it's important.' The boy hung his lamp on his belt and went off into the workings.

Half an hour later women at their doors saw Caspar speeding down the hill and up again to his house. Even under the pit dirt they could tell his face was pale and haggard. No one could detain him. There was a little knot of women on the road outside his house; they talked in low, hushed voices, and as he ran inside their faces were grim.

That evening, when a reporter from the paper was present downstairs with several visitors and every one of the previous eighteen, Caspar appeared before

216

them. In his arms were three glories. His eyes alight with triumphant pride, he said:

'Look! Look now! Three lost years have been given back to me! A miracle it is. Yet people there are who say there is no God.'

And to Enid, privately and allowing himself a trim humour on this famous day, he said: 'Well, Enid, my girl, surely a day in the cemetery is better than a month in the seaside?'

His fame increased. His history as father of twenty-one was related in the paper, together with all about that time when he had so bravely rescued Dai Dry Dock from under a fall of roof in the pits. Gifts were showered on him from mansion and cottage. Enid bore twice again, but one at a time. Then, strangely, she stopped. So the number remained at an aggravating twenty-three. But even in this there seemed a benevolent Will at work. For after the last birth the bad times began and Caspar went on the dole like nearly all the valley miners. The earth was too crowded already and, it seemed, did not know what to do with all its sons and daughters.

However, by then Gomer, Morfydd and Olwen, married to valley persons, began to produce. Every time a child was born to them he went down joyfully to the house concerned, carrying a small Bible, a loaf of home bread baked by Enid, and a bunch of flowers.

MOURNING FOR IANTO

The day Ianto was to be buried blew cold and dour, the upper hills already covered with thin snow. His ten friends filed up the front garden of the cottage, looking very black in stiff clothes that had been withdrawn from boxes under beds, each wearing a flattish bowler hat pressed down tight over the ears. Ianto was going to be buried with what ceremony his cronies could muster; they had already paid for the coffin.

The hand bier they had hired was laid outside the door, which was opened by a cross-looking woman whose only sign of mourning was a pair of jet earrings, angrily swinging now. She was Ianto's landlady, a widow and maker of medicinal concoctions that were of dark reputation.

'You've come for him, I suppose,' she said, her feet stepping restlessly, as if she were longing to insult them.

Ianto had died owing her much money. He had been her lodger for twelve years. Though she herself was not a smell of violets in the nostrils of the village, no man could say she had never paid her way in life, and none could say she spent her money swilling herself daft in the inn. She eyed the collection of men on her doorstep surlily now: the famous boozers well-known for miles for their drinking competitions. 'Well,' she added, 'he's no sparrow for you to carry.' She screeched when they scratched the coffin against her wallpaper.

They could see that she hated the way they claimed Ianto. Yet, soured, she would have no concern with his burial, would not contribute a farthing. Dying, Ianto had requested his old friends to bury him, and to mourn for him the same night in the taproom of the Red Lion, placing a full pint for him in the middle of the table. 'I'll be with you in spirit, boys,' he had croaked.

Men of the local farms, they had taken the morning off and were prepared to make it a suitable festival, albeit a sombre one. Some of them were married to respectable women, the others wedded, like the deceased himself, to the buxom XXX ale that made their meeting in the Red Lion roaring programmes of fighting, sing-songs, storytelling, and various competitions. Four took up the handles of the bier after they had gently rested and strapped the coffin thereon.

'Aye,' one sighed, 'the old dame was right: he's no bird.'

But they were sturdy men, and in relays surely they'd manage to carry their loved burden the four uphill miles to the cemetery. A hearse from the town would have been the thing, of course, but that would have been costly, and there was tonight's mourning in the Red Lion, as requested by Ianto, to be considered. Their pooled resources had left about thirty-five shillings free for this, and the money was safe in Merlin Evans's pocket now. A hearse or thirty-five shillings' worth of ale? Well, no true pal of Ianto would have hesitated. The four carriers staggering up the steep lane outside the cottage concentrated their thoughts on the coming reward.

'Funny it is,' gasped one presently, 'he ate so small, yet a man of tidy bigness he was.'

'Don't waste your breath talking,' panted another, sweating.

The others were already well ahead of them up the lane. Below, the grey cottages of the village scrambled among the bare wintry trees like forlorn sheep. Snow threatened nearer, preceded by icy drops of sleet; the wind blew. It was unfortunate that no more burials could be accepted in the crowded village churchyard; everyone had to go now to the cemetery opened by the county authorities four miles away, up amongst the hills, in a draughty green lap that this morning would surely be covered with snow.

At the top of the lane, though their half-hour was not yet completed, the four carriers complained of weariness. 'Oi,' they shouted to the others, 'come and take your turn now. Sweating like old 'osses we are.'

The others returned in shocked protest. 'Giving in 'fore we're started, are you!' remarked Gomer Beynon severely. 'He didn't ought to be heavier than a bunch of dandelions if you had any guts for the job.'

Redly truculent, one of the carriers, Ivor Roberts, shouted: 'This old lane's steep and stony as the way to Heaven. Quarter-hour for those chaps on steep roads, half on flatter. So there! And,' he declared suddenly, 'I want a drink.' He took out his heavy watch. 'Pubs,' he added obstinately, 'will be opened in five minutes; the Duck in the Mouth's just round there, behind Williams's farm.'

'Can't start drinking,' protested Ellis Richards, though weakly, ''fore Ianto's buried. Now, now, it wouldn't be proper at all. Work first, play after.' The others nodded severely.

'You carry him for a bit,' growled Ivor, still panting, 'and your tongue'll be dry enough to take to water! . . . Why,' he demanded, gazing at the others balefully, as though one of them was to blame for some grave hitch in the proceedings, 'why didn't someone bring a bottle of *cold tea*?'

But his angry irony was lost on his pals. Indeed, there had been no real objection to what he had had the courage to suggest. Only they thought it fitting that in such a solemn activity as a funeral they should demur a little. But the morning was truly cold and dismal. A short, quiet call at the first inn on the way to the cemetery would put fresh heart into them for their melancholy task.

'Well then,' said Ellis, with an air of giving way to a fractious child, 'well then, shall it be *one only* at the Duck?' His face, frigid as a preacher's, looked round at the cluster of men, black-clothed as crows. 'The wind,' he added grievously, 'is high and drying to the throat.'

Some of the men, indeed, were coughing as if their chests were very weak. 'The day,' lamented swarthy Ebenezer Powell, 'is cold as the bald patch on top of the world's head. Let us take a short comfort, as Ellis says. Ianto would have been willing.'

So they laid the bier tenderly near the hedge and tramped across a field to where, in a tiny hamlet, an ancient inn crouched under chestnut and beech trees. In the snug oak-veined taproom they sat in two black rows either side of a long, fresh-scrubbed table. The innkeeper was surprised at this invasion and exclaimed looking at their best clothes:

'Going to a wedding you are?'

'Ten pints, quick,' Merlin Evans, the treasurer, ordered sternly. 'We are burying a pal and got no time to waste jawing.'

'*Eleven* pints!' Ellis said significantly. 'One for the middle of the table.'

They drank in silence, each staring now and again at the tankard placed in memory of the deceased. The silence became oppressive. They finished their drinks.

'What,' muttered Llew Lewis, wiping his dejected moustaches, 'what's to be done with that there full pint?'

No one knew. They stared at it in depression. 'A pity to waste it,' mumbled Gomer Beynon, scowling. 'Ianto wouldn't like good ale wasted.'

But no one liked to touch the tankard and drink its contents alone. They waited in uneasy nervousness for someone to speak up. It was Gwilym Watts, lean and not long released from jail, who suggested: 'Tell you what. Order nine pints more and put them with that one for company.'

So once more the treasurer doled out, sternly but not unwillingly. Heartened, the mourners presently trooped out into the cold again. Snow met them, thin but promising a greater abundance. The hills were curling into white waves. The mourners thought disconsolately of the cosy room they had just left. Would that Ianto had died some warmer week!

'Hurry up now,' Ellis exclaimed, 'else the storm will nip us like a fox at a chicken.'

Another four grasped the handles of the bier and began to trudge, quite briskly at first, a length of flat road under a stout hill. Soon, however, there was a climb—a hard one, until the decline into the next dip in the hills began.

They panted and snorted. The snow thickened; it ran into their eyes; it trickled down their necks; they sweated. Llew Lewis's tongue began to hang out like an exhausted dog's.

'Oi,' he gasped, 'help now! A small breakfast I had this morning and no nourishment is in me.' So someone had to replace him.

The changes became constant. All complained of the unexpected weight of the bier; all cursed the callous snow. When they reached the next dip, where there was a hamlet and the Bunch of Grapes, without debate they rested their burden under a white-filled elm and hurried across to the inn. Merlin took out his bag of money.

Warmed again, in a room full of brass ornaments and pictures of Victorian celebrities, they bustled into cheerful conversation. The tankard in the middle of the table did not oppress them this second time.

'You remember, chaps, how Ianto climbed tower of church and hung Betty Prichard's red petticoat on spire?'

'And Betty knocked him into duckpond with her broom. Aye, a lad he was in those days. 'Ow did he get 'er petticoat, asked parson, and wouldn't let Betty come to church after that.'

'Aye, Betty Prichard,' sighed Edwin Thomas, full of regretful memories. 'Where's she now, I wonder? Went away to Cardiff docks and never came back. Pretty and quick as a squirrel she was. Skin pink as a wild rose . . . I was going to court her once,' he added defiantly to his pals' ironical smiles.

'The snow,' observed Llew Lewis, peering broodingly out of the window, 'lies heavy on everything.'

But they had to set out again in the bitter, bitter cold. The greater part of their journey was still before them, and the snow was now stampeding upon the steep landscape. But they were determined; the sad job had to be done. Were they not the only human connections poor Ianto had possessed in the whole world?

Entering a village mid-way to the cemetery, without further ado they sheltered the bier in a convenient cart-shed and hastened into the Black Cow, a good pub well-known for its rich, potent stout. Their faces blue and red, they sighed with satisfaction. But after the third round, Ellis, studying his watch with difficulty, urged them to their duty again. Outside, the wind seemed to have become ominously fierce, for the weakest of the mourners staggered as they went into it.

'Let us bury him tomorrow!' Gwilym bawled, 'and stay here now mourning for him.'

The others were shocked. To postpone such a sacred ceremony as a burial seemed to savour of blasphemy. They criticised Gwilym harshly. Gwilym, always truculent under certain circumstances, flung off his coat, struck a fisted pose, and invited someone to hit him.

'We will leave the rude ruffian behind,' said Edwin delicately. 'No esteem has he for the sad business we are doing today.'

Gwilym staggered after their offended backs, shouting in fear that he'd be left behind in the bleak, snowy village. At the next call, in the Crooked Billet, he wept and was obedient. Here, however, a long-standing grievance between Ebenezer Powell and Rowland Price broke out once more. Ebenezer had, three years before, sold a pig to Rowland which the latter declared defective. Presently they were hustled out by the indignant landlord, for blows were struck.

The party staggered on, fairly familiar with the whitened road. Some were slower than others and lagged behind. But all knew, instinctively, they would meet in the Rose and Crown near Lord Gilfach's place, and afterwards in the Travellers' Rest, the last inn before the cemetery. And so it was. The treasurer's bag of money was empty, but they scraped sufficient between them. And still they sacredly if vaguely observed Ianto's request for a memorial tankard in the middle of the table.

At last, two hours late, they trailed into the cemetery, wavering black-and-white figures panting untidily into the snowy place. The parson, who had been waiting for them in the cemetery keeper's cottage, complained severely, though he was not really offended. On such a cold morning the keeper had provided him with a bottle of his favourite cherry wine, and he had been sitting by a large fire reading a detective novel. But he looked in doubt at the cluster of swaying men outside the cottage.

'The storm seems to have knocked you about!' he remarked.

Ellis, their spokesman, kept on saying: 'Beg your pardon, parson,' and bowing; Gomer Beynon kept turning round and round, a human weathercock in the wind; two others had collapsed exhausted under snow-laced yews, and the others lurched about dazedly. The parson peered up and down the broad cemetery path.

'And the coffin?' he enquired suavely. 'You have taken it to the graveside?'

Ellis stared at him with glassy eyes. 'Ianto,' he said with heaving solemnity, 'Ianto was a good man, one of the best. All the way up the chaps been grieving sore about him. He didn't ought to have gone so soon!'

'The coffin?' repeated the parson.

'One of the best! Earth's poorer for his going, parson, b . . . b . . . but'—Ellis seemed about to weep—'but Heaven's the gainer.'

The parson's benignity was thinning; he muttered to himself. But Ellis began to reach an inspired eloquence:

222

'Who should want a better pal in this world than Ianto! A kind word for everybody, and always a smile on his nice mug! He'll teach the angels in Heaven! Begging your pardon, parson.' His voice sank. 'And we have come now, his old faithful mates, to lay him to rest.'

'The coffin?' the parson asked suspiciously.

Ellis, as though overcome by his grieving eloquence, stared in a tranced way about him. Merlin slouched up to him. 'Parson wants the coffin,' he whispered with care. Ellis chid him gently. 'All in good time, all in good time,' he said, very dignified. 'Form procession to the grave now.'

Rowland Price, who had been listening near by in perplexity, suddenly gave a frightened shout.

'Hey, hey, chaps—coffin's not here!'

The disorder that ensued was human but deplorable. Each reproached the other for this awful carelessness. Harassed abuse was exchanged; Ebenezer again struck Rowland. The parson slammed the door of the keeper's cottage and disappeared. After a while someone attempted a reasonable discussion. Where had the coffin been left? In which pub backyard, by what hedge, under what tree? But no one seemed certain.

Light snow was still falling; the heavens frowned. It was dinner-time and there was no food and no money. Home was four miles away through the snow. And somewhere, lonely and snow-covered, the coffin of poor Ianto lay abandoned. Depression crept across the ten mourners. Like Job, hopeless and overcome, Ellis collapsed to the bitter cold earth and lamented weepingly:

'For why is man born? There is no sense in the behaviour of things. Everything is wicked and even the bosom pals of a man have forgetfulness in their hearts.'

'Come now,' heaved Llew Lewis, 'wasting time you are down there. We got to go back and find our Ianto.'

THE NATURE OF MAN

Though Catti found that Dan the carrier fitted her nature like a key fits its lock, in the end she chose Selwyn, who was the fishmonger in the little market town six miles away. She decided (though in a temper) that her trim body, her smooth calves, her cowslip-yellow hair and her mouthful of glittering teeth deserved something better than Dan's half-a-crown cottage slunk down at the edge of a lonely wood and smelling of mice and winter mildew. The evening she made up her mind she went down to the cottage where Dan had lived alone since his parents' death, and from the patch of garden shouted at him through the open window:

'Come on out of there, you old sluggard, and listen to a lady.'

When the great hook of his nose came out of the door, she went on:

'Give me back the broidered spread I broidered last winter. No wedding for you and me, you snail. Month after next I'm marrying Selwyn the Fish, so there!' And she snapped her fingers at him, still in a temper.

Dan, swarthy of hair and skin as a gipsy, bared his yellow eyes. Just by the front door was the butt that caught the thatch drippings. In a flash he scooped a pan of water and sprung it over her as, too late, she jumped back.

'Go and marry the dirty mackerel!' he shouted in fury. 'Be off!' He scooped another panful.

She picked out a stone from the black loam and threw it at him, hitting his chest. She dodged the second lot of water but did not leave the garden. He remained on the doorstep, his muscled belly heaving up out of his loose-strapped corduroys. But he threw no more water; as the month had been dry, a pity to waste it on this baggage of a turncoat.

'The banns are going to be read next Sunday,' she screeched. 'A tidy wedding I'm having. So there! Good riddance of a courter that got no more ambition than a rabbit!' Her yellow hair sprang about like wheat in wind: his yellow eyes danced in answering rage.

'Go and marry a shifty townee,' he roared. 'A couple of bad eggs, the both of you.'

'Jealous!' she sang in vengeful delight. 'Give me back my broidered spread. For wife, one-legged old Mari is proper value for you.'

Six yards between them, and approaching no nearer, they continued in abuse. But he had no intention of yielding up the spread of blue cloth, embroidered with jays, red lilies and flying swans, which she had given him not

224

long ago, saying it was for their wedding bed. One day it might fetch a good price in the market.

At last, with final jeers at the stick-in-the-mud blockhead, his poverty and his paltry cottage, she went skipping into the road. Dan's pony, from the paddock beside the cottage, watched her speculatively as she climbed the short height to the village. The evening was darkening. Dan slammed his door, lit a candle, and with an oath stamped his foot on a cockroach.

Her complaints were the uproar of love kept waiting. Dan, with his country slowness and caution, had dithered because of his inability to decide whether to buy a motor-van before marriage or not. For himself he was satisfied with the old pony and cart, and he clung obstinately to them. But Catti's taunts at his lack of ambition had kept him fixed in a dilemma, so that the date of their wedding was for ever being postponed.

Also she wanted him to move out of the ancient cottage that had belonged to his family for two hundred years, and go to live in the market town where, so she declared, his carrier business must surely grow, aided by a motor-van. But he was quite satisfied with carrying for the village, and his legs were like roots in the cottage of his fathers, where his childhood smelt sweet.

They had courted for five years, walking in the woods and nearly always quarrelling, like demons that cannot part. She was an orphan and milked the cows up in Trecornel farm. He knew that on market day Selwyn the fishmonger had cast his greedy drunkard eyes on the way Catti skipped about the town, her bosom before her like a basket of peaches.

But he was startled to find that this time her threats were true. She married the fishmonger and went to live above his shop, in the babbling town that was divided by azure streaks of river and where there was a famous ruined castle and a cinema opened three evenings a week. The day she was married she passed Dan's cottage on her way to the town; she passed in a tumbril in which was piled all her belongings. And though she saw him scowling behind the window curtains, oddly she did not scream a taunt or demand her broidered cloth on which she had spent months. She only showed her beautiful teeth in derision. Dressed in a grand gown and wearing stays, she was stiff with a new haughtiness.

That evening Dan chopped off the head of one of his best fowls, snatched out the feathers and entrails, roasted it before his fire and ate it in his hands. A gallon of beer went down his throat. Drunk, he sang songs to himself, in the shadowy candle-lit cottage, old rude songs that maligned women.

The first year or two of her marriage Catti queened it in the town, silks on her limbs which before had known only the bite of flannel. But soon her yellow hair began to fade and lie in limp untidy hanks about her thinning face.

225

Up over the fish shop the marriage did not prosper. Selwyn, whose mouth always hung open like a little boy's, had no more brain than one of his dried sprats, and only in the whisky of the Shepherd's Staff inn across the road did he find some meaning to life. But perhaps it was the lack of harmony in his home life that drove him across the road oftener, so that the fish shop, never expertly managed, began to smell with stock allowed to go stale.

Upstairs, Catti tried to forget things by making herself fine clothes, which was a delight she had always coveted. But now she began to look like a dressed-up scarecrow, very gaunt, and all the untrammelled beauty of the old days was gone. Sometimes she wept, oftener she fell on Selwyn like a tumble of bricks, her tongue and fists full of hard blows.

Meanwhile Dan, as if in vengeance, began to prosper. He bought a motor-van on hire purchase, but he would not move from the dark black-beamed cottage where he stewed a pot for himself just the same. The colour of a smoked ham, and the great hook of his nose proud as a psalm, he began to look fierce and cruel. Shunning the inns now, he spent all his spare time carving knobs of wood into the likeness of animals. He bought himself an oil lamp, a set of knives, a chimney clock and, in a fit of extravagance, a gold ring.

Neither would he look at another woman. With his motor-van he was able to get round to half a dozen villages, collecting and delivering fowls, eggs and vegetables all day long and every day now. As he prospered, some unmarried women, braving the fearsome cast of his face, endeavoured to be to him the lost Catti. But his manner with them remained stony.

Once when he passed the fish shop in his green van and saw Catti coming out of the door, sharp and angular as scissors, he leaned out and bawled, derisive: 'What price the stale mackerel are today, Mrs. Fish?'

She gazed after the bowling back-firing van with dilated eyes.

One blowy November night, about four years after her wedding, he slowly looked up from his wood-carving and saw her face staring in at the window. His lips drawn back in a grin and his hawk's beak poised over the wooden fox, he resumed work. She tapped the pane and called through the wind: 'Let me in Dan, let me warm myself by your fire.'

'Be off!' he shouted. The door was unlocked but she would not enter it unasked.

'The wind is cold, Dan, and there's no food in me.'

He looked up only once more, saw the dejected chin and the naked fleshless bones of her cheeks and answered: 'Shift yourself off. Back to your husband. Don't you stand there. Shall I call the policeman, then?'

She banged her fist against one of the lattice squares, smashing it. The blood

226

ran down her hand. 'The night is frozen,' she wailed. 'Drive me back in your motor, Dan!'

He blew out the lamp and locked the door. She heard him tramp upstairs to the bedroom. So over the road that wound through the skeleton wood she returned, walking the six miles to the town. She had set out whimpering to the place of her youth, after a bitter scene with Selwyn, who had drunk the day's takings, such as they were.

About a month later she appeareed again, bedraggled and shivering. He grinned as she shouted her news through the window, for he knew already. 'Selwyn is bankrupt, the shop closed today. No home have I got, only a mattress on the floor. Let me in, Dan.'

He shouted back: 'Mackerels got the deep ocean to dive in. Or walk the town you can with bells on your toes.' He dare not close the curtains in case she smashed the window again. Eighteen-pence the other pane had cost him.

Though her shriek had lost its old bounce, she demanded: 'Give me my broidered spread. Money it's worth.'

'Warm it keeps me at nights,' he jeered.

'I will cook, sew, clean and wash for you,' she begged again. 'For no wages. And I will sleep on the mat of your hearth.'

'Cosy ditches there are by the road,' he laughed. Once more he locked the door, put out the light and tramped noisily upstairs.

She pressed her cheek against the wall of the cottage as if for warmth. And she crept down the black road. A week later her husband disappeared and she was fed and housed by the parish until she found low work in the kitchen of the town's hotel. The humiliation of this gnawed at her, for still she remembered the pride of her fine body and yellow hair, her silks and the soft strut of her bosom. And one bitter night in January she set out again to the place of her childhood, stealing there like a lean homeless hound, and obeying a need she could not control. Frost paled the road, the trees were crackling and writhing.

Dan was counting the month's money, ready to take to the bank next day. A crisp whisper of notes, pools of silver, an army of copper. His brown hands grasped the money, his beak took up the smell of the cash, now more delicious to him than the old perfume of her flesh. He did not turn when he heard her ghostly tapping on the window, but he scooped up a shower of silver and let it drip in the lamplight. He grinned.

'Dan,' she called, humbly, 'Catti wants to come in. Thirty-two she is, and you thirty-six, next birthday. Let us waste no more years, Dan, and let the years be pretty again. Fatten me, Dan, and put the cold out of my breast.' She tapped the window gently; he did not look round. But he sang out:

'Go and find your haddock of a husband, down in the briny sea.'

She called: 'Your nice house I will sweeten, and cook you dishes every day. Gone is the old mischief and the evil old temper. You was for me and I was for you, Dan—don't you deny it now.'

Putting the money in a leather bag and with never a glance at her, he shouted: 'Be off. The tail end of a flatfish I do not fancy.'

'Open the door,' she wailed.

He put out the light, locked the door, and tramped upstairs. Bag of money under the bolster, he stretched into the flannel quilts. Soon he was fast asleep among the warm feathers. Top of the quilts was her spread, bordered with the jays, red lilies and flying swans. Under it he slept all night like a hog.

In the morning he opened the front door and her body fell at his feet. Her blue face and hands gleamed with frost, her ashen hair crackled. He propped her against the frozen water-butt, locked the door and went in his van up to the policeman's cottage in the village.

'What do you think that old Catti has done, Emrys!' he complained. 'Died on my doorstep! Best for you to speak on your 'phone and tell the parish to fetch her in their ambulance, for I am full up and very busy with crates of eggs and two dozen of poultry from Powell's farm.'

The next market day he sold the spread cheap for ten shillings, so that memory of her should be quite wiped out. Catti was buried by the parish, and though in spring Dan painted his cottage outside a bright green, drank goat's milk every day, bought himself a new black suit, and another watch, he became ill of a wasting complaint. The flash had gone out of his eye, the whip out of his tongue. His wood-carvings became clumsy and dropped from his dulled hand. He shuffled about as if there was nothing in this world to urge him put one foot before the other. Death's last stroke took him in the winter as he was driving the van down the village hill when he ought to have been in bed: the van crashed into a tree.

There was nobody to claim his money. Or the silent desolate cottage, where the rats began to leap on the empty bed.

A PEARL OF GREAT PRICE

The rector of Brwmstan, a man of sinewy and restless limbs, was forever waging war against iniquities. He itched to keep the flesh of Brwmstan pure. Very angry he became if a maid fell or a man got hauled up for one of the offences, and the ledge of his pulpit was worn from the thumps of his fist. For no less than eight busy inns were scattered about the little straggling village. It was a place of deep, ancestral and unreformed drinking. Eynon, the bygone bard, wrote that Satan himself often came up from the hot to drink the strong black Brwmstan beer.

So that he might never lack fuel for his sermons, the villagers, who admired their rector, kindly continued to bathe in their foulnesses, and the church was always obediently full on Sundays. In the taproom of the Malt Shovel a farmer would say in respectful appreciation: 'Very good sermon there was on Sunday. Unclean bats hanging in stables, the rector called us. And leaky pots of dirty liquors.'

Brwmstan—it is called that because of a sulphurous spring in the vicinity—is tucked away under the fat golden roll of Cawrfil mountain where the vale broadens. Nothing had happened there for hundreds of years, not since the flying pig, whose image is carved on the church pulpit, flew out of the clouds one day in the sixteenth century and spat poison over the crops. Now it is known for its well-flavoured ducks and the tomb of an old warrior (who killed thousands of the heathen English) which lies under a huge black cedar in the churchyard. A wheezy bus from Gafr Coch prowls up there in the morning and again in the evening.

Except for his housekeeper the rector lived alone in the thick house beside the mildew-tinted church, his only corporeal pleasure a bottle of port and books in Latin. It was a mystery why he had never married. Perhaps women were afraid of his eagle's nose and swinging limbs swooping round a corner as if looking for prey; perhaps they feared the hard primitive authority in him. In round black hat and flapping black cloak he was like some fierce bird come down from the thundery rocks top of the mountain where no one ever went.

But at last his old housekeeper, Mrs. Olly Bevan, grumpy and a bad cook to the last, died of nothing at all. There was no one in Brwmstan to take her place. He sent to his friend the Dean of Gafr Coch, and presently there arrived Maudie, with best references. She came from the far side of Cawrfil mountain, a district where the people have the salt of the sea in them, and the sea's deep rolling strength: a fine carnal creature, big and blond and young. But she looked meek. Bashful peeps she seemed to take at the world, blue peeps coming up sideways from under dropped lids.

The modest mien of her face pleased the rector. But it was nothing compared to her cooking. A pie made by her came from the oven grand as the world out of the darkness in Genesis. Angels could have eaten her roly-poly puddings with pleasure. Accustomed to Mrs. Olly Bevan's messes, at first he ate with astounded gratification. Yet, after a while, feeling the seductive warmth lave his guts, his eyes narrowed and gleamed. He fully recognized that Maudie was the tailed temptress sent to molest him, gleaming of flesh and talent in her hands.

One evening, after eating of one of her best dinners, he brooded long over his port. Then he called Maudie into the study. She stood meek before him. Her downy neck curved down plump, her peeps were humble. But a warmth thrashed out of her that made him start and bridle in his chair.

'Do you,' he muttered, 'say your prayers every night, Maudie?'

'Every morning too, indeed,' she replied with surprising readiness.

He suddenly banged his fist on the arm of his chair. 'Pies and sauces of the world, corrupt meats and gravies, pah! You think to bring before me the juices of the flesh, do you!'

Maudie thought he was complaining of bad cookery. 'Roast pork I'm giving you for lunch tomorrow,' she said in a hurry. 'Tasty and beautiful I'll cook it, I promise you. And a cherry pie you shall have that'll lay in you as if it wasn't there.'

'No!' he shouted, cantankerous. 'Tomorrow you will bring me a few dry biscuits and a slice of white cheese. Surely you have been cook to the devil himself!'

For the first time since arriving she opened wide at him her milky blue eyes. Reproach was in them. 'My references,' she rebuked, 'you read. Cook to Lord Ithon I was, before he fell off his hoss.'

'That old ruffian with his bastards like blackberries!' he snorted, and shot a suspicious look at her. But, as suddenly as he bellowed fire, he simmered down, seeing her so meek. 'Simple meals I require, Maudie,' he said fretfully.

'Thin you are, church-minister,' she said then, quite lovingly. 'And eat you must. The coffin is a bare larder. A leg of pork, with steam rising from the crackling, keeps the feet out of the grave.'

'Back to the kitchen,' he shouted, 'back.' But after swallowing another glass of ripe port he called her again. 'Brwmstan,' he warned, shaking a long bony finger at her, 'is a place of damnation. The rector's housekeeper must look neither to left nor right.'

'Indeed yes,' she babbled at once. 'Shy I am, and content to sit at home cosy by my kitchen fire.'

Yet the next day she did not obey him in the matter of the dry biscuits, and though at first he scowled at the leg of pork, he ate of it abundantly. Its aroma was such that it might have been cooked in the kitchens of Heaven and stuffed with onions and herbs of Paradise. And for the first time for years he went to sleep in the afternoon, a deep rosy sleep, his reading glasses slipped down the fierce curve of his nose and the volume of Cassian's Dialogues fallen to the floor.

It was that same afternoon that Peter Bach went into the kitchen to ask for a glass of water. On Tuesdays and Fridays Peter Bach came to tend the rectory garden. Though he wasn't really little, he was called that to distinguish him from his policeman father, Peter Mawr—Big Peter. Little Peter, just come into the twenties, was trim and cheerful as a blackbird's whistle. His face was a cherub's. No tale of him had yet reached the rector's Black Book.

After this and that politenesses had been said of the weather and the garden, Maudie went back to her work at the sink. Peter laid down his glass of water and shot his hand up under her skirt, stroking her leg that was as warm as summer or her fresh cakes out of the oven.

'Ten o'clock tonight,' he whispered, 'I'll be by the tomb under the cedar. Slab of stone big as a bed there, and tree keeps any rain off.'

She reared back, heaving. Her downy neck stiffened up like a sawn's, she bared her eyes full and indignant. 'Slab of stone!' she derided. 'Under it I'd put you in half a tick, you ugly frog.'

Yet, as the church clock struck ten into the quiet night, she ambled across the kitchen garden, the great cabbages bursting at her feet. Aided by a mulberry tree she climbed over the short wall, stepping on to the flat tombstone of the farrier's family the other side. The purple shade of the cedar received her.

In the front of the rectory an oblong of light shone on to the lawn. Inside, turning over a crusty, pock-marked page, the rector was reading: 'At mass, in the very act of contrition, the old stories flaunt before my mind, the shameless loves . . .' He lifted his head, his nostrils awake. Some said the rector had second sight and could detect evil five miles off. But there was no sound except the sigh of the summer breeze in the trees. He went to the window. A young moon was sliding up from under a cloud. He could see the green church, the dark bushy hair of the trees and the bright roll of the mountain-side. He stood peering out. Then he went back to his book. But its words tumbled over each other untidily.

The next day Maudie gave him a meal, including one of the famous local ducks, that was as a psalm of praise. And for the first time—for she was not one to forget that she worked in a rectory—she sang at her tasks, though it was not a frivolous song she sang but a hymn. Her little pink mouth let out the words in soft elegant claps, very musical.

And when she attended to him at his meal, though her eyes were still cast down so modest, her plump body gave off a glow healthy as a field of wheat in the sun. She even dared to chat, bringing in the fowl: 'There now, there's a pretty duck, excuse me. Smells lovely and his fat was laughing in the pan as he roasted.'

'Fowls,' he grumbled, and there was a wail in his voice—'today I am preparing my Sunday sermons and you feed me full of fat fowls!'

'Eat now,' she coaxed. 'A comfortable belly will make sermons jump out of you fresh and full as eggs.'

But, before eating it, he seemed to whimper over the duck. And all that day he was restless, walking in and out of the study into the garden where, closing his eyes as if in a trance, he would sniff up the warm blue air sensitively. What was in the day, what witch's menace! He pulled down books off loaded shelves and read of the lamentations and the trials of saints encumbered with the body. The two sermons took very long to compose.

Maudie, deaf and blind to his reproofs, gave him Teify salmon in the evening, a bright salad, and hot tartlets. Afterwards, bringing his port on the silver tray which she had polished to a diamond glitter, she chattered in her new courage: 'My Lord Ithon drank two bottles of port a day. Gouty he was and liver very bad. But there's a merry one all the same! Day before he fell off his hoss his britches he split from a joke that Canon said to him.'

And from under her dropped eyelids she peeped up at him.

But the rector wailed at last: 'I forbid you to mention Lord Ithon's name again! Now that he is dead the virgins of the county sleep safe in their beds. Chatter, chatter.' He ground his teeth.

'Very good, church-minister,' she said meekly. 'But there's a funeral he had! Over a hundred wreaths there were, and Canon Williams, he preached by the graveside till everybody was crying sore.' She turned to go, but came back humble, her neck curved down and from its downy slope the glowing corn-smell coming. 'Excuse me, please now, but my Bible I've lost coming here. A little old copy you don't want have you got? After washing up, I am sitting down for a while by the fire, and cosy for the night a chapter puts me.'

He gave her a Bible. He knew that she put nearly all her wages in the Post Office savings-bank. She dressed with a neat subdued taste proper to a rectory, and on her evening out she visited the sexton's wife (who however had not been without blemishes in her time) and helped to make skirts for the South African Mission. *Was* she the tailed temptress? Or a pearl of very great price?

One Friday just after harvest had begun Peter Bach turned round from the raspberry canes and found the rector before him, black and sinewy, spread like some awful eagle. 'Well now,' Peter stammered, 'a jump you gave me!'

The rector, finger pressed on nostril and eyes narrowed, did not speak for a full minute, keeping the brooding gleam of his gaze on the frightened young man. But when he spoke, it was kindly: 'Peter Bach, are you without ambition?'

Curly-haired and foolishly good-looking as a girl, Peter Bach's cupid lips trembled. 'I couldn't come to choir-practice Wednesday because Shinkin's threshing machine broke and . . .'

'The world,' said the rector, 'is full of wonders. They are within your grasp. Do you not wish to become a sailor of His Majesty's Navy?'

'Hoping I am to be a policeman like dad later on, and . . .'

'The country needs sailors more than policemen,' declared the rector testily. 'Have the young men of Brwmstan lost all their patriotism! Not one is in the Services. I would be willing to do all in my power for you,' he hinted.

Peter Bach, uneasily scratching his head, said: 'Ships rock about and sink.' And warily he reminded the rector: 'Best tenor I am in the choir; don't I sing solo in the anthems?'

'Ah,' grunted the rector impatiently, moving away, 'ah, would that I were your age again!' Yellow pouches were under his eyes, as if the temptations of Maudie's rich dishes had been too much. And all that day and the next he was restless about the house, unable to settle to book or to meditation.

On Saturday night he went up to bed at his usual hour, but before midnight there he was noiselessly going downstairs again and into the dining-room back of the house. He sat in the dark at the window, looking into the summer night that was so clear that the long view over stooked field and pasture was visible. Ears pricked, once he leaned forward in the chair. The church clock tolled midnight.

Harvest finished with praise from all. Summer had laughed, and wept not too much: the grain was handsome. Orchards bowed heavy, haystacks smelled rich. On the Saturday set apart for the final celebration there was great all-day drinking in the eight inns. From the vans coming from Gafr Coch the women bought food in tins, fashionable new stays, whips and tops for the children, and other luxuries. The god of fertility not forgotten, according to ancient

233

custom a labourer climbed up the tall pole on the Green and tied a bunch of wheat to the top.

Laughing came all day from festive throats, and bells and trumpets from the little fair on the green. After the inns closed there was to be a dance in Obadiah's barn. But all that day, while the moon lay down behind Cawfil mountain, the rector had strode about in dark distress. In the early evening he stalked to the kitchen.

'Pack your nightshirt,' he commanded, 'and get ready to catch the bus to Gafr Coch. Quick now. Take this letter to the Deanery. It is important. The dean's housekeeper will put you up for the night. Come back in the morning bus.'

So stern and menacing was he that Maudie, though her jaw dropped, jumped to obey. He hung round her like a demon, hurrying her, bundling her out of the house. He went with her to the bus, he shook his finger at her: 'Don't you lose the book the Dean will give you. It is valuable. I need it for my sermon tomorrow.'

Her pink mouth open in fear, the bus took her safely away.

At midnight the moon, coloured like a bull, came up splendid. Out of him a wicked red light poured into the world. And as the hour struck, the rector, naked, stern and denunciatory, blew out the candle and climbed into Maudie's bed. Shutting the moonlight out, loose-hanging curtains were drawn tidy over the half-open window. Distant sounds of a banjo came from Obadiah's barn. The church clock struck a quarter.

His fury grew. Was he to be thwarted! Then, long past the hour, there were creeping sounds below the window. A hand thrust aside the curtains and in a quick shaft of moonlight Peter Bach jumped into the room.

'Couldn't come earlier, Maudie,' he whispered. 'There's a job I had chucking Jane Roberts off!' He smelled of beer and smoke like a young Satan.

The rector made the slow breathing noises of one asleep. Old-fashioned, feathery and pompous, the bed was in shadow. Peter Bach was busy throwing off his clothes. And he stepped to the bed, yawning like a married man. The hump under the bed-clothes had not stirred. 'Hoy there, wake up,' whispered Peter, giving it a push with his fist. He threw back the coverings and jumped in.

'No one there is like my nice Maudie,' he murmured. And sidled up.

Two long sinewy arms gripped him. In terrible wrath a hairy body bore down on him. Peter Bach's first yelp of surprise was followed by a bellow of fear. 'Ow, ow,' he screamed, 'oh, mother, mother!' He struggled like a caught salmon. But the punishing arms and legs throttled all his movements. A wild animal escaped from a circus was in Maudie's bed! Maudie, bitten to death, was lying under the bed! He bawled for help.

He was thrust out sprawling on the floor. The animal drew itself up on the bed, a horrid shape black with hair. Noises of fury came from it. Peter Bach leapt up and dashed for the window. After him scrambled the beast. Down the edge of the conservatory, to the water-butt, on to the ground. Two naked figures with frenzied limbs flying. High in the sky the moon looked down in red amazement.

'I will flay,' a voice bellowed in words at last, 'your evil skin from off you!'

Peter Bach, jumping over the meadow beyond the rectory, recognized the voice and understood. The rector charged after him, losing ground a little but scuttling fast in his awful wrath. Whimpering in terror, Peter cried back over his shoulder: 'Oh sir, oh sir! I'll never touch Maudie again. I'll join the Navy, I'll go as a sailor.'

'You'd use my house for your goat's business, would you!' yelled the rector.

Past old Shinkin's farm they streamed. Down the slope where mushrooms slid up to the moon's glow and cow-pats darkly circled the grass. 'Mother!' screeched Peter, slipping on a pat and tumbling down the slop. 'Ow, ow.'

'I will clean this village of its beastliness,' yelled the rector.

Bottom of the slope was a big pond. Peter Bach jumped up and with a yelp plunged headlong into the shiny green water. And thus he escaped, thrashing his way across. For the rector hated cold water as the devil hates salt. He pranced raging on the bank, shouting across. He would purge Brwmstan of its foulnesses, he would protect the white virgins and enclose them in walls.

Peter Bach, dropping green slime, disappeared into the moonlit bushes the other side. And as far as the people of Brwmstan knew, the moonlight ate him for ever. By the next afternoon he was gone, though some months afterwards someone received a postcard from Gibraltar where he was serving in a dreadnought.

And when Maudie, faithfully holding the valuable book to her bosom, returned from Gafr Coch by the morning bus and the rector thundered to her of his discovery, she collapsed and made full confession of all her misdoings, the whole taking an hour to tell. But her shame and repentance were beautiful. Peter Bach's fault it was, she sobbed, he wouldn't leave her alone, no indeed.

'What are we to do about you now!' he exclaimed, pale but masterful after the episode of the night.

Cast down before him in wonderful contrition, she babbled: 'I don't know, indeed.' But she peeped up at him humbly, with wet blue peeps, and her rich neck curved under him obedient.

'You must be saved from yourself,' he announced. 'I will marry you. It is the only way to keep you safe from ruffians.'

'Very well, church-minister.' She rose, and her bosom came out proud as peonies. 'A good woman I'll be. And now your lunch I must cook. A lunch fit for a king it will be, I promise you.' For she was of those who recognize true power.

And, to the brief scandal of the people of Brwmstan, he married her, the Dean of Gafr Coch officiating. But so like a lion was he, roaring his noble contempt of the world, that the couple received all manner of presents from the farmers, including a fresh-cured ham and a plump goose. For all that, some months afterwards Farmer Shinkins was heard to complain in the Malt Shovel taproom: 'Very dull the rector's sermons are getting, surely? Shout and kick at us any more he don't. Yet,' he added, staring in an aggrieved way into his beer, 'bundles of sin and evil we still are, surely, surely now?'

NIGHTGOWN

I

She had married Walt after a summer courtship during which they had walked together in a silence like aversion.

Coming of a family of colliers, too, the smell of the hulking young man tramping to her when she stepped out of an evening was the sole smell of men. He would have the faintly scowling look which presently she, too, acquired. He half resented having to go about their business, but still his feet impelled him to her street corner and made him wait until, closed-faced and glancing sideways threateningly, she came out of her father's house. They walked wordless on the grit beside the railway track, his mouth open as though in a perpetual yawn. For courting she had always worn a new lilac dress out of a proper draper's shop. This dress was her last fling in that line.

She got married in it, and they took one of the seven-and-six-penny slices of the long blocks of concreted stone whipping round a slope and called Bryn Hyfryd—that is, Pleasant Hill. Like her father, Walt was a pub collier, not chapel.

The big sons had arrived with unchanged regularity, each of the same heavy poundage. When the sex of the fifth was told her, she turned her face sullenly to the wall and did not look at him for some time. And he was her last. She was to have no companionable daughter after all, to dote on when the men were in the pit. As the sons grew, the house became so obstreperously male that she began to lose nearly all feminine attributes and was apt to wear a man's cap and her sons' shoes, socks, and mufflers to run out to the shop. Her expression became tight as a fist, her jaw jutted out like her men's and like them she only used her voice when it was necessary, though sometimes she would clang out at them with a criticism they did not understand. They would only scowl the family scowl.

For a while she had turned in her shut-up way to Trevor, her last-born. She wanted him to be small and delicate—she had imagined he was of different mould from his brothers—and she had dim ideas of his putting his hand to something more elegant than a pick in the pits. He grew into the tall, gruff image of his brothers. Yet still, when the time came for him to leave school at fourteen, she had bestirred herself, cornering him and speaking in her sullen way:

237

'Trevor, you don't want to go to that dirty old pit, do you? Plenty of other things to do. One white face let me have coming home to me now.' He had set up a hostile bellow at once. 'I'm going to the pit. Dad's going to ask his haulier for me.' He stared at her in fear. 'To the pits I'm going. You let me alone.' He dreaded her hard but seeking approaches; his brothers would poke jeering fun at him, asking him if his napkins were pinned on all right, it was as if they tried to destroy her need of him, snatching him away.

She had even attempted to wring help from her husband: 'Walt, why can't Trevor be something else? What do I want with six men in the pit? One collier's more work in the house than four clean-job men.'

'Give me a shilling, 'ooman,' he said, crossing his red-spotted white muffler, 'and don't talk daft.' And off he went to the Miskin Arms.

So one bitter January morning she had seen her last-born leave the house with her other men, pit trousers on his lengthening legs and a gleaming new jack and food tin under his arm. From that day he had ranged up inextricably with his brothers, sitting down with them at four o'clock to bacon and potatoes, even the same quantity of everything, and never derided by them again. She accepted his loss, as she was bound to do, though her jutting jaw seemed more bony, thrust out like a lonely hand into the world's air.

They were all on the day shift in the pits, and in a way she had good luck, for not one met with any accidents to speak of, they worked regular, and had no fancies to stay at home because of a pain in big toe or ear lobe, like some lazybones. So there ought to have been good money in the house. But there wasn't.

They ate most of it, with the rest for drinking. Bacon was their chief passion, and it must be of the best cut. In the shop,where she was never free of debt, nearly every day she would ask for three pounds of thick rashers when others would ask for one, and if Mr. Griffiths would drop a hint, looking significantly at his thick ledger, saying: 'Three pounds, Mrs. Rees, *again*?' her reply was always: 'I've got big men to feed.' As if that was sufficient explanation for all debt and she could do nothing about it; there were big, strapping men in the world and they had to be fed.

Except with one neighbour, she made no kind of real contact with anyone outside her home. And not much inside it. Of the middle height and bonily skimped of body, she seemed extinguished by the assembly of big males she had put into the world off her big husband. Peering out surly from under the poke of her man's cap, she never went beyond the main street of the vale, though as a child she had been once to the seaside, in a buff straw hat ringed with daisies.

Gathered in their pit-dirt for the important four-o'clock meal, with bath

238

pans and hot foods steaming in the fireplace, the little kitchen was crowded as the Black Hole of Calcutta. None of the sons, not even the eldest, looked like marrying, though sometimes, like a shoving parent bird, she would try to push them out of the nest. One or two of them set up brief associations with girls which never seemed to come properly to anything. They were the kind that never marry until the entertainments of youth, such as football, whippet-racing, and beer, have palled at last. She would complain to her next-door-up neighbour that she had no room to put down even a thimble.

This neighbour, Mrs. Lewis—the other neighbours set her bristling—was her only friend in the place, though the two never entered each other's house. In low voices they conversed over the back wall, exchanging all the eternal woes of women in words of cold, knowledgeable judgment that God Himself could have learnt from. To Mrs. Lewis's remark that Trevor, her last, going to work in the pits ought to set her on her feet now, she said automatically, but sighing for once: 'I've got big men to feed.' That fact was the core of her world. Trevor's money, even when he began to earn a man's wage, was of no advantage. Still she was in debt in the shop. The six men were profitless; the demands of their insides made them white elephants.

So now, at fifty, still she could not sit down on the sofa for an hour and dream of a day by the seaside with herself in a clean new dress at last and a draper's-shop hat fresh as a rose.

But often in the morning she skulked to London House, the draper's on the corner of the main road, and stopped for a moment to peer sideways into the window where two wax women, one fair and one dark, stood dressed in all the latest fashions and smiling a pink, healthy smile. Looking beautiful beyond compare, these two ladies were now more living to her than her old dream of a loving daughter. They had no big men to feed and, poised in their eternal shade, smiled leisurely above their furs and silk blouses. It was her treat to see them, as she stood glancing out from under Enoch's thrown-away cap, her toe-sprouting shoes unlaced and her skirt of drab flannel hanging scarecrow. Every other week they wore something new. The days when Mr. Roberts the draper changed their outfits, the sight of the new wonders remained in her eyes until the men arrived home from the pit.

Then one morning she was startled to find the fair wax lady attired in a wonderful white silk nightgown, flowing down over the legs most richly and trimmed with lace at bosom and cuffs. That anyone could wear such luxuriance in bed struck her at first like a blow in the face. Besides, it was a shock to see the grand lady standing there undressed, as you might say, in public. But, staring into the window, she was suddenly thrilled.

239

She went home feeling this new luxury round her like a sweet, clean silence. Where no men were.

II

At four o'clock they all clattered in, Walt and her five swart sons, flinging down food tins and jacks. The piled heaps of bacon and potatoes were ready. On the scrubbed table were six large plates, cutlery, mugs, and a loaf, a handful of lumpy salt chucked down in the middle. They ate their meal before washing, in their pit-dirt, and the six black faces, red mouths and white eyes gleaming, could be differentiated only by a mother.

Jaw stuck out, she worked about the table, shifting on to each plate four thick slices of bacon, a stream of sizzling fat, ladles of potatoes and tinned tomatoes. They poked their knives into the heap of salt, scattered it over the plate, and began. Lap of tongue around food was their only noise for a while. She poured the thick black tea out of a battered enamel pot big enough for a palace or a workhouse.

At last a football match was mentioned, and what somebody said last night in the Miskin taproom about that little whippet. She got the tarts ready, full-sized plates of them, and they slogged at these; the six plates were left naked in a trice. Oddments followed: cheese, cake, and jams. They only stopped eating when she stopped producing.

She said, unexpectedly: 'Shouldn't be surprised if you'd all sit there till doomsday, 'long as I went on bringing food without stoppage.'

'Aye,' said Ivor. 'What about a tin of peaches?'

Yet not one of them, not even her middle-aged husband, had a protuberant belly or any other signs of large eating. Work in the pit kept them sinewy and their sizes as nature intended. Similarly, they could have drunk beer from buckets, like horses, without looking it. Everything three or four times the nice quantities eaten by most people, but no luxuries except that the sons never spread jam thinly on bread like millionaires' sons but in fat dabs, and sometimes they demanded pineapple chunks for breakfast as if they were kings or something. She wondered sometimes that they did not grind up the jam pots, too, in their strong white shiny teeth; but Trevor, the youngest, had the rights to lick the pots, and thrust down his tongue almost to the bottom.

At once, after the meal, the table was shoved back. She dragged in the wooden tub before the fire. Her husband always washed first, taking the clean water. He slung his pit clothes to the corner, belched, and stepped into the tub. He did not seem in a hurry this afternoon. He stood and rubbed up his curls—still black and crisp after fifty years—and bulged the muscle of his black

240

right arm. 'Look there,' he said, 'you pups, if a muscle like that you got at my age, men you can call yourselves.'

Ranged about the kitchen, waiting for their bath turn with cigarette stuck to red-licked lower lip, the five sons looked variously derisive, secure in their own bone and muscle. But they said nothing; the father had a certain power, lordly in his maturity. He stood there naked, handsome, and well-endowed; he stood musing for a bit, liking the hot water round his feet and calves. But his wife, out and in with towels, shirts, and buckets, had heard his remark. With the impatience that had seemed to writhe about her ever since they had clattered in, she cried: 'What are you standing there for showing off, you big ram! Wash yourself, man, and get away with you.'

He took no notice. One after the other the sons stripped; after the third bath the water was changed, being then thick and heavy as mud. They washed each other's back, and she scuttled in and out, like a dark, irritated crab this afternoon, her angry voice nipping at them. When Ieuan, the eldest and six foot two, from where he was standing in the tub spat across into a pan of fresh water on the fire, in a sudden fury she snatched up the dirty coal-shovel and gave him a ringing smack on his washed behind. Yet the water was only intended for the dirt-crusted tub. He scowled; she shouted: 'You blackguard, you keep your spit for public-house floors.'

After she had gone into the scullery, Trevor, waiting his turn, grunted: 'What's the matter with the old woman today?' Ieuan stepped out of the tub. The shovel blow might have been the tickle of a feather. But Trevor advised him: 'Better wash your best face again; that shovel's left marks.'

From six o'clock onwards one by one they left the house, all, including Walt, in a navy-blue serge suit, muffler, cap, and yellowish-brown shoes, their faces glistening pale from soap. They strutted away on their long, easy legs to their various entertainments, though with their heads somehow down in a kind of ducking. Their tallness made it a bit awkward for themselves in some of the places down in the pits.

Left alone with the piles of crusted pit clothes, all waiting to be washed or dried of their sweat, she stood taking a cup of tea and nibbling a piece of bread, looking out of the window. Except on Sundays her men seldom saw her take a meal, though even on Sunday she never ate bacon. There was a month or two of summer when she appeared to enjoy a real plate of something, for she liked kidney beans and would eat a whole plateful, standing with her back to the room and looking out of the window towards the distant mountain brows under the sky, as if she was thinking of Heaven. Her fourth son Emlyn said to her once: 'Your Sunday feed lasts you all the week, does it? Or a good guzzle you have when we're in the pit?'

She stood thinking till her head hurt. The day died on the mountain-tops. Where was the money coming from, with them everlasting pushing expensive bacon into their red mouths? The clock ticked.

Suddenly, taking a coin from a secret place and pulling on a cap, she hurried out. A spot burning in her cheeks, she shot into the corner draper's just as he was about to close, and, putting out her jaw, panted to old Roberts: 'What's the price of that silk nightgown on the lady in the window?'

After a glance at the collier's wife in man's cap and skirt rough as an old mat, Roberts said crossly: 'A price you can't afford, so there!' But when she seemed to mean business he told her it was seventy bob and elevenpence and he hoped that the pit manager's wife or the doctor's would fancy it.

She said defiantly: 'You sell it to me. A bob or more a week I'll pay you, and you keep it till I've finished the amount. Take it out of the window now at once and lay it by. Go on now, fetch it out.'

'What's the matter with you!' he shouted testily, as though he was enraged as well as astonished at her wanting a silk nightgown. 'What d'you want it for?'

'Fetch it out,' she threatened, 'or my husband Walt Rees I'll send to you quick.' The family of big, fighting males was well-known in the streets. After some more palaver Roberts agreed to accept her instalments and, appeased, she insisted on waiting until he had undraped the wax lady in the window. With a bony, trembling finger she felt the soft white silk for a second and hurried out of the shop.

III

How she managed to pay for the nightgown in less than a year was a mystery, for she had never a penny to spare, and a silver coin in the house in the middle of the week was rare as a Christian in England. But regularly she shot into the draper's and opened her grey fist to Roberts. Sometimes she demanded to see the nightgown, frightened that he might have sold it for quick money to someone else, though Roberts would shout at her: 'What's the matter with you? Packed up safe it is.'

One day she braved his wrath and asked if she could take it away, promising faithful to keep up the payments. But he exclaimed: 'Be off! Enough tradesmen here been ruined by credit. Buying silk nightgowns indeed! What next?'

She wanted the nightgown in the house; she was fearful it would never be hers in time. Her instinct told her to be swift. So she hastened, robbing still further her own stomach and in tiny lots even trying to rob the men's, though they would scowl and grumble if even the rind was off their bacon. But at last, when March winds blew down off the mountains so that she had to wrap round her scraggy chest the gaunt shawl in which her five lusty babies had been nursed, she paid the last instalment. Her chin and cheeks blue in excitement, she took the parcel home when the men were in the pit.

Locking the door, she washed her hands, opened the parcel, and sat with the silk delicately in her hands, sitting quiet for half an hour at last, her eyes come out in a gleam from her dark face, brilliant. Then she hid the parcel down under household things in a drawer which the men never used.

A week or two later, when she was asking for the usual three pounds of bacon at the shop, Mr. Griffith said to her, stern: 'What about the old debts, now then? Pity you don't pay up, instead of buying silk nightgowns. Cotton is good enough for my mussus to sleep in, and you lolling in silk, and don't pay for all your bacon and other things. Pineapple chunks every day. Hoo!' And he glared.

'Nightgown isn't for *my* back,' she snapped. 'A wedding present for a relation it is.' But she was a bit winded that the draper had betrayed her secret to his fellow tradesman.

He grumbled: 'Don't know what to do with all you take out of my shop. Bacon every day enough to feed a funeral, and tins of fruit and salmons by the dozen. Eat for fun, do you?'

'I've got big men to feed.' She scowled, as usual.

Yet she seemed less saturnine as she sweated over the fireplace and now never once exclaimed an irritation at some clumsiness of the men. Even when, nearly at Easter, she began to go bad, no complaint came from her, and of course the men did not notice, for still their bacon was always ready and the tarts as many, their bath water hot, and evening shirts ironed.

On Easter Bank Holiday, when she stopped working for a while because the men had gone to whippet races over in Maerdy Valley, she had time to think of her pains. She felt as if the wheels of several coal wagons had gone over his body, though there were no feeling at all in her legs. When the men arrived home at midnight, boozed up, there were hot faggots for them, basting pans savoury full, and their pit clothes were all ready for the morning. She attended on them in a slower fashion, her face closed and her body shorter, because her legs had gone bowed. But they never noticed, jabbering of the whippets.

Mrs. Lewis next door said she ought to stay in bed for a week. She replied that the men had to be fed.

A fortnight later, just before they arrived home from the pit and the kitchen was hot as a furnace, her legs kicked themselves in the air, the full frying-pan in her hand went flying, and when they came in they found her black-faced

243

on the floor with the rashers of bacon all about her. She died in the night as the district nurse was wetting her lips with water. Walt, who was sleeping in a chair downstairs, went up too late to say farewell.

Because the house was upside down as a result, with the men not fed properly, none of them went to work in the morning. At nine o'clock Mrs. Lewis next door, for the first time after thirty years of back-wall friendship with the deceased, stepped momentously into the house. But she had received her instructions weeks ago. After a while she called down from upstairs to the men sitting uneasy in the kitchen: 'Come up; she is ready now.'

They slunk up in procession, six big men, with their heads ducked, disturbed out of the rhythm of their daily life of work, food, and pub. And entering the room for the last view, they stared in surprise.

A stranger lay on the bed ready for her coffin. A splendid, shiny, white silk nightgown flowing down over her feet, with rich lace frilling bosom and hands, she lay like a lady taking a rest, clean and comfortable. So much they stared, it might have been an angel shining there. But her face jutted stern, bidding no approach to the contented peace she had found.

The father said, cocking his head respectfully: 'There's a fine 'ooman she looks. Better than when I married her!'

'A grand nightshirt,' mumbled Enoch. 'That nurse brought it in her bag?'

'A shroud they call it,' said Emlyn.

'In with the medical benefits it is,' said his father soberly. 'Don't they dock us enough every week from our wages?'

After gazing for a minute longer at the white apparition, lying there so majestically unknown, they filed downstairs. There Mrs. Lewis awaited them. 'Haven't you got no 'ooman relation to come in and look after you?' she demanded.

The father shook his head, scowling in effort to concentrate on a new problem. Big, black-curled, and still vigorous, he sat among his five strapping sons who, like him, smelt of the warm, dark energy of life. He said: 'A new missus I shall have to be looking for. Who is there about, Mrs. Lewis, that is respectable and can cook for us and see to our washings? My boys I got to think about. A nice little widow or something you know of that would marry a steady working chap? A good home is waiting for her by here, though a long day it'll be before I find one that can feed and clean us like the one above; *she* worked regular as a clock, fair play to her.'

'I don't know as I would recommend any 'ooman,' said Mrs. Lewis with rising colour.

'Pity you're not a widow! Ah well, I must ask the landlady of the Miskin if she knows of one,' he said, concentrated.

ALICE'S PINT

Evans Cockles, who was giving up business, sold his donkey to Griffiths Fruit and Vegetables, who had just come to the vale. The very first day that Griffiths took her out with the cart, Alice—that was the moke's name—drew up sharp and unbid outside the Rose and Crown, which is half-way up the vale.

'Hoy,' Griffiths shouted, twitching the reins, 'come on now, gee up.' Alice looked round, gave a little belly-shake, but did not budge. Griffiths flicked the whip. 'Go on, gee up with you, now then!' Alice only whinnied protestingly. Griffiths lashed the whip and roared: 'What's the matter with you, you god-damn little *crab*? Shove off, will you!' Alice whined a bit but stood firm, her hoofs sturdily clamped to the road.

Griffiths was the more surprised because so far on the round she had been docile and obedient enough, trotting quite eager from one street to another. The lay of the vale was as familiar to her as it was to P.C. Dai Daniels, now standing on the corner with a cynical grin on his blue jaw. At last, when Griffiths's face was getting red as boiling beet-root, Dai strolled over and said officially:

'She won't budge till she's had her pint.'

'What!' spluttered Griffiths.

'Her pint of beer. She's been used to it for five years now, to my knowledge. Evans Cockles was always stopping here, for a pint for himself and a pint for Alice, all the year round.'

Griffiths exploded, for he was neither a generous man nor much of a drinker. Whip in hand, he attacked Alice with bitter venom, until P.C. Dai trumpeted warningly: 'Hold on now! Stop. A donkey's got feelings same as the rest of us.' Griffiths took the hint. All the time Alice's hoofs hadn't budged, though she vigorously shook her head up and down as if in astonished protest against all this fuss over a pint of beer.

There was nothing else for Griffiths to do but go in the Rose and Crown for Alice's pint, which was poured into a flat earthenware bowl kept specially for her.

Alice, with Griffiths holding the bowl, drew the beer up gratefully, her middle-aged grey lips content in the rick liquid. Griffiths was cursing about this expense to each business day, for the Rose and Crown couldn't be avoided on his round.

But Alice's big silver ears closed and opened in shivering delight while she drank. She had another trick too. The beer finished, she lifted her head high, set back her lips and, displaying all her teeth, gave a long, gurgling laugh. Griffiths started back in astonishment from the laugh. He gazed at Alice with sobered dread now.

She, briskly shaking her body, was ready to begin business again. And during the rest of the round she trotted the streets with stylish niceness, stopping prompt at customers' doors and taking corners tidily and undirected. On her way back from the top of the vale she never stopped at the Rose and Crown. It was afternoon closing time by then, anyhow.

'The old donkey that I had in Pontypridd,' Griffiths grumbled, however, 'was teetotal as a Baptist minister and never laughed from one Christmas to another.'

It did not seem proper that a donkey should be so intelligent. What next would Alice do? Yet in everything else she was an orderly example to all workers. Let Griffiths, on starting the round, load the cart as much as she liked, she never staggered. There was her pint to look forward to half-way up the vale and, after it, there was the abiding tonic power the beer gave. Alice asked no more of life.

Little did she know that, though she had triumphed over her new owner, another threat to her bit of pleasure was brewing.

It was a time when the vale was filling up with new houses, and to one of these came Mrs. Maud James. She was a woman who Spoke and a great one for organising meetings against this and that, which she did very well, being herself very public-looking and with a deep, stern voice. She called herself a lover of animals, was strict teetotal, wore big furs, and usually a pheasant's feather stuck up like a sword from her hat.

One day she was passing the Rose and Crown while Alice was about to enjoy her beer. Griffiths, who by now had come to accept this little interlude in the day's busniness and even took a half pint himself, was just carrying the bowl out. Mrs. James stopped short. Her nostrils twitched. She peered into the bowl.

'Surely,' she boomed, 'you're not giving that poor animal *beer!*' Griffiths nodded. Mrs. James swelled. 'What a scandal! Doing it for fun, I suppose. You disgusting man,' she said severely, 'are you intoxicated yourself? That donkey needs water. It's a shame he should be taken advantage of——'

'Alice is a lady, ma'am——' Griffiths began, stopping on the kerb.

'That makes it worse if anything,' declared Mrs. James, flushing. She worked herself up indignantly. 'Look here, if you don't stop this I'll report you to the——'

246

Alice stretched her head to them and gave a loud neigh of impatience, her eyes devouring the withheld bowl.

'Budge from here,' Griffiths was trying to explain, 'she won't without her beer.'

'Nonsense. I never heard of such a thing. It's you drunkards of men, not satisfied with intoxicating yourselves, but you want to make the very beasts resemble you.' Now she was well away on one of her favourite themes. The feather in her hat quivered in fury. 'Do you starve that poor animal? It looks bony enough. Just as drunkards starve their poor wives and children——'

'Here,' Griffiths began to growl, 'put a brake on it. Who's blooming moke is this . . . All right, Alice, my girl, I'm coming.' For there were pitiable neighs now.

Mrs. James refused to be silenced, and by now a few people had gathered round. While Alice thirstily drew up the all-too-brief pint, she appealed to them: 'Don't you agree this is a scandal? Intoxicating a poor animal——'

Alice, perhaps attracted by Mrs. James's fur, lifted up her head from the emptied bowl and swerved it quite near the woman. Her lips pulled back, she uttered that long, gurgling laugh up and down the stretch of her neck. And all her grey belly shook, and her high, pointed silver ears, quivered.

Mrs. James started back from that strange, antique laugh, with its wild echoes of champing teeth, rubbed tough sinews, and clashing bones. Besides, those evilly gaunt teeth were dangerously near. The little knot of people had tittered.

'There!' said Griffiths. 'See what Alice thinks of your teetotal ideas?'

But, undaunted, Mrs. James's anger was renewed. She filled her lungs, heaved, and let loose: 'It's wicked. As I thought, you give this wretched beast drink to get fun out of it. You probably do not water it, so that it's obliged to drink anything. I *know*. This has been a most disgusting sight. I shall report you. Your cart looks overloaded to me too. It's not enought to make this creature a beast of burden but you'd make it into a sot too——'

Alice suddenly dropped a steaming load.

'—yes, a sot,' heaved Mrs. James. 'It's the most scandalous ——' But the burst of laughter which came from the people discomposed her at last. She began to back away, not without various threats, however.

Alice began to give sundry indications that she wished to resume the day's business now. Her soft, gleaming eyes looked round enquiringly. She stamped a hoof. Briskly she whisked her tail in the steam.

Someone in the crowd remarked: 'Seems that Alice has got a back answer for everything, same as all her crew.'

247

THE DARK WORLD

'Where can we go to-night?' Jim asked. Once again it was raining. The rows of houses in the valley bed were huddled in cold grey mist. Beyond them the mountains prowled unseen. The iron street lamps spurted feeble jets of light. There were three weeks to go before Christmas. They stood in a chapel doorway and idly talked, their feet splashed by the rain.

Thomas said: 'There's someone dead up in Calfaria Terrace.'

'Shall we go to see him?' Jim suggested immediately.

They had not seen any corpses for some weeks. One evening they had seen five, and so for a while the visits had lost their interest. When on these expeditions they would search through the endless rows of houses for windows covered with white sheets, the sign that death was within, and when a house was found thus, they would knock at the door and respectfully ask if they might see the dead. Only once they were denied, and this had been at a villa, not a common house. Everywhere else they had been taken to the parlour or bedroom where the corpse lay, sometimes in a coffin, and allowed a few seconds' stare. Sometimes the woman of the house, or maybe a daughter, would whisper: 'You knew him, did you?' Or, if the deceased was a child: 'You were in the same school?' They would nod gravely. Often they had walked three or four miles through the valley searching out these dramatic houses. It was Jim who always knocked at the door and said, his cap in his hand: 'We've come to pay our respects, mum.'

At the house in Calfaria Terrace they were two in a crowd. The dead had been dead only a day and neighbours were also paying their respects, as was the custom: there was quite a procession to the upstairs room. The corpse was only a very old man, and his family seemed quite cheerful about it. Thomas heard the woman of the house whisper busily on the landing to a neighbour in a shawl: 'That black blouse you had on the line, Jinny, it'll be a help. The 'surance won't cover the fun'ral, and you know Emlyn lost four days in the pit last week. Still, gone he is now, and there'll be room for a lodger.' And, entreatingly: 'You'll breadcrumb the ham for me, Jinny? . . . I 'ont forget you when you're in trouble of your own.' The dead old man lay under a patchwork quilt. His face was set in an expression of mild surprise. Thomas noticed dried soapsuds in his ear. Four more people came into the bedroom and the two boys were almost hustled out. No one had taken any particular notice of them. Downstairs they asked a skinny cruel-looking young woman

248

for a glass of water and to their pleased astonishment she gave them each a glass of small-beer.

'It didn't seem as though he was dead at all,' Jim said, as if cheated. 'Let's look for more. In November there's a lot of them. They get bronchitis and consumption.'

'It was like a wedding,' Thomas said. Again they stood in a doorway and looked with vacant boredom through the black curtains of rain sweeping the valley.

'My mother had a new baby last night,' Jim suddenly blurted out, frowning. But when Thomas asked what kind it was, Jim said he didn't know yet. But he knew that there were nine of them now, beside his father and mother and two lodgers. He did not complain. But of late he had been expressing an ambition to go to sea when he left school, instead of going to the colliery.

Jim, in the evenings, was often pushed out of home by his mother, a bitter black-browed woman who was never without a noisy baby. Jim's father was Irish, a collier of drunken reputation in the place, and the whole family was common as a clump of dock. Thomas's mother sometimes made one or two surprised remarks at his association with Jim. They shared a double desk in school. Occasionally Thomas expressed disgust at Jim's unwashed condition.

Again they set out down the streets, keeping a sharp lookout for white sheets in the windows. After a while they found a house so arrayed, yellow blobs of candle-light like sunflowers shining through the white of the parlour. Jim knocked and respectfully made his request to a big creaking woman in black. But she said gently: 'Too late you are. The coffin was screwed down after tea today. Funeral is tomorrow. The wreaths you would like to see?'

Jim hesitated, looking back enquiringly over his shoulder at Thomas. Without speaking, both rejected this invitation, and with mumbled thanks they backed away. 'No luck tonight,' Jim muttered.

'There was the small beer,' Thomas reminded him. A wind had jumped down from the mountains and as they scurried on it unhooked a faulty door of a street-lamp and blew out the wispy light. When they had reached the bottom of the vale the night was black and rough and moaning, the rain stinging hot on cheeks and hands like whips. Here was a jumbled mass of swarthy and bedraggled dwellings, huddled like a stagnant meeting of bats. A spaniel, dragging her swollen belly, whined out to them from under a bony bush. She sounded lost and confused and exhausted with the burden that weighted her to earth. In the dark alley-ways they found a white sheet. A winter silence was here, the black houses were glossy in the rain. No one was about.

'Let's go back,' whispered Thomas. 'It's wet and late.'

'There's one here,' Jim protested. 'After coming all this way!' And he tapped at the door, which had no knocker.

The door was opened and in a shaft of lamplight stood a man's shape, behind him a warm fire-coloured interior, for the door opened on to the living room. Jim made his polite request, and the man silently stood aside. They walked into the glow.

But the taste of death was in the house, true and raw. A very bent old woman in a black cardigan clasped at her stingy throat with a geranium brooch, sat nodding before the fire. Thomas was staring at the man, who had cried out:

'It's Thomas!' He sat down heavily on a chair: 'Oh, Thomas!' he said in a wounded voice. His stricken face was though he were struggling to repudiate a new pain. A tall handsome man, known to Thomas as Elias, his face had the grey tough pallor of the underground worker.

The boy stood silent in the shock of the recognition and the suspicion prowling about his mind. He could not speak, he dare not ask. Then fearfully the man said:

'You've come to see Gwen, have you! All this way. Only yesterday I was wondering if your mother had heard. You've come to see her!'

'Yes,' Thomas muttered, his head bent. Jim stood waiting, shifting his feet. The old woman kept on nodding her head. Her son said to her loudly, his voice sounding out in suffering, not having conquered this new reminder of the past years. 'Mam, this is Thomas, Mrs. Morgan's boy. You remember? That Gwen was fond of.'

The old woman dreadfully began to weep. Her face, crumpled and brown as a dead rose, winced and shook out slow difficult tears. 'Me it ought to have been,' she said with a thin obsession. 'No sense in it, no sense at all.'

Thomas glanced secretly at Elias, to see if his emotion had abated. Three years ago he used to carry notes from Elias to Gwen, who had been the servant at home. It seemed to him that Elias and Gwen were always quarrelling. Elias used to stand for hours on the street corner until he came past, hurry up to him and say hoarsely: 'Thomas, please will you take this to Gwen.' In the kitchen at home, Gwen would always toss her head on the receipt of a note, and sometimes she indignantly threw them on the fire without reading them . . . But Gwen used to be nice. She always kept back for him, after her evening out, some of Elias's chocolates. Once or twice she had obtained permission to take him to the music-hall and gloriously he had sat between her and Elias, watching the marvellous conjurors and the women in tights who heaved their bejewelled bosoms as they sang funny songs. But Elias, he had felt, had not welcomed those intrusions. After a long time, Gwen had married him. But before she left to do this, she had wept every day for a week, her strong kind face wet and gloomy. His mother had given her a handsome parlour clock and Gwen had tearfully said she would never wind it as it would last longer if unused. Then gradually she had disappeared, gone into her new married life down the other end of the valley.

Elias looked older, older and thinner. Thomas kept his gaze away from him as much as possible. He felt shy at being drawn into the intimacy of all this grief. The old woman kept on quavering. At last Elias said, quietly now: 'You will come upstairs to see her, Thomas. And your friend.' He opened a door at the staircase and, tall and gaunt, waited for them to pass. Thomas walked past him unwillingly, his stomach gone cold. He did not want to go upstairs. But he thought that Elias would take a refusal hardly. Jim, silent and impassive, followed with politely quiet steps.

In a small, small bedroom with a low ceiling two candles were burning. A bunch of snowy chrysanthemums stood on a table beside a pink covered bed. Elias had preceded them and now he lifted a starched white square of cloth from off the head and shoulders of the dead.

She was lying tucked in the bed as if quietly asleep. The bedroom was so small there was nowhere else to look. Thomas looked, and started with a terrified surprise. The sheets were folded back, low under Gwen's chest, and cradled in her arms was a pale waxen doll swathed in white. A doll! His amazement passed into terror. He could not move, and the scalp of his head contracted as though an icy wind passed over it. Surely that wasn't a baby, that pale stiff thing Gwen was nursing against her quiet breast! Elias was speaking in a hoarse whisper, and while he spoke he stroked a fold of the bed-clothes with a grey hand.

'Very hard it was, Thomas, Gwen going like this. The two of them, I was in the pit, and they sent for me. But she had gone before I was here, though old Watkins let me come in his car . . . I didn't see her, Thomas, and she asked for me ——' His voice broke, and Thomas in his anguish of terror, saw him drop beside the bed and bury his face in the bed.

It was too much. Thomas wanted to get away; he wanted to run, away from the close narrow room, from the man shuddering beside the bed, from the figure in the bed that had been the warm Gwen, from the strange creature in her arms that looked as though it had never been warm. The terror became a nightmare menace coming nearer . . . Unconsciously he jerked his way out to the landing. Jim followed; he looked oppressed.

'Let's clear off,' he whispered nervously.

They went downstairs. The old woman was brewing tea, and in the labour seemed to forget her grief. 'You will have a cup,' she enquired, 'and a piece of nice cake?'

At this Jim was not unwilling to stay, but Thomas agonizedly plucked his sleeve. Elias's heavy step could be heard on the stairs. Then he came in, quiet and remote-looking. He laid his hand on Thomas's shoulder for a second.

'Do you remember when we used to go to the Empire, Thomas? You and Gwen used to like that Chinaman that made a white pigeon come out of an empty box.'

But Thomas saw that he was not the same Elias, who, though he would wait long hours for the indifferent Gwen like a faithful dog, had been a strutting young man with a determined eye. He was changed now, his shoulders were slackened. She had defeated him after all. Thomas sipped half a cup of tea, but did not touch the cake. He scarcely spoke. Elias kept on reminding him of various happy incidents in the past. That picnic in the mountains, when Elias had scaled the face of a quarry to fetch a blue flower Gwen had fancied. 'Didn't she dare me to get it!' he added, with a strange chuckle in his throat. 'And then she gave it to you!' He sat brooding for a while, his face turned away. Then, to Thomas's renewed terror, he began to weep again, quietly.

The mother, hobbling across to her son, whispered to the two boys. Perhaps they would go now. It was only yesterday her daughter-in-law had died, and the blow was still heavy on her son. She had stiffened herself out of her own abandonment to grief. The boys went to the door in silence. Jim looked reserved and uncommenting.

But outside, in the dark alley, he said: 'I wonder how she came to chuck the bucket! The baby was it?' Receiving no reply, he added with something like pride now: 'My mother's always having them, but she's only abed for three days, she don't die or nothing near it.' Thomas still stumbling silently by his side, he went on: 'Perhaps he'll marry again; he's only a young bloke . . . I never seen a man cry before,' he added in a voice of contempt.

But for Thomas all the night was weeping. The dark alley was an avenue of the dead, the close shuttered houses were tombs. He heard the wind howling, he could feel the cold ghostly prowling of the clouds. Drops of icy rain stung his cheeks. He was shivering. Gwen's face, bound in its white stillness, moved before him like a lost dead moon. It frightened him, he wanted to have no connection with it; he felt his inside sicken. And all the time he wanted to burst into loud howling like the wind, weep like the rain.

'Shall we look for more?' Jim said. A roused, unappeased appetite was in his voice.

Thomas leaned against the wet wall of a house. Something broke in him.

He put up his arm, buried his head in it, and cried. He cried in terror, in fear and in grief. There was something horrible in the dark world. A soft howling whine came out of his throat. Jim, ashamed, passed from wonder into contempt.

'What's up with you!' he jeered. 'You seen plenty of 'em before, haven't you? . . . Shut up,' he hissed angrily. 'There's someone coming.' And he gave Thomas a push.

Thomas hit out. All the world was jangled and threatening and hostile. The back of his hand caught Jim sharply on the cheek-bone. Immediately there was a scuffle. But it was short-lived. They had rolled into a pool of liquidly thin mud, and both were surprised and frightened by the mess they were in.

'Jesus,' exclaimed Jim. 'I'll cop it for this.'

Thomas lurched away. He stalked into the rough night. All about him was a new kingdom. Desperately he tried to think of something else. Of holidays by the sea, of Christmas, of the nut-trees in a vale over the mountains, where, too, thrushes' nests could be found in the spring, marvellously coloured eggs in them. Jim, who had seen him weep, he thought of with anger and dislike.

At the top of the hill leading to his home he paused in anguish. The bare high place was open to the hostile heavens, a lump of earth open like a helpless face to the blows of the wind and the rain. He heard derision in the howls of the wind, he felt hate and anger in the stings of the rain.

OVER AT RAINBOW BOTTOM

Sian Shurlock's cottage was over at Rainbow Bottom, in the lee of an ancient quarry which glowed a rosy tan in the sunset. Everything, except Sian's husband, flourished with great exuberance there. Twisted ropes of foliage, hung with huge pink and white trumpets of convolvulus, writhed like plumed and garlanded serpents down the quarry's face. Trees and flowers took their ease there with fertile pleasure; It was an early place too for thick-blooded blackberries. Stout toads and frogs leapt about a pond of rich green slime, and the spiders were big and muscular. The cottage itself, white and fat-stoned, was squared about with buxom hedge of black yew crusted with myriads of silver-shivering webs. An apple tree on Sian's round of lawn bore chubby fruit cheeked like prize babies.

It was a cottage to be happy in and Sian Shurlock suited it. She would often sing at her work, in a peculiar voice that couldn't be called musical in the concert-hall sense. But it had a strangely enticing quality; it it was both nude wail and provoking laughter. It made the rare pedestrians—for Rainbow Bottom was right off the main road—stop outside the cottage to listen. Independent by nature, she made up the words to her own tunes. Nobody could make sense of either.

In the country a woman cannot bury four husbands before she is forty without causing remark. People did not say that Sian disposed of her four in an illegal way—there was old Doctor Matthews and certificates to prove they died of simple and acceptable complaints; one, heart failure; two, poisoned leg; three, consumption; four, heart failure—but after the death of the fourth they did not expect she would tempt Providence a fifth time. Besides, Sian herself had announced that she was tired of men letting her down.

And she had had to buy another grave—which also meant two marble tombstones—and the expense had seemed to sober her. True, there would be room for still another husband, in addition to herself, in the new grave, but why should she be crowded thus? 'No,' she had said, 'expecting I am to lie alone with my dear Edgar, that was my quietest.' She had always insisted that her fourth husband turned out to be her best.

'But what is she going to do,' asked Tomos Tomos in the Unicorn taproom, 'at the Last Trump when the other three next door rise up too and make claim on her? Christian it's not.'

'These days,' said Jonas Gammy Foot stolidly, 'been proved it has that rise up we don't.'

Tomos, his nostrils quivering with what looked like fright, suddenly announced: 'Started singing again she has, whatever! And dropped her black. Passing her way I was this morning.'

Edgar had been buried only two months. In strict mourning Sian had kept silent over at Rainbow Bottom. Very quiet the cottage was in that drowsy warmth among the quarry's lush foliage. If you listened you could hear the delicate whirr of azure butterflies, or tread of a fat spider scurrying across a trembling web to snatch some unwary fly, and afterwards perhaps the champ of dry jaws chewing a wing or a leg. Sian judged that two months of this quiet was sufficent.

So that morning, after a breakfast of green bacon, two fried eggs and shop strawberry jam piled thick on her own beautiful snowy bread, she began singing in her odd way. Her voice throbbed with a throaty wail that seemed to call both hungrily and promise soothing delights. But the words were any old nonsense that came to her mind:

> 'Rubies, queen's heads and men's pound notes,
> The flue wants sweeping and oven won't hot,
> And merry milkmaid in size six shoes
> Tugs old man's beard round by Cuckoo's Knob,
> Twt, twt, twt,
> On a bladder of lard his will he wrote,
> Soda do clean and soap do wash,
> Very dear they are, too dear for old Emma Jones,
> Hob y derri dando!
> Three ribs he broke, there's fish in his boots,
> On toast the eyes of frogs do shine,
> Come in, come in, no money it costs,
> Ay, ay, ay, ay . . .'

And she came out into her garden in the sunny August morning, a basket for blackberries in her hand. Her mourning gone, she wore a dress barred with yellow and mulberry rings like a wasp's back. She was light-footed and her gleaming eyes were alert; her long slender legs and arms, her lively body and lithe neck were to match. She was like a brilliant insect or thin gorgeous beetle going brisk to some thieving task.

Soon the blackberries' purple blood had stained her thin fingers that, oddly enough, could never grasp light but gripped too furious, with a tenacious bite. They were fingers that would squeeze the very last drop out of lemon or udder. As she finished singing a little smile lurked on her heart-shaped small mouth. But, agile among the briars, she began again, her voice full of that old magic. And Tomos Tomos appeared up the lane. He stopped and listened, an uneasy torpor come into his honest eyes. Only when a bee zoomed warningly into his face did he lift his legs again.

Sian had seen him out of the tail of her wren-bright eye. But she took no notice of him. He disappeared slowly and as if unwillingly. She went on singing. And soon the postman came. He had not been to Sian's cottage since he had delivered the undertaker's bill for Edgar's funeral, submitted a week after.

'There you are, then, Johnnie Post,' sang Sian without surprise. 'A fortune from America you've brought me?'

Sheepishly he handed a letter. His red ears twitched. Unmarried—not like Tomos Tomos—he was young as a colt, unfinished about shoulders and hips. Sian treated him with short shrift, even though he lingered, mouth open and eye staring.

'Bit of hot weather staying,' he mumbled. 'Redding your apples are.'

'And waiting for their letters people are!' she pointed out, slamming the gate and skimming up the garden path with the full basket. 'Be off now.'

It was a letter from the Monumental Mason, sending an estimate for the tombstone, lettering inclusive but a marble dove to rest on the stone extra. Sian frowned for a moment as she sat in her cosy parlour. Marble was dear, but white was not so dear as black. A dove she could do without too.

And soon she began to sing again, going out to pick the leaping asters for her walnut table. Then presently over the road, where people so seldom came, strode a sailor, blue trousers flapping round his ankles.

'Back you are, then, Emlyn Pugh!' Sian sang, seeing him loiter at the gate. 'Ship in port, is it then?'

'Aye,' said Emlyn, shifting his feet, shy and looking down. 'Fortnight's leave.'

'Going for a walk you are,' she suggested. 'Well, no nice lanes there are on ship, no doubt.' And, one big puce aster dangling from her hand, she went inside, carefully shutting the front door. After a moment's hesitation he went on to see the new bull at Mafeking Farm.

She threw wide the windows, she opened the door. Her singing throbbed out into the blue air, shaking the dried, curled leaves on the climbing rose-bush:

> *Wet is the sea and cockles are cold,*
> *The devil would like this blackberry pie,*
> *Back leg is off my dear one's chair,*
> *Hoity-toity, oh!*

256

Dull is the brass, the lamp it smokes,
Money do dusters cost, and polish and oil,
Cheaper to be dead, and those that live
Shall handsome stones and marble dove buy,
Ay, cheaper to be dead!'

And up the road, looking vacant and glassy-eyed, hurried a stout man in homespun and a billycock hat. It was Oswallt Prosser, Insurance. As a rule he never came that way on his rounds. He too loitered uneasy near the yew hedge, listening to that singing. Finally he forced his unwilling legs a few steps beyond the cottage, but went back and, perspiring, unlatched the gate and walked up to the open door. All the time, Sian, in her parlour, kept singing her nonsense. And, still singing, she appeared in the doorway.

'Morning, Sian Shurlock,' he stammered. 'Passing I was, and wondered if a bit of business we could do these days.'

Sian looked rebuking. 'Now then, Oswallt Prosser, knowing you are very well that I belong to the Globe and Timeglass Company. Very tidy they treated me, thank you, and paid up quick for my poor Edgar.' She craned her white neck and her lively foot gave a pirouette. 'Besides, nothing else is there for me to insure now.' And her black eyes flashed, derisive.

'Hot it is,' he mumbled. 'Out canvassing I am. A little glass of small beer you don't want have you got?' His eyes went past her desirously into the rosy coolness of her spick-and-span parlour.

'Not a drop,' she said, preparing to carefully shut the door. 'Be off now on your rounds; the wrong way you've come surely!' And with forbidding politeness she asked: 'Mrs. Prosser keeping well, is she?'

He turned, scowling, away. Half an hour later she was singing once more, waking the drowsy toads and frogs in their mossy nooks about the pond and disturbing the myriad spiders at their elegant silver labours in the quarry.

'The teapot is broke and almanack says Friday,
Pancakes for supper, thin as a weasel's tail,
The old fox in his hole got a limp hind leg,
Nothing else is there for me to insure now,
Hanky-panky, ah!'

She had come out into the garden again, in her dress of mulberry and yellow rings. The rector, carrying a sheaf of parish magazines, approached, but stopped, listening, in the shade of a hazel. He frowned, stayed a little longer, then, pursing his lips, egged himself back in the direction he had come. The noon sun looked out of the sky like a lion.

But in the afternoon she was quiet, taking a nap on the chintz sofa, where poor Edgar had suddenly breathed his last one afternoon in the June heat-wave. In the early evening, however, her voice rose again, and with extra vigour, while she plucked a few ready apples off the tree over the front round of lawn. She could even be heard over at Mafeking Farm, disturbing the labourers who had just finished mowing a field of barley. Dusk was soft as peach-bloom.

And over Rainbow Bottom road, wandering with a puzzled look on his lean brown face, came Ted Thomas, late sergeant of the Hussars.

Jaw down, he stopped and listened. He did not go to the front gate, for, accustomed to service on the North-West Frontier, he was a wary man. He crept round noiseless in the hedge's shadow, reconnoitred from the quarry's depths, and then, brushing aside a web from under his very nose and greatly annoying a spider who had just been getting ready to scuttle out to an entangled fly, he peered into the garden from a certain gap in the hedge. Sian went on singing: Ted listened in profound meditation. There was no pleasure in his face. Only a damatic vacancy, like one under the influence. Suddenly, with that decision for which military men are famed, he strode away from the hedge, straightened himself smartly, and plunged off the way he had come. The singing followed him: Ted went faster.

He was staying at the Unicorn. He had come to the district to rout out old acquaintances after twenty years' absence. Forty and single, he had no relations. That night he asked soberly in the taproom: 'Hoy, who's living over in Rainbow Bottom now, then?'

No one spoke for a minute or two. Ted added in the gathering stupor, while the oil lamp jumped: 'That woman that sings . . . A name she's got?' he demanded with sudden truculence, in the silence. He began to glare round at the yellow-shadowed faces hanging dismayed in the clouds of shag-smoke.

At last Tomos Tomos, his voice rattling like a choke in his stringy neck, shot out: 'Sian Shurlock she is. And not long buried husband number four.'

'Four!' started Ted, and his jaw dropped.

There was another sudden and oppressive silence. No one peered at Ted. Then Jonas Gammy Foot, with dainty tact, enquired soft: 'Funny things you've seen in those foreign lands, Sergeant? Us by here don't see nothing 'cept a cow with cloven hoof, p'raps, and healthy pigs struck sudden with the swine fever. These big Indian snakes,' he encouraged, 'artful they are as they say?'

But Ted Thomas only shook his head. Plunged in deep thought, his scorched cheeks sucked in and his fuzz of bleached hair upright, he even ignored his beer. Seeing him thus, the others left him alone, squeezing up their eyes as they looked at each other. Harvest was discussed. But Ted slowly

258

lifted his head, inclined one ear towards the window, while his nostrils twitched. He finished his beer, got up, and swung out.

The night was fair. A crow's mile lay between Rainbow Bottom and the Unicorn. But Ted thought he distinctly heard the singing. He set off smartly, wishing he had his mare, Goldcrest, under him. And, sure enough, when he got to Sian's cottage and looked in at the gate, there she was at the open lamp-lit window behind the apple tree, rubbing something into her hair and happily singing:

> *'Say it does the hair keeps bright and glossy,*
> *Half a crown the bottle and smelling of violets,*
> *Half-past nine and time for bed and sleeping.*
> *Good-night to Friday, oh!'*

He strode up the garden path and knocked. Unafraid, the lamp shining behind her on glossy wood and bright wool-worked cushions, she opened the door, smiling pleasantly.

'Sian Shurlock you are?' he said, in his excitement going back to the sing-song of his boyhood. 'Ted Thomas I am. Sergeant of the Hussars till last week, but brought up on Neifion Farm back over the hill by there.'

'The way to the Unicorn you want?' she asked, demure.

He looked at her, in her yellow and mulberry ringed gown, and her long fingers white on the door. 'Nice home you'got,' he said, hoarse and pathetic. 'In India I been for twelve years.'

'And the Queen of Sheba I am,' she tinkled. 'Come on in then, Sergeant Thomas.'

She sat him on the flowered chintz of the sofa; she brought glasses and a pint of fruit cordial made by herself. She was teetotal as the cock top of St. Michael's spire. Her black eyes were lively as a young girl's and there was fun in the sleek stretch of her white neck. She did not need intoxicants.

Neither did Ted. Military discipline and the arid plains of India had taught him austerity. A cosy cottage in his native country and a cheerful wife were all he required now. A soldier makes up his mind quickly. After praising the cordial, and his spellbound eyes fixed immovably on her, he said:

'I got my pension, and I been putting by. Close on two hundred quid in the bank. A drunkard and a spendthrift I am not. A hoss was my pleasure only.'

Sian sat folded in on her little smile. Her dangling feet waltzed happily. But she said: 'Content I am as I am.'

Ted strained. He said: 'Clean I am in the house, a good riser in the morning, and can sole shoes good as any cobbler.'

'No doubt,' she said.

259

He tapped his chest. 'I got tattoos. On here and on my back. Best collection in the regiment it was.'

'Let me see,' she said.

In a moment he had stripped to the waist. And he was a treasure-house of beautiful pictures. She gazed at them in excitement. On his hairless chest the centre show-piece was the Leaning Tower of Pisa, with a jug of flowers, galloping horses, crossed flags and a parrot in splendid array about it. Around both his arms coiled a brilliant serpent. More wonderful still was the Lord's Supper occupying the main stretch of his flat back, complete in every detail down to the upset salt-cellar. At Sian's shrill exclamation of delight behind him, he said proudly:

'Aye, in Canterbury that was done, when I was a trooper. Not many like it there's in this country today. Chap that did it is dead now.'

'There's colours!' she cried. 'There's brightness! There's lovely!'

'Look at them all day and all night you can for ever!' he suggested earnestly. He pointed to four photographs of tidy-looking men, ranged on the mantelpiece in frames to match. 'Bad luck you've had till now, p'raps?'

She nodded. Her black round eyes were alert, as she sat with her fingers scratching the back of her hand. She smelled nice of hair lotion and her little pink tongue came out thoughtful between her pretty pointed teeth. But it was plain she was still doubtful.

'What's the matter with you?' she asked suddenly. 'You are delicate?'

'A bout of malaria I had,' he confessed. 'That's all.'

Her black eyes whirred. They seemed to have no lids.

'The winter is coming,' she tinkled. 'Your feet I must keep warm soon as the owls begin to hoot.'

In the morning she wrote off to the Monumental Mason to accept his estimate. And concerning the lettering, she wrote, let there be a good space left underneath, as the stone was for a new grave with only one in it. She decided to have a marble dove too, a black one. The letter done, she made a plate of apple-tart, unlocking a cupboard to get some cloves. On the top shelf were bottles of high green, dark purple and tawny stuffs: Sian understood how to brew not only the showy plants of the hedges but also the small demure simples lurking under them. Ted came again in time for dinner. In the sunshine she saw the wan sapped light in his eyes; even in the summer he looked whipped by cold. Her happy feet waltzed as she laid the meal. Not even her four husbands had seen those feet bare: they had little stretches of delicate skin, like webs, between the toes.

She closed the door. She sang no more. And no one else came over the road to Rainbow Bottom.

THE PITS ARE ON THE TOP

Snow whirled prettily about the bus in the bright noon light. Through a hatch in his glass cabin the driver gossiped with a policeman so enormously majestic that the flakes seemed nervous of fluttering on his blue cape; they just melted away in the fiery red of his face. The bus, a single-decker, was slowly filling up; in a few minutes it would begin its steep journey up the vale, right to the top where the pits were.

A girl entered with her young man. They sat near the front. Something of the bright, chill shine of the morning was in her oval face: he was dark, sturdy-looking and brisk, though his face had that azure pallor of the underground worker. As the couple entered and found seats together a little interested silence fell over the other passengers, who, except for the district nurse, were all married-looking women. Everybody, of course, knew that Bryn Jones was courting Dilys Morgan: perhaps they had come down to the shops that morning to buy the engagement ring.

The couple settled, interest was withdrawn from them and conversation resumed to more important matters. There was a youngish, serious-looking woman with a wreath on her knees. It was composed of red tulips, white chrysanthemums and two long-tongued orchids which were the colour of speckled toads. She eyed the wreath with uncertainty and went on with her complaint:

'Fifteen shillings, and in the summer a bigger wreath than this you can get for seven-and-six. The price of flowers! And soon as I've taken this up I've got to come down again and be fitted for my black. Potching about!' She spoke as if she wanted to administer reproof to someone or something.

'It's bronchitis weather,' sighed a fat woman with a large basket on her knees. Top of the bulgy basket was a loaf of bread, a bag of cakes and a tin of peaches. 'Did he—' she asked the woman with the wreath, hesitant, 'did he *think* he was going?'

'No. A hearty dinner enough he ate and spoke as if it was no different a Sunday to any other. Then he went to lie down on the couch in the front room. Middle of the afternoon my sister heard him coughing but didn't take no notice and went on making the cake for tea. About five o'clock she went to call him—and there he was!' A frown knitted her brow and she touched the closed mouth of a tulip with an uncertain finger. She was wondering if the flowers were quite fresh.

'It's a wonder,' said the fat woman, 'that they didn't open him up.'

'But the plates,' said the district nurse, who had her black maternity bag on her knees. 'He had the X-ray plates took not long ago and they didn't show anything.'

The fat woman did not like to dispute with the district nurse, but, pushing the loaf more firmly into the basket, she said judiciously: 'Oh aye, the plates! Funny though for him to go off so sudden: a young chap too. I wonder,' she turned again to the woman with the wreath, 'your sister didn't *ask* for him to be opened up, like Joe Evans and Dai Richards in my street was, when they went. It's worth it for the compensation. The pits got to pay for silicosis, haven't they!' Indignation had begun to seep into her voice, before it subsided into doubt: 'Of course there *is* a lot of bronchitis about.'

Another woman, who was nursing a baby voluminously wrapped in a thick, stained shawl, said: 'There's two men got it in our street. You can hear them coughing across the road. Jinny James's 'usband one of them, and *she* do say it's the silicosis.'

'What d'you expect,' said another, 'with their lungs getting full of the coal-dust and rotting with it.'

'They can always have plates taken,' said the district nurse officially, and looking down her nose. She leaned across to the woman with the baby. 'How's Henry shaping?' she asked, peering at the pink blob of face visible in the shawl's folds. She had brought Henry into the world.

'I just been taking him to the clinic,' said the mother and whispered something in the ear of the nurse, who nodded sagaciously.

A woman, thin and cold as an icicle, climbed hastily into the bus. A crystal drop hung on the end of her nose. She wiped it away with the back of her hand and, having settled into her seat and nodded to the others, she exclaimed rancorously: 'Not a bit of tidy meat in the butcher's! Only them offals, as they call 'em. And my man do like a bit of steak when he comes from the pit. I rushed down to Roberts's soon as I heard he 'ad steak. "Steak," he said to me, "someone's been telling you fairy-tales—"' Something mournful in the air of the bus arrested her, and her roving eye then saw the wreath. Ears pricked, she asked sharply: 'Who's dead?'

''Usband of my sister Gwen Lewis,' said the woman with the wreath.

'Gwen Lewis . . . let me see . . .'

'That stoutish piece,' helped the woman with the baby, 'up in Noddfa Street. 'Usband worked in Number One pit. He went sudden Sunday afternoon, lying on the front-room couch. Been coughing and had trouble with his lungs. A young fellow too.'

'Not the silicosis,' exclaimed the thin woman, 'again!'

262

'Well—' said the woman with the wreath, 'we don't know.'

'He ought to have been opened up,' repeated the fat woman. 'Gwen Lewis could get her compensation from the pits if they found the coal-dust had rotted his lungs.'

'He had plates taken,' said the district nurse, 'months ago and there was no sign.'

'He's in his coffin now,' said the woman with the wreath. 'The doctor said it was bronchitis. My sister don't want to go out or anything.' Something of the finality of death seemed to oppress her too, hold her locked. 'I had to buy this wreath for her. Fifteen shillings it cost.' She examined a chryanthemum; the petal-tips were slightly darkening. 'I do hope it's fresh,' she went on worriedly. 'And I've got to come down agan this afternoon; my black isn't ready.'

Taking out a red and white spotted handkerchief, the young man with the girl covered his mouth and coughed hard. His girl had sat still as a rabbit; she seemed to look round at the others without looking round. Her ears were flushed.

'It's bronchitis weather,' sighed the woman and pursed her mouth as Bryn Jones coughed again.

The baby suddenly let out a bawl, ferocious and astonishing from such a small leaf of a face.

'He wants his titty,' nodded the thin woman, smiling bleakly.

'Oh, a hungry one he is,' said the mother in a disconsolate way, as if she were complaining.

'What does he weigh now?' beningly asked the district nurse.

Two men jumped on the bus, followed by the conductor, who clipped the bell. The driver put away his pipe. Solid and red-faced among the whirling snowflakes, the policeman stepped back. The thin woman gazed out at him with a kind of disagreeable respect. 'He don't look as if he's got a crave for steaks,' she nodded, speaking to her neighbour as the bus moved safely off. 'And I don't blame him, out in all weathers like they are.'

The bus began its whining climb up the steep slope. The hard prune-coloured hills each side of the vale were beginning to hold the snow in their wrinkles. Sitting in the recessed back seat, one of the men who had jumped on last thing plucked the conductor's sleeve and said: 'Hey, Emlyn, heard what happened in the cemetery on Saturday night—you know, when them incendiary bombs fell?'

'What?' said Emlyn vaguely, examining his row of tickets.

'Well, you know old Matt Hughes, the cemetery keeper? Well, after them incendiaries fell he went all round the cemetery at midnight to see that everything was O.K. And who should be coming down one of the paths in the dark but two funny-looking chaps, and each of 'em carrying a tombstone under his arm. "Hey," said Matt, "what you're doing walking out of 'ere?" The chaps was hurrying, but they stopped and said: "Hell, it's getting too hot for us us 'ere with them incendiaries falling." "Oh aye," said Matt, "they *is* a bit dangerous. But what you're doing carrying them tombstones under your arms?" "Well," said one of the chaps, "there's the Home Guard at the gate, and we heard that people got to have Identity Cards nowadays, haven't they?"'

The conductor gave a subdued guffaw and called: 'Fares.' Down the bus, where the man's tale had carried, there were smiles. The fat woman tittered. Bryn Jones's neck reddened and swelled with interior mirth, though his young lady did not seem amused . . . Out in the rushing snowflakes a woman had hailed the bus, but it stopped much further up the road and she was obliged to pant through the windy flakes. 'What,' she shrilly scolded, climbing in, 'is the matter with the damn buses? Why can't they stop when they're asst to?' Her snow-wetted eyes glared at Emlyn the conductor; she wore a man's cap skewered to a bun of hair by an ancient hatpin. Sitting down, her gaze pounced on the wreath and she asked, breathless: 'Who's dead?'

'My sister Gwen Lewis's 'usband,' said the woman with the wreath and gazed down heavily at the expensive cluster on her knees. The fat woman added for her:

'Last Sunday. The young fellow went into the front room after dinner and—' She gave the history. And the woman in the man's cap was sure it was the silicosis: a man in her street had gone off just the same and he wasn't thirty. She agreed he ought to have been opened up, even though the district nurse said the X-ray plates had been negative and the woman with the wreath said the doctor said it was bronchitis.

'It's *proof*,' added the woman in the cap, 'if you open 'em up.'

'*Of course*,' assented the fat woman vigorously, and shoved the slipping tin of peaches further into her basket. 'I wonder she didn't think of the compensation.'

'I've got to go back this afternoon,' lamented the woman with the wreath, but fluffing herself out a little, 'to see about my black. What a potch it is, and snowing like this. My sister, she can't do a thing but sits there by the fire all day, poor 'ooman.'

'The New Inn!' shouted the conductor, roused to his duties by the scolding, though everybody knew every stone and post of the place.

The girl and her young man rose and passed down the silenced bus. He strutted a little, chest before him. She, rather skimped, went looking and not looking, her ears pink. As they stepped out of the door the married women nodded to each other knowingly, with a little grimace of the mouth and lowering of the eyelids. The bus swung on.

Bryn spat as soon as he was out of the bus, then coughed again, in the bright, sharp air. Dilys opened her small fancy umbrella and held it against the snowing wind. She shivered. She was slight, unlike the dumpy older women in the bus. But there was a tenacity in her body and in the way she put her face into the wintry air. 'Goodness me,' she said with a worried kind of irritation, 'I wish you'd do something about that cough.'

'Hell, it's nothing,' he barked. He wore no hat. His shoulders were broad, his limbs and hand thick and hard. The snowflakes turned into a grey liquor in the warm grease on his brisk black hair. The faint bluish pallor of his face was a little more evident. This week he was working on the night shift.

They went down a side turning. They lived in the same street. But before they reached it he put his hand in hers and stopped her against an old building where there was shelter from the whirling flakes and wind. It was a bakehouse, and the oven was inside the wall: they could feel the heat coming out. He would not be seeing her again until Sunday. 'What's the matter?' he said.

'It's those women in the bus!' she exclaimed in a little burst of half-curbed hysteria.

'What's the matter with 'em?' he asked, mystified.

She frowned, trying to concentrate. She did not quite know. But she struggled to know. He tried to help. 'Talking about opening that bloke up?' he suggested.

'No,' she almost wailed. 'It's . . . it's their *way*. Sitting there and . . . and talking, and—' No, she couldn't express it. But she went on: 'And looking at me when we came out, looking at me like as if I'd soon be one of them . . . even,' she added, the hysteria getting a hold, 'carrying a wreath in my lap!'

He was a bit shocked. 'Dilys,' he said, 'they're not bad; they're not bad women.'

As suddenly the hysteria coiled down. But she spoke with bitterness: 'No, that's the worst of it.' She knew she had failed to express the fear knotted deep in her.

With a thick finger, grained with coal-dust, he brushed a stray snowflake off the tip of her nose.

'Ooh,' she said. 'It felt like a biff.'

'Just a bundle of nerves you are!' he said in a loving, gratified way. Then he coughed.

'That cough!' she cried, the irritation returning. 'Why don't you wear a hat and a muffler?'

'Oh, shut up,' he growled, squirming in her irritation. 'Didn't you hear it's bronchitis weather?'

After they parted in their street she felt—for she was not one to stay ill-tempered and sulky for long—that she was lucky really. He was in a reserved occupation, and he was a good miner, with a place of his own down under. They were going to be married in three month's time. He would be by her side for her to look after him.

WEEP NOT, MY WANTON

He delighted in his sister Gwen, always following her about or expecting her to follow him. Vehemently alive to injustice, he would be bellicose if she, who was three years older but no taller—Gwen was inclined to a rosy thickness—was given either a bigger or a smaller share of food than his. Very careful to defend all his rights equally with hers, and hers with his, he could not bear her to possess anything importantly different from his possessions. But now, after by accident discovering her one morning when she was stripped to the waist, he had taken it into his head to be jealous of her mysteriously announced breasts, lying there like two small pale pears.

He had run unexpectedly into her room before breakfast and stood arrested for several seconds, seeing the strange new things.

'What are you staring at!' she exclaimed, reddening and snatching up a towel. 'Go on out; you've got no business in here.'

But he approached, big eyes immensely startled, and lifted a hand to the unripe fruit with their fragile pink lips. Fascinated amazement had been his first reaction. 'Let me see!' he cried, stretching a finger.

Gwen stamped her foot. Even her darkening yellow hair seemed to frizz up with anger, and in her confusion her anger became hysterical. 'Go away!' she shrieked. 'Rude. Go out of here—'

He pulled at the towel. 'Let me see,' he cried, in sharper excitement at this denial and resentful of the enwrapping towel.

She gave him a violent push. Her face was unusually hostile and threatening; she might have been defending something he was never, never going to be allowed to share. The result was a burst of truculent rage from him. Squirming on her, he gave the towel a sudden hard tug. It flicked away from her grasp. For a moment again he saw the white pink-starred wonders she had so secretly acquired.

He wanted to ask how she had got them, from where, and when: he felt his own front deficient and at a disadvantage beside that of Gwen who until now had seemed to share his life and all that was in it. 'You've been hiding them from me!' he shouted in a passion of reproach. It seemed a treachery in her.

But, raging too, she was cowering away from him, covering herself with her arms and crying out, the towel on the floor, stamped by his feet. She seemed to rear like a wild pony; fire came out of her eyes. Suddenly in the doorway appeared their mother, bothered in a morning irritation, her voice like a smashing dish.

'Now what's the matter—'

'He's following me about,' Gwen cried, 'and wants to stare at me.'

He shouted, though with a little under-wail: 'I want two of those like Gwen's got.'

Gwen's hands covered the shapes. For a second his mother stood startled. Then she drew away from him in sharp protection of Gwen. He saw it and his resentment grew. Allies, they were hiding something from him.

'Let me see 'em,' he beat up into rage again. 'She won't let me see 'em.'

His mother advanced, most darkly an enemy. Advantageously imprisoning him in her strong thick arms, she swept him up, laid him struggling across Gwen's bed, and smacked his taut buttocks several decided smacks. At the same time she announced indignation and horror. Wicked, wicked ruffian. Let *that* teach him to respect his sister, and *that* give him manners.

Meanwhile Gwen was dressing and watched the punishment complacently. He was pushed out of the room. But later over breakfast, while in sulky brooding he bent his head over a plate of porridge and spitefully resolved not to eat it, she said: 'I'll show you where the cowslips are when we come out of school.' He heard the patronizing in her voice. He did not reply.

He felt she had removed herself into the kingdom where grown-ups shifted in their cunning power, like wolves and kings and disasters in the history books.

Yet he could not let her go. She had belonged to so many of his activities. The two school buildings on the low hillside were divided by a wall: one harsh bell clanged for both, but the children scudding up the slope from the black and green valley separated and entered two gateways foreign to each other. At the mid-morning intermission he suddenly left off chasing the ball that Dan Richards had pulled from his pocket and climbed the wall—which was forbidden—to stare down into the other gravelled yard, where knots of girls paused in talk or swooped about uttering short squawking shrieks in the patched spring sunshine.

For the first time the fact of their separation by a wall opened slowly in his mind. There was something, something . . . Meditatively he half lay on the wall, staring down, and let a mouthful of spit fall out very slowly, watching its silver, sun-shivering progress down into their yard. Dark, unresolved thoughts went like shadows of cloud over his mind, never staying.

His gaze searched for her among the bunched noises, her tawny hair and brown frock. There she was, strolling arm in arm with a girl, very deep in talk. What was she talking about to her friends, their heads so close together? Then, swerving in their stroll and as if aware of their intent gaze, they saw him perched above on the wall. Gwen's friend burst into a kind of laugh that made him at once scramble off the wall in deep shame. There was a secret mockery in that laugh. And again he was startled by a sense of betrayal.

Sums vexed him, but the red shape of Great Britain on the map brought thought of trains and the seaside. He was so satisfied with his colouring of an oak-leaf into his copy-book that he bragged of it to Dai Daniels next desk who still had chilblains large as walnuts on his fingers. Asked to spell Dublin he stood up and gave it two b's, and Mr. Matthews said it was strange what a duffer he remained in spelling. Llew Jones asked twice to leave the room during the Welsh poetry lesson, thus strengthening the opinion that there was something the matter with him.

Running home, he remembered the tumult of the morning. A scowl came into his face. At tea Gwen asked him if he wanted to go and pick the cowslips. She looked at him cautiously over a tipped teacup. He shook his head, but stared fixedly at the soft rise of her frock.

Brinley Williams' brother had a ferret at Number 4. His mother called out: 'Mind to be home before dark,' and as he was going out, without a word to Gwen, his father was arriving from the colliery office. in the loud voice that he used for his two children, as if they were deaf or too stupid to hear a quiet voice he called: 'Well, whiskers, what are you scowling about?' He hated to be called whiskers, and going past his father in silence, he tried to repair the loss to his dignity by pausing to examine the sky with a cold and haughty calm.

At Number 4 he found that Brinley's brother had taken the ferret on a ratting expedition in which Brinley was not allowed, so they went down the back garden to look for frogs in the damp grass behind the currant bushes. There were no frogs and they climbed the lilac tree till it groaned, and Brinley made water in an old tin and poured it on an earthworm they found coming out to greet the evening. Presently he said: 'My sister's got two pears growing on her up here.'

Brinley had a sister a bit bigger than Gwen and so perhaps knew all about these things. But he only said: 'My grannie in Gilfach got a blackbird marked on her arm. She has! Been there for ever.'

'Has your sister got pears growing up here?'

Brinley rolled on the grass and yawned. 'I dunno. Shall we go down to the railway by the signal box?'

But he would not go, lying in heavy meditation now, picking the edge of a nostril. The blue spring evening thickened in the garden; he could smell the blood-red wall-flowers, the earth under the currant bushes, and the day-warmed houses growing blue as the darkening grass about him. Brinley, bored by this lack of adventure, jumped up and said he was going to drink a glass of ginger pop. He did not invite his friend indoors but, to make him envious, set the musical box going in the back parlour and from behind the geranium-pots watched him go past with a jeering grin. Above everything else, even the ferret, the musical box was coveted. There were other treasures too in Number 4, which was a rich family.

The thin waltzing melody in his ears, he went home. The evening was coming down between the houses. An unknown woman hurried past him, a veil over her face and the wings of a grey bird spread on her hat. He felt her excited haste waft over him like a warm scented wind, and he loitered, staring after her with idle curiosity. Where was she going so hastily, why did she smell like flowers and wear a veil? The tapping of her heels died away into the dusk.

At home company had arrived: Aunt Becca and Uncle from down the valley, with some snapdragon roots for the garden. His mother was laying supper. At his entrance he sensed their extra interest at once; all eyes were turned on him mockingly. Except Gwen who was sitting with her head down and as though she was carefully counting the freckles on her arm. His father roared: 'So there's the chap that wants things like his sister!'

Auntie Becca made tittering wet sounds through her teeth, then suddenly sang out jeeringly: 'A petticoat he'd like to wear too, p'raps, and have a plait down his back. Well, well, there's a boy!' When she used to sweep him up into her arms her skin smelt of floor-polish.

His aunt had a lumpy face, dismal as a mistake: in it were drab treacherous eyes sunk far back, a small squeamish mouth, and a colour like dried figs: the whole was finished off by a nose. She always had indigestion bad.

'A medal,' croaked Uncle Caleb, who had pores all over his face each containing a speck of soot, 'a silver medal I won for sprinting when I was your age. At the Sunday school sports in Coronation Field.' His big shag-stained moustache was lifted critically towards the boy. 'A bantam boxer I was too. Ah, ah.'

He tried to cross his enormous legs, failed, and sat breathing heavily, wondering when his brother-in-law would bring out the beer. Becca had married him in a hurry.

'I never heard such a thing!' his mother said, vaguely lifting the lid of the cheese-dish, giving the wedge of cheese a push, and replacing the lid. 'Not in my life.' She turned a mildly scolding eye on her son, met a fixed stare, and went back to the pantry.

'Gentlemen,' roared his father, 'treat their sisters with respect.' But there were crinkles in his face as if he was laughing.

'Yes indeed,' Auntie Becca said, very crossly. 'What next! Mrs. Evans the Boot Shop's boy stole his sister's doll and went to bed with it cuddling like he was Rudolph Valentino or somebody. What,' she addressed him with despotic directness, 'did you think you was going to do with a bosom like Gwen? Hey?'

He gazed back at her balefully and in silence.

Gwen said nothing either, and kept her head on one side modestly. But she might have been licking her chops over her superiority. Had she gone over entirely to the enemy's camp! He would like to put handfuls of live ants up Auntie Becca's clothes, and into Uncle Caleb's mouth toss, one by one, sheep's droppings.

His father was concluding like a policeman: 'Don't let me find you up to those tricks again, my lord. They put blackguards of little boys in reformatories.'

'Gracious,' said his mother, holding up a bottle to the light, 'I thought I had more pickles than this! Come to the table then.'

He and Gwen did not sit up at the table. Tea was their last big meal. Presently they would have milk and brown bread before bed, though they no longer undressed downstairs before the fire, fighting on the hearthrug in their warm flannelettes. Still she would not look at him, and he hated her aloofness and her new mysterious air. They had been sheltering her against him as if he was an enemy. She was puffed up proud as a pan of dough. Anger filled him. And also a sullen regret. His eyes goggled on her relentlessly, but still she would not look.

He lay listening to the noises of the night. Gwen came up and he half rose in bed and leaned towards the wall. Patter, patter of her feet, a thud, a creak of her bed. He lay back. His father and Uncle Caleb scrunched down the gravel, talking: the front gate clicked. When his father came back, would he start playing the piano in the front room while his mother, angrily and uselessly, exclaimed to him to stop? Sometimes, wakened, he and Gwen would meet on the landing and listen in delight, pushing each other for fun, enjoying the knowledge that their father was drunk. But if their mother discovered them there she was always more angry than at anything else.

He got out of bed. Walked with caution out to the landing. Downstairs was like the bottom of a dark deep well, where his mother and Aunt Becca sat talking in secret, everlasting talking, complaint rocking in their voices same as in the hymns in chapel. Shut off, they sat under a black basin of mourning. Why were they always scolding and careful of this and that? Why didn't they go out to the public-house too, where people thumped, and fell about, and sang at the tops of their voices?

The new nightshirt, long so as to allow for its shrinking and his growing, caught in his feet; he bunched it up in one hand and opened and closed Gwen's door cautiously with the other. Yellow bits of light from the street-

271

lamp came between the slats of the blind. Her bed was dark and silent in a corner. He thought he heard her move, but she did not speak, and climbing on the bed, he called hoarsely: 'Gwen!'

She did not answer; he leaned over her and felt her breath curling soft on his cheek. He put out his hand and fumbled at the folds of bed-clothes, drew them back, and sought for the top of her nightshirt where the string was loose in the opening. His hand delved down and felt at last, in anguish of curiosity, the strange soft warm things. It was same as putting his hand into that nest of thrush's eggs they had found over in the Dimbeth Valley.

All the time she did not stir. And then she whispered, though almost she sounded like a grown-up: 'Oh, you nuisance. What's the matter with you?'

'I want to feel them,' he whispered back in great anxiety.

Her arms came up and pulled him down, as she did in their play, but with something new, rougher and stronger. He was beside her in the bed now, warm and magic and secret, same as in a dark tent with the rain and wind beating outside. He liked her soft moist smell like grass and he felt he could tell her stories for ever. She was nice again and back with him.

'Won't I have them too?' he asked.

But she did not tickle his sides, she did not playfully twist and pull his hair. Yet she crushed him as if she were about to do these familiar things, and vast, globes of silence, he felt her breasts press him down. He heard the spit rising and falling in her dark throat, and the soft fragrant champ of her teeth. Above her cheeks, that smelt of fresh grass, he heard her lashes rustle like rain.

'Hush,' she said, crooning, 'hush.'

And she pressed him to her and her soft hair fell thickly on his mouth. He felt she wanted to press him into silence, withholding what he had come to seek, conversation and knowledge. But he did not want that.

'Won't I have them too?' he insisted.

'No, boys don't have them.'

He hesitated, while the information sank in. Then he said shrilly: 'Let me feel again.' And struggling out of her arms his hands swarmed over her, going now by the bottom of her nightshirt.

Suddenly she gave him a fierce hostile push, thrusting him across the bed. 'Go out of here!' her voice lashed. A furious acrid criticism came off her like a whip.

Amazed, he accepted it at once. He scrambled off her bed, went back to his room, climbed quickly into bed and lay with startled wide open eyes. In deep thought he gazed at the bars of light in the window. Some people passed on the pavement, and there was a laugh.

His lips formed her name. Gwen. But even her name had a different sound. And dimly he knew she had gone from him for ever.

THE ZINNIAS

'The country,' Owen said, 'is there!' He pointed to where the scarred mountain humps yielded to a vista of vague crab-coloured flat land. 'We can walk to it easy.' My father's been there and brought nuts and blackberries back. We can *explore*,' he urged, adding in bitter familiar knowledge of them: 'There's nothing on these mountains. Come on.'

Emrys, the cautious one of the two, gazed sceptically towards 'the country'. It seemed so far away. But he too was a little bored. It was the second week of the holiday and already the delights of black pit river, railway line and the everyday mountains had palled. Why couldn't he go to the seaside like some of the other boys in his school? But his mother, dropping pit singlets in the tub and sweating in the steam, had shouted: 'I'll give you seaside on the backside if you don't clear out. Go on, go up the mountain for a walk with Owen next door.' But she gave him a penny, and Owen also produced a penny.

'D'you know the way there?' he asked, doubtful.

''Course I do,' Owen said boldly. 'Come on. It's the *country*, like you see in those books in school. Birds and squirrels. Bats and flowers that anyone can pick. Let's go!' he cried, becoming shrill in these visions. 'P'raps we can catch a squirrel.'

Emrys felt for the penny in his pocket, and twitched down his jersey in decision. 'Come on, then.'

'Hey, not so fast!' ordered Owen, since he felt boss of his adventure. 'You can't run there.'

Two small boys already smudged with the day, they scampered down the bald mountain slope and then went with sedate secrecy between the long blocks of grey dwellings—who knew but some obscure power might withhold this country trip from them. They passed over the purple-speckled road skirting Bwlch colliery with its stack belching and its screens clattering. Then across a path on the huge loose tips of slag and waste, menacingly steep but which they negotiated nimbly as monkeys. Owen declared this was a short cut.

The other side of the tips was a kind of unused land, broken and stagnant, where the derelict buildings of an abandoned by-product experiment stood gloomy even in the yellow glow of the August day. Their clear knowledge of the district ended here. Emrys was for exploring the fascinating ragged buildings, but Owen was still obsessed with his country vision and its free fruit and flowers for everybody. 'Over there!' he kept on pointing instinctively. 'There!'

Up alien paths winding over slopes still bitten to the rock by colliery activities, down strange roads where the detached houses now made defeated efforts to be not as their neighbours were. The morning drooped into a pink afternoon. 'Over there!' insisted Owen. 'See, the rich are living by there.'

'I can smell the country already,' Emrys said valiantly. 'Let's buy a bottle of pop and a cake.'

'There'll be a farm in the country,' Owen bustled, 'where we can have tea and tomatoes.'

But the solid groups of stone houses dragged on and on, and it was plain that the paradise was not yet. Soon there was another colliery, and all the black ruinous waste about it, and the familiar grit and the clanking wagons. 'Hoy!' A scowling man looked out of a little shed. 'You keep off this railway or you'll be summonsed.' They hurried. 'We got to go over that mountain,' panted Owen. 'See!'

The mountain was only a small disembowelled hill, grey-coated and lumpy with rocks. And the other side was full of the same old rows of miners' dwellings. But, far away in the ceaselessly enticing distance, a whitish road went out of the place. It began winding houseless round the opposite hill's flank. A few skimped trees lagged along it.

'There!' Owen pointed triumphantly. 'You see!'

'I'm hungry,' Emrys flagged. 'I'm thirsty.'

He insisted on going into a parlour-shop they found among the dwellings below. The woman, who had a moustache, gave them a glass of home-made small beer and a rock cake each. 'Travelling you two esquires are?' she asked the strangers. Owen, though very cautiously, said they were going to see the country. 'You want to go to Carmarthenshire for that,' she replied, scratching an armpit. As, intimidated by her moustache, they meekly went out she gave them another cake for nothing.

Refreshed, they went on with more belief. Both instinctively shrank from asking for information. The country magic was surely to be found round the corner, and its mystery must not be discussed with strangers. Grown-up strangers, who often possessed such depressing powers, particularly must be avoided. They found the lonely whitish road with undelayed certainty.

Its length, yielding nothing of interest, was a trial. But it led at last to flattish open land over which the sullen presence of the mountains still brooded. But there were glimpses of broken-hedged rough fields, clumps of trees, and a white farmhouse perched uneasily on a far eminence. There was also a crooked road of scattered big houses nestling among bushes and green patches.

And at their feet a curly brook of clean water tumbled and chased itself in true holiday fashion. Of flowers there were no signs yet. Two birds dodged a way up the brook. Undoubtedly it was the country, for there were no long rows of houses, no pubs or chapels, and the air was silent and smelled different.

'It's the country!' said Owen softly. 'We'll see a squirrel in a minute. Hush.' Their first advance was as if on tiptoe.

The little place was drowsily empty in the afternoon sunshine. They spent an hour vainly searching for a squirrel. There was not even a cow. Only a morose-looking old horse too weary to bend to the grass in the flowerless fields. Not a nut or a blackberry could be seen, or remarkable coloured bird. The white farmhouse seemed far away as ever. Polite because of their consciousness of being strangers, they expressed no criticism of this country thriftiness. Perhaps here, too, happy things had to be stoutly sought and fought for, as at home.

'P'raps there's fish in the river?' Owen said hopefully. 'There's some fish that's coloured like rainbows. I'd like to take a fish home.'

'It must be past tea-time,' Emrys began urging. 'Didn't we ought to be starting back? It'll be dark—'

'Look!' suddenly whispered Owen.

They had come to a gate wide open before a sweep of gravelled road. On one side was a dark, high hedge, on the other a large stretch of the greenest and softest grass they had ever seen. But it was something else that had caught Owen's darting eyes. Flowers! They grew in two big round patches cut in the grass, and the dazzling splendour of their colours was startling.

'I told you!' hissed Owen in triumph. 'I told you there were flowers in the country. We can take 'em home. Come on.' He ran on the velvet grass. Emrys followed more slowly. But his eyes too were entranced.

Their bare, dirty knees went carefully among the zinnias set in mathematical precision in those circles on the elegant lawn. Colours of blood, of money, of cat's eyes, of dark oranges and grapes. Snatching and pulling, they piled the stiff, well-bred flowers into their arms.

'We'll take 'em all,' Owen said placidly, and waded into the second circle.

Their dazzled eyes had not noticed the villa far back behind a short wavy hedge. But they heard a car grinding to a sudden standstill on the gravel. A squat man in a black trilby hat got out and stood for a moment as though stunned.

'What's the matter with him?' Emrys muttered, taut-kneed.

The man advanced with the peculiar agonised heaves of a frog. His precious zinnias, his darlings, that only this year he had brought to perfection! He was one of those who find in cultivation of such flowers ease from the frustrations of a hostile world. All day long in his city office their colours lay in the pit of his stomach, which otherwise was a disappointed one.

From the shorn circles two pairs of round eyes watched his advance. A yellowish flush swelled and drained in his face, never an agreeable one, as his employees knew only too well. The fury of his voice was the more frightening for the anguish in it.

'What are you doing?'

'Picking flowers to take home to my Mam!' Owen said, mechanically. One penny-coloured bloom fell from his loaded arms.

At the ensuing bellow Emrys dropped his bundle and ran. Owen chucked his down and followed. Two dirty, ragged small boys in startled flight across a sunlit lonely lawn. Their knees flew swift.

When at last they saw there was no pursuit, Owen babbled from the foam round his mouth: 'I thought . . . I thought the country flowers was for everybody. They wasn't in a shop . . . I got a stitch in my side!' he wailed.

'Come on,' panted Emrys. 'It'll be dark soon.' Over his shoulder he glanced fearfully into the first still shade of evening. 'I don't like the country.'

And up in the villa the cultivator of zinnias—they were now heaped on a table—was storming at his wife, who liked her drop of drink but not, for some years, him. The zinnias tragedy was made the occasion for a return to one of their many disputes. In his anger he finally swept the flowers off the table. His heel stamped them into the carpet and their broken colours ran into each other uglily, like ill-matched dyes.

PLEASURES OF THE TABLE

I

'We had arrived,' Sabina sang out, 'at the third chapter. Where Mr. Darcy's manners disgust the Meryton ladies.'

Flora, propped up in the tall chair, did not reply, and her cousin, easing herself the other side of the fireless hearth, began the evening's reading. Though she was very hungry, she read for an hour in that piercing, dominant and avaricious voice which, coming from such a shabby and even dingy old lady, surprised people. Totally unsuited to Jane Austen's prose, the voice was so shrill that it carried through the thin, rickety wall to next door, where Mrs. Flook remarked to her husband: 'She's begun again. I wonder poor Miss Flora can stand it every evening, ailing like she is.'

But Miss Flora, besides being too short-sighted now to read herself, was hard of hearing. Really it was very kind of Miss Sabina to go and on, entertaining her cousin with their beloved author's works.

Tonight, however, Flora appeared not to be listening at all. A cushion lay on the chair under her head, and over her head a tattered bandanna silk square was spread, completely covering her face. In her lap her yellow hands lay very still. Flora might have been taking a nap. But Sabina was not incommoded by this seeming lack of attention. During the last few years there had not been many evenings when she missed reading a chapter or two of Jane Austen. Not only had it become one of her habits which it would upset her to break, but she obtained great personal satisfaction in going over and over again those wonderful scenes familiarity could not stale. Jane Austen was a haven of security in an oppressive world. Flora could attend or not; it did not matter.

Otherwise they were a quarrelsome couple, bound together by habit, necessity and the remnants of a great esteem. Peering resentfully, Flora was apt to drool: 'Sabina, it looks to me as if you'd got the lion's share of the pudding again.' A purple-red would mottle Sabina's face. 'Take it, Flora, take it all—' and she would push her plate across the table, her fingers scuttling like crab claws and her acrid voice so haughty that poor Flora's feeling of being ill-used, because her wits were not quite what they had been, would fritter down to a grizzle: 'There's no need to get offended, dear. But I don't seem to have enough to eat. Can't you make a bigger pudding?' 'We can afford to, can't we!' Sabina would reply harshly. And behind her pince-nez her flat eyes sidled:

they might have drawn their occasional malevolency from the brutalities of life itself.

But in the evenings such irritations vanished from their day. Jane Austen calmed them. Her works held something of their old rightful world. The very volumes were inherited: the thick pages with spacious margins, and grandpapa's bookplate with its engraving of 'The Priory' where every year right up until they were twenty-three they had spent an unforgettable summer month. These months had set a standard towards which they must always aspire. Ay, 'The Priory' with its oval pond, weeping willows and stone balustrades! Mistresses of such a domain, still in reverie they swept about the yew paths, cutting a bloom of the clematis trailing from the grey urns, sauntering to gather the morning's roses. Those were the days when the world was sane and safe.

At eight o'clock Sabina closed *Pride and Prejudice*; they kept country hours. 'Well, Flora,' she called shrilly, 'I'm going up to bed now. I'll just have a slice of bread and cheese. It's not worth laying supper.'

She did not wait for a reply. She went into the dark, damp larder. Her hand knew exactly where to find the toffee-tin containing crusts, and the wedge of cheese. She ate in the darkness, under the slate tiles of this lean-to, tearing the crusts with her rimed and much-ringed hands, biting into the block of cheese, and knowing in hostility the empty shelves around her. But tomorrow she would be fetching the pensions. Hers and Flora's.

Singing out 'Good night, Flora,' but without a glance at the unmoved figure in the chair, she took her candle and tramped upstairs. Next door, Mrs. Flook, eating pressed beef and pickles with her husband, heard and remarked for the hundredth time: 'Goodness, how her voice carries!'

But the two houses, sagging to each other as if for support in their decay, were so cheap: the Flooks were only tenants but the cousins were owners. People came and went next door, but the cousins had been there since paint, new brick and unrotted wood gave the twin houses that flashy and sprightly look such architecture wore in the century's first years, with the Boer War over and people expecting to settle down to prosperity. The village too was still a true village then, and no scatters of bus-tickets, cigarette cartons and paper bags blew over the Green. Who would have thought the slovenliness of the town would have reached so far! Now self-confident villas, racing motor-cars and bustling young men with squealing shrimpy girls used the place as a convenient 'country' retreat. The cousins, having bought their house with half their capital, deplored. But this vulgarity had also brought to them a brief season of prosperity.

Sabina lay in her bed. Her teeth lay on the grime-blotched marble washstand. She was still hungry. Her gums gripped together, she thought, as was her wont in bed, of the past. Of the lodgers they had had. She cackled, she frowned. Mr. and Mrs. Stevenson, indeed! A man of his age and a slip of a girl! Coming for their beastly weekends, too wary to go to an hotel. But at last she had given them to understand what she thought of them. . . . But there had been proper lodgers too, though they had never stayed long. Clerks in the town who wanted to live in the country and caught the morning bus with their breakfast still in their mouths—for, she had to admit, neither she nor Flora liked getting up so early.

All in all, the lodgers had brought money. There had been good food in the house then. They could even afford a daily cleaner. This was a tremendous relief; both she and Flora found pails and scrubbing-brushes abhorrent. Flora indeed had complained quite recently of the dirt in the house, when no one ever came to see it.

Hearing Mrs. Flook tramp upstairs next door, she screeched loudly: 'Flora, aren't you coming to bed? Flora!' And, like a reproachful parrot: 'Flo-*ra* darling, you really must come up!'

II

'Flora, nine o'clock . . . Flo-*ra*!'

Her cousin, whose bedroom was next to hers, did not reply. But Mrs. Flook's broom could be heard. Sabina yawned and lay for a while in the greyish feather bed, staring musingly at the stained violet serge skirt flung over the brass bed-rail. She'd wear her sage-green today, to fetch the pensions and to . . . She chuckled. Her tongue stroked her dry gums; she opened her eyes wider, wider. The ashen October light crept into them.

Out of bed, she slipped her teeth in. She'd need them today, she chuckled to herself. Going downstairs, she opened the door of the back room and stood pondering for a minute, hulked forward as she gazed vaguely into the dim room. She heard Mrs. Flook go out to her shopping.

An hour later Miss Sabina herself stepped out into the morning, carefully locking the front door. She had spent some time on herself, and when she reached the Green the passers-by were startled. Miss Sabina at any time abroad in the air was now an unusual sight; the cousins seldom went even to church nowadays, and everybody, including the Rector, had given up calling on them, respecting their obvious wish for complete seclusion in their poverty. Miss Sabina's only trip was a weekly visit to the post-office-shop across the Green, where she collected her own and Miss Flora's old age pensions and bought their meagre food.

Today she had dressed up. There were daubs of crimson on her bony cheeks. Her lean neck was white with powder. A heavily braided green skirt of billowing proportions flowed from a saffron blouse and a waist-belt of linked fanciful metals. For protection against the October chill a plump coat of copper-tinted bombazine reached down to her hips. Her corsage contained numerous antique ornaments, her large hat masses of faded flowers, a blue bird and a yellow plush apple. Angular and tall, she swept along with surprising energy to the Post Office and greeted the postmistress with a smile of piercing but deferential sweetness. She took out of her bag the two old age pension books. The postmistress, stamping the books, asked after Miss Flora's health.

Miss Sabina's high voice broke in a breathless cackle: 'My cousin is much the same. Nothing serious, but I doubt if she will leave the house now until the winter is over.'

Miss Andrews made a sympathetic comment and paid out the two pensions. Miss Sabina looked at the clock. And a few minutes later two gossipers on the Green were surprised to see her climb into the twelve-thirty bus for the town. It was the first time in living memory that either of the cousins was known to leave the village. What in heaven's name had happened?

Miss Sabina herself displayed no discomposure. She was too delighted. Her bright cheeks became quite puffed in excitement and her eyes sidled about observantly, now gaily, now scornfully. Those common new houses on Cuckoo's Ridge! Oh, they had built a public-house at Gallow's Tree corner! Luncheons and Teas! A little thread of saliva came from the corner of her mouth. . . . She turned to the conductor, pointing a be-ringed finger. 'You see that Georgian house, young man? A bishop was born in it. Look at it now— *Teas Provided!*' Her own long woe was verified in that example of the world's decadence. The sprawling lack of design in the town's suburbs drew from her a hiss of contempt. But already she was smiling. Ten minutes later she stepped off the bus, hungry as a hawk.

Oblivious of heads turned to her, she was obliged to ask a constable the way to Grant's restaurant, for this new town with its crowded traffic confused her. At last she found Grant's, which was re-built and smartened unrecognisably. This did not upset her; it even pleased her. She swept down the long, shining dining-room and chose a table under an energetic palm. A perked-up waitress, divided between amusement and respect for age, stood beside her. Miss Sabina settled her pince-nez and, with no betrayal of her almost stupefying hunger, pored carefully over the ample menu card. She gave her order with ceremoniously remote little enquiries as to the exact nature of the dishes.

She ate. She ate a soup, a grilled sole and a steak garnished with mushrooms and small golden potatoes; she hesitated over a fancy cheese, rejected it, and chose a striped ice strewn with nuts and pieces of fruit. She drank a half bottle of claret; she took coffee, and then, brightly telling the waitress of her chest's condition, she ordered a brandy. The bill came to twenty-five shillings; Grant's had not become expensive in its modernity. Benignly she chatted to the girl about her job, left her sixpence, and made at once for the bus-station.

She chatted even more to the bus-conductor on the return. Yes, she had seen some changes in her thirty-five years in the district; and not at all for the better, young man. Progress, ha! Had he ever read Jane Austen? Progress indeed!

Her arrival at the village came all too soon. As she descended on the Green and stood collecting herself, for a few moments a shadow seemed to banish the brave crimson flags on her cheeks. She stood musing, her gaze sidling sideways. Then, hulked forward, she sailed across the Green, her skirts swishing. Down the lane and under the weary oaks to the two houses sagging against a grey sky.

Mrs. Flook was picking the last chrysanthemums in her front garden. Miss Sabina seldom permitted herself gossip with her neighbour. But today the acid parrot voice sang over the fence, patronising: 'A moderately fine day, Mrs. Flook. Those yellow chrysanthemums are pretty.' The cousins' garden was a dreary mass of weeds.

Mrs. Flook, after a moment's half-averted glance, said: 'Take them to Miss Flora, will you? Is she better? I have not seen her about lately.'

'It is very kind of you, Mrs. Flook. My cousin is no worse, but I doubt if she will leave the house this winter.' A few more courtesies followed. Miss Sabina sailed to her front door with the yellow flowers, inserted her key, and could be heard screeching: 'Well, Flora, I haven't been long, have I? . . . Flo-ra!'

III

At last, in November, the Rector called. There was a local charity which allowed winter coal to the needy. He knocked three times before Miss Sabina came to the door, which, however, she threw back wide, immediately crying: 'Come in, Mr. Brayshaw. You find me disarranged, I fear. My cousin is not particularly well today.'

They grey, flat eyes, lying back in loose clots of flesh, pounced inquisitively on the parcel he carried. She ushered him into the front room, and she seemed to stoop in a kind of fawning obeisance. She was wearing her old violet skirt and a blouse, dirty and torn. But her voice was lifted in its parrot's

281

note of shrill energy. Next door, Mrs. Flook, realising the Rector was within, felt relief.

Mr. Brayshaw's nostrils had quivered as he entered. A resigned-looking man, he undertook his parish duties with an efficient perfunctoriness. The village, corrupted by the town, had become nondescript; the old influential families had long departed; his own interest had dwindled. Going into the parlour with its marbled chiffonier, huge vases crammed with dry dusty grasses, and photograph frames inset with mildewed plush, he did not sit down but launched at once, even hurriedly, into the formal business of the coal. He found the cousins needed and would accept the gift as usual. He indicated the parcel. That year's glut of fruit had encouraged Mrs. Brayshaw to make a tremendous amount of jam. Perhaps Miss Flora was well enough to indulge in some? And would she care to see him? He spoke as if he held his breath.

In the sullen November light, filtered through smudged panes and curbed by curtains hanging stiff with dirt, Miss Sabina spoke vivaciously. Accepting the jam with praise of Mrs. Brayshaw's housewifely industry, she rambled into an anecdote about a jam-making incident in her grandpapa's house 'The Priory', lost herself in it while she showed her gums in a cackling laugh, broke off, and said with a sudden exquisite hint of old-world etiquette that her cousin was resting, but perhaps he and Mrs. Brayshaw would take a dish of tea with them one day?

The Rector took up his hat. He wanted to tell her how he felt sorry for the cruelty of their lot, how he admired their brave battle in a changed world alien to their traditions. But there seemed no opportunity. Miss Sabina herself was so very talkative. Out in the dark odorous hallway there was a sense of closed doors and silence. Above the stairs one strip of mildewed wallpaper curled down scroll-wise.

The ton of coal was delivered in the middle of November. But people began to gossip about Miss Sabina's weekly trip to the town on the day she collected the two old age pensions. A villager had seen her in Grant's restaurant bent over a succession of dishes and eating so rapidly that bits of food dropped unheeded on to her clothes. A half bottle of wine on the table, there she sat fixedly unconscious of everything but the task in hand, yet about her a majestic remnant of an old familiarity with the pleasures of the table.

The weekly meal over, she never dawdled in the town but hastened back to her cousin. As she crossed the Green anyone could see she was anxious to get back, even the four women talking one Friday, in voices pitched to careful criticism, under the hollow oak that refused to die and every year put forth tough bunches of leaves on cancerous, staggering branches. In those voices was the unwilling admiration and the uneasy contempt such feel for those who have fallen from their class and will not recognise the fall:

'She's been for her meal again, I s'pose. How can she do it on her old age pension? Mrs. Bryant saw her sitting like a duchess in Grant's with wines and brandies . . .'

'She must be blowing her own *and* Miss Flora's pension on one meal! But is it right she takes the charity coal when there's others needing it?'

They frowned uneasily over the problem. 'I shouldn't wonder,' mused one, 'that they got a secret bit of money put by. Unless she's starving poor Miss Flora, that never could say boo to a goose.'

Miss Sabina, voluminous skirts hurrying, passed dauntlessly into her lane. From wandering rough-edged clouds dribbled the last wan light of afternoon. Dead leaves drove over the oak's splayed feet and the wilted grass. Voices sunk in suspicion, the women prowled closer over their subject:

'Her neighbour Mrs. Flook was saying she wondered if Miss Flora has had a stroke or something. Miss Sabina's so brassy, a person could be falling to pieces under her very eyes and she wouldn't notice it.'

'Living to themselves like that, they get withered. Feelings die in them. You remember, even when Miss Sabina used to go about a bit, she always talked about food. But I don't suppose Miss Flora knows how she stuffs herself at Grant's.'

'Someone ought to get the district nurse to call. Poor Miss Flora! Mrs. Flook hasn't seen or heard her for weeks.'

'Miss Sabina's not likely to let the district nurse in, even though she took the charity coal. No one's allowed in. Have you seen the window curtains? Heaven knows what it's like inside.'

They nodded, but backed away in immediate uneasiness from this thought of domestic dirt. They began to try to place the date of Miss Sabina's hat.

A fortnight later, Mrs. Flook, deliberately in her front garden when Miss Sabina returned from the trip that had become the talk of the village, asked if it was true that Miss Flora had had a stroke. Miss Sabina blinked her eyes in surprise. Then she rustled in dismissal. She had that benign air of one who has enjoyed a good meal.

'Stroke!' she sang. 'Certainly not. My cousin is still indisposed but hopes to be about soon. She requires rest and quiet, and *that* I see she gets.'

Mrs. Flook glanced at the stains down the flowing green skirt. Miss Sabina briskly poked a rusty umbrella towards the Flooks' part of the roofing. 'A tile is slipping out there, Mrs. Flook. You'll have the winter rains in.' And she sailed up to her door, unlocked it, and screeched out the usual greeting to her cousin.

Mrs. Flook, a nervous, childless woman, was not quite satisfied. She often listened carefully to that dominant voice coming through the rickety damp-weakened wall. 'What, you've laid the tea! You should *not*, Flora . . . What's that? Speak up, my dear . . . No, sit there . . . No, dear, no, you must *not.*' Rest and quiet, indeed—hard of hearing though Miss Flora was! But strain her ear to the wall though Mrs. Flook might, she never could catch the ailing woman's part in these parrot conversations.

That Miss Flora was downstairs and not bed-ridden was proved however by the evening's reading, which still came from the back room. Promptly at seven the voice was raised, swift, like a proud turkey swelling its long neck: '. . . "Its greatest elegancies and ornaments were a faded footstool of Julia's work, too ill done for the drawing-room, three transparencies, made in a rage for transparencies, for the three lower panes of one window, where Tintern Abbey held its station between a cave in Italy and a moonlight lake in Cumberland." . . .' Miss Sabina was now deep in the calm luxuries of *Mansfield Park.*

One Friday morning early in December, the neighbour heard Miss Sabina burst into song. This had never happened before. It was a cawing rooky noise that yet followed a definite and happy melody. Mrs. Flook, pausing startled on her broom, could not catch the words. Then she remembered it was the morning when Miss Sabina drew the pensions.

Miss Sabina was dressing for her trip to the town, heedless of the spitting rain, the low, angry clouds and the bitter wind.

IV

The double rat-tat was impatient. It announced the demands of a bustling world that would be denied no longer. It was repeated. Next door, Mrs. Flook listened. It was she who had given information that Miss Sabina undoubtedly would be home at that hour. She had not been able to stay her tongue any longer, and there had been a conference. The rat-tats went on, the letter-box was rattled, the door was thumped. Broken light came from under the scudding clouds. Dusk would be early. The knocking went on.

At last the door was flung open. And there Miss Sabina stood, drawn up like a war-horse, her long bony head swerving back. 'Do you not know,' she exclaimed with trembling hauteur, apparently addressing a great hostile mob, 'that my cousin is seriously ill?'

The gas-man had retreated half a step, his nostrils twitching. Then he clanked down his bag inside the doorway. 'I've been 'ere,' he said, frowning, 'three times. The meter's got to be emptied, ma'am.'

He was plump and reassuringly middle-aged, a family man: not like those impudent young fellows the Company sent sometimes. Her glance sidled, curled round him, withdrew into flat silence. Then she stood aside. But, as he stepped into the dim hallway, swiftly she began chattering, in a torrent. She was obliged to go out a great deal now, to fetch things for her cousin. Mind the mouse-trap under the bottom stair. Oh, if the mice came upstairs! She and her cousin put traps all around their beds.

She opened the little door under the staircase. There was the gas meter. Heedless of her chatter, he unlocked it. Pennies, pennies, oh such a lot of them! She stretched out her hand in playful greed.

Half in the alcove, bending on one knee, he counted the coins. He had lit a torch; the yellow shaft of light fell on her stained green skirt and long bony hands. She bent over him. Behind her was the closed door of the back room. She chuckled jovially now. Had he found any dead mice in there? She had found a frozen one in the larder only yesterday. Still he did not reply, counting the pennies. Mice, she went on, did not get much nourishment in her house; why did they come, only to die? The almshouses were full of them, so she had heard. But mice couldn't be fed on the old age pension.

He muttered something and she bent down further into the yellow stare of the torch and screeched in his ear: 'My good man, do not mumble. This is a country of free speech.' And derisively she cackled: 'Let us be kind to each other, let us eat, drink and be merry, for tomorrow—'

But he was getting up, pouring the pennies into the bag. Snapping out the torch, he heaved his plump solid body up into the dusk, lifted his head without looking at her, and sniffed. 'There's gas,' he said suddenly— 'there's gas leaking 'ere.'

She crouched against the door of the back room. 'Oh no,' she said animatedly. 'It's those mice. Dead mice—'

He pointed a definite finger. 'In there! It's dangerous, ma'am. You get so used to the smell you don't notice it.' At last he stared at her, forcing his guarded eyes full on her.

She seemed to crumple. Crouched against the door, she called again in a high-pitched but beseeching voice: 'Oh no, my good man. It's the dead mice.' She laid a finger on her lips. 'Hush. My cousin is resting in here; she is very ill.'

'All the more reason, ma'am, for me to stop the leakage.' Suddenly he went a menacing step towards her. 'D'you want me,' he demanded quite roughly, 'to get *the sack*?'

Her eyes turned on him like a hare's.

'The Company'll sack me if it's found that I've neglected—' But she was kneeling against the door now, beating her hands on it. 'He is here, Flora, he is coming! Keep still, there is nothing to fear. We shall not be parted. Do not look—'

His hand was on her shoulder; he gently thrust her aside. Crumpled, she grovelled on the floor. He stepped over her and opened the door. An exhalation met him like a blow. He went in a wary step or two. Lace curtains like ancient cobwebs entirely draped the window. But in the filtered light he saw a figure propped in a tall chair, a dirt-rimmed cushion behind its head. Covering its face was a tattered bandanna square and in the lap shrunken blue hands lay, very still.

He backed out of the room. She was standing on the bottom stair, one bony hand against the mildewed wall. Once more she had drawn herself up proudly. Yet it was as if she was tottering. She was babbling something about old age pensions being too small. But those hare's eyes were no longer aware of the gas-man heaving past her.

He ran out, leaving the front door open, sped down the weed-filled garden and beckoned to four waiting women skulking against the hedge in the ragged light: they included Mrs. Flook. Then he hastened to the policeman's cottage across the Green. By the time the women had entered the house, Miss Sabina had mounted the stairs and was in her bedroom. She had fallen on her knees, and the women's arms lifted her and laid her on the bed. They used the small compassionate words that soothe the stricken; they promised that all would be well.

EDITOR'S NOTE

Apart from their regular and widespread appearance in anthologies, the short-stories of Rhys Davies (1901–78) have long been out of print and his books found only in second-hand bookshops. The hundred stories which he published in ten collections and eight private press editions during his lifetime, together with one that appeared posthumously in the magazine *Planet* in 1991, are once again made available in this new comprehensive edition of his *Collected Stories*. They include all the stories he chose for his *Selected Stories* (Maurice Fridberg, 1945), *Collected Stories* (Heinemann, 1955), and *The Best of Rhys Davies* (David and Charles, 1979). Not collected here are a few which appeared in magazines during the author's lifetime but which he chose not to publish in his books, often because they were early versions or reworkings with which he was not satisfied. The purpose in republishing these stories is to demonstrate, for the student and general reader of today, the achievement of Rhys Davies as a writer of short-stories and one of the most distinguished Welsh practitioners in this literary genre.

I am grateful to Dr. Dai Smith, Chairman of the Rhys Davies Trust, of which I am Secretary, for suggesting that I should undertake the task of compiling this edition. The Trust, a charity which I founded in 1990, has as its principal aims the commemoration of Rhys Davies and the fostering of Welsh writing in English. Its patron is Mr. Lewis Davies, the writer's brother, whom I should like to thank for his remarkable generosity, warm friendship and kind co-operation. I should also like to thank members of the Trust for their advice and encouragement.

All enquiries regarding copyright on the work of Rhys Davies, whether short-stories or novels, should be addressed to me in the first instance.

Meic Stephens